D0307588

Frank Delaney

Novelist, broadcaster and journalist Frank Delaney was born in Tipperary, Ireland. His non-fiction works embrace James Joyce, John Betjeman, Boswell and Johnson, the European Middle Ages and the Celtic civilizations. He has lived in Britain for twenty years, where he broadcasts frequently. *At Ruby's*, his eighth novel, features Nicholas Newman, who also appears in the highly acclaimed *Pearl* and *The Amethysts*.

AT RUBY'S

'The plot twists and turns . . . it engages and grips, detached and stealthy as a work by Ian McEwan. Delaney has his own way with language . . . economical and restrained, expressing perfectly the details of a situation without heavy description. Above all, it is the details and nuances of Newman's relationship with Claire that keep the pages turning.' *Sunday Tribune*

PEARL

'The build-up of menace is deft and convincing. Something exceptional and utterly gripping.' *Daily Telegraph*

'Delaney has skilfully concocted a blend of adventure thriller and psychological mystery.' *The Times*

'A wonderfully appealing book. The inexorable rolling out of psychological discovery has a precision and power that echoes Delaney's beloved James Joyce.' *Good Book Guide*

THE AMETHYSTS

'Delaney effortlessly hooks the reader . . . This mix of John Fowles-cum-Ian McEwan turns flammable.' *Guardian*

'A compelling novel written with pace, verve and imagination.' *Mail on Sunday*

'A psychological thriller as harrowing as it is absorbing . . . This novel may prove unforgettable.' *Sunday Telegraph*

FRANK DELANEY

AT RUBY'S

HarperCollins*Publishers*

This novel is entirely a work of fiction.
The names, characters and incidents portrayed in it are
the work of the author's imagination. Any resemblance to
actual persons, living or dead, events or localities is
entirely coincidental.

HarperCollins*Publishers*
77–85 Fulham Palace Road,
Hammersmith, London W6 8JB

www.**fire**and**water**.com

This paperback edition 2002
1 3 5 7 9 8 6 4 2

First published in Great Britain by
HarperCollins*Publishers* 2001

ISBN 0 00 651491 X

Typeset in Meridien by
Palimpsest Book Production Limited, Polmont, Stirlingshire

Printed and bound in Great Britain by
Clays Ltd, St Ives plc

To Sue Bradbury

Underneath the lantern by the barrack gate
Darling I remember the way you used to wait,
'Twas there that you whispered tenderly
That you loved me, you'd always be
My Lilli of the lamplight,
My own Lilli Marlene

LILLI MARLENE

i like, slowly stroking the, shocking fuzz
of your electric fur, and what-is-it comes
over parting flesh . . . . And eyes big love-crumbs

E. E. CUMMINGS

1

Claire's history attacked within days of our wedding. We retreated to bed. It helped, and even when we came to know each other's bodies utterly it continued to prove the best way of calming her. We lay there as the old addictions raged through her. While she shivered I tried to keep myself calm and objective and tender to let her know I was caring for her – and, in part, to study the pattern of her distress.

First she reached for the comfort, the whispering, the huddling down, the burrowing for warmth. Next we had the desperation, the clutching: 'Nicholas, do you love me?' and, 'Nicholas, you won't leave me, will you?' Lovemaking, inevitable and, I think, essential, took her to the peak of her awful mountain where, still weeping, she always fell asleep.

The attacks occurred more frequently than I admitted to myself. Typically I came home from the practice and found her swaying in a chair, cold and astray. At such a moment she was without prettiness, she looked dank and empty, no trace in her pallor of the sunny, funny girl. She wouldn't look at me, she turned her head away. If I knelt and took her face in my hands she closed her eyes.

I cancelled any friends scheduled for such a night and raised her gently from where she sat. We ate nothing, drank nothing, took off our silent clothes and walked through the rooms to bed as the sun set through the windows of Chelsea. Did my arms around her body reach her mind? I don't know, and I asked myself again and again, Am I losing this gamble, the gamble that marrying her might get her life (and mine) under control? In my lower moods it looked bleak: eight months married and we had days when she shuddered more than ever.

She fought alongside me, she knew I wanted her healed more than I wanted anything else. And, it's true, the pattern had patches of improvements – plus one standard moment which brought encouragement, because it released her. I possess some old genetic luck from somewhere. Whenever she launches herself upon me with that terrible hunger, that wildness and gasping, my body always gets ready for her quickly. It needs to; Claire has screams inside her head that no woman so young should ever have heard. I have learned to hold her immovably in her desperate straddle across me as wave after wave breaks over her and she digs her fingers into my shoulders and begs me to help her. How can I describe the love I feel for her at such moments? I can't – my words would fall short.

Her sleep when she subsides hits her like a coma. I slide softly down the bed, flip-flopping out of her as I make her limbs comfortable. She is gone from me then and therefore has become more vulnerable than ever and I am held willing prisoner by her head cradled in my arms.

Sometimes while I'm watching over her my mind takes on a sudden clarity and I am visited by a brightly lit glimpse of my life and my shortcomings. I curse myself again for my incurable reticence. And sometimes, to ease my own pain, to talk myself up out of this sudden pit, I wander through a catalogue of other loves. They are impersonal and therefore undemanding: the gold screens of Italian churches; the taste of pistachio ice-cream; willows overhanging childhood's river bank in Herefordshire; in a hotel outside Belfast the wooden pillars built from the paddling wheels of a linen mill; the walnut fascia and leather seats of my father's old Alvis car; that absolute silence of the sedges in the Sologne; the suddenness of a spark from the fire at Rye and its fizzing

2

upon the stone hearth; a rainy, roasted-apples smell of wild briar; seaweed's green and brown blisters; the unexpected delight of a doodle on some eighteenth-century architect's drawing.

These and myriad more adored privacies course through my mind. I know such thoughts add up to my way of loving myself, such as it is. Whether Claire will ever know is something I can't say, because I'm too awkward (or do I mean too selfish?) to speak them. Which means – she may never know. I may never be able to say what I want to say to her, may never succeed in sharing these small glories of my inner life with her, except perhaps piecemeal and inadequately.

Once or twice I tell her by accident, if it happens that someone at dinner raises a topic touching one of my passions. Afterwards on the way home Claire loves to call me 'You dark horse!' and laughs with delight as I expand on the passion for her privately. But that's the only gift of intimacy I have and it's a poor enough one. I have never been able to find the good, the salving words, during those needful times when we're glued together in desperation.

All I can do is hope that above the noise of her pain she hears the gasping of my own heart as I die inside her and that when she is old and I am dead she will remember the bone of my jaw as I bury my face on her neck. I have no other means of telling her the force of my love.

2

At some moment in the night she twists away from me and I'm free to rise. I know that by next evening she will be alert again, grinning, doing her Charlie Chaplin walk, making rude jokes or mimicking the people she met on her adventures along the streets of the world that afternoon as she shopped for the meal she meant to cook.

So far I have never left our bed without checking her sleeping face. Without quite knowing the reason, I find myself, as I look down at her, wondering about the emotions behind prayer. This must be what it's like having children.

Great advantage of a combi-boiler is that the shower never runs cold. In the bathroom mirror I once saw bruises on my chest where Claire butted me with her head and beat me with her fists and I thought irrelevantly, Purple heart. Then I looked sardonically at my pale face and my lank hair and I thought, No, Nicholas, the purple heart is awarded for bravery.

Yet I must defend myself here against my own self-accusation. I knew what Claire was like when I fell in love with her, I knew her addictive condition. But I went ahead and married her, I who had avoided all commitments in the past because, as I told myself, I disliked hassle and had enough problems looking after myself.

Usually after the throes of a bad night I bring Claire her morning tea and usually she doesn't wake up. I tiptoe here and there. After a month of marriage Claire began to call our bed her 'sanatorium'. So I called it 'the Intensive-Claire Unit', which made her smile.

4

Great advantage of always wearing black is that you never need to haver at the wardrobe door. If the day ahead contains meetings I leave a note on the pillow or the breakfast bar and go.

As I did on the morning of Richard Strafe's board meeting. Bright sunshine, calm streets and my mind dwelt on the suddenness of Claire's relapse last night. I thought, I wish her tremblings would show signs of easing off. And I wish I knew what brings them on. Does she suffer premonition perhaps? I used not to believe in premonition but now I think I do.

Easy to say it afterwards but I know I felt some sort of edgy current in the boardroom that morning, something restless as I walked in. Conversation flourished; people greeted and smiled. But ease never arrived and the atmosphere felt jagged. No identifiable tension showed; powermongers never allow that. To show tension is two things: a sign of weakness and a signal to enemies. Those great beasts standing around me, many of them from commerce's top plateau, had long since cloaked or cured all such flaws.

However, one mask slipped.

I watched him, as I always did, from the moment I saw him. He was a man I often thought about. Hair almost albino blond and cropped close as a doormat. Big, unpuffy face, all bone. Big nose, a peasant's nose. Anthropological guess? He had Polish blood perhaps, certainly eastern European. At base, this looked like a coarse man even though he had built up a deep lacquer of shine. Eton, Oxford, LSE, MIT, the Harvard Business School – how often he sang me that list, too often for a man who seemed so confident.

Incongruously, he had one of those voices higher than you expect. It wasn't piping or fluting exactly, but it wasn't, as it were, fully broken, there was no throat in it; on the telephone you might have thought him a woman.

He had hands, though, that could split a tree. In one of

the stories he told me about himself a family's Alsatian dog attacked him on a beach somewhere in Italy. He said he grabbed the dog's collar and while the owners watched he twisted it like a garrotte until the dog gurgled and keeled over.

On those same violent hands he wore prelate's rings today and he also flaunted gold engraved cufflinks. I peered at them: one said 'Richard' and the other said 'Strafe'. Chutzpah? Or bad taste?

I sort of liked Strafe; he made me curious about him. Behind his power, beneath the strutting, I glimpsed the word 'lonely'. He always sought that extra quarter hour from me at lunch; at dinner he ordered a brandy too far. Generosity has many uses, such as the buying of fellowship. I haven't tried it myself.

Strafe's contrasts also interested me. No matter how mixed or senior the company he could be as foul-mouthed as a pimp and he showed that same sort of motherfucker aggression towards business rivals. And yet he presented himself with such elegance – for instance, he wore a Hublot watch, had his shoes made by Pietro Forno in Florence, sent flowers to colleagues' wives to thank them for dinner. I remember looking at him one day during a meeting and thinking, Something in this man wants to be a star, a dandy – and something else in him is dragging him down.

I found all of that absorbing. He was, I agree, hard to handle, but I have a kind of obeisance in me, probably born of desire to be liked, and that helped with Strafe. Two years now since I joined his board and other than some mild, snide needling he hadn't turned his guns on me. Nor did I wait in apprehension that one day he would. I thought, Worry about it when it comes, if it comes; I can't go around fearing I'll ignite his famous rage. And anyway, who can ever tell what pulls someone else's trigger? I mean – that morning it was the bright tie that Strafe wore.

6

'Richard, what d'you call that colour?' Clay Massey asked him along the table. 'Is it mauve or violet or purple – or what the hell is it?'

I remember thinking a mild, Oy-oy, what's this? because Clay, the oldest person there and the richest, had an air of agreeing with everyone. That was his specific life-device and it obviously worked for him; he was arguably the country's most senior boardroom figure. Shrewd of Strafe, and accomplished, to get as heavy a hitter as Clay Massey on his board. To the investment community that came over as a coup and, of course, Clay's name brought in other big guns.

Strafe looked down at his tie. 'I think it's called "heliotrope".'

Clay said prissily, 'Oooh!' and the table sniggered. I came alert. Boardroom banter's not unusual but this had a warp.

Strafe's acumen was slow that morning. He said, with a query in his voice, 'Ye-es' and looked at me, slightly puzzled. 'That *is* heliotrope, isn't it, Nicholas?'

Everybody stopped to listen to this exchange. I thought, What's this about? Surely this is the boardroom of a large public company and not a boys' gym?

'Missoni?' I offered, attempting to take it out of this zone of taunts. Claire had given me a red-and-yellow-slashed Missoni tie for Christmas.

Strafe, looking for the label, glanced down and fiddled.

'Yes, you're right,' he confirmed rather innocently. 'It is a Missoni.'

Clay Massey said mock-soothingly, 'Well, that's all right, then. But can we have a chairman who wears *heliotrope*?'

Strafe stroked his tie down the snow of his shirt. He turned his head and looked out of the window. The table cooled. People opened their folders.

Clay Massey ignored the mood – or else didn't get it, or maybe didn't care. Strafe, who had pointed ears like a lynx, remained standing, looking out across the rooftops at nothing. I saw the moment Clay decided to move in harder. He opened his mouth, ran a finger along the ridge of his lower teeth and stared at Strafe. Then he spoke.

'Richard, you've simply got to take off that tie. I'm not voting anything through today while you're wearing heliotrope.' Clay had a heavy tone and a heavier chuckle. 'Anyway, where the hell did you get it? Some "model"? Two flights up and ask for Daisy?'

Before the implication of the 'joke' hit me I had the thought, Clay Massey looks not unlike Henry Kissinger. Then, because of the extraordinary stiffening that seemed to seize Strafe like a sudden frost encasing his body, I recoiled, realizing Clay had cut too close to Strafe's bone. The boardroom recoiled too – this time nobody as much as smiled.

Strafe turned and looked at me. I think he hoped I was tracking whatever game might be running. He expected me to say something but I leaned back and said nothing. Better to wait, see how it broke.

Some clock somewhere chimed. Strafe sat down and opened his own folder. His mouth a closed slit, each nostril a dark little hole, he drew a huge, slow intake of breath.

'Is this a board meeting?' he asked with sharp unhumour. 'Or a fashion inquiry?'

Clay Massey said, 'Isn't that up to you, old boy?'

Strafe reached inside his jacket and for a flash I thought he wore a gun. No; he took out his pen and uncapped it without hurry, all slow movements to steady himself.

'Gentlemen.' He raised his large blond bone of a head and looked formally around the room. 'Thank you for attending our May board. There are twenty-two items on the agenda, including two committee reports. I intend that we finish at five minutes to eleven.' Strafe was ten years younger than me.

Clay Massey called out, 'Point of order, Chairman.'

Clay half-winked at me. I moved not a muscle of my face.

Strafe looked at him and spat, 'What is it?'

I know women who thought Richard Strafe handsome. Yes, I could see the sexual attractiveness, that driving warmth, the energy, the ability to quicken. But – I read a biography of Bobby Kennedy once where the writer reflected, 'How often does he make his wife cry?'

Clay Massey rapped the table.

'This is important!'

Strafe said, 'Yes?'

Clay, looking to the table like an actor, raised his voice to the notch marked 'crucial'.

'Chairman, what *are* you going to do about that tart's tie?'

Strafe's reaction electrified us. In a reflex action he snapped the barrel of his pen. Ink flooded his hands. Somebody hissed a nervous intake of breath. He jumped up, looked at Clay Massey for one boundless moment and left the room, a man with his safety catch off.

They say if you can't be good, imitate a good man. Ditto, if you can't be cool, act cool. Strafe wasn't like that. I thought of following him – but to what end? To say, 'Cool it, Richard, it's only a joke'? I didn't – because I sensed it wasn't. Also, I wanted such distance as I had from Strafe. And anyway nobody else moved so why should I be the one?

While he was gone nothing happened. Clay Massey yawned. The secretary who shorthanded the minutes blotted the spilt ink, rearranged Strafe's folder a little and then superfluously checked the pages of her own notebook. One or two of the big tigers fidgeted but remained surprisingly calm. I now think they must have smelled some agenda even if they couldn't define it. My thoughts turned to Claire, still in bed, I hoped, curled up safe and warm.

After about two minutes Strafe returned. Same tie, different face, taut and bleak. He had dried the ink on his fingers but failed to remove the stain. With no more than thin control of himself, he took on the board like a drover. He slammed a small clock down on the table and his aim of finishing at five minutes to eleven was neither challengeable any more, nor in doubt.

The agenda turned out as on wheels. Some of the tigers contributed easily, speaking in voices that betrayed no hint of the violence I felt in the air. Clay Massey made some appraising contributions at well-judged intervals. Strafe scarcely acknowledged any of them. Down the agenda he rolled, a juggernaut that nobody in the room could equal or halt. He did not look at Clay again.

Violent people often have a pedantic streak. At twenty minutes to eleven Strafe intoned, 'Any other business? Which as you know,' he chanted, 'is always the last item on an agenda.'

He looked to every person there except Clay Massey. Clay lounged deeper in his chair, his arms resting on the table. The liver spots made his hands look like toads. Not a word came from anyone else. I checked each face as Strafe addressed them. Of the eight non-executive directors, five belonged in the country's top fifty captains. But not a word did they say, not a smile nor an eyebrow raised. By sheer force of personality Strafe had run down whatever animal he felt stalking him.

The executive directors, who saw Strafe every day, relaxed. Their faces bore that placid, exhausted relief of athletes after effort. The secretary sitting beside Strafe groomed her hair, her rising arms lifting her breasts – and the shiny air was full of knives.

3

In the milling around afterwards one or two people did that thing of raising their eyebrows and smiling wryly, with looks that said, 'Whew!'

Strafe nodded at me and then beckoned. Before I could get to him another director intercepted me and said, 'Congratulations. Haven't seen you since your marriage.'

'Thank you.'

Strafe, his voltage still flickering, called over, 'Nicholas, will you ring me?'

I watched him walk into his office. His huge shoulders said, I've won, but I've not finished.

And Clay Massey offered, 'Lift back to the office?'

He and I walked slowly down the stairs together. His posture told me not to mention the clash with Strafe. Therefore, I told myself, Prepare to be bored. Every time I meet Clay he gives me advice that I neither solicit nor want.

On the street as his driver drifted over to us, Clay shifted his demeanour a little and said, 'Isn't Strafe, my God, an animal?!'

I laughed but didn't engage. The car stopped beside our legs. Clay clambered into the back seat.

He complained, 'Nicholas, you won't know about this yet. But. When you get. Older, eeagh! Every – bloody – movement – hurts.' He hauled his legs into place.

The chauffeur diced with Park Lane and as I was thinking, Here beginneth the lesson, Clay began.

'D'you know I've never, Nicholas. Been able to do what you do.'

11

'What's that?'

Although I wanted to like his avuncular air he irked me. He never once put any business the way of Bentley Newman, yet he had known me for at least ten years. And I think he knew my partner, Elizabeth Bentley, for four times as long, almost since she founded the practice. Plus, Clay was well aware that we had made something of a reputation designing out-of-town shopping malls. Two board meetings back he irritated me by preachily condemning 'the dough-nut effect' of such developments and then he went on, as he put it, 'to air the hole-in-the-middle symbolism of the doughnut'. Come to think of it, a clash with Strafe happened that day too, but milder, almost like a warm-up bout for this morning.

Now Clay insisted, 'Well, I've never been able, I mean, to do that. Sit through a meeting and say nothing? I mean to say – well! Yeah, I thought that was. Well, a very *good* performance of yours.'

What you mean, I thought, is that you don't much care for the fact that I didn't come in on your side against Strafe.

'Oh,' I said. 'Wasn't it rather wet of me?'

'No. No-no. Look on it as a gift. Now you see.' He wagged his finger. 'In the boardroom, you know, it's different, well, as if. What it is, I mean. You can choose. Spectator or player – there it is.'

I was crystallizing my thoughts. In my late-reacting way I could see on my inner screen the word 'surprise' – surprise that Strafe should have been so enraged by gibes at his tie. Some deep nerve tweaked? Or couldn't take a tease? Or didn't see it as a joke?

'That's the wonderful thing. That's what it is,' Clay Massey spoke on. 'About, you know – having the self-discipline to remain silent. That *is* self-discipline. So that when you do contribute – and, Nicholas, I'm sure you probably shall one day – then your words will carry more weight.'

12

'I didn't think you were exactly boxing flyweight,' I said.

'But *you* don't like Strafe?' He used one of those disapproving intonations.

I have a rule. Bad-mouth nobody. That way my words can't get carried onwards. Better for business.

'He's – interesting,' I ventured.

'*That's* what you call it,' Clay said. And laughed. With an edge.

I looked at him. The large frames on his spectacles made it difficult to read his eyes. He wore gold golfball cufflinks. Would Claire like him? That was my new benchmark. Yes, I think his calm would appeal to her.

'What *was* going on back there?' I asked. 'He seemed sort of –'

'There were other agendas,' Clay rapped.

At that point I should have asked, Do your 'other agendas' include suggesting that the head of a large public company buys whores? But I didn't ask and that's where I fall down in the moral courage stakes. I was, however, ahead of Clay Massey's next remark.

'Perhaps,' he said, with a thoughtful air, 'perhaps you and I. You know where I am. Yes, we should talk. We should talk about, ah, a number of things. Yes, come in for a bite of lunch one day, Nicholas. I mean I know we have interests in common. And the other thing is, d'you know – ?' He paused, withholding someone's name. 'No, you don't know him, I think – one of my main board directors. He wants to retire at the end of this fiscal.'

Quickly I said, 'Not a chance, Clay. Kind of you to ask but I'm over-committed as it is.'

He looked surprised and I thought, Good for me. Clay has a reputation of promising directorships to people. He picks their brains, strings them along and then doesn't deliver. I don't want to be subject to that kind of disappointment.

Looking straight ahead, he nodded and I felt his antennae

withdrawing from me. The shrewdest men are those who rumble that they've been rumbled.

Fact: the Bank of England has the best drivers in London. Clay Massey poached Ron from that pool. Like a swan slipping through swine Ron did a glide to the kerb outside my office. I climbed out, spoke my thanks and goodbyes – and never saw Clay Massey again.

4

If premonition contributed, no wonder Claire and I had slipped back the previous night into her desperate rhythms. The telephone on my desk rang at a quarter to one and Roy Jewell, Strafe's finance director, said, 'Message from RS, listen to the news at one o'clock.'

'Oh?'

'RS says he'll call you.'

Roy Jewell unsettled me. I never knew whether to view his face as a smile or a sneer. Strafe admired him. How could a man as driven as Strafe admire someone so clammy? And he's so nasal. I guessed he rendered Strafe useful services.

The World at One led with the story. They told sharp details and the old feelings of dread hit me again: stomach going blaah! and hands shaky.

Ten minutes after Clay Massey dropped me, a motorbike slid in behind his car. Ron had reached their office. Eye-witnesses described 'a tall, thin courier, wearing leathers' and riding a bike with 'silver lightning flashes on the petrol tank'. And, I wondered, one of those sinister helmets, black and glinting like Darth Vader? The biker dismounted, parked, pulled a gun from inside the tunic and unexcitedly shot Clay Massey in the forehead as he looked up out of the back seat. I imagined the receding, mottled brow, the rosebud of blood.

Listening to the other details cushioned the blow. Clay Massey, I learned, was born 'Massermann' and had fled Hitler's Germany; a rabbi spoke of the shock, of Clay's 'tireless charity'; someone from the Institute of Directors called him a 'ground-breaker'. The BBC reporter said the police had 'as yet no definite line of inquiry'. After which a chief superintendent talked specifically and solely about the setting-up of an incident room.

I thought, Christ, what's going on?! and sent out for an evening paper. There it is – banner headlines. Is my name mentioned? No, only that Clay was emerging from his chauffeur-driven car after a board meeting. They had a photograph of Ron the driver. Newspapers live off such thin details.

My office diary listed one meeting – at three o'clock, therefore an afternoon (the relief!) for drawing and thinking. Soon Claire will ring. On my private line. She is like my skin now – how I savour my own inner term for her, 'beloved young wife'. I am feeling appalled about Clay Massey, appalled, so I will concentrate my thoughts on my work and on Claire.

God, how my life has changed! I will weather her storms. With her, standing by her and for her. I must do so, not just because I love her but because I was in some ways the agent of her worst experiences. Since the past that kept attacking her was a past she and I had, in part, made together, therefore we had to conquer it together. I believe it was a factor in our decision to marry: how could it not have been? *Who killed him? Who?*

After a bad time she sleeps for hours. I want her to sleep, I want her cures to come as naturally as possible. Last night was a bad one, so today she will have slept. I decided to delay telling her about Clay Massey and then play down my involvement in the matter. Not difficult, because my own natural protector, my delayed-reaction system, hadn't yet let the shock reach me. It would, though, it would.

At last my private line rang. I smiled as I lifted the phone. Instead of sleepy, loving Claire, Richard Strafe shrilled at me, 'Hey-hey?! What about THAT, then? Jesus-Peezus!'

'Richard.' And I thought, Play this level.

'The old prat!' He almost shouted it.

I enquired lightly, striving for composure, 'Bit ageist of you?'

'No, he was past it. Long past it. And you left the meeting with him? Shit, it coulda been you.'

I shuffled a little. 'Indeed.'

'But, Jesus! Get ahold of the plaudits, have you heard them?! Fuck – for such an old hypocrite!'

'The media didn't think so.'

'What do they know?! But, hey, what about the share price? See it? Where's the fucker? Up! Gone fucking up. Not down.' He chuckled. 'Tells you everything, no?'

I should have said, It tells you what a few astute phone calls will do.

Strafe said, 'But what was he up to? Getting totalled like that? Wasn't he always banging on about errors of judgement? I'd call that some fucking error of judgement.'

'Have the police been in touch with you?'

The piping timbre shifted a touch but he came straight back at me. 'Why would they?'

'All known associates, the news said. Covers you and me.'

Strafe didn't budge. 'Yeah, well. I'm glad he's dead. I'm always thrilled when someone I dislike dies.' He laughed. 'Takes a bit more pressure off the system.' Then, 'We still doing Uzès next week?'

'Wednesday, I believe.' I made a sound like a man checking his diary.

'I've got a meeting Paris Tuesday.'

'I'm on the early one to Montpellier.'

'Marseilles is easier,' he said. 'No flight, though.'

Strafe always did that; he always manipulated himself astride the facts one should know oneself.

He continued, less shrill now. 'You'll like this new place,

17

Nicholas. I thought of you when I bought her. Hey, I was gonna fly myself down there. You be game?' But before I could resist he said, 'But naw, no dice. The frogs. As usual. Air space, that shit, too much aggro.' He rang off.

Funny: I'd never asked myself what social class Strafe came from. Difficult to say. The soaring ease and the claims of education suggested middle but the vocabulary placed him lower. Might it have been that he dropped a notch by choice? To do business with whom he did business?

Quick meeting: the draughtsmen (they're on the Cardiff job) had progress to report. One of them, Bernard, hums tunes when he's nervous. I kept looking at my watch: no word from Claire yet.

At about half past three I went back to my own office and telephoned her.

'Have you finished your meeting?' she said, wide awake but her voice foundering.

'You all right?'

'Nicholas – you were in the car a few minutes before – before he was –'

Jesus! How did she know? She always does that to me, she always knows more than I think she does.

'Claire, it's-okay-it's-okay.' I slowed down my words, dropped my voice. 'It's okay. His office was two streets away. I wasn't anywhere near. It's okay.' I waited a moment, then changed my tone. 'How did you find out?'

'I rang you – Mary Strait told me – in detail.'

My rage rarely sparks. When it does I see magnesium flares. For now I held it and talked to Claire, talked for five, ten minutes. Down. Down. Calm down. She eased, enough to resume whatever she'd been doing. We agreed our arrangements; pick her up after work, go straight home to Rye.

'You're sure you don't want to stay in London?'

'No,' she said. 'I'll be glad to get home.'

18

'Claire, you all right?' She needs to work. The life she's leading during the day isn't fulfilling her, shopping and sleeping and chatting to too few friends. She needs a job to do. But is she up to it yet?

'I'll be fine.'

With my promise to be punctual leaving the office we rang off. She doesn't lack courage – but I still knew too little of her to read her as deeply as I needed.

Hunger hit me, born of shock and anger. My secretary, Lemon, stood chatting with Mary Strait, who seemed to spend less and less time at a drawing board. I beckoned; Mary Strait came and stood in my doorway.

'Close it.' My magnesium flare burned in the distance.

'So much for open-plan,' Mary Strait said as she pulled my door behind her.

I said – she knew what was coming – '*Why?*'

Not a budge. She looked straight in my face. I should never have slept with her, I should never have done it, what *was* I thinking of?

'Why what, Nicholas? Why do the stars keep on shining? Why does the sea rush to shore? Why is Lemon wearing socks with ducks on them when yesterday she was wearing teddy bears?'

Old rule. A clever dog doesn't foul his doorstep. And I broke that rule.

'You know why.' Her eyes looked cool and opaque.

Mary Strait applied for a job. Superb credentials. She wanted 'to come home to England'. So I hired her. The following night I bedded her. Then I took her to France. The same weekend I met Claire. Mary Strait was there. I dropped Mary Strait. Not knowing that she was a nut-cracker. Not knowing she was Elizabeth's niece. Not knowing that to a woman like Mary Strait there is no such thing as the past, that things must always continue as before.

She raised a look of innocence and sighed. 'I will know why, Nicholas, if you tell me.'

Axiom: If you go to bed with a woman and don't handle it well she'll know how to get inside you, how to light your anger and how to stoke it. I wanted to scream, You bad bitch! Why did you tell my frail, vulnerable Claire about Clay Massey, about my being in his car minutes before he was shot? *And* I bet you exaggerated it. When you must have known I would want, I would *need*, to break it to Claire gently. The same scream continued, You *know* how frail Claire is because I was stupid enough to tell you, you jealous bitch! But I knew I'd never say any of that.

Instead I snapped, 'This interview's ended.'

It hurt her in the eyes. Tough. She can expect that if she's forever going to make me pay.

As she left she threw back over her shoulder, 'And how's *Claire* today? Is she *well*?'

I asked Lemon to prepare my lunch. Still heaving with anger, I stood aside as she laid the cloth, the napkin, the fruit, the yoghurt on my desk. On her way to fetch the water and the rye bread she answered the phone, buzzed me and I heard her voice in two dimensions, on the phone and from the outer office.

'Someone called "Hamer"? Says you'll know.'

'Who?'

'Someone called Ruby Hamer.'

Good God! 'Lemon, put her through.'

'Darling Nicholas.'

More fervently than I meant to sound I said, 'Ruby! How *are* you?'

My God! How long? It must be, what, eight years? Could it be ten?

'Not well, darling.'

'Oh?'

'A dear friend of mine has just been killed.'

20

Such pennies always drop, don't they? I knew it as I said it: 'Not Clay Massey?'

'Yes, darling. Darling, this is terrible.'

I tried to listen between the lines. Her voice had a crack in it. Possibilities began to approach like stacking aircraft, too distant to define.

'Oh, Christ, Ruby, I'm sorry.'

'Darling, I knew him very well.'

'I was in the car with him.'

'Oh, my God, darling, were you hurt?'

'No, it wasn't like that. He gave me a lift back from a meeting. I got out two streets earlier. It's awful. My hands are still shaking.'

And my body. And my soul. But how did Ruby Hamer know Clay Massey?

'Oh, darling, I'm glad you're all right.'

'I expect there'll be the funeral?' Say something, say anything, stop my head jangling.

'I don't do funerals, darling.' Still that slight European accent, attractive. She hesitated. 'Could I see you, darling?'

'Yes, of course, I mean – yes.' I paused. 'Sorry, Ruby, I'm a bit frazzled.' I jumped back because I knocked over a glass of water with the telephone cord.

'Of course, darling.'

'Yes. No. I mean – well, yes, it'd be lovely to see you.' Could it be eight years? Certainly not more. 'When would you like?' But she was younger than me then. At least I think she was.

'D'you have a gap now, darling?'

I paused, listening to her breathing. 'I take it this is urgent, Ruby?'

Pause. 'You heard about my lease?'

'Ah!'

'I may have to close the club, darling.'

'We can't have that, Ruby. When do you have to be out?'

21

My antennae jangled and said to me, This isn't the full story.

'It's complicated, darling.'

Indeed.

5

Ruby's club had the fabulous lustre of the nineteen-thirties, all ersatz and flesh. Prewar Berlin, perhaps? Somewhere in Lebanon or Beverly Hills? She hung it sumptuously with black and white brocade, lit it mysteriously in silver. In the foyer, a ruby as big as a fist sat behind thick glass in a chrome strongbox. Was it genuine? She swore it was.

When I first knew Ruby she asked no questions. She simply gifted to me her heart's unreserved affection. Or so it felt. And with her thighs absorbed all my force. I spent a crucial weekend of my life in her bed. Fled shaking to her from the office, stayed Friday night, all Saturday and Saturday night.

During those long hours I lay listening to the sounds of the club below. Now and then Ruby would materialize in the dim bedroom. She'd gossip of some newest arrival, or somebody else's mood, or complain about the barman or the band. Or just make some hot chocolate.

Almost the most healing thing of all – she dressed and undressed openly and didn't mind that I stared. She even, as she said, let me into 'the secrets of Sellotape'. I knew she was watching over me and I had never fully thanked her.

She sent me home on Sunday evening. An hour later, when I was still no more than paces away from a breakdown, the doorbell rang. Ruby had come round in a cab, her arms filled with flowers and food. I don't know why she did it.

Will she still have that bloom on her skin like the royal family women? She'll be fleshier, perhaps? Not a lot, I bet.

The club looked weak and stale in daylight, like all morning-after places in every set-'em-up-Joe movie. Ruby had restored the original Mayfair cornices but you don't see them at night. She had her own mythology now. It said that every evening of her life Ruby danced a naked solo at her club. Always wore a ruby, she claimed, and then one night as she danced, a punter called out from his table in the shadows, 'You're not wearing your ruby!' Ruby, nude as a beach, raised a hand to kill the band, held the pause, swung her hips in a one-two and answered sweetly, 'Oh, yes, I am!' They applauded her for ever and she danced on, famous. We all need myths.

En route I fantasized. *I will stand at the open door. She will turn to greet me and I will say, 'Ruby, that's not fair!' because she will be wearing a white silk robe with, I know, I just know, nothing beneath it. Ruby will pad across to me. As I bend to kiss her cheek she will draw me in deeper and kiss my mouth. I will say, 'Ruby, stop it! I'm married and respectable.' And she'll laugh, 'Just testing, darling!'*

Under house lights and a spotlight or two she was sitting alone at a table, thumbing through sheet music.

'Mr Nicholas Newman!' She laughed from where she sat. 'Let me look at you!'

'I don't stand up to scrutiny.'

'Come on, darling! Let me take off my spectacles and look in your eyes.'

She wore a simple straight grey dress with a tiny lace collar, probably her own crochet. And, as ever, lovely shoes, dark red silk, high, high heels. The frames on her reading glasses matched the colour of the shoes.

'Mmm. Bit wiser, darling – but you haven't lost the old things.'

'What old things, Ruby?'

'Oh, you know. The vulnerability.'

'I'm not vulnerable.'

'No, darling,' she cooed in a mock soothe. 'Of course you're not.'

My turn to scrutinize. 'Couldn't you try to look a bit older, Ruby? For decency's sake?'

'Oh, darling, sweet of you but when I have to meet anyone I am like an old actress. I tug and I pull until I'm in shape, and then I paint and I paste and I dress up so that I will look like a younger actress, and each day it gets a little more tiring to do. And each day it takes a little longer. Growing old in Mayfair.'

We laughed, she in her excitement, I in mine.

'Nonsense, Ruby!'

On the table lay one of her constant companions – a paperback novel; Ruby reads more books than anyone I know. I looked at her closely, felt again free to stare at her as I did in the darkness of the old *demi-monde*. She threw her version of the same look at me and for a moment we said not a word. Impossible not to smile at her. I had made love to this woman more than thirty times and she never made me feel guilty. And now she smiled back.

But my bones rattled. In my brain I muttered, I hope to Christ this isn't about something else. Which meant I knew it was. So I went along with the false reason.

'What's this about the lease? Who's the landlord?'

'The Burgh Estates.'

'Ah, yes. Not entirely sensitive.'

'No, darling,' she said. 'And I don't want to close down.'

'London wouldn't be London without Ruby's,' I said.

A telephone rang on the wall. She took the call and apologized with her face: something about a new piano player.

While she was talking on the phone something bizarre zinged down from the sky into my head. It was one of those eerie frissons that I have lived off – even survived by. What can I call them? I reach for the word 'psychic' even though

25

I know nothing of it nor do I believe in any of that suspect whirl of the clairvoyant or extrasensory. Nevertheless this is the vision that splashed itself like a rainbow across Ruby's upturned chairs on her round tables.

Jerusalem houses a museum to the Holocaust. They call it Yad Vashem, it's intelligent and sombre. Something in the gardens there chilled my jaded, gentile heart. From a rock outcrop a branch of railway line reaches out over the shrubberies – and stops in mid-air. It's a piece of exhibition genius because on this awful overhang, this siding to nowhere, waits a freight wagon, a cattle truck, one of those in which the Nazis dispatched the Jews to the camps. The truck bears all the banal stencils of its functions: serial numbers, railway data, weights and measures.

Looking at it, I froze, then turned away. This occurred long before Claire. I had gone to Israel to offer some rash and useless, misdirected, delayed-shock homage to the memory of my dead lover, Madeleine. In her lifetime I had dishonoured her by not respecting the sincerity of her feelings for me. I believed – I still believe – that my uncaringness killed her.

Every time I think of that wagon hanging out there in the sky everything else around me becomes a metaphor; that's how powerful the exhibit is. In my own pursuit of the smooth, beautiful life, I had, until I met Claire, been on a single track to nowhere.

The image plunged back at me as I sat in Ruby's. Why? What's the connection? Or is it that Ruby's club is a metaphor? Of what – of love won and lost in Ruby's torch songs? A fantasy of being wanted when Ruby sings 'Love for Sale' or 'Stormy Weather' or 'I'll Wait for You'?

Dreams. Ruby watched her customers dreaming them. I, who dreamed daily of this new life with this new wife, I was among the dreamers who had passed through Ruby's club and, indeed, through Ruby herself. So why, I asked, does that awful freight wagon haunt me again now? I calmed down and settled for the dismissive thought, Christ knows.

Ruby finished her phone call and reached to a side table for a flask and its beaker. I knew what to expect: her great hot chocolate. I sat back, pleased but uneasy. Something in Ruby's manner plucked at me.

She took a breath and spoke. 'Darling, it's dreadful. About Clay.'

Was this it? All my old systems fired up. Was this the true agenda? Reluctances which I thought I had abandoned went on red alert. I even moved back in my chair. So much for my fine thoughts about nobility of purpose, acknowledgement.

'Ruby, I know about this sort of thing –'

'But did you know he was a Jew, darling?' I began to answer but she pressed on, sounding somewhat desperate to tell me. 'Did you know *I* was, darling? Or "Jewess" as your friend Strafe would say.'

I almost exploded. 'Jesus, Ruby! How do you know Strafe?'

'I won't talk to you about Richard Strafe. Not yet, darling.'

'Why not?'

All her playfulness had gone. But not her appeal. She finished pouring the chocolate and sat down.

'Darling, how much do you know about me?'

'Ruby, I know very little about anyone.'

'Don't be evasive, darling. I can't stand it if you're evasive. Darling, those years ago. We didn't part well, did we?' She rubbed her forearms as if cold.

I should have said, Ruby – my fault. At the end I had not returned some of her calls. I said nothing.

'Never mind, darling, that was a long time ago. I always knew we had – a connection, my father would have called it.'

27

'Yes, I suppose we did.' I drank the chocolate, fat and sweet on my tongue. Her brown eyes steadied on me like a mother or a victim. Move the subject on. 'Ruby, I'm a little surprised to find –'

She interrupted; Ruby always knows what's coming next.

'To find that I'm a Jew? So was I, darling.'

'But – ?'

'I've given up – some things.'

'You mean you stopped sleeping with some clients?'

I realized I was jealous.

She shrugged it off. 'I don't dance the way I did.'

Did she sleep with Strafe? My mind screamed the question. Shit, I won't be able to bear it if she slept with Strafe! Instead I said, 'My wife's Jewish.'

She ignored it. 'People sometimes ask me to dance. I tell them it's sweet of them to ask. So I sing to them.'

It seemed as though her face kept changing while I looked at her.

'Ruby, begin at the beginning.'

She lit a cigarette. Claire's going to smell the cigarette smoke from my hair.

'No, darling, I won't begin at the beginning. I won't begin at all . . .'

'You must understand – I mean, Strafe –'

'I'm afraid of him.'

She said it as simply as dread. I often feel tears at the back of my eyes but they never fall.

'But –'

'Darling, Strafe comes in here. Alone.'

'Alone?'

'Alone. He sits over there.' She pointed to the empty air beside a pillar.

I looked. The pillar's silver paint was flaking. I thought, I'm flaking too.

'Ruby?'

'Yes, darling.'

'Please. Like I said. Begin at the beginning. It's the only way I can function.'

She shook her head. 'No, darling. Because. Well, because I have a favour to ask. It has to come first.'

I halted, apprehensive. Checked my soundtracks. Most of them said, Be careful.

'Okay. Ask.'

'It may be difficult.'

'Say it, Ruby.'

'Will you meet me in Berlin?'

'Is that a line from a song?'

'I knew you'd say that, darling. Please?'

'Is this serious?'

'Yes, darling.'

'What's it about?'

'It's about me, darling, and it's about. Oh, it's about many things. Please, darling?'

'Is it about Clay Massey?'

'It might be, darling.'

Why didn't I say, Ruby, no, not for me? I didn't say it because this power that Ruby stores in her body had some control over me. There was one hour we spent together when I simply lay with my head resting across her thighs . . .

The resentful part of me fought back. 'You'll have to tell me *some*thing.'

'Darling, you're the only one I can ask.'

Why did I believe her? Why did I take her at her word? I suppose because you do tend to believe someone if she once saved the life of your soul. I looked at her all the time. Between drags on the cigarette she pressed her upper teeth down on her lower lip, leaving a mark like a rail.

I thought, I know about Ruby's 'lease'. It's a lease on someone's life. It had better not be my life. So I sat as silent as I can. It's one of the few things I do well, sitting silent. We simply looked at each other. I put my hand out and rested it on her bare forearm.

Ruby stroked my thumb.

'I remember those hands,' she said. 'Big hands.'

'Ruby, tell me –'

'Please, darling. Please?'

'But – Berlin? Are you sure?' I pressed, my reluctance escalating.

'Please.' She added quickly, 'I will go any day you can. Out and back in a day.'

'Only Berlin?'

'Only Berlin. I promise, darling.'

I stood up, bent over her chair, kissed her and walked away.

6

Mary Strait sang out as I walked through the door, 'Nobody knew where you were.'

'I must have missed the search party,' I said.

'Meaning your wife?' Mary Strait replied.

Hal Callaghan, the practice manager, came to my drawing board. He picks his teeth twenty times a day with a triangle of cardboard.

'Surprised you came back, Chief.' He squinted at his triangle.

How does he do it? How does he gauge that line between friendliness-as-usual and insolence? And how, for such a crass individual, does he pack so much into one question? 'Surprised you came back': meaning (a) You were at lunch with a well-known 'hostess'; (b) You dog, you're a first-time, newly married man and, therefore (c) 'Are you now going back to old ways, the wild times you had when I knew you first – *Chief*?'

'Hal, have we got a file on the Burgh Estates?'

'Aha! So it wasn't personal?'

'No, Hal, it was professional.' I am blessed with a dull voice; it gives me a level tone.

'Whose profession, Chief? Hers or yours?' He strolled away with a cackle.

I owed him – I owed him some serious heavy duty for his treachery. Seventeen months earlier Hal had machiavellied the crucial meeting which castrated my majority share-holding. Legally he did it blameproof. But according to the true rules of comradeship, favours, crises, triumphs, he had behaved like a thug.

31

I said, 'Ruby Hamer's losing her lease. She's got a new property. She wants Bentley Newman to be the architects; she's spending three-quarters of a million.'

Hal turned back and whistled. 'I always knew it. Women are sitting on a goldmine. See that remark by the oldest woman in France? She's a hundred and five and she said the only wrinkle she ever had was the one she sits on. Yeah!' He chortled; his lewdness will nail him one day. 'But Chief – hey!'

His inflection sought more urgent attention. I raised my head to look at him. However much he irritated me, I had the nous to know when Hal got it right.

He said, 'How're you gonna get this through the dames?'

Right again. We had recently become politically correct, thanks mainly to Mary Strait's days in California. And, also due to her, we had voted to hire two new female architects. Impeccable credentials and iron politics: we now had an office full of attitude.

I shook my head. 'Bloody hell!'

Hal wandered off saying, 'I'll take soundings.'

He didn't need to. Mary Strait rapped on the jamb of my door.

'Nicholas, can we talk about St Peter's Terrace?'

'What is it now?' – a project driving us all crazy: subsidence; client kept changing his mind; planning permission only partially granted – in other words business as usual.

She clicked her teeth. 'Chiswick have come back to us. They say the original application wasn't filed according to their spec.'

'And?'

She shrugged. 'They want us to go through the whole application process again.'

'At this stage?'

She pouted. 'I've said "no" to them. Incidentally –'

'Incidentally what?' Here comes the real agenda.

Every day I voiced inner regret about Mary Strait. Mostly I regretted that I didn't have the voting clout to get rid of her. She closed the door.

'Not good talk about your little venture forth this afternoon,' she said.

'Oh?' – playing for time.

'The hostess with the mostest' – more sarcasm than irony. 'Not good.'

I said, 'We do renovations of buildings. I believe it's a thing architects do. You may have heard of it. And I've known Ruby Hamer longer than I've known most of the people in this office.'

'Not many of us like that the Senior Partner was having lunch with a –'

'With a what?'

'You tell me? Tart? Or do you prefer your core harder?'

'We did not have lunch and she is not a tart.'

'Does Elizabeth know?'

'Ah. Auntie's little helper.'

The gloves had come off long ago. Why didn't she tell me in those first weeks that she was Elizabeth's niece? I know why. Elizabeth wanted me to marry Mary Strait. That was what Elizabeth liked to do, she liked to control people's lives. So I had scorned two women – talk about hell and fury. In my defence I had rumbled their wheeze. The two of them set me up. Elizabeth had never retired. She wanted back in but couldn't because she had long ceded me her shares. When they voted my shareholding down, Elizabeth recovered five per cent. Civility took a holiday.

No use arguing. All my own fault. I made the first move, I took Ms Strait to my bed like some unreconstructed Swinging Sixties buck. Subsequently she duped me as much as I used her, so we ended up all square in my eyes. But not, I suppose, in hers. Never mind. I know that if and when I manipulate my shareholding back to above fifty per cent it will be goodbye Mary Strait and don't bother to write.

Now she stood for a moment, watching me draw. Would she mouth one of her usual platitudes? Yes, she did.

'You know, it's such a shame, you are so brilliant and yet you can't take control of your life.'

'I thought the problem was that I am too controlled.'

'Too much control is no control.'

I said, 'I'm sorry – I seem to have fallen behind with my self-help books.'

When I reappeared from honeymoon Mary Strait had taken a month's leave. Now she demanded, 'Are you going to go through with this, Nicholas?'

'Since when do we select our clients on so-called morality?'

'People will feel demeaned.'

'Well, you shouldn't.'

She said, 'What's that supposed to mean?'

This could turn into screams. Oh, what the hell. Luckily she walked away.

'I'll put it to the meeting,' I called after her. 'I'm a democrat.'

'Incidentally.' She turned. 'Several of us think that your secretary shouldn't be asked to act as a kitchenmaid.'

'Is Lemon herself among the several?'

She murmured, 'She will be.'

I replied, more blithely than I felt, 'Then I will simply hire a secretary who doesn't mind preparing my meals.'

Claire rang at half past four and said she was ready when I was – which I have always taken as, 'Please come home as soon as you can.' I signed some letters.

Just before I left, a detective with a colourless voice rang. Would I come to the police station and give a statement. No. I wouldn't. He pressed. I am law-abiding.

34

In the car on the way to the flat I prepared some difficult ground. Would I tell Claire about Ruby? How could I not?

7

On that short drive from the office shock began to drift in like smoke. Post-traumatic, post-whatever you want to call it, I knew by the way I recalled horrors. I thought about Philippe Safft. I thought about his face and his striped shirt and his relationship with Claire and his death last year in front of our eyes, stopping the bullet he hoped was for me. And I thought about Claire, how she knew enough to run from the house on the Seine. Philippe and I had only his uncle in common. I didn't resent Antony. My rationale ran, Okay, so he introduced Claire to drugs and then Philippe kept up the supplies but if it hadn't been for knowing Antony Safft I'd never have met Philippe and if I hadn't met Philippe I'd never have met Claire. QED.

She waited on the steps; I could see her, down the street. I wish she wouldn't do that. There have been days when she's waited outside the door like that for up to an hour, like a child locked out. It also means I can't ring her if I'm delayed.

Lovely late sunshine again. Look closely. How is she? That, even in these few months, had become my first, most urgent question. Impossible to predict her. Anticipate one mood – find the opposite. Madeleine had been like that. So, of course, had my mother.

Claire looked fine, smiling and light-hearted, and her hair, the barometer of her state, swung bright and clear. So far so good. She had recovered since our Clay Massey phone call. As I drew in she hiked her skirt a little and raised her thumb and eyebrow like a saucy hitch-hiker.

I hopped out and opened her door, partly because I

wanted to kiss her. Who is this young and beautiful woman I married? I hardly know her. Half of the time, I wish to protect her. Half of the time, I despair of her. All of the time, I wish to know her more and more.

'How was your day?' I asked.

'Rotten – good – very good – a little rotten again – then good – now excellent.' She ruffled my hair.

If this weekend goes well I can probably get her back up onto that plateau where she becomes merry and industrious. We'll cook together and she'll prattle, she'll make me laugh, spinning flights of outrageous speculation into the lives of the people we know. She'll paint her toenails some amazing colour (once it was stripes of silver and lilac). While the nail polish is drying she'll waddle around the house with white things flapping between her separated toes. Every time she walks by me she'll flap her arms like ridiculous wings. I would never have known it of her when I first met this leggy, soignée woman.

As she tugged at her seatbelt I said, gingerly, 'Listen. I've got to go to the police; they want a brief statement. Why don't you wait here for me –'

'No-no, I'll come. I'll sit with you.'

She said it wearing her firm attitude. Since that's what I want to encourage, I gave in.

Here's Horseferry Road police station – ah, the walls inside are beige-grey, I could have won a bet on that. Posters of many desperations shouted, *Missing: Have You Seen This Man?* And, *Incident – Can You Help?*

At what point do the police cease to suspect one? Certainly we were treated courteously but none the less they convey an air. Doubt. Watchfulness. When I needed a lavatory (my gut proved unequal to a tremor of fear) a policeman escorted me – and waited.

This wasn't like the cop shows on television. Assorted police drifted in and out. They asked each other questions, confirmed requests, passed back and forth pieces of paper; they checked who was rostered over the weekend, whether there was overtime.

Two detectives dealt with me. They talked among themselves about street measurements, the make of Clay's car, the missing 'firearm'. Once or twice they made dilatory notes.

The immediacy of the place ambushed me. Or perhaps my delayed-reaction system had decided it was time I faced the day's events. I sat there, aware of two sensations. My mind was as clear as light – and my mind was as fuzzy as smoke. I could smell the acid of my own breath. The unease accelerated, taking me out of plumb; I had an image of myself as a door half-wrenched off its hinges.

Ten minutes in, they began to ask questions, halting and convoluted. I tried to answer and they wrote things; this is going to take all night.

I interrupted them: 'Look, wouldn't it be simpler if I wrote out a statement?'

The officers looked at each other enquiringly.

'Yeah,' they agreed. 'Yeah. Let's do that.'

'A pad?' one asked, pulling out the drawer at his waist.

'Ask Barry,' the other said. 'No, I'll do it,' and she left the room.

Claire looked less anxious than I feared; just a touch of pinched face; she's trying to keep a grip. The detective came back with the pad.

I began to assemble my thoughts: tea arrived.

'Mmm, your handwriting,' Claire whispered.

Full marks for effort.

'All architects write in Egyptian lettering,' I murmured.

'Are you okay?' she whispered.

The detectives heard the note in her voice and half-smiled. I said, 'We're recently married,' and the woman nodded. Claire wore the blue moleskin trousers I love stroking.

After a minute or two I began to shake. Shock was hitting hard. I could see it coming. Like a landslide, all rocks and huge splinters. I almost put the pen down. In distress, try to press down on each toe in turn inside your shoes, then release all together, five toes at a time. Difficult to do, but it switches the focus, makes you aware of the ground beneath your feet, grounds you. But what does a house look like when the landslide has passed through it?

Claire whispered to me, 'Why are you leaving so much space between the sentences?'

I whispered back, 'You'll see.'

Finished. I handed over the document. They read it together. Then, as I expected, they started to question me on each phrase I had written. Soon I was inserting extra sentences for their clarification. Claire got the point of the spaces I had left. The detectives leaned back and nodded, their officialness and suspicion evaporating.

My face tingled as though a little roasted. But my being began to swing carefully around to Claire. She seemed relaxed – until they asked for details.

Her eyes darkened. That's the worst sign – when her pupils dilate. I'm selfish; if Claire is unhinged my own stability wobbles, whatever my outward calm. If she crashes, mightn't I? It's a feeling I hate more than almost anything. And I know that some of my effort on her behalf stems from a desire not to have that feeling anywhere near me. Unworthy attitude – but at least honest.

At half past seven, with two unappealing hours of my life gone by, I asked, 'Might that be it?'

The officers looked at each other; perfectly ordinary, plain-clothes CID people, he a little more comfortable than her.

He began to say, 'Yeah, I don't see why not' – but she said, 'Better check with the Boss.'

Trying to force their pace, I stood up, stretched and walked around.

The Boss, double-breasted and cold, came in. He nodded to us, looked at the statement, looked again at Claire, eyes roaming a little unnecessarily all over her.

'You Mr Newman?'

I nodded.

Pause: deeper look at the clipboard.

'You didn't see the assailant?' Archaic language the police use, nineteenth-century.

I make an empty gesture. 'No, I got out of the car earlier,' I said.

He scanned the statement. Claire reaches behind her neck and boxes her hair up in her hands, a sign she's uneasy.

'No sense of anyone following you? The noise of a motor-bike behind you, or that sort of thing?'

I lifted my shoulders. 'Sorry.'

He looked unpleased. Anxious to please him I said, 'I'm sure I'd probably have noticed the lightning flashes.'

Quick as hate he said, 'How d'you know about the lightning flashes?'

I said, 'It was on the news.'

He knew that, he just wanted to see whether I did. Next, he read aloud: *'I have known Mr Massey for at least ten years, always in a business capacity.'* He – dlok! – clicked his tongue in his open mouth. 'Why d'you say that? "Always in a business capacity." Eh?'

Feeling invaded by his tongue on my words, I said, 'Because if I knew him any other way I might have more to offer.'

He asked, 'D'you know his family?'

'Not really.'

He looked at me very hard sideways and said, 'Ye-es.' Then he read on through my statement.

'This board meeting?'

'Yes.'

'Regular event?'

'Every month. Usual sort of thing.'

'Nothing *ab-normal* at it?' He made it two words, emphasizing the 'ab'.

'Routine.'

'H'm,' he said.

Claire tried to catch my eye and the Boss saw her do it.

'Did you know him?' he asked her.

'He was a business associate of mine,' I said.

'I'm asking her.'

'No,' Claire said. 'Not at all.'

He looked at her with disbelief – as he did at me.

'You haven't signed this statement,' he said, not an inch of give in his voice.

The male CID officer said, 'We were still adding bits and pieces, sir.'

I reached for some grip on myself, bent to the table and signed. Claire's discomfort increased. Nothing she did, nothing she said – just a movement in the ether surrounding her. If, as the healers believe, we all have an aura, Claire's was now darkening into black. I handed over the statement. The Boss looked from Claire to me – but he didn't know what expression to put in his look. She rose and stood beside me. Her arm nuzzled mine in a 'Can-we-go-now?' plea.

'We know where to find you,' the Boss said. He had the policeman's trick of question-and-statement in one inflection.

'I've given all my details,' I said. My body ached.

'He was a colleague, rather than a friend, Massey,' the Boss said.

'A distinguished man,' I said. I thought I'd try his inflection trick. 'You know of course who he is.'

'Was. His widow's on her way – d'you want to meet her?'

I disliked 'Massey' and 'widow' and 'was' – circumstances being forced too suddenly on a body still warm. Also, I disliked the naked old trick of testing for guilt.

41

'No. I'll get in touch with her.'

He didn't answer. I thanked the two officers, who then ushered us out.

The street glowed yellow in the May evening light.

'Let's walk for a bit,' she said.

'Where's the car?' I answered my own question with, 'No, let's – no, you're right.'

My head was empty of thought; it contained only sensation.

We set out, unsteady, bathed in sunshine. Seconds later, a police car swooped by, bearing Lynne Massey to the building we had just left, the first journey of her future.

'She was his second wife,' I said meaninglessly to Claire.

No reaction, not even a nod.

I said, 'I'm sorry.'

'Why doesn't life ease up on us?' she said.

8

London traffic has become a daily freak. Average speed three miles an hour. Comes down to two on the Friday evening exit. But I no longer care too much because this gives us talking time.

'D'you want to stop for supper?'

Claire said, 'Maybe when we get nearer home. Let's see how we go.'

'Or shall I ring Mrs Lydiard?'

'No need – I've done that.'

'How was she?'

Claire shrugged. 'She doesn't like me. You know she doesn't.'

'No-no-no. She likes you very much.' I'm not anxious to have that pathway opened up; Mrs Lydiard's kept Rye since I bought the house.

I changed tack; 'I had a go at Mary Strait.'

'She always answers the phone.' Claire heated up. 'Nicholas, you'll have to get a switchboard and a full-time receptionist; the practice is too big –'

'What did she say?'

'More what she didn't say – made a mystery of where you were – as if she wanted to give me the impression you were off somewhere being nefarious.'

Oh, Christ. Therefore this is not the ideal moment to mention Ruby. Or Berlin.

'What did you say?'

'I fought back – wished her a lovely weekend – said you and I would do our long walks thing – come back and sit by the fire – cook oysters on a griddle, that sort of thing – said how lovely the house is.'

'Well done, you.' Then I broached a subject I dreaded, but it helped her to have me mention it. 'Did you get much paperwork done?'

'Some.'

My nerves felt like a piece of netting. Must keep my eyes on the prize, the prize being to ease Claire into better phases – from queen of sorrows to Goldie Hawn. I know I'm doing it so that I'll feel less pressured. But she'll feel better too. The M25 had some choice idiots aboard; I had to brake hard three times behind the same car.

'Slow down, Nicholas. Let him get away from us.'

I did but he slowed down too, creating a huge gap between him and the one in front of him. He seemed to watch us in his mirror. In my own rear-view the queue of traffic stretched thick and long. I slowed further and the car behind hooted. The driver ahead gave me a fingers sign and accelerated. I swore at him.

'Please don't use that word,' Claire said. 'I feel it demeans part of me.'

I made a calm silence – to stop her mood plummeting. The traffic eased. I said, 'Sorry. Mustn't – you know. I must calm down.' She stared straight ahead. In a moment she began to whistle, a sign of fighting her mood.

When I first met Claire, on the war-blackened streets of Oradour-sur-Glane, I formed no immediately deep idea of her. What I later discovered chilled me – that such a young woman, with that limber walk, could already have lived such a turbulent life. Her inner landscape had been as blasted as the village where we met.

She was an only child of a family that once visited Hell. Her mother, Fran, survived Ravensbrück, sent there from France by Klaus Barbie's men in 1944. Himmler nominated Ravensbrück as the depot for all the furs confiscated from

Jewish women across Europe. At the age of nine Fran was put to work restitching fur coats and stoles into garments for Germans. Fran lost two fingernails – and watched her emaciated mother die of stomach ulcers in their shared bunk.

Claire told me that Fran, safe, married and warm in domestic Kensington, hid her one and only pregnancy bump lest she look plump. And could never bear to have another child for fear of looking fat. When Barbie was convicted in 1987 Fran went into a psychiatric hospital for four months – and Claire, who was seventeen, started to take drugs. Before I met her she was already trying to climb out of those ruins. She says it's impossible to do it alone.

I remember looking at her on the streets of Oradour and thinking, Something or someone's broken her nose but it hasn't damaged her profile. And she wears so many rings on her hands. And I thought, How did she come to know this village? It's famous only to the French because they're somewhat ashamed they let the Nazis torch it and its people. De Gaulle ordered that Oradour be preserved as it was the day the Panzers left it, so that 'the world should see and understand'.

But what about us, the children of the war? Claire, thirty years old, strode like a supermodel between those charred walls. She looked cool, blonde and angry – and splendid, because we have to hide our ruined parts, we allow no commemorative display of the damage done to us. That was my last such thought before I fell in love with her.

We have talked about Oradour-sur-Glane many times since then. She's obsessed with the age of the soldiers who did it – boys of fifteen, a sergeant of twenty-five. I fought off a spooky connection – Claire and those Waffen-SS: all so young, but already astride such horrors. For myself, I had no doubt that the damage in her attracted me.

She stopped whistling. I loved that she could whistle.

'Nicholas – I had it again today – that was what I meant when I said "rotten, good, very good".'

The traffic eased. We edged through the slipshod terraces of south London.

I took her hand. 'Poor you. How was it?'

'Like before – same sequence – first I got the feeling – the drifting and the goodwill towards everyone – and the well-being – and then I got the physical sensation – the sense that I could feel my veins – and then I got the bloody longing again.'

'Are you all right now?'

'It's not getting easier. Was I awful last night?'

'You're doing wonderfully.'

'I'm afraid I'll start dreaming about it again.'

She took her hands away to fix her hair and I waited, then reached for her again.

'That's the worst part – when you start to dream about it – you feel the letting-go – and then the peace – and you wake up and you're disappointed and cold and your head starts to –' She sighed. 'I've been trying to describe to myself the progress of one of my episodes, I feel that if I can I'll somehow begin to control them. If I could only establish what triggers them.'

I wanted to tell her that her 'paperwork' was doing this to her, that she should drop it and start a career. Instead I said, 'Put on some music.'

'I can't if you're holding my hand' – and we laughed. Another 'moment' safely navigated.

Mozart, she chose, the clarinet quintets. She could as easily have chosen George Michael or Doctor Hook or Divine Comedy. And that, too, was why I loved her. The music washed through the car and through our souls. I postponed any mention of Ruby. But I knew I must tell her soon. Part of my deal with Claire – never hide difficult matters.

How did I know the Ruby business would cause problems? Instinct – similar to the instinct that kept me off this 'paperwork'. Claire had set herself the task of recovering family property the Nazis had confiscated. She disliked that I took no part in it – didn't say so outright but my avoidance angered her.

Had she asked me why, I'd have pretended I wanted her to feel the accomplishment for herself. Which would have been a lie – what I really wanted was distance from all that. The past slings enough at us without needing to be asked.

Truthfully, I disagreed with her doing it. The claims, the legalities, the excavations of histories made tragic long before she was born could offer nothing but pain. Even if she is successful, and in today's rush to confess other people's crimes she might be, I doubt she'll feel better. She'll feel hollow, I know she will.

Mozart ended. So did the motorway.

'What did you fix with Mrs Lydiard?'

Claire said, 'The usual. If we decide to eat out, what's in the fridge will keep.'

South of Ashford, off the A2070, we headed for Warehorne. Between Snargate and Appledore we know an ancient pub with a jolly signboard of a fat lady in a straw hat – the Captain's Wife. The roads of the southern marshes always kept such inns, catering to the coast. This has preserved its interior, with tables made of halved tree trunks where the raised brass rims prevent drinking glasses (or the coins in shove-halfpenny) from sliding to the floor.

They serve country-generous food, more dollop than *haute*. Claire loves it – massive slappings of fried plaice in breadcrumbs; T-bone steaks that flop over the side of the oval dishes. I can never finish the meal they put before me – it's too much. Claire habitually devours hers, no trace of her mother's eating diffidence.

By now the landlord recognized us – or pretended he did.

Friday's easy for tables. His greatest trade comes on Saturday and Sunday nights from the local people. As usual, we had a drink in the bar and then he called us. We filled the fourth of his ten tables.

I rarely look at other diners – no longer interested in sexual opportunity. Anyway, down here you only find elderly locals, or couples like ourselves escaping London for the weekend.

Claire said as soon as we had ordered, 'Now, Nicholas.'

'Now, Claire.' We laughed at her 'business' tone.

'The office.'

'What about it?'

'Mary Strait.'

'What about her?'

'It's time to start "the campaign". I think we should try to get your shares back.'

'If you say so' – but I wasn't patronizing her. Claire knew useful strategies; she could not have worked so long alongside Antony Safft, or lived with his nephew, without learning some tricks. Also, she blamed herself because I had been tending her recovery the day the practice voted me down. Led by Mary Strait. Abetted by Elizabeth. Betrayed by Hal. Oily Hal.

I looked at her closely. Amazing that her face had remained so still after all her horrors. Still so lovely after all the dogs she'd laid down with. First she cold-turkeyed herself out of addiction. Then – my fault – got force-fed the drugs she'd kicked. Which meant starting all over again.

At the table now she made that same hand-to-throat gesture I saw the night I first dined with her in France. She remained so unchanged. I assumed familiarity would shrink her value – that combination of freshness and natural tranquillity. So far it had not.

'Haven't you got bigger fish to fry?' I asked.

48

The wine at the Captain's Wife may best be described as 'a liquid contained in a bottle'. But we always drank it, if with mirth.

'Have you seen the amount of paperwork?' she asked. 'They want everything in quintuplicate.'

I replied in my mock-acid, explain-everything voice, 'They're Germans, dear.'

She didn't answer. Her face, looking at someone behind me, had changed to alarm, then to something like horror. I turned around in the direction of her glance.

At the corner table beyond us stood a young man. He stared at us, as stunned as if clubbed on the head. Next he began to approach. He looked slightly younger than Claire, perhaps mid-twenties, dashing in a louche sort of way, wild curly hair and a navy sailing pullover with a high rollneck, you can buy them in any Breton *coopérative maritime*. Professional crewmen live around here, working the yachts of the Channel marinas.

'Claire!'

She went white, then looked at me with the same pleading fear of old.

The young man rounded my chair to reach her.

'Come on, Claire! Don't put your head down like that.' He paused. 'Claire, there was a time when you wouldn't. Unless I asked you.'

It all happened too fast for me to nip it. Claire covered her face with her hands, sat up, shook her head and screeched her chair back from the table.

The young man joshed my shoulder.

'How well do you know her?' he asked me belligerently. 'Because I know her really well. Don't I, Claire?'

I said, 'I'm her husband.'

'Husband? Fuck that!'

'Oh? Am I so appalling?' I asked, hoping for irony's rescue.

'Her *husband*?! I don't fucking believe it! You must have loot. Christ – Claire! If you fucking knew – !'

'Hey, hey! Language!'

'Sunshine, leave it,' he said to me. 'Just – leave it.' Then he called her again, 'Claire!'

She shook her head, covered her face with her hands.

'Claire! Come on! You gotta talk to me. Come ON!' His accent was public-school, adjusting streetwise. 'Claire! Have you forgotten –' He leaned in past me, trying to pluck her arm.

I rose to my feet. 'Back. Please.'

'*Jawohl*, dickhead! Cool it, okay?' He stepped back, eyeing me. 'D'you know about her? Do you? Do you? D'you know about Claire?'

I took a step towards him. 'Look –'

'Because I know about her. Don't I, Claire? I'll tell him if you wish, I'll tell your *husband*!'

As I quickened he moved to the door. For a moment or so he stood there. Then he shook his head: 'Husband? Jesus! Claire, you're something, you really are.' Then he half-shouted to me, like an angry child, 'If you only knew!'

He left the restaurant. The others in his party paid the bill and followed. None of them looked at us.

I stared past Claire's shoulder through the window. The young man with the curly hair roamed the car park noting down numbers.

'Is he a policeman?' I asked.

Face behind her hands, she shook her head. 'No, no. Of course not.'

'Then why is he taking down all the registration numbers?'

In the voice she uses when addressing blunt truth Claire said, 'I expect because he wants to trace us and get in touch with me.'

'But who is he? What an extraordinary performance!'

She closed me down. 'Please, Nicholas. Can we not talk about it now?'

When she does that I feel completely controlled. It endangers us. I finished my food – she didn't. We drove home in silence.

Church Square always has a welcome. The house looked lovely. Claire disappeared, had a shower and came to sit by me.

'I suppose I had better expl—'

I said, 'No. Go and play something on the piano.'

She did, two Schumann pieces, known since school. Soon we hit the floor. When I woke, Claire had covered me with her robe and gone to bed.

9

We had a thoughtful weekend with no heights reached and no depths plummeted. I slept a great deal and each afternoon Claire and I went to bed, more affectionate than frenzied. I took Monday off, worked at the drawing board in Rye. On Tuesday morning in London Claire came with me to Clay Massey's funeral – another shock for me.

I said, 'Why?'

She said, putting on a black jacket over a crammed black bra, 'I knew him.'

'But you never –'

'He was my case historian. At least that's what I called him.'

'Your what?!'

'He helped me with what you call my "paperwork".'

'But – when I gave that statement to the police?' I could scarcely get the words out. 'You said –'

'None of their business,' Claire said. 'At least not yet.'

'How often did you meet him?'

'He's hugely involved. With the politics of it and everything.'

'Why didn't you tell me?'

'I have tried to involve you.' She shrugged on the jacket. 'Haven't I?'

I should have said, 'Come on, Claire' – but I let it drift.

'Clement' they called him in the prayers. A man of presence, they said, a good man, of charity and thoughtfulness. But he hadn't told me he knew my wife. Oh, well. I reflected that perhaps, yes, he had generally tried to be 'clement'.

Same name as my father, 'Clement' – Clement Newman.

In the gathering afterwards we inspected the wreaths laid under the soulless brick cloister. I offered my condolences to Lynne Massey and a grown-up son. Small talk, little comfort; I said I especially enjoyed the board meetings when Clay attended; his ease made things easy.

She said, 'But Clay always got his own way.'

Surprised at her disloyalty I almost made one of those uncontrollable gaffes, I almost said, Well, he didn't get his own way this time. Luckily she was still speaking.

'You were the last person with him. And Ron.'

I nodded. 'I tried to ring you.'

She seemed to lose it a little. Words came rapping at me like knuckles. 'How could he do it to us? To people like us. You don't expect this in our kind of lives. When murder gets into a family you can't get it out. We thought we'd all had enough from history.'

Nothing you can say to that. I was probably the only person present who had been to a murder victim's funeral. But that was long ago, in a different world, and I was Madeleine's only close mourner (although to my shame nobody would have guessed it from my conduct). But, like it or not, I had, so to speak, experience. Therefore my cold, base self looked with interest at the Massey family's response.

Two more grown-up children joined Lynne. They all manifested that particular kind of shock in which people have lost their own meaning. The English don't express grief well. We don't rock back and forth. Nor do we vocalize. When people neither weep nor wail is it because they have no sound left to make? Their pitiful stillness almost oppressed me. I turned and looked out at the green sward and the landscape with each tree and flower growing out of someone's ashes. And even though I had not known Clay Massey well and did not feel any deep loss I took care not to look at the crematorium chimney.

Clay's son, Todd, walked over and introduced himself.

I asked, 'Are you in the family business, too?'

'Depends what you mean. Will you help me?'

He said it aggressively and I knew he didn't mean the supermarket trade.

I said, 'I can't, I'm no good at that sort of thing.'

As I began to move away he rapped back at me, 'So you let your wife take the brunt of it?'

This, I thought, has to be sorted out. I looked at Claire but found her withdrawn. Did she overhear?

'What do you mean?'

'I mean that my father was devoting a great deal of his time to advising your wife. That's tricky business. The least you might do is help us find out who killed Dad. But from what I hear you're too concerned with your social life. Too worried about your image. Won't get your hands dirty.'

He glared at me. I turned away: his gibe sprang from grief, with its added smear. There ought to be no reason why murder relatives feel shame. But they do. They also feel anger.

Staying near but not connected to them, we walked at the same pace as the family towards the outer area where hearses parked. From behind me Todd Massey suddenly spoke.

'Who did it?'

How did I know he was speaking to me? I half-turned and made some sort of vacant gesture. We reached the pavement outside. Standing behind me, he pressed.

'I believe you have some experience of this sort of thing.'

I said, as calmly as I could, 'Yes, well, I don't think there's any such thing as what I'd call experience of these things –'

He said, in a rising inflection, 'Yes there is – we've just had it now, haven't we? This is experience, isn't it? Isn't that what this is – experience? And you were with Dad. Did you and your wife bring this on us? Did you?'

Oh, Christ's eyes! Where are all these angry young men coming from?!

I turned, ready to answer. Changed my mind. Suddenly he and his mother were quite off the leash in distress but they turned it towards each other. She was grieving deeper and deeper. All I could do was say, as one does, 'If there's anything I can –'

Todd Massey said, 'There is. There's plenty you can do. But you won't, will you?'

I said, 'But isn't this a matter for the police?'

Fortunately a sibling in her long black coat and tear-stained face claimed his attention. Claire, through all this, said nothing and we avoided each other's glances.

Drifting to the gateway, I crashed into Richard Strafe.

'I didn't expect you,' I said.

'Always do the right thing, Nicholas. Speaking of which – ! Who? Is? This?'

He stared like a boy at Claire. Of course, he knew perfectly well who she was, but nevertheless I did the introductions. Strafe said, 'Oh, boy!' and retained her hand. Claire looked half-pleased, half-nervous.

He was like an actor with her, taking over her space: 'My *dear*! What is someone like *you* doing married to *him*?'

To me he said, 'Jesus, this *is* tasty. You baby-snatching bugger!'

Always difficult – the compliment wrapped in vulgarity. I let it go.

People milled around and past us, in and out, Clay Massey's mourners leaving, another heavy funeral arriving. Boardroom London is a village. Strafe held Claire's arm. I didn't like his grip.

Nobody knew much about Strafe. Perhaps none of us knows much about any of us. The point is – if you go looking, if you ask questions, you can find out about people. Or can you? I hadn't known Clay Massey was Jewish. But I wasn't somebody who asked such questions. I remember thinking when I married Claire, Will I now challenge the casual anti-Semitism I hear every day? I haven't, not noticeably.

Hang on. I *did* ask about Strafe. When he invited me onto his board. Yes, I did ask around and got vague answers, generalizations. He's very bright. Doesn't mince his words. Very tough. They said, Don't know him well, don't much like what I do know. Not English, but not sure from where.

I took a long look at him; he still held Claire's arm.

'Nicholas, your wife's my speed!'

I laughed, minus humour. 'I happen to like her, too.'

Strafe said, 'I've got some entertaining to do soon. You'll lend her to me?'

'Doesn't go out without a chaperone. Anyway, where's your own wife?'

'Dumped her. Boring.' Then he whispered, 'I bet you keep fit.'

I had to stop this line of talk.

'Have the police seen you?' He didn't like it. I pressed him. 'You realize,' I said, 'that people, some of them here today, know how hostile you were to "the deceased". As the police call him.'

Strafe didn't budge. 'Yeah, I been telling them.'

Part of me admired his candour. My own central feeling revolved round a kind of dim rage: murder had got near me again.

I took Claire back on my arm. Her eyes were excited.

Strafe asked her, 'You spending the rest of the day with him?' indicating me.

Claire enjoyed the compliment. Across the road, where cars were leaving and others trying to park, someone waved – Ruby. I thought she said she wasn't coming.

Claire saw her too. 'Who's that?'

Strafe said, 'That, my dear, is Ruby. Poshest tart in town. What's she charge for an overnight these days, Nicholas?'

10

During that afternoon I tried to draw. Unable. And unstable.
My mind wouldn't focus. I have never had a chemical
addiction. Those who do, such as Claire, have told me that
focus is the problem. No focus.

Not quite knowing why, I became acutely uneasy and
stepped out of the office for a break. I walked to Marsham
Street and stood by the kerb where Clay Massey died. Yes,
I looked for bloodstains. No, I found none.

Focus. I replayed the events of last Thursday's board
meeting, the short car drive afterwards. Did I say or do
anything that might have brought Death calling by? I used
to think myself too prosaic for such thoughts. What I had
not expected was the ingredient now released – Fear. That
gave me the answer to my lack of focus: I was simply and
clinically afraid.

Of what, I could not say. Unknown forces? But I had
known those before. This was new.

Across the road a skateboarder knelt to adjust his knee-
pads. Too old for a skateboarder. Street too busy. Odd.

I stand and inspect. Behind me loom the high granite
portals of Clay Massey's head office. Is that dark patch on
the pavement a bloodstain? Or oil? Stalin, I think, said
he wanted his enemy reduced to 'a patch of grease on
the earth'.

Lamp-post. No professional driver would park where a
door might be obstructed. So (I paced) I'm in the wrong
place. No marks on the pavement here. Kerb a little high.
Where did they kill him? Claire's 'case historian'! What else

did I *not* know about my wife? At that moment a courier roared by in a black shiny helmet. Life loves laying it on.

My breath shortened. Not so that anybody would notice. Just – try for a little more breath. I squatted. Here I am at the scene of somebody else's death, somebody else's crime. Mustn't let the police see me. Murderers always return to the scene of the crime. The police know too many clichés. Breathe slowly. Look for details.

I'm directly outside Clay's office door. Wonder if his son's watching me from some window. So – the bottom edge of the car door cleared the pavement by about an inch. I see. Enough to let the door swing back? Ye-es. Breathe again, don't gasp, just – breathe. Nostrils now – intake, feel the air's coldness in the nose, out again, slowly. Don't gasp.

No car parked here now. I stand again.

A cloud covers the sun. Is this the place to pray for the soul of the departed? Christ, my hands are shaking! And my legs. I'm terrified. Of what? I don't know. All I know is that I feel like whimpering.

I step back from the empty kerb, hoping that by looking up at the sky I will change my mood. It sometimes works for me. Shouldn't be surprised if there isn't some simple physiological reason. Maybe they'll discover one and it will be the new health tip – tilt your head back and you'll release a feel-good hormone.

Suddenly I'm aware of something coming at me from the side. With the rattle of danger the skateboarder hurtles past and pushes me so hard I spin off the pavement and out into the street. I bounce off a passing car. The car is going slowly, no damage done – to it or me. How long did it all take? Two, three, five seconds.

The motorist stops, jumps out.

'Hey – you okay?!'

'Yes, fine.' I hadn't fallen.

58

He came over, frowning. 'He pushed you. I saw him. Go after him?'

'No, no. I'm fine.'

The motorist looks into the distance. 'Shit!' He cranes his neck. 'Hate to see them get away with it.'

I shake my head. 'It's okay, really. I'm fine.'

The motorist says, 'An old bloke got shot round here last week, must be gangs or something.'

'I hope I haven't damaged your car.'

He checks it – minutely: 'Naw. S'okay.'

Why is it that terror removes fear? Or is it a different adrenalin? Like vodka after wine?

I walked back to the office and went to the lavatory, stood resting my head against the chrome towel dispenser, seeking coolth. My mouth had gone dry. I waited, hoping nobody would come in. Slowly I felt better, then roused myself. Decision taken: I will not tell Claire about the skateboarder. Nor will I tell her about Ruby or Berlin – yet. Anyway, I have three hours of opera ahead of me tonight. Good thinking time.

And she looked lovely when we met, her green beaded dress. As part of what she called her 'wifely duties' she had taken over the ordering of tickets. Tonight brought *Otello* at Covent Garden.

Over our drinks she seemed withdrawn.

'Are you all right?' My mantra to her.

'Yes, sure.'

Clipped tones. Hair piled up. Bad signs. I looked around: don't like this Covent Garden refurbishment and, dammit, they had a large enough budget. Someone's going to skid and tumble on these stairs.

'Did you take a rest?' I asked.

'Yes.'

No, she's not all right. Oh, I get it – Ruby. Strafe's remark. Oh, Gawd. In the car from the funeral she had said nothing.

I put it down to distress. To reach her I did what I always do when she's aloof in public – I chatted, perhaps a touch manically. Which is wrong; a man's wife shouldn't cause him to gabble.

'My mother told me the story of Olivier playing Othello. On about the fifth night he was apparently brilliant beyond belief. The audience wanted curtain call after call. But while they were still baying for him he locked himself in his dressing room. The actor sent to fetch him, I believe it was Anthony Quayle, could get no response. He knocked and hammered on the dressing-room door and Olivier merely shouted at him to eff off, go away, leave him in peace. Finally Olivier unlocked the door. He was in tears.

'Quayle said to him, "What's the matter, Larry? You were wonderful, you transcended any performance ever given anywhere. By anybody."

'Olivier said, "I know – but I don't know how I did it." True story.'

Claire smiled thinly. The call bell saved my face.

She watched the stage keenly. I wondered how much of the jealousy in the plot would reach her. She responded to none of it. Then I recalled that Ruby never asked me about my marriage or my wife. Is this some sort of lousy, jealous triangle brewing?

At the interval I joked, 'You're the supersubtle Venetian and I'm the barbarian.'

The joke didn't work; she iced me by saying, 'The line is "erring barbarian".'

I touched her arm and said, 'Claire, what's the matter?'

'Nothing's the matter. If you're going to quote from the play quote it accurately. I happen to know it very well. You wouldn't like it if someone cut a line from one of your drawings.'

This could escalate. I bought another drink for us. And as I edged back from the bar life had another little tweak at me.

A woman walked over, in full view of Claire.

'Nicholas, hel-*lo*. How *are* you?'

Andrea Jack, predator and party-giver. I had successfully avoided her for years. She put a hand on my arm.

'Wasn't that the most extraordinary weekend? Last time we met.'

I had to think.

'Edwina Kovak's, d'you remember? Who was it said they always knew it was an error to go to East Anglia?'

'Oh, yes. Yes.'

'Are you alone?'

I said, 'No, I'm – I'm –' and then Claire walked over.

'People can die of thirst,' Claire said. 'Aren't you going to introduce me?'

As ineptly as a schoolboy I said, 'This is Andrea Jack, this is Claire.'

'You might have said "my wife" – and which are you called? "Andrea" or "Jack"? Useful to know.'

I had never thought of Claire as rude.

'Wife? Nicholas, I didn't know. Congratulations. And to you – Claire, did you say?'

'I didn't. He did.'

'Girls have been trying to marry Nicholas for years. Well done, you!' She chuckled.

Had Andrea been rude, Claire would have coped with it better. Instead, the goodwill jarred her, made her realize she'd been unpleasant. She walked away.

'Excuse me,' I said.

Andrea grinned. 'I'd be jealous too if I'd married you.' And added, with irony, 'Good luck.'

Claire didn't drink her drink; she had gone to the auditorium. I swallowed mine and went after her. In the seat she looked as if about to weep. I caught her arm and tucked it into mine.

In a bright voice I said, 'Did I tell you that "Othello"

means "one by whom you can swear" and "Desdemona" means "ill-starred"? Or maybe you knew?'

Claire put her head on my shoulder.

In Sheekey's afterwards she seemed easier.

'You're going to "feed on nourishing dishes",' she quoted.

The shell began to crack. She reached for my hand.

We sat for a while in silence, until she said to me, 'What's the difference between jealousy and envy?'

'Claire, listen. This morning. The funeral. Ruby Hamer's an old friend. She's also a client. But anyway. A man like me, if he hasn't married before, you must expect to run into his past now and again. Andrea Jack is just someone who was on the same social circuit for a while.'

'But there is a real difference, isn't there? Envy's more dangerous. Mother says, she says it was envy that caused the Holocaust.'

Claire has the power to make you address what she raises. I said, 'The difference is, at least I think it is – envy is, what?, isn't it wanting what someone else has? And isn't jealousy the sort of, I don't know, extreme form of protecting what you have?'

The ice had all broken by now.

Claire said, 'I'm useless.'

'You're lovely. And I hate funerals.'

She said, 'We don't do them well, do we? We never acknowledge what they're for. What I find is, there's an odd comfort, weird, isn't it, when something's over. Is that callous?'

'What about Strafe?'

She laughed. 'Talk about a wolf!'

'By the way. Just so's you know. That's all part of the Ruby connection, talk of coincidence. She knew Clay Massey particularly well, I mean – she rang me about an hour after he died.'

Claire looked at me. 'I didn't know she rang you.'

'That's why I went round there.'

'You what?! When?'

Too late – too bloody late. Clumsily handled. The ice rolled in again and formed a huge floe. Within minutes Claire was on that floe and drifting away, leaving me, marooned, on the cold shore.

In the car I tried. 'Hey, listen. This can't start happening. It's too soon. We're too newly wed. Come on, you're my *bride*.'

'Why didn't you tell me?'

'It wasn't like that.'

Back in the flat, the slamming began. In anger I grow cold before my flare blazes. Claire's different – she makes noise; she slams things down on surfaces, she shoves everything around brutally, closes doors like a gale, all without saying a word. I counted five, six, seven, eight slams until I discovered that life had contributed its bit to the coldness – the boiler had gone out.

When I surfaced from it Claire said distantly, 'There's an urgent message from Rye.'

I played it back. *'Sir, it's Mrs Lydiard here. Just to tell you the police rang me, there was an attempted break-in, nothing to worry about, there's been a spate of burglaries and as you know the house is very secure, the police said to me it was like Fort Knox when they went round there, but ring me if you're anxious, I don't retire until two in the morning as you know, old habits die hard, best wishes, yours sincerely, Carol Lydiard.'*

Sweet when people treat answering machines as though they were writing letters.

'Mrs Lydiard, I'm not too late, am I?'

'No, I've got my feet up and I'm watching a video. How is Mrs Newman, she well?'

'Yes, thank you' – I forbore to add that the same Mrs Newman, still keeping her distance, was now walking around in nothing but green, lacy French knickers. She often flashed her goods when angry with me. Erotic, all that hot, naked ice.

'How serious was the break-in?'

'Oh, nobody got in. I think the scullery window took a little pressure but the grilles carried the day. All's well, as they say.'

'Good. We'll be down at the weekend.'

'Oh, yes, I thought you might, because there's a message from Miss Bentley, she's going to be in Tenterden and wondered if you and your wife were free for lunch on Sunday.'

At that news I sucked a tooth. Sooner or later I knew I would have to face the ordeal of dining with Elizabeth and Claire across the table from each other.

11

Rang Claire next morning from Montpellier airport, to say I'd arrived safely. Four feet away from the telephone a woman stood combing a sitting man's hair. Claire didn't answer. I left a message on the answering machine. Checked with the office. Lemon told me Strafe had rung and confirmed the meeting.

This journey intrigued me. Strafe had bought a dilapidated chateau. When he first told me about it I thought, Cliché, but I was wrong. Strafe intended commerce. He had begun to pursue a series of such projects and had already bought two others. Renovated and fully restored, they would become conference venues to international organizations seeking something different. The European Union had preleased one of them for an economic summit two years ahead.

Empty autoroute: bright sunshine: roadworks at the Remoulins junction. Why can't we manage our roadworks as efficiently? The French keep everything moving – including the workmen. She *must* be there. Why didn't she answer? Still encased in ice, that's why. If she had to get up for work, go out to an office or any form of employment the ice would fall away in the chafing heat of the world. She must get herself occupied. Does she slam when I'm not there?

This is how we lived. I worked five days a week, based at the practice or, like this, visiting sites. Claire, wishing to be near me, always came to London during the week. On her good days she rose at ten or eleven, dappled and dabbled about the flat, met a friend for what she called 'a retail lunch' – in other words they went shopping. I could expect three, four or five phone calls from here, there and everywhere. On her bad days she stayed in the flat – ten, fifteen, twenty calls.

Her friends – I had scarcely met any – never came across as nourishing. I encouraged her to see her parents more often. David liked theatre matinées, which worked beautifully – until Fran began feeling claustrophobia. For one short period I persuaded Claire to become a tourist and she brought back hilarious reports from the Tower of London, the Old Bailey, the Royal Mews. But that, too, palled. I began to feel like one of those bachelors in an American romantic comedy whose pretty niece has come to stay and he doesn't know what the hell to do with her.

No, this has to stop. She could read law? Why not? Or what else? Not interested in medicine. She loves the theatre – anything there? The tollbooth shimmered like a heatwave. What's she doing now? Will she go shopping today, or to the gym? She should go to Aylesbury, spend a night or two with her parents. Her patience with her mother, her tenderness, makes me wince with shame that I don't have such a gift. In Remoulins there's a man scooting along the street as though in a walking race. Claire's the only person I have ever known who walks faster than I do.

Strafe had chosen the Hotel Robinson, just down the road from the Pont du Gard. His hallmark yellow Porsche sat there.

'You drove over?'

'Don't be stupid, Nicholas.'

'But the Porsche?'

'Check the plates.'

I laughed. 'So you're going to have a Porsche in every country where you do business?'

Strafe put on his wicked look. 'Where's your wife? I hope she's here?'

'Afraid not.'

'Pity.'

I tussled for some advantage.

'Heard from the police yet?' I asked. 'You hadn't the last time we spoke.'

'They never showed.'

I gave the knife another little twist. 'They'll get to you. I had to give a statement. Have you heard any developments?'

He shrugged. 'Nothing.'

Strafe looked immovable.

I tried one more twist. 'Any idea what's the status of their investigation?'

He flinched with impatience. 'Oh, listen to him! "Status"! He knows all the jargon. Of course, I forgot, didn't I? Nicholas is a veteran of these matters.'

Very creepy being spoken of in the third person to your face.

I tried one more time to plant the knife.

'Unsatisfactory to have a board member murdered.'

'It *still* hasn't upset the share price.'

A journalist friend of mine once interviewed John Ehrlichman, the disgraced Nixon aide, to whom he put violent questions – nefarious White House practices, Watergate, lies, deaths and other things. He told me Ehrlichman swatted him aside without shifting an eyebrow. Richard Strafe had the same ability.

I kept trying. 'Nevertheless,' I said, 'big fuss over Clay's death.'

'Yeah. Typical.'

He took my frown for puzzling at what he meant.

'Those people exaggerate everything. Look at the way they've rewritten history.'

'What about history?'

'You know what I mean.'

Strafe has sharp and powerful antennae. Sometimes he

picks up a signal from an inexact source but with enough strength to alert him. Somehow I found the courage and said it.

'My wife – whom you're kind enough to admire. She doesn't look it, but she's Jewish.'

Strafe grinned at me, his lizard eyelids shutting and opening. No reply – and I felt feeble.

Which he picked up, because next he cried, 'Hey. I need to talk to you about the fees you're charging. I'm paying you a fortune.'

Now, at least, I had an arena in which to release other feelings.

'Any idea what the *un*talented practices would charge you?'

He laughed. '*Un*talented? What do you call your lot?'

Time to jab. 'Sometimes I call us not perhaps particular enough about our clients.'

It hit him. 'Well, let's see how good you are today.'

He sulked and I rang down a silence by reading the menu. Any traveller would call this place an ordinary, holiday hotel, out in the countryside, near a major tourist attraction. But the French don't confine good food to the stars of Paris or Lyons.

Strafe switched on his power. With the force of a turbine he briefed me on the job. I made pages of notes; once more his energy amazed me.

We drove separately to the site. Strafe drove ahead of me. In that, too, he applied the pressure, hammering the Porsche. For the first half-mile I tried to keep up in my hired Peugeot. Then, I thought, No, slow down, make him wait for me. Not only that, I deliberately slowed down to relish the Pont du Gard. Every time I see the size of those arches and the width of the span I marvel. And they did it without steel or concrete.

Three miles on, Strafe parked in the tumbledown gate to

a long avenue of heavy trees. I had not seen him so excited. Over lunch he had talked of his battle with the French law of entail.

'They're impossible. Fifteen families on this one,' he said. 'Everyone wanting a scratch off it.'

Cicadas clicked in the heat; I love the Midi. Exotic trees of ancient gardens held their own against encroaching wilderness. The avenue fell dim. Weeds on the gravel quietened our footsteps. Ahead the ochre path disappeared in a sharp elbow.

Which we rounded. And I stopped dead. Like some massive, golden dower house of Heaven, the chateau stood five hundred metres away, blinking in the sun.

I gasped. Utterly splendid. Didn't know they had anything like this south of the Loire. The sheer *size* of it. And the *ornateness* – ohh! Echoes of Brissac? And a little theft perhaps from Chambord? The little domed minarets? It most reminded me of Cheverny. It had that same calm parade of windows, the escutcheon medallions and then the high-shouldered shiny roofs. Oh, God! This is more beautiful than any woman. Had Strafe not been with me I'd have wept.

My mind on fire, I almost ran down the slope. I had not enough eyes to look with. How did they do it? That façade has to be early seventeenth century. Let's see. One, two, three, then a high arch, then four, five, six – they built it as a series of linked pavilions. And then the last two pavilions, slightly apart at each end, east and west – they're probably later.

A northern architect? Possibly. But the pagoda? Seventeenth century too. Or eighteenth. Hold on: those outer pavilions – they could be eighteenth; I'll know when I get nearer. The tiny slates shone like ravens. I wanted to lick the creamy gold stone.

'She's lovely, eh?' Strafe said. 'The Japs'll fucking eat her.'

You can't see the river until you get down to the terrace. Ah yes, I see – they diverted the Gard. As they did with the Cosson at Chambord. French landscapists manage water better than anyone (except maybe the Chinese).

But surely this must be one of the biggest chateaux in France? That façade has to be nearly two hundred metres. The stone looks like parchment. No trace of brickwork, real or painted. A pure building; that stone might have been dressed by a laundress. The mason must also have sealed it. With what? The house's papers may say.

I wonder who the architect was? Could it have been le Camus? No, too early. Was it too late for Leonardo da Vinci? Oh Christ, wouldn't it be wonderful if it were Leonardo! Or Bougier? It might be Bougier, this is a mason's work.

Through the central archway I could see what was still a passable parterre. A young red deer came legging out like a shy girl at a dance.

'Bang! You're dead!' Strafe yelled.

The animal swerved away down the parkland. Beauty and the Beast? Yep – Richard Strafe's the owner of this wonderful house.

We walked the terrace first. Many of the long windows had been boarded up from the inside. I counted. Six per individual 'pavilion', therefore twenty-four either side of the archway – forty-eight French windows in the entire façade. Only one had broken glass, at the farthest, the west, end. It looked as though a bird had crashed into it; the French have not acquired the British national habit of vandalism. This stone was cut like silk.

I walked away and stood far back on the westerly mound. Strafe watched me; I tried to ignore him. The chateau watched me too. This is like the trick Palladio pulled off in Venice. No matter where you stand, the front doors of his three churches across the Giudecca seem to look you in the eye. Same effect here.

Then I went back to where Strafe stood and began to measure. Each window stood twelve feet high and twelve wide. That was the secret of the placid symmetry.

'Who was the original architect?'

Strafe said, 'How should I know?'

'D'you realize it might have been Leonardo da Vinci? Or the great Bougier?'

'So long as it shoves up the value.'

'The Japanese will love it,' I said but he missed the irony.

'Yeah, but will the French let me fucking do it?' He jigged about.

I squinted along the façade's length. So far no bulging. No subsidence, at first glance.

'There's roof damage at the back,' he said. 'When can you have the show on the road?'

'I'm not doing this one without a survey.'

'Aren't you a surveyor?'

'I mean a French surveyor.'

'That's more costs.'

'It's the best way.'

'You're trying to fuck me over.'

Is this the famous rage appearing? If it is – what do I do? Do I walk away? No. I love good buildings . . .

A trick I learned from Elizabeth: in an edgy negotiation, lower your voice. Give your opponent a problem hearing you. Added advantage with a man like Strafe: he mistakes it for menace. I spoke without looking at him.

'Richard, I want a French surveyor on this. You will be glad of it –'

'What'you saying?'

'Because you do not begin to have an idea of how the French heritage *départements* will hold you up –'

'I can't fucking hear you!'

He came and stood right beside me, craning his neck to listen. I pressed on like a metronome.

71

'So what you're going to do is – you're going to hire a French surveyor. One that I recommend, who does a lot of conservation work.'

'But the French bend the rules more than anyone! You some kind of dickhead?'

I walked away. He muttered something. I didn't hear it and I didn't want to hear it. Inside the gateway he came and stood beside me.

As if nothing had happened, Strafe said, 'I'm going to make this into the pool area.'

'No, you're not. That is a late seventeenth-century parterre needing very little restoration. Nobody's going to let you take that out and put in a swimming pool.'

I was going to have such pleasure denying him the crasser requests.

'Can't we pretend? When they've inspected, who gives a fuck? After the final inspection?'

I lied, but not much. 'In France the conservation authorities inspect every year.'

Strafe had in his hand a huge key.

I said, 'There's your marketing gimmick.' The teeth of the key formed some old emblem.

He looked at it and lit up. 'Oh? Yeah. Good idea.' Strafe had a boyish side.

Glorious interior. Somebody had loved it and possibly spent all their money – maybe even their life – on retaining its condition. Curtains remained, some a century old I guessed, and a threadbare carpet clung to the horseshoe staircase.

Long, long hallway; rooms radiating off – chambers, anterooms, libraries. The first salon I entered had a painted ceiling, a joy of cloud-blues and deep reds, white swags of silk so realistic they might rustle. And a door, as delicate as a tea-plate, picked out in dark blue, light blue and primrose.

Through that door came a ballroom, still with its blue and

saffron colours intact; it ran the width of three salons, in parallel to the front hall. Again, the condition excelled what could have been expected. Perhaps this house had been locked up to preserve it.

Benign air though, inside and out, and scarcely musty. The sad thought crossed my mind that it would serve Strafe's purposes admirably. He had a genius for property and I feared he would insist on a headlong surge towards commerce. How can I control that?

The solution came to me. I called as I walked towards him down the ballroom, 'I hope your budget's up to it.'

'Yeah?'

'Biggest restoration I've seen. This is as big as any house in England.'

'Cliveden?'

'Much bigger.'

'Jesus!'

'Have you actually bought it?'

'What the fuck you saying? Of course I've bought her. Fucking nightmare when you don't have a word of French.'

Slightly touching that he called all his properties 'she' or 'her'?

'It's possible, you know – to get substantial grants.'

He was instantly alert. 'How much?'

'Up to seventy per cent.'

'On all of them?'

'Yep.' I exaggerated the figure. What I didn't tell him was that any grant he accepted bound him hand and foot to the conservationists – which suited me fine.

'Are you saying to me that I can get the French to pay for up to seventy per cent of all this work? Including your exorbitant fees?'

'I'll certainly give it a try.'

'And you speak enough French?'

'With a little help.'

73

Strafe whooped. Then he did this disconcerting thing I'd seen him do before. He dropped to the floor and began doing impossibly heroic press-ups.

We stayed a couple of hours at the site. I agreed to have a drink with him in Uzès. We sat in one of the cafés at the Place aux Herbes. Strafe gazed into the falling sunlight.

'This square, those pillars. As old as my place?'

'Six hundred years older. This is tenth century.'

He did not look pleased. I watched him, sidelong. Nothing in him remained still; not his fingers nor his feet nor his hands. He twitched all the time. In profile the shelving cheekbones made him gaunt like an alien. He had unhappy eyes.

Strafe was booked into the Entraigues in Uzès. I opted for La Regalido in Fontvielle, almost an hour away.

'Dinner?' he asked.

I shook my head. 'Must check in.'

'Cancel it. Stay here.' He wanted company. But he'd have angered and bored me. I lied.

'I can't. I'm meeting friends of mine.'

'Oh, come on. See them another time.'

I sensed pleading and I am not good with pleading; it gets to me.

'Sorry. I really can't.' I felt myself wincing.

'Maybe I should come with you. We could talk some more over dinner.'

I softened. 'Come for dinner tomorrow night.'

'Okay. But stay now. Be my guest.'

'I can't, Richard. They're expecting me.'

He gave in, disappointed. As I turned to leave he held out his hand. I shook hands with him and he held on with both hands.

'Nicholas. You'll do this brilliantly. I know you will.' He said this looking straight into my eyes. I almost blushed with the force of his charm.

74

12

La Regalido grants sweet privacy. And glowing light. For years when I've come down for the May or September corrida in Nîmes I've reserved Sarriette, a room with high ceilings and a clever sense of width. Have they redecorated it? No, thank Heaven, the same Provençal palette of yellows, lemons and light blues. And the same Monsieur Michel, tall, cheerful, competent and bald, addressing everything and everyone. I once watched him surreptitiously at the huge market in Arles early on a Saturday morning. No housewife there bought her fruit so fastidiously as did M. Michel.

The month of May in Provence brings cherries. Lavender scents the villages. I like this time in the south – my first alfresco meal of the year. Childish of me, but I enjoy watching La Regalido's hydraulic lift when they bring the *chariot des fromages* up the rear steps to the garden.

Smells of pine and cooking; I planned my life under these trees. Not once but several times, carving my solitary future. All changed now: not solitary any more. Or has it changed? Claire's not speaking to me. Feast or famine. Twenty calls a day or silence.

I ordered the courgette soufflé. Then the *rognons de boeuf*. When the French cook beef kidneys all the coarseness disappears. Nowhere else in France have I tasted them so tender.

How am I to break Claire's ice? Maybe I should write her a letter? And perhaps the words will reach her as I write them down. How shall I address her? 'My love'? 'My darling'? 'Dearest Claire'? I crossed these out. Yes, I *must* be emotionally retarded if I can't actually decide how to address my own wife.

It's the gap, isn't it, that defines intimacy? It's the width of the gap between oneself and the other person. And the ease with which we cross it. She's better at crossing it than I am. Wish she'd cross it now.

The thought took effect. Claire phoned as the main course arrived. I took the call at the reception desk. She prattled cheerfully, as though nothing had happened, and I went along with that. Elizabeth Bentley has a saying, trite but useful: 'You have to work with what you have.'

We kept the conversation brief. Claire's 'tarty friend' Lucinda (whom I had never met) was about to arrive for a drink.

'And my main course has just come.'

'A man's gotta eat,' she cracked in her John Wayne accent. 'Speak later?'

That's better.

Tomorrow is the anniversary of my parents' wedding. What was that day like? Was my mother unmanageably fretful? My father said that when he saw her at the church he almost burst into tears she looked so – so . . . He never finished the sentence. The day after he married her, he went back to the war – the war that would kill him with its wounds thirty years after it ended. A week after the wedding, my mother went back to an old lover. And had lovers thereafter.

Between bites, between courses, I made notes. Today I have seen the most beautiful house I have ever been privileged to see. Excited, I listed the people I needed to talk to, the offices I wanted to telephone, the officials I must meet. At the next table a couple as old as dried fruit spoke unceasingly to each other, they talked and touched all the time. He had a cream silk pocket handkerchief, she had thin black Duchess-of-Windsor arcs instead of eyebrows and lips pursed like petals. I had a feeling I had seen them here in the past, on those long, lone evenings under these trees, before Claire's arrival ripped the chart of my future to shreds.

Sometimes I think back with a shiver to that day the Berliners lifted her in Rye. They stuffed her full of heroin and hauled her across Europe. So cruel. And it will prove tragic, if I can't recover her. It wasn't Claire's fault that Antony robbed Jewish bank accounts during the war. It wasn't Claire's fault that Antony gypped his German 'partners'. And that Philippe went on doing it.

I don't know how much she knew – and I don't think she's told me the whole story. Certainly she had met the Berliners long before they snatched her, my bones say she had. As I now know, she doesn't tell me everything. Although when we talked it through, she said she knew that by making me his executor Antony had set me up. Thanks, old pal. But I mustn't get negative at night or I won't sleep.

Three little cubes of Chaumes; then an apricot *galette* followed by camomile tea with those dense chocolate truffle balls that glisten when you bite into them. Across the garden the night caved softly in. When I called again, no reply; Lucinda had come and they'd gone out. I left a message; now she had to call me back; we had poor timing that night.

The evening stretched on. I worry over what she does when I'm not there – she digs up the past, she calculates what the Nazis wrenched from her family. What could she do with her life, what might she take up to occupy her? Evenings like this, when she's with a friend, they're better, she's safer.

Late diners flooded into the garden. I returned to my table and ordered a fresh pot of camomile. Finally Claire's call came and I took it in my room. We talked about the day.

'Tell me about Lucinda.'

She laughed. 'Lucinda has golden eyes and a nice line in oral sex.'

'How d'you know that?'

'She told me.'

'Is that what you talked about?'

'Nicholas, you know what girls talk about.'

'Did you cook?'

'No, we went to Colson's. Lucinda had never been there. Of course she'd read a review of it, she reads all the colour magazines and the restaurant reviews.'

'Nice evening?'

'Yes, you know how pleasant they are. We went and stood in the Gun Garden afterwards. There was the highest wind I've known for ages; you'd have loved it. The trees were whipping.' Claire's tone improved. 'Nicholas, I've been walking through the rooms. Time to redecorate.' She had her business voice on.

I joked. 'Don't give me a hard time. I've had that all day.'

'How was he?'

'Vile.'

'I'm thinking of going to Aylesbury.'

'Good idea,' I said. 'I could pick you up from Heathrow.'

'Mother knew Clay Massey. As I expect you might have guessed.'

'Oh, dear.' But I let it pass. Didn't want to raise any spectres from this distance. Claire picked up my discomfort and moved on.

'You know, this could be the most beautiful house on the south coast. Lucinda and I talked about it, she thinks it's a great idea. Oh, and there's another house for sale in the square.'

Claire's voice is quite sing-song. I had mixed feelings at her domestic eagerness: dismay, yet some kind of cautious delight. 'Achievement,' the psychiatrist said; 'that's what we want, get her into a way of life that will give her a sense of achievement – what they call "tangible success".'

How often, though, had she tried things and suddenly given up halfway through in anger or tears or both? Okay, let her redecorate; it might take her mind off that wretched 'paperwork'. Her mother knew Clay Massey? Oh, hell! Plus – if she redecorates it will home-make. I asked myself once or twice, Did I marry Claire because I wanted tradition? A home with a fireside and a wife? As Hal cracks, 'It's nice to have a wife to put your feet up on.'

I never really had home comfort. The chintz armchairs of my childhood were icebergs, with Mother too flighty, too jerky to make a placid hearth.

We chatted on until Claire felt sleepy. It grew into one of our good talks. The feelings between us got easier again. As my caution drops, my affection rises. She made me laugh.

'Nicholas, has it occurred to you – Richard Strafe and Mary Strait: the names are very alike. Do you suppose they are by any chance related?'

'Tell you what.' I warmed to it. 'Why don't we do a little matchmaking? Strafe's looking for a wife. He told me he dumped the last one.'

'He "dumped" her?'

'His word.'

'My! What a lovely person.'

13

Next morning I spent enjoyable hours among the officials of Uzès. The planners on the continent of Europe have a simple rule for the Englishman: send the fool farther. Always one more office to visit, one more form to fill, one more fee to pay. It doesn't bother me too much. Hopeful travelling, pleasant arrival. And so much coffee. One small breakthrough: a municipal architect announced he'd once been to a lecture of mine.

I got to the chateau at about three.

Strafe said, 'Where's this inspector?'

I wagged a folder at him. 'Do you want me to suggest contractors?'

'Is this guy someone we can shaft?'

'If you don't have a French contractor it slows up everything.'

'I have to have her up and running in a year.'

He poked at the sheaf of documents on planning and conservation I had picked up during the morning. I held them out to him.

'Expect a lot of inspections. I mean – a lot.'

Strafe looked bored. 'So?'

'And at every inspection, work has to stop until the inspector's certificate is issued.'

Not strictly true in practice, but it can happen, I've seen it. I briefed him on what I'd found: the competent authority; the probable timescale; the local contracting power for this kind of work; the likely planning level.

'It'll go up to national government.'

'That high?'

'Given the importance of the building.'

'I'm not paying any bribes. If you pay bribes, you bear the cost.'

'I never said a word about bribes.'

Strafe changed direction swift as a fish. 'Is your wife coming down?'

'Not sure yet.' I was completely sure, having spoken to Claire that morning, her voice still sleepy.

'Keeping her to yourself, are you?'

I ignored it.

'Where are we dining tonight?' he asked.

Aha! So he forgets things. Or does he merely check them out?

The inspector arrived, a formal little man in his hound's-tooth jacket; *M. Gerard Imbert*, his card said. There came a moment when he stood on the far side of Strafe and I couldn't see him because Strafe's bulk masked M. Imbert. But he possessed true force. I loved his control – he gave Strafe no room, no place to go.

M. Imbert and I conversed busily. I played a fiercely straight bat, relaying the essence to Strafe. M. Imbert, I sensed, would like me less if he saw me taking advantage of my client's linguistic disadvantage. Therefore I spoke respectfully of the project, of 'M'sieu' Strafe and of la France's official requirements. The world divides into two kinds of planning official – those you can work with and those you can't. M. Imbert and I liked each other.

I confess to one oily patch, a kind of gush; I told M. Imbert the chateau seemed to me as glorious as 'la France' herself. Gravely he agreed and I realized he meant it. As, I realized, did I.

We quit the site at four o'clock. Strafe had the sense to thank the inspector.

'Well?' he demanded as M. Imbert drove away.

'He's sticky,' I said. 'Likes his details but he wants to get it right. So that's okay.'

'I didn't like him. We're gonna have trouble with that little fucker.'

I said, 'Dinner tonight? Remember?'

'Yeah, sure.' Again he hit me with that most dreadful of charms – the one based on loneliness. He put his hand on my shoulder and said, 'Thanks again, Nicholas.'

Strafe watched me drive away. I felt his eyes on my neck. Perhaps I'll put Mary Strait on this job. Whew! What are the dangers in that? I'll try and gauge it tonight over dinner. Wish I were dining alone.

Strafe didn't keep the appointment. Seven thirty came. Eight. Half past eight. At which moment I wrote him off and ordered the gourmet *carte*.

A wedding party partied on. The warmth of the night unsettled me. Half past ten, half past nine at home. Eleven o'clock, ten at home. I edged out of La Regalido's tiny car park and then rang Claire.

'Where are you?'

'Just passing Montmajour. I'm driving into Arles to walk around.'

'You must bring Fran an Arlesian *galette*; she talks about them.'

'One *galette* coming up.'

'Oh, hey – no Mrs Lydiard today.' She sounded irritated.

'Has she rung? Perhaps she's ill.'

'Not a word.'

'Most unlike her,' I said. 'She's fabulously reliable.'

'I don't find her so.' On this subject Claire was terse.

'Oh?'

'No. There's something about her.'

I changed the subject. 'What time you going to bed?'

No, the irritation is in me, because I haven't told her about Berlin tomorrow and I feel guilty.

Claire said, 'I'll be up for a while. How's Strafe?'

'*Quelle question,*' I said. 'He was supposed to meet me for dinner.'

'And?'

'Not a word. He didn't telephone, didn't appear. I'm rather relieved. He keeps mentioning you, asks if you're coming down, makes lewd remarks about you.'

'Oh – do tell. I love lewd remarks about me.' (Actually she didn't.)

'I don't want to tell you until I'm looking at you.'

'Give me a hint.'

'I'll tell you in bed.'

She squealed.

I parked down by the Rhône and from the car rang Ruby. As the call went through I thought, No, she'll be at the club. But she answered.

'Oh, darling, how kind of you to ring.' She coughed a little. 'Where are you?'

'France, the south. I've been down here with Richard Strafe. He was to have met me for dinner tonight. But he didn't show up.' Why did I tell her? What was I testing?

Silence from Ruby. She began to cough again. I waited. When she had finished she began to say, 'Darling, the thing is –'

'Ruby, I need you to tell me. I know you know something.'

Ruby had seen me in many moods; she knew me well enough to read me. The line quietened as she thought. When she spoke again her voice had grown flat.

'We meet in the airport – Berlin-Tegel, I mean? Ten thirty?'

'Or thereabouts.'

'Each of us waits for the other, darling? The old spy trick?'

'Why Berlin, Ruby?'

'Darling, not on the phone.'

At the cafés of Arles the people sat under the trees. I want the smell of cooking and Gitanes at my funeral. Walk first, phone Claire later. How shall I tell her about Berlin without distressing her? No. Call her now.

'Where are you?'

'On the streets of Arles. Would you like something by Lacroix?'

'Give my love to Princess Caroline. Or is it Stephanie?'

'I might buy myself a suit of lights.'

'What's a suit of lights?' she asked.

'You know – what the matador wears.'

'By the way. I will definitely go to Aylesbury.'

'Terrific,' I said, grateful of the distraction. 'I'll get to you there about seven.'

'That's what I thought. Good night, lovely Nicholas.'

'I'm not the one who's lovely,' I growled. Thus did I fail to tell her about Ruby and Berlin.

One day I may live in Arles: van Gogh's face; Glanum, where it looks as though the Romans left last week. The *Arènes* gates are open. Excellent. Of course – *Pentecôte* at the weekend, they're preparing. This is the best time down here. I saw some years ago the *Transhumance*, when they take the sheep up to the pastures for the summer. And the bullfights, can't talk about them in England where we value animals more than humans. The young Nîmois matador, Dennis Loré, fought here six years ago. A packed and hostile crowd – Arles versus Nîmes, so to speak – and his first bull turned Loré over three times. Then he came back, his torso a broad tube of white bandages, and took his second bull like a musician. Arles hailed him, they carried him shoulder-high into their streets. The Arlesian woman beside me wept. These stone bleachers were hauled into position by Caesar's slaves. I sat for a moment and savoured the place; I love it – and the amphitheatres at

Nîmes and Orange, their symmetry, their miraculous acoustics.

Down the sloped streets I drifted. Asylum door stands wide open. Poor Vincent. I have never liked Gauguin, for his unkindness to mad Vincent. Don't much like Gauguin's pictures either. But Vincent – ah! Even in the dusk you can see why the gnarled van Gogh perspective is a triumph.

Somewhere I heard a car engine roar. Bizarre experience breeds unerring instinct. A moment later Richard Strafe and a woman walked into the courtyard. Arm in arm and animated, they stood in the centre and looked around them at the pillars, the rows of windows, the trees with their bark flaking like leprosy. Yellow light caught the woman's full-flowing, frizzy hair.

They sauntered towards where I lurked. From my shadows I strained to hear. The biscuit-coloured stone warmed my back. Strafe's voice carried to me. He was speaking in flawless French.

14

So he lies! Surprise, surprise. File it away for future use. Richard Strafe lies. In this case he did it to check my honesty. Strafe understood every word I had spoken to little inspector Imbert.

Such nerve and its implications kept me awake. My face creaked with tiredness at Tegel in the morning. Ruby played it straight: dark glasses and no lavish show. She didn't kiss me; she asked for a coffee. We sat at the most ubiquitous tables in airport Europe – circular and zinc-topped. She drank two killer coffees; I drank one.

Until Clay Massey's funeral I had never seen Ruby out-of-doors. At her club she's taller. In the airport she looked short and a touch chubby. The journalist who compared her to Raquel Welch had a point. I felt my tongue move when I looked at Ruby's lips. Her bearing imposed silence which I tried to respect. She carried no luggage, just a square leopardskin handbag. Her cream linen suit looked young, brittle and rich.

Over coffee I began, 'Now, Ruby. Time to ask some –'

She shook her head. 'Later, darling.'

The silence continued.

When we rose to go she opened her handbag. I, thinking she meant to pay for the coffee, began to protest. Wrong assumption. Instead of a purse Ruby pushed a piece of paper across the table. I read it: '71, Spannungstrasse.'

'This is where we're going?'

She nodded. 'Near the Zoo, darling.'

In deference to her I hired the newest 5 Series BMW; I

wanted to drive it anyway; I'm sick of the way the Saab's snow flanges scrape every traffic ramp. Not to mention the steep entrance at Rye.

In the car, Ruby put out a hand and touched my thigh. All the old comfort flooded back, followed by guilt about Claire.

'Ruby, please tell me –'

'Darling, be patient. You will learn many things today.'

'What sort of things?'

'Not yet, darling.'

During the lines of traffic Ruby gazed out at Charlottenburg and distant Berlin. She wore a mood I had never seen in her, profound and indefinable. I wanted to ask, 'Ruby, what are you thinking?' – but didn't dare. Men assume they can fathom a woman they've slept with. Not necessarily true. We drove along Bismarckstrasse and towards the Tiergarten.

Call Spannungstrasse dull. It has some shops, a sex boutique or two and great grey ranges of anonymous European buildings. We found number 71. Ruby made me drive to the far end of the street and return. She pointed out a parking bay directly outside.

The meter had twenty minutes. I switched off the engine and climbed out as Ruby looked the building up and down.

She opened the car window. 'Darling,' she called eventually, 'tell me what the name on the plate says.'

Was this Weimar's best planning? If so, be glad Hitler didn't win – lumpen, highflown and unappealing.

'"Zurich."'

'No, darling. It can't be.'

I looked again. 'Oh. Sorry. "Zurück." Z-U-R-U-C-K.'

From the car she pointed, and so I tried the tall, immovable door. She indicated a small notice I hadn't seen. *Zustellung Verboten.*

'Deliveries forbidden,' she translated.

I said, 'And no doorbell. No knocker. They do not expect

visitors. Weird or what?' I tapped the brass plate. 'Zurück, what is it?'

She stared at the building.

Like a gunslinger I whipped out my mobile. 'Let's try for a telephone number.'

Directory Enquiries on my mobile said – No Zurück listed in Berlin.

'Police, then. Central Berlin, please.'

Ruby shied away, as though fearing I'd hand her the phone. 'Please, darling, no.'

'*Sprechen Sie* –' I began and the voice cut into me.

'I speak English, what is it?'

'I'm on Spannungstrasse, and I'm trying to find out why the company at number seventy-one will not answer the door.'

'Spannungstrasse? Just one moment.' Dead sound filled my ear. Then, 'Why do you wish to know?'

'I need to speak to them.'

Ruby half-climbed from the car and, white-faced, waved to stop me. The line went dead.

'Oh, darling, you shouldn't have.'

Her hands shook.

'But I thought –'

'Can we go, darling? Please? *Now?!*'

As my seatbelt clicked home I heard the siren. A screaming police car braked fast to my window. Two officers climbed out, halting me with brutal, flat hands.

One rapped in 'voss-diss' English, 'Turn off your engine. Get out of the car, plizz. Now.'

I stood. They examined the ignition key. One held out his palm for my passport; the other lurked half-behind me. The first read the details into his carphone and then spoke to me in English.

'Plizz, why do you want to make all enquiries?'

I said, 'I'm a businessman, I want to know –'

Stuck for a reason, I stopped. They looked at my passport, then looked at me. One had a small white scar-gash in an eyebrow. The first cop handed me back my passport, tapped my car roof and made a 'drive-on' gesture. Without a word they left as abruptly as they came.

'What was all that about?' I asked the morning air. They irked and baffled me but I was glad they ignored Ruby.

Ruby's demeanour said – Say nothing. She reached into her bag. Another piece of paper. Her face was still pale. I patted her hand.

'Sorry, Ruby.'

Zurück. Strange name – bad vibe.

15

I first saw Ruby in her club. Some Japanese clients took Elizabeth and me there after dinner.

Elizabeth said, 'I think I must be too old for all this,' and then squeaked, 'That's a *real* ruby' – the rock above the door.

Think of people as buildings. Elizabeth is a sexy, lacy, old manor house. I imagine Claire as a sumptuous yet minimalist riverside apartment. And Ruby? Ruby can only be a nightclub.

From that first evening, I knew what she'd done. She'd pulled that old trick – find the one thing you do well and cash in on it. Singing was Ruby's trick – with added personality. She belted out torch songs, she hovered over ballads, she drooled Gershwin, Hoagy Carmichael, Johnny Mercer. Ruby could be as stylish as Peggy Lee, as memorable (and not as irritating) as Billie Holiday, as smooth and dangerous as Dietrich. In flashes, not all at once – otherwise she'd have been a megastar. But she also added wit. And of course she put on the ritz – or, rather, took it off.

That night, she began with a zinging tour of her repertoire. She was like Bach – every tune she held seemed to run others beneath it. Dragging the last phrases of 'The Very Thought of You', she came on louche as well as smouldering. She turned 'Mad About the Boy' into something that could have been sung by a dowager or a doll. Then she coasted into her production number, 'Mister Wonderful'. I'd never have noticed that song in a thousand miles of car radio. For years after I couldn't hear it without bursting into flame.

As always she began cold. *Why this feeling?* Ruby holds out her left arm and peels off the long glove. *Why this glow?* Long red glove – gone. *Why this thrill?* Second glove peeling off. *When you say hello?* Glove off and gone, naked arms raised like sex. *What's this strange.* Her hands reached behind her. *And tender magic I view? Mister Wonderful, that's you.* Gown gone, in a pool of glistening red satin at her feet.

She was four phrases in and the band picked it up. Ruby stood there in a one-piece black number, fishnet stockings, garters and high-heels. She should have added up to some kind of cliché – hands on her hips and her cleavage a bow wave. But no – she had a kind of rude innocence. The band slogged on, lazy jazz with Ruby waiting for their next bar. Customers, glinting deep in the shadows, sat forward and waited.

Ruby steps it out. She's on the edge of the darkness. I see her profile. My thought is, That's a girl's face. But a woman's body. I sneak a look at her now, beside me in the car. And I look away. *Why this joy when you touch my cheek?* Ruby turns her back to the folks and pats her behind. The folks laugh like kids. Never was a song so double-meaning – but so good-humouredly, because now she places a hand on her heart and when she takes it away again she hauls the black one-piece from her torso like she's unveiling a plaque. Underneath she's wearing a criminal black satin bra and high-cut knickers, she still has the garters and the fishnets and I realize I'm counting what she's wearing.

The band hits a phrase of marching music. Ruby goose-steps across to a lone silver chair. She's into the chord change like a snake. She unhooks a pin and shakes out that head of chestnut hair, it falls like a cataract. Wheeee! She hikes a leg up on the chair and plants it there, hurling the Wild-West-saloon garters to the shadows. By magic she's able to slide the first fishnet off her leg without taking off the shoe. Everybody laughs. Now she's dragging the phrases.

Elizabeth Bentley, age then mid-sixties, winked at me. I remember my young surprise that she enjoyed it so much.

Ruby's in high-heels now, two garments left. In the car beside me this morning in Berlin she's sitting grave as a child, her profile solemn, the chestnut hair on her shoulders tied loosely in a grey velvet ribbon. But in my memory's eye I see her sashaying forward centre-stage in the full white light, the hair pinned behind one ear, falling over her face on the other side. The band behind her is shoving and sobbing; I can see the instruments gleam from the dusk.

Oh, there's much more I could say. She's tender now, and she's a woman undressing for a lover she's afraid she'll lose. With an air of regret she tugs at the knickers. They open at the side and she's wearing a thong. As frail as all women she turns fully away from us and off comes the bra. We're looking at the most vulnerable sight in the world, a woman's naked shoulders.

Ruby raises a hand. The band holds it. Silence. Ruby's alone now, her back to us. Deeper silence. The spot picks out her upraised hand. We, the audience, hold our breath. Ruby goes into that old teenage gag – she mimes like a hugging couple seen from the back, her hands caressing her spine. Now she's singing unaccompanied.

She's whispering. *Mister Wonderful.* She murmurs it. *Mister Wonderful.* Deep, slow pause. *Mister WON-derful!* Her back's still turned to us. She's loafing the words, using them, dragging, thrilling. Moving up into a shout. *I – LOVE – YOU!*

A hand flashed and her thong flew through the air. Ruby turned to the audience and for a split instant we saw all of her. Or did we? No, we saw no more than a subliminal glimpse of any naked woman since time began. With drums and saxes and stabbing mutes the lights crashed a sudden death and Ruby had gone.

I thought I glimpsed her bare, departing shape. But I knew I only imagined it. Like every man there I wanted to have seen it. And like every man there I knew that she sang that song to me. The old clichés are the best. Which is why I sent her a huge garland of flowers next morning: 'Wear these around your neck.' Ruby, do I love you?

Outside the window of the car I'm looking at the new skyline of Berlin and the fantastic concentration of towers. We didn't bid for any of Potsdam's resurrection. I could never build on Hitler's earth, not after my parents' war – his courage, her infidelities.

Ruby says, 'Follow the signs for Lindenberg, darling. The Hamburg signs,' and holds out the little map like a gift.

'Do you know how to get there?' I looked at the paper. '183, Magda Zemendstrasse.'

'Yes, darling. It's up in Weissensee. Quickest through Potsdam onto Unter den Linden.'

Someone draws a good chart.

Somewhere over there is Norman Foster's born-again Reichstag. No time to go and view. Behind us we leave the ruins of the Berlin Wall and worse, the cellars of the SS and Hitler's bunker, where at four o'clock in the morning of 29 April 1945, with the Russian guns half a mile away, Goebbels and Bormann witnessed Hitler's 'political testament'.

> But before everything else I call upon the leadership
> of the nation and those who follow it to observe
> the racial laws most carefully, to fight mercilessly
> against the poisoners of all the peoples in the world,
> international Jewry.

Ten pages of anti-Semitic rant. Deny that, Strafe. Must quote it to him some time. What's the point? He'll only say, 'Forgery.'

I think with anxiety and anger, *Nicholas, don't get into all this again!*

Up through Alexanderplatz, onto the Berliner Allee, turn

93

right into Lindenberg. Ruby navigates, thickening on the local pronunciations: she must have some working knowledge of German. A last right turn – Magda Zemendstrasse.

Here is deep suburbia. On Sundays the neighbours call *Guten Tag* to each other from the lawns where they bask. At Christmas they have drinks in each other's houses. Ruby's deep in thought; Ruby, what are you thinking? Along the long length of the *strasse* the structures change their nature – detached houses, apartments, large gates indicating estates or larger houses, then detached houses again and finally more apartment blocks and a parade of shops.

'Ruby, who was Magda Zemend?'

'She was a wonderful singer, darling. Operatic. In the generation after Mozart.'

The numbers – perfect, German precision. I drove unhesitatingly to 183, an apartment block.

'This is one eight three.' I stopped the car.

Ruby looked straight ahead. 'Describe it to me, darling.'

'It's an apartment block. It's got six floors. Probably built some time around 1850.'

She sat rigid as a steel bar, but the image of her fluid body wouldn't leave my mind. While we were driving through the locus of the worst horrors ever planned by civilized man I recalled Ruby stripping. Why? Ruby was never lewd. Only those who didn't see her performance called her pornographic. Ruby was a class act.

I suddenly realize – I do love this woman, I've loved her for a long time. Not *in* love. And not a love that threatens Claire. Nor will it destabilize my life. Claire, I murmur in my mind, there's no need to be jealous. No need.

Ruby spoke in a voice full of stress. 'Tell me about the fourth floor, darling.'

I owe her the privacy of not looking at her face.

'I'd say each apartment runs the length of one floor. Judging from the decor of the windows.'

'Yes, darling.' She might have meant, 'That is accurate.' Or she might merely have been acknowledging that I spoke.

'The fourth floor windows are painted in a kind of cooking-apple green, Ruby. They have lace curtains inside.'

'Tell me what the windows are like, darling.'

'They're tall, Ruby. Casements, probably the originals. In some cases I should think the glass is the original.'

'Darling, what's the entrance door like?'

She was right to call it an 'entrance door' – because neither 'entrance' nor 'door' did it justice. On a wide portal, carved foliage drifted like a Black Forest faience across the lintel. Deep inside that, set back about six feet, a pair of oak double doors, tall as a church, stood guard.

'It's an impressive entrance, Ruby.'

'Yes. Impressive, darling.'

I said nothing. She lit a cigarette. I looked again at 183. Wealthy middle Germans, the kind we pay our VAT for, the kind who pay their VAT for us – they live here. What did they do in the war, daddy? No, what was it the comic books said? 'For you, Fritz, the war is over.' Me. too.

Ruby blew smoke. I sat and looked at the building. Seeing nothing. Waiting. Then it came, the zigzag crack of lightning even though she spoke it soft as a sigh.

'Darling, Richard Strafe was born and grew up on that fourth floor.'

I said nothing.

'You're surprised, darling?'

'Well – yes.' To put it mildly.

'Be surprised again, darling. That fourth floor is also where I was born and grew up.'

'Wh-*at*?'

'True, darling.'

16

We don't always have to say something. Especially when there's nothing to say. I sat there and gripped the wheel. Ruby drew on her cigarette. The street remained quiet. Two, three cars drove by – nothing else. A woman in a suede jacket, blue jeans walked towards us, wielding her dog on a leash reel. Crisp white hair: I wondered if she had ever worked for Hitler.

Ruby finished her cigarette. She knew I wanted her to speak. I didn't want to carry this load. Claire would have helped, merely to hear her voice.

Ruby whispered, 'Drive, darling. Please.'

She had locked herself into herself; I could see her as through a glass booth. After two minutes I drove the car into a small, empty road, switched off the engine and took her hand. We sat there. Slowly, she composed herself.

'Thank you, darling,' she whispered.

'You did it once for me,' I said.

So she did. The police still hassling me over Madeleine's death. My guilt at my own callousness. Nobody I could tell. Ruby took me into the soft ridges of her body, no questions asked. And now I, who had a thousand questions, asked none.

Eventually I drove towards the airport. Five hours to kill before our flight. At a junction near Westhafen I turned down towards the canals and saw a good-looking restaurant.

'Ruby, to quote your own words – "you must eat".'

The public trouper carried her through. She took my arm

as we crossed the road, went to the ladies' cloakroom and emerged shining, picked up the menu with its green lettering and canal boat motif. Was she going to raise the subject? Would she allow me to?

I ordered her a drink; she slogged it down.

'Thank you, darling.'

'Ruby, this is all I ask. That one day – and soon – you will fill in the blanks.' She nodded.

Nobody else came to the canal boat restaurant. Our waiter had troubles of his own. The quiet of the day brought a comfortable silence.

I studied her face. From Ruby's deep looks she might have been Russian. Or from any of the old generations east of Berlin. Her nose was large, yes, but no cosmetic threat. Extraordinary eyes: in certain catches of the light the irises glistened like tears.

I have a wife at home who is as blonde as a Saxon and who also has brown eyes. And my mother had brown eyes. Ruby Hamer and her brown eyes.

We left Westhafen, full of dumplings or *schnitzel*, whatever – I can't cope with German food. Soon, past the Volkspark, I swung onto Müllerstrasse. Large silver cars and black saloons and trucks ran with us as though on rails. Are there no poor Germans? Or undisciplined German drivers?

If you're being followed you sense more than you see. Somebody was following us. I sensed it. Then I thought, But I often think I'm being followed and it's always nonsense. I checked the mirror. No, there *is* a car. He's keeping his distance. Am I making this up? I've been so wrong in the past. A silver-grey something. Driver, nobody else.

Quandary. Solved by the fact that I didn't wish to alarm Ruby. This, I told myself, is the decision: Okay, so you're being followed. Take no evasive action. It must be obvious I'm driving to Tegel. So what? I'm taking a flight back to London. Is that worth following? See if anything happens at the airport. I bet nothing will: often, all you have to do is think the thought. By the time I reached the airport tunnel the silver-grey follower had evaporated. My own 'so-what?' serenity surprised me.

I returned the BMW, having first dropped Ruby at Departures. That way round I could ring Claire at her mother's house. From which there was no reply; Friday afternoon – out for a walk, or shopping in Aylesbury? They resist technology, have no answering machine. My gut shifted a little; I should have rung Claire this morning but I cheated by telling myself she'd be asleep.

Ruby had checked in. She told them to hold the seat number beside her. We found the same coffee bar; for fun I chose the same table we had that morning; she smiled.

People walked past, nobody-people, meaning nothing to us. I suddenly missed Claire, apprehensive at the guilt I will feel when next I see her.

'Ruby –'

She guessed. With a heave of her shoulders she sat up and launched into a stream of long monotone.

'My grandfather Alexander, a young man, refused to leave Germany. He married the daughter of his father's business partner and they wouldn't leave unless the old people came too. My grandmother was called Hana.'

I began to interrupt but Ruby wagged a finger and pressed on fast.

'Everybody knew and was devoted to everyone else. They could hardly distinguish as to who came from which family. So. My grandparents would not leave unless everybody else came too. In nineteen forty, when their baby Liese was born, Liese was my mother, the young couple, Alexander and Hana, they were in their early twenties, they didn't want to go. Why should they? Many families were like that.'

'Are there photographs?' I asked. What my eyes can see keeps me sane.

'Most Jews lost all their mementoes. I have no souvenir of my own family, not one.' She was unusually stilted.

I nodded; I have some of my father's shirts, and my grandmother's furniture. My stomach heaved. Tough combination – Ruby and her past. I decided to hold up the story a little.

'My wife tells similar things,' I said. 'As you might expect.'

Ruby looked at me like stone and said, 'So you *could* have married me, darling.'

I shrugged meaninglessly and smiled at the compliment. Ruby didn't smile and I said, 'Please. I didn't mean to interrupt.'

Ruby folded her hands with their – always – ruby nail varnish.

'Now we come to the next generation. The one after the war. Do you know about the properties, darling?'

Oh, Christ! Am I going to be drawn into this morass whether I wish it or not? Claire and her bloody 'paperwork'.

'My grandparents' apartment. One eighty-three. The one you saw this morning. It happened to Alexander and Hana, too, darling. The knock on the door. Ten o'clock in the evening. My grandfather, he went down. On the doorstep is a man, a sort of stranger but Alexander thinks he recognizes him. Then, yes, he does recognize him – he lives on the next street or the one beyond that. He says to my young grandfather – and has the decency to half-apologize about it – he says, "I am sorry, my friend, but this is ours now." Alexander, he knows well what this means but thinks he'll try it on anyway and he asks, "What is yours now?" The man is a little embarrassed and from the shadows beside the door step two ugly boys in uniform, boys of about nineteen or twenty, and they say, "Your apartment is his now, so get out, *Juden*." By now Alexander remembers the neighbour's name and he also knows that this scene is being replayed hour by hour, day by day across Germany at that time. On the stairs Alexander stops and he returns and asks the soldiers, "But where will we go?" and he is told, "There is transport." Of course Alexander has also heard all the rumours but he goes upstairs and tells his young wife, Hana. "Hana," he says, "there is a member of the Nazi party downstairs with two soldiers and he wishes to step in and inspect our home. We have to go outside while he is doing it and we have to go on a bus to an office and do some new registration." Of course, he is lying – because he is confused and because he wants to save his wife pain, because their baby, Liese, that is my mother, she is in a cot, three months old and asleep, she has been awake all day, the little thing, with a chest infection and has only got off to sleep now and what are they to do? It is a bitterly cold night. Hana says to Alexander, "I know the wife of this man. She will look after Liese while we are out." And so the parents go down to the street leaving baby Liese asleep. It was a great mistake. But maybe it was not. Hana believed – must have believed – they were coming back shortly. But Alexander and Hana were taken away that night. There was no bus, they were made to walk to the train station and from there they were taken to the camps.'

When I'm stressed I whip off my spectacles and polish them. It's a habit that irritates me. Ruby watched me do it now. A psychologist would say it's a message that I'm not seeing things clearly. Sure thing. Ten thousand questions rocked me. But Ruby has amazing command. As I opened my mouth she headed me off.

'One moment, darling. Let me finish. The German family came in and they found the baby Liese and didn't know what to do, they had children of their own and here was this Jewish baby – a baby rat, if you believed the propaganda they believed.'

'Ruby –'

Her eyes became opaque. Gazing at me, she bit into the flesh of her thumb's mount. The teeth made marks like cogs. I reached for her hand. Her spasm of chagrin passed.

She said, 'Darling, they've called our flight.'

Ruby spoke no more to me that day. At Heathrow she reached up and kissed my mouth with her open lips. Then she was gone from me, jinking through the public like a jogger. I chose not to follow. Ruby had a right to manage her own feelings.

17

The machine trashed my ticket. A fat, cheerful girl in the car-park bureau liberated me. My concentration shimmered like a haze.

Strafe – born *there*? Same building as Ruby? Shall I follow Ruby to her club? Call Aylesbury again. No reply. But if he and she were born in the same apartment . . . ? I drove too fast through the tunnel; I made myself slow down.

Sunshine and tarmac, that's what England looked like that evening. I tried to force Berlin from my mind. Travelled back in memory to Provence. Fields of lavender. Black bulls on the Camargue. Dipping flights of pink and black flamingos. Black bulls in the *Arènes*, too, and the matador looking down his sword as though sighting a rifle. I got to Aylesbury about half past seven.

Claire's father opened the door. Pleased to see me but – what's this? – surprised.

'Nicholas, hello. How nice.'

I like David a lot. Admirable restraint; he converses only when moved to.

'You're marrying me for my father,' Claire said.

'Yep,' I agreed.

Pleasantries in the hall; the dog, Bruce, to be patted; a drink to be accepted.

'Fran's out at her bridge evening.' He was waiting to ask, 'What can I do for you?' or, 'To what do I owe this surprise?'

'I came to pick up Claire.'

'Claire's not here.' Did he look a little baffled? Too polite to show it.

'Where is she?' – thinking she was visiting a neighbour or something.

'Last time I saw her was with you. At the opera.' He looked at me carefully. 'Phone?'

Old familiar feeling. Of chill. I went to the hall and rang. No reply from Rye. Fear, like cold gripe, closes my eyes. No reply from the flat, either.

Choke the thought, Nicholas, choke it, there will be a logical explanation. Open your eyes. Shake your head. Now close your eyes again, nobody will see you. Steady. Go back to your drink. You know what your fear is, you know what it's always been but you must accept that the thing you fear has already happened and that lightning doesn't strike twice and that there is nobody who any longer has any reason to kidna— *Stop!*

David would never ask that crass, clichéd in-laws' question, 'Everything all right?' – no, not by so much as a raised eyebrow.

'I had better go,' I said.

'Of course. Lovely to see you. Send Claire our love.' I noted the 'send', not 'give'. Yes, I *am* paranoid.

Now. Deep breath. Problem on a site is often a problem in a drawing. Problem in a drawing is *always* a problem onsite. I drove away from the house and cleared Aylesbury, then drew into a hedge-screened lay-by to think. Claire said she would go to her parents. She didn't go. Thinking is like drawing – best done in straight lines. Imagination comes before and after thinking – and no matter how much imagination you possess or employ, you still have to draw in direct lines . . .

Worst-case scenario. Why should I leap to that possibility? And why is Clay Massey's wise-owl face dancing before my eyes?

There's usually a simple explanation to most mysteries, isn't there? She's with Lucinda. Of course she is, Lucinda of the golden eyes, the nice line in oral sex. They're talking about the refit of Rye. No. I know she isn't. Don't ask me how I know – I know.

Images flow like spooling film. Claire breaking down in tears when she's spoiled what she's cooking; Claire insisting on driving, then hitting a bollard; Claire making a hair appointment and forgetting it – again; Claire losing her chequebook and credit cards and telling the bank – again; and then finding them all – again. Me folding her in my arms. Me saying it doesn't matter, it doesn't matter. And it doesn't. Not now it doesn't.

I checked my pulse. Still in sinus rhythm. I'm on top of the game – so far. Don't panic. Traffic belted by, heard but not seen. A metaphor in itself, danger near, but invisible. First thing is to establish – *to establish what?!* Ring again. And ring every five minutes, press the 'redial' button. Both numbers. No answer, not one. Not from London, not from Rye.

Chelsea was quiet, warm and empty. Has she been here? No. Did she come by the flat on her way to Aylesbury? No. No clothes tossed on the bed. No drawer or door a smidgen adrift. No knickers on the floor, none of her sexy spoor.

One down, one to go. I rang Rye again. No reply.

What if she's not in Rye? I drove the journey in two hours. Senseless driving, cutting in, cutting out, cutting up.

What am I going to do when I get there? Reach for the practical. To do something is to calm things. But what is there to do? I may find a number for Lucinda. And food. Mrs Lydiard keeps a good fridge. Never trust those who say they can't eat under pressure; they're making a big mistake. She'll have baked a small ham. We have jars of preserves. Or cold lamb. I like mint jelly. Rye gets a belly-soft Brie from somewhere, try that with onion. Maybe Mrs L.'s made a sherry trifle. Thus did I try to keep my thoughts sane and light. And failed. I am a martyr to worst-case scenario.

The house stood in darkness. My blood and my bones turned blue with cold fear. I switched on all the lights in the hall. What am I looking for? That old cliché – 'signs of a struggle'? No sign. In the kitchen no traces of food or drink consumed recently. Nobody's been here. I know now that my fears are irrational. This is what happened. Claire got a return fit of her jealousy over Ruby and decided to cool me. But she's never done that before? Always a first time for everything. Yes, much more plausible explanation – and that must be why am I subsiding; the panic is easing. I opened the fridge, checked the food, planned a sandwich. And listened as this dreadful, whining anxiety abated. I did a mental count. We spoke last night. She left for Aylesbury at crack of dawn this morning. Only she didn't. So there must be an explanation. She decided not to go. Did something else. But what?

I tried our bedroom. No sign of life. This is baffling. But I am not distraught, no, I am *not* distraught. I stood in the hallway and polished my spectacles. Somewhere a band played, some fête or gala. I went to the Long Drawing Room. Through the window, lights from afar winked and blinked. Out there winds the Channel and then the long, low, dark bulk of France. I need a lighthouse in my life to keep me from hitting these rocks.

Then my breath caught: I couldn't breathe.

There's someone in this room. I quarter-turned my head. A still body lay full-length on the couch. Not asleep, I know sleeping bodies. But still, very still, and I see the pale white feet. My nose is full of my cold breath. In the darkness behind me something rustles. The couch is long enough for me, and therefore long enough for Claire.

'Hello,' she says. 'Don't be angry with me.'

18

Her eyes looked rough. She'd had a bad time. Self-inflicted? Dreadfully, I hoped so. I can cope with self-inflicted. Keep it cool, that's what I try to do.

'You okay?'

'Yes.'

'Any danger?'

'No.'

'No problems?'

'No.'

'Claire?'

'Yes?'

'You all right?'

'Yes and no.' Her usual answer when her history bites her spirit.

'How marvellous to see you,' I said and meant it with all my heart.

I steered her to bed, helped her to undress, couldn't wait to hold her. We lay in the dark and she curled up in my arms. I gave her one of the homoeopathic sedatives she liked. She simply fell asleep without saying a word. I rested my hand on her cheek. Let us not speak of anything contentious tonight. Let us just accept that the past has pounced again. *Let us be lovers and marry our fortunes together*.

From time to time I dozed. She rolled away and I covered her bare shoulders. I checked the clock – a few minutes after four, the hour of the wolf. In the kitchen I found myself urgently ravenous, the sudden hunger that makes me tremble. I made two giant sandwiches of cheese, tomatoes, ham, onion and mayonnaise, mixed a mug of hot chocolate and went to sit in the Long Drawing Room. Sometimes the sky down here comes up green at dawn.

The connected and the unconnected. Separate them. So that a natural priority may emerge. Strafe? Jesus God! Strafe and Ruby, what about that?! I used my fingers to count. Clay Massey. Ruby's call. The skateboarder. Berlin. Zurück. Had we been followed? Too much for me, too much. A crisp ridge of onion wedged in my teeth.

Left anything out? Clay Massey and Claire? Don't forget the hostile young man. Christ, yes. From Claire's past. *'Husband?'* he jeered. What's his connection? Is he a stalker? That's all we need. Is he out there now, on the hill, with binoculars? Jesus, why think that? A stalker – Claire followed by a stalker? There are new laws. But a stalker in my life? I mean, that's bloody ridiculous. 'Nicholas Ridiculous' a boy called me in school. I hit him so hard I was sent home. His parents phoned mine. They met. Inconclusively.

In the light of the window I saw a pad on the table beside my chair. Claire had been taking down telephone messages. 'RS 1.' 'RS 2.' 'RS 3.'

The dawn began to leak into the sky, in pewter and silver blades. Will there be green streaks? I reached for the telescope; the brass mount is still stiff; I must get it fixed. Out somewhere in the English Channel that I wish I could see from here, there will be a container ship dragging itself off somewhere. What was it? An Alexandrine, wasn't it, 'that, like a wounded snake, drags its slow length along'.

Figures of speech. I thought about Ruby and tried to digest the connection between her and Richard Strafe. Is that a transferred epithet? Figures of speech.

Almost without thinking I rewound the answering machine – and recoiled.

'Hello sweetie, this is your friend and mentor –' Clunk; the

107

phone had been picked up. That was 'RS 1'. Dare I listen to 'RS 2' and 'RS 3'?

'It's me again. Don't hang up, there's a good girl –'

Red rage lit the back of my eyes. Did Strafe ring from France? When he was supposed to be with me? Why didn't Claire tell me?

'Sweetie, listen. Your old man's in Germ—' Again the clunk of the machine. In my head the pieces clunked too. Strafe told Claire about Berlin and Ruby. Hence her violent lapse.

The mild thought was, How did Strafe get my home number? The worrying thought, What did he say to Claire about me? The murderous thought, If he damages my wife I will kill him. I don't know when. Or how. But I will. But will I? Will I be able? No, I won't. The worst thought of all appalled me: How did he know about Berlin and Ruby and me? Strafe is one of those men who grooms his face all the time, stroking, smoothing.

Claire appeared in her white tee-shirt, looking like a ghost first, then like a little girl. I stood to hug her. Affection's still an effort, except at sex. And even then I find it so difficult to sustain after the act, as it were. Which is why I'm able to feel tender if Claire falls asleep.

'Are you all right?'

'Nicholas, I couldn't face Aylesbury. I wanted to stay here.'

So we're going to ignore it all, are we?

'Shhh! I understand.' Claire put her head on my shoulder. 'Oh, Christ! Your father! I'd better ring him.'

She looked up at the clock – ten to seven. 'He'll be up and about, let me do it,' and moved like a woman in a dream, faint, drifting and quick. When she begins to clatter around, less like a marionette, I'll know she's feeling better. The Berliners fed her adulterated crack – it attacked her motor function.

'Dad, it's me.' I heard her say, 'No, it was a muddle, that's all, I muddled things, how are you both?'

When she finished she turned and said to me, 'You know this is the weekend Elizabeth's coming?'

I groaned. 'What are we cooking?'

'Duck. She rang and told Mrs Lydiard.'

'She *what*?'

'Yes. Yesterday.'

'Elizabeth did?' I shook my head. 'I don't believe it – well, yes I do.'

'Nicholas, I'm scared of her.'

'Of Elizabeth? No. No need.'

'She's a dragon.'

'I'm used to that fire.'

'She doesn't like me.'

'Now, Claire, come on. You don't know that.'

'Nicholas, have you slept with her?'

'Of course not.'

'People think you have. People think that's how you got your professional reputation. That you were her young lover and that she had all the contacts.' Her voice was getting up, like a threatening wind.

'Claire. Look at the age difference between Elizabeth and me – and think of the age I was then. Was it likely that I would have gone to bed with someone as much older than me as Elizabeth Bentley?'

'Well – she doesn't like me.'

I said, to close the matter, 'If she doesn't like you it's because you're tall and leggy and sexy and very beautiful. Elizabeth is a control freak who dislikes bright, pretty women and who has to have everything her own way, she's fantastically political and she brings politics into everything and that really is the bottom line. Now make me a cup of tea.'

'Give me a hug, Nicholas.'

I thought, Claire, I'll give you a million hugs. But I didn't say it and the hug was a failure. We sat, looking

109

nowhere, both tired. Who says you have to be alone to feel lonely?

At half past nine in the morning I went back to bed. The grey overcast skies still hid the sun. Claire hadn't joined me in bed by the time I fell asleep. Nor when I awoke.

In the kitchen Mrs Lydiard said, 'Miss Bentley rang. About this evening.' Here we go. The first twist. 'She wants you to call her at this number.'

I rang, expecting somebody's home. Elizabeth was staying at a small hotel called Snave Dower somewhere beyond New Romney. But she was 'out at the moment'.

'Mrs Lydiard, do you know a hotel called Snave Dower?'

'Ooh, indeed I do, sir. Very exclusive. Over beyond Lydd, you go to New Romney, turn towards Brenzett and then you take the signs for Ivychurch and you turn right into the marshes and it's there, in a wood, near St Mary-in-the-Marsh, there are roadworks there at the moment.'

Mrs Lydiard is a journalist's dream; she always tells you more than you ask.

'How exclusive is it?'

Mrs Lydiard switched back into her old hotel mode and thought aloud.

'Covers? They do lunch and dinner, about thirty covers, and the set menu – the *set* menu, mind – sixty pounds a head. Not including wine. I'm surprised, sir, you haven't heard of it.'

'I have now,' I said, wondering at the same time, What is Elizabeth playing at? Let me guess. She'll cancel dinner and invite us over there and I'll pick up the tab.

Or she'll cancel dinner and come for lunch tomorrow because her curiosity will get the better of her and she's never been to the house in Rye.

Or she'll do both.

While I was trying to second-guess Elizabeth Mrs Lydiard asked quietly, 'Have you a moment, sir?'

'Of course.'

'The duck, sir? How shall I – I mean, Mrs Newman – ?'

'Oh, whatever.' Glide over the hidden agenda. 'You know best.'

'Thank you, sir.'

Telling myself, Claire needs time, I thought, yes, I will go out for a walk. One look across at the Gun Garden and the people milling through it and I thought, Stay indoors. Draw, read – do anything. Not a day for braving the tourists. I was the one who needed the time. If only to close down parts of my mind.

We met in the bathroom later, Claire still distant.

'Mrs Lydiard asked me about the duck.'

Claire's eyes hooded a little. 'Oh, that's all sorted.'

The phone rang and as I left the bathroom to take the call, Claire said, 'But I know she doesn't like me.'

I groaned – but allowed myself a smile to hear Elizabeth say, 'Nicholas, dear, I'm not very well and I wondered whether you and Clara might have dinner here with me. They tell me it's not very far.'

Now if I could find a bookie to take the bet that I'll be picking up the tab . . .

It broke the ice a little with Claire. She laughed as I dissected Elizabeth's stratagems. I persuaded her to wear a Versace dress I bought her in Paris, hip-short, red and clinging, with a see-through top.

'That's more like it,' I said. 'Elizabeth will hate that.'

'But shouldn't I wear something more formal?'

'No. Fight fire with fire.'

She looked at me. 'Nicholas? Do you love me?'

'Of course I love you. Don't be silly.'

'Then will you look at these? Please?' From her dressing table she lifted a manila folder. Her 'paperwork'.

'Claire –'

'Please, Nicholas?'

111

'Why don't we both pretend we never had a past?' I said.

For a minute or so she stood with her face pressed to my neck and I stroked her spine. The folder lay on the bed like a little beige cadaver.

Clear night and empty roads. Snave Dower had Tudor windows. Elizabeth stood alone, bleached and theatrical, by the huge fireplace. When we came in she walked towards us. From five paces she said to me urgently, 'Nicholas, dear, there's a very private party in a separate room, very private. Who d'you think it might be?' She spoke as though Claire hadn't come.

'Elizabeth, how should I know?' I bent to kiss her ivory skin.

'Well, you *live* down here. Now where's your wife?'

I said ironically, 'Right here, Elizabeth.'

In the otherwise empty hall Claire had been standing beside me when Elizabeth kissed me.

'Oh, my dear, you look charming. I could never wear a dress like that, never had the confidence.'

One thing's for sure about Elizabeth – she never fails to entertain. Claire rose to it and said, 'Thank you.'

Astounding food: grilled oysters with apricots; quails and *foie gras*; Elizabeth chose the claret, a 1980 Pomerol of which (annoyingly) I had never heard.

'Now tell me about you two, are you happy? He's frightfully self-centred, you know. And vain, aren't you, dear?' she said. From there on Elizabeth soared.

'How d'you stand all that minimalism, Clara dear? We gals like a bit of clutter, don't we?'

'He used to love girls whose families had a big house in the country, or a flat in Paris or Vienna. Or one of these journalists with mascara – of course, journalists, they can be *so* useful.'

'D'you know who I met a few days ago, Nicholas?

112

D'you remember Valerie Mells, was that her name, Lord Portumna's daughter? Oh, [to Claire] they were in *all* the gossip columns.'

'When Nicholas came to work on a Monday morning we laid bets on what name he'd be linked with *that* week.'

'D'you remember that girl, not the one who [pause] died, she was Madeleine, wasn't she, no, what *was* her name, Isobel something, gosh, didn't she turn out spectacularly? Or was that someone else?'

'And the thing I loved, Clara dear, was the number of times Nicholas's love affairs brought us some big client or other.'

My heart sank. I had long expected this. My bones warned me. Elizabeth homed in like a heat-seeking missile on Claire's retrospective jealousy. That's Elizabeth. Her negative side is her strongest.

In due course I brought easier topics to the table. The evening straightened out. I think Elizabeth knew she'd gone too far. Soon she called up all her magic. Her safer reminiscences made us laugh. I watched her closely. Red patches glowed on her cheeks; her eyes had grown large. When she's on parade Elizabeth's hands glide through the air like the hands of a wicked queen.

For coffee we moved to the linenfold drawing room. On extravagant chairs I ordered herb tea and went to the flower-tiled lavatory.

On the way back I stopped near the door, out of sight, to eavesdrop. Claire had finished some remark and I half-heard Elizabeth's immediate question, 'And your own life, dear? D'you take any drugs now?'

I rattled into the room. Elizabeth saw my glance – and my fury.

'Do excuse me. I've left my shawl upstairs.'

Agile as ever, she rose and ran. We waited half an hour and then knew, as one does, she was gone.

113

In the car Claire asked, 'How much?'

I handed her the receipt. 'Tell me. I couldn't bear to look.'

Claire read it out. 'Four hundred and seventy-nine pounds. For three of us. The old bitch!'

I felt an immediate stab of discomfort. Elizabeth's part of my bedrock. I tried to soften it.

'Well, we were warned that it was "exclusive" –'

'It was almost worth it to hear that parade of your past.'

The note in Claire's voice didn't bode well. She wound down her window and looked out at the marshes. I thought her lovelier all this evening than she had ever been. I kept wanting her and wanting her . . .

She wound the window back up again. Plonked her feet on the dashboard. Drummed her heels like a little Russian dance. Began to sing like a wild child, no words, just, 'Ob-la-di, ob-la-da, ob-la-di-AH' – and shouted on every 'AH'. I said nothing.

Suddenly she stopped singing and drumming and said, 'Nicholas, I don't think we should have married. You don't want to be tied down. We should just have had an affair and then remained friends. Millions do it. It's always on television.'

Only one way to handle it, only one way to fight that sudden plunge in the pit of my stomach.

'Claire.'

'Yes?' Truculent. 'Or are you sure I'm not called "Clara"? Who was Clara anyway?'

'Take off that dress.'

She turned her body round towards me. Looking hard at my mouth she began to unfasten. Few trees grow on these marshes. I found a farm lane, reversed under some willows. Should a car come along I would see. I caught her face, began to kiss her. She gripped my hair. The erotic rage between us, her jealousy, my need, often rescued our bad times.

Headlights swept the sky. I raised my head out of Claire's neck. The car drove past but I heard it brake. It turned, came back, stopped a little short of the lane.

'Hold it, Claire. Shhhh.'

She sat up. Slam of distant car door. A man came down the lane and shone a torch. Lock all the doors. Switch on my engine and beams. We might be on his land. Or he might be a policeman. Claire has dropped her red dress down to her waist: my hands are tracing her shapes: she's so warm and smooth.

He didn't run away; he stood there, switched off his torch. I recognized him but grasped Claire's face to my shoulder – the curly-headed young man. Who mocked *'Husband?'* that night at the Captain's Wife. Stalking us. Am I psychic?

He went without murmur or gesture and revved off.

'What was that about?'

'Some bloody Peeping Tom,' I said as the magic ebbed.

Nor did it flow back next morning – because at ten o'clock I heard a car outside and then the doorbell and then the voice of Elizabeth Bentley speaking into the entryphone. Trust Elizabeth: always tries to have the best of all possible worlds. She stayed to lunch – and tea.

19

Not for days did Claire speak to me thereafter. Not a word. Not a reply to a remark or a telephone call or a question. Thank you, Elizabeth: such a performance. While I cooked she told Claire every detail of the Mary Strait affair.

On Sunday night, I shook Claire's shoulders.

'Speak to me, Claire. That's the past. We're the here and now.'

And I said, 'You're playing into Elizabeth's hands. She'd love to split us.'

And I implored her, 'Claire! Tell me what's bothering you. Please?'

She walked away and locked herself in the farthest room. In which she slept. Nor did she emerge next day, Monday of the Whitsun Bank Holiday. My feelings mutated from anger through concern into loss – in my ribcage lodged a pain. On Tuesday morning I took the decision; let her cool down. Work calms me. I would have to live with the worry of her being alone. If – when – she wants to float back to me, I'll welcome her with open arms. She knows that. This has happened before.

The drive to London, the office day, the solitary night – they seem like a haze now, a kind of fuzzy coma. Too many angles, too many problems, too many knots to untangle. I put my mind to my drawing board and my computer screen and said, 'No calls – except my wife,' who did not call. What is she doing down there today? Oh, she'll go for a walk, she'll have a bath, she'll browse the town – again. And she'll work on her 'paperwork'. I feel certain that's what's disturbing her. She must – she *must* – give it up. That was a long time ago and you can't go home again. Home's different now for the Jews of Europe. And besides, it was only bricks and mortar . . .

Strafe telephoned me on Wednesday. My heart rattled. What should I say to him? Rip into him for telephoning my wife?

I failed again, managing only a mild, 'You didn't show up for dinner.'

'What you talking about?'

'Last week. La Regalido. Fontvielle. Near Arles.' I said it all softly, almost humorously: a client is still a client.

'What you saying? That I was supposed to be meeting you for dinner last Wednesday night?'

'So you said.'

'Oh.' No apology, nothing. 'Did you get anywhere with the conservationists?'

'Yes. And it's bad news, I'm afraid. We'll have to deal with Paris. The building is listed as a national treasure. The only one of its kind so far south. And they won't de-list it.'

'Will that hold things up?'

I said, 'It mightn't. We have some connections.'

'Use them. Lunch?'

I said, 'Okay.'

'How's your wife, she still living with you?'

I riposted, 'How do I know you'll show up for lunch?'

'A week Friday. L'Arlésienne.'

I said, '*I'll* certainly show up.'

He put the phone down. My fear passed, leaving me hungry. The day continued. Claire never rang and never answered the phone, never returned one of my loving messages. My good sense told me, Be consistent. Keep telling her you love her. Be patient. If you love her – then, love her.

Any routine offers succour. I relished the details of the

117

day. One of the architects wanted us to buy a new software package, purporting to list the building regs, dimension for dimension, in any country of the world that has building regs. In our dreams.

My secretary, Lemon, had a new romance. She also had a new tie – *Dan Dare, Pilot of the Future*; 'A barrow on Brick Lane,' she said, and I said, 'I had a Dan Dare tie once.'

I overheard Mary Strait trying to pull some of Aunt Elizabeth's strings and jump the twenty-year queue for Glyndebourne's waiting list; she was telling someone she had developed 'a passion for opera'. Hal Callaghan beaded his bulgy eyes on the new 'draughtsperson' as she, abetted by Ms Strait, insisted on being called.

Bernard, the most sober of them all, the one who hums when he's stressed, came to tell me of being smitten by the Home Secretary at some dinner. All because when he told the Home Secretary what he did, he was asked if he designed that wonderful sphere, cone and cube in the City? Being Bernard, he did not take the credit for himself (as several of the others would have done). He attributed it to me and the Home Secretary said that I must be 'a very interesting person, and I said to him yes I suppose you are'. Bernard seemed miffed that I looked less than giddy with excitement.

About five o'clock I checked the diary. Empty. Claire and I, loving each other's company, resisted social engagements in London; therefore people had stopped inviting us. There had been a brief flurry directly after we married. 'They all want to see, dear, whether you'll stay with each other' was Elizabeth's verdict on that.

Those months of peace gave us a chance to form some sort of life. I had never lived with anyone. Claire had, with Philippe Safft, and then he got himself killed. And nearly took her with him. And me. We had all of that to address, too. Post-traumatic bloody everything. That's why it felt as though the world were granting us time to settle down.

Evenings of the working week we spent simply; either we cooked or ate out. Which we rarely did in Rye, except at Colson's, a tranquil old inn with delicious fish and charming management – and fifty yards from our front door.

Before marriage I feared the constant company. How in God's name am I going to live hour by hour day by day with another human being? Not a problem. Claire's lightness of being, coupled with her dependence, kept me emotionally active. On her high days she stimulated me. She sifted several newspapers; she became a kind of evening bulletin, full of ideas and curious angles. On her low days I became her protector, a role I loved.

Only one aspect of cohabiting proved difficult – having to account for my movements. Since I was seventeen and went up to Cambridge, no one asked about my life. If they did I told them little. Now I had to answer – ordinary, everyday – questions. But above all I could not withhold. I found that difficult.

Tonight – nothing to do. No wife with me; nobody to go home to, to go out with, to look at. I checked the office invitations. Melchior's Gallery. Yes, why not?

Gallery nights need careful judgement. You have to make the buzz, yet not invite so many people they can't see the walls. I drifted around. Good draughtsman, energetic colour, strange choice of subject – human heads as landscapes; there was one I might have bought. If he can work on a larger scale I might commission him. Make the client pay.

Standing before 'Vermilion Lobe on Perspex' a woman mused aloud, 'Mobile phone art?'

'Thank you,' I said. 'I've forgotten to switch off mine.'

I reached into my pocket and pressed the button.

'Shame on you,' she said.

'You'll succumb.'

'My brain's already scrambled,' she said.

Large-ish, attractive. I looked closer. Weight problems, I'd guess. Shrewd face, lazy but tough-minded. Glossy, with a tint of cheap. Not a fool; aware of her bargaining chips.

'Buying?' I asked her.

'I might,' she said. 'Just to spite my husband.'

'That's not very nice,' I said lightly.

'*He's* not very nice.' She nodded at the painting. 'It'd jack up the settlement – it's the most expensive picture here.'

I said, 'Ouch!'

'You should know,' she said with a slight boom of triumph.

'Should I?'

'I'm Diana Strafe.'

'Ah.'

Boy, oh boy!

'No cheap imitations,' she said. 'The only one in the phone book.'

'How d'you know who I am?'

'You're my husband's tame bit of lifestyle. He used to joke about you.' She eyed me. 'I don't think I would.'

'Would what?'

'Would have joked about you.'

'What did he say?'

'Oh, I expect you can guess. That he was the only property developer in London who had to ring *Hello!* magazine to get hold of his architect. That his architect dressed in black like an undertaker. That sort of thing. I hear you've married?'

'Indeed.'

'Congratulations. Happy?'

'It wasn't in *Hello!* magazine.'

'Richard told me. In one of our "mediations". He said

120

you'd just got married and he didn't see why I mightn't marry again. D'you see much of him?'

'He was at Clay Massey's funeral.' I said it deliberately, to see whether anything registered.

Something did. But I'm not sure what.

20

Too much poison afloat. Vague danger is dangerous danger. The ether smelt of phosphorus, orange and acrid. Strafe, Berlin, Ruby, Massey – something had to give. But who would give it? It had better be me, if only for peace of mind.

The night passed badly, riven with sour thoughts. It got worse. Failure arrived, dragging its litany. I have pledged so much to Claire, invested so much in this relationship. What does a man do when he fails? Why do I always fail at feelings? I began to understand something. In me, reluctance means fear of failure. I had always been reluctant to marry. When I met Claire I overpowered myself. What is she doing now? Is she awake? Long white limbs. Shocking fuzz electric fur. No. Stop.

We deny fiercest that which we know deepest. Which is why I denied so furiously to myself that I hankered after the 'home' thing: the fireside, the Labrador, home cooking, slippers – the whole Homes & Gardens, Badger's-house-in-The-Wind-in-the-Willows bit. Which explains why I travelled so hard and far in the opposite direction: minimalism, chrome, glass and abstracts. Nice one, Nicholas.

Claire didn't return my calls that night. Not one. Out of ten. Tender messages. Pleas. Appeasement. Once she picked up the phone but after twenty seconds of silence replaced it as firmly as a slap in the face. To think I hadn't yet told her about Ruby and Berlin: I thought, Perhaps I never will. She knows. Strafe.

Not much sleep. In fact, no sleep. At four I got up and sat there. Thinking about failure. Feelings of uselessness and how to fight them. If there were something I could do, a step I could take to cure this feeling of futility, what would it be?

Go for a walk. The night's clear and pleasant and now the streets have emptied. Were this Paris I could go to that all-night place by the Pont St Michel. Full of cabbies and students and sometimes the whores.

I wanted to walk. To test my delayed-reaction system. It often yields the solution some time after I've aired the problem. The phone rang – Claire!

No. Ruby.

'Hello, darling' – as calmly as though it were the bright afternoon.

'Good God. Everything all right?'

'No, darling.'

'Ruby, what is it?'

'Please. Could you come round, darling?'

What did she think she was doing? Ringing me at that hour? Claire, were she here, might have answered.

Ruby buzzed me in. Cigar smoke from that night's business. I clanged the little French lift. How many customers walked past those *trompe l'oeil* curtains in any one night, week, year and never knew the lift was there? Ruby's own idea, it has to be said.

She lay in bed, propped high and reading.

'Come in, darling. So nice to see you.'

I waved my fingers. The bedside radio breathed jazz.

'Come and kiss me.'

'Ruby, you're astonishing.'

I kissed her on the cheek.

'Mouth, now, darling, just gently, I'm a little lonely tonight.'

I kissed her on the lips, first lips I had kissed since Claire's.

'Thank you, darling. Now, sit.'

I pulled over her *bergère* chair.

'Darling, I promised you.'

'Oh?'

'The rest of the story.' She raised herself on her pillows, wheezing. 'You're so kind to me, darling, you never say to me, "Ruby, you must give up smoking" – I like that about you, darling.'

'I'm not in a position to tell anyone to give up anything.'

She rearranged her pillows. I waited.

'Spannungstrasse. Remember?'

'Not easy to forget, Ruby.'

'This is what I have been given to understand, darling. It is the headquarters of an organization whose purpose is to stop Jews getting their homes back. Do you know the procedure?'

I had gathered some idea, watching Claire at a distance. But I'm not going to speak to Ruby of Claire's private life.

'There is a claim form. Very painful, but that is to be expected. Very bureaucratic but very painful. There are committees of politicians. That claim form is filed with lawyers, some in Europe, some in Israel. But, darling. In some cases recently –'

Ruby stopped and I felt the cold again. My mouth dried, as it does when I battle with Claire.

'Darling, people who have filed claims have had unpleasant things happen. Accidents, some fatal. Clay Massey. You know, darling.'

'But was he –'

'He helped in these claims. I mean, darling, he was, you know, on committees. He knew things.'

I looked at her. The eyes had clouded again.

'You understand what I'm saying, darling?'

'Ruby, how much do you know?' In my mind's eye I saw Claire's manila folder.

'Very little, darling.'

124

'Why are you telling me tonight, Ruby?'

She didn't answer. The radio singer sang 'Cry Me a River'. We listened. For a moment it was the only sound in London.

'You used to do that song.'

'Still do, darling.'

'Why are they called torch songs?'

'Carrying a torch for someone, darling.'

We sat for a moment. *You can cry me a river. Cry me a river. I cried a river. Over you.*

'Ruby, what happened in Berlin? I mean – after your grandparents left.'

'It's very painful. Hold my hand.'

Plump fingers. But not puffy. Nor worn. We sat there; the song finished.

'The baby – Liese. She was my mother. I told you that, darling.'

'Yes.'

'They brought her up, she grew up with them, she was their housemaid.'

'But she was living in her own house, so to speak?'

'And when she was sixteen she was made pregnant by the father of the family and I am the child that was born. I was born in my own home.'

Like one of the three monkeys I sat with my hand across my mouth. When I make that gesture I think it comes from two things – being dumbstruck; and fearing I will make an inappropriate remark.

'Ruby.' I thought before I spoke. 'Strafe?'

'Yes, darling.'

'Was that the family?'

'Yes, they were called Straffenberg. He shortened it.'

I nodded. 'Not unusual.'

'But do you know what "Strafe" means in German?'

I shook my head.

'It means "punishment" – see?'

'Oh, Christ.' I was in danger of losing my composure here. 'Is he the son of that family?'

'Yes, darling.'

'So he is your –'

'Half-brother –'

'But that apartment – it rightly belongs to you?'

'I don't know, darling. I'm trying to find out. Clay was –'

'Is that why you went to that office in Berlin, Zurück?'

'Yes, darling.'

It fitted. She wanted to know whether her claim endangered her. And asked me along for protection. I could understand that. I held off the noise beginning in my mind, the scream, *But what about Claire?!*

'Ruby, we discovered nothing. So how can you find out?'

'There's someone who knows.'

'Are you saying that you in fact – that you have definitely entered a claim?' Don't know why I questioned her.

'He lives in Switzerland.'

'Ruby, have you? Have you made a claim?' Is she too frightened to say 'yes'?

'He's a doctor, darling. Or so I've been told. But he's under threat himself. They've told him so. He's followed everywhere he goes, every minute. He's watched all the time and his house has microphones. And his telephone is listened to. His letters are opened. Everything.'

'Why doesn't he tell the police? Why don't you all tell the police?'

Ruby looked at me. 'You called the police in Berlin, remember?'

'Why is he so important?'

'He worked his way into Spannungstrasse and found out everything. But he can't tell anybody. He once tried to post a letter and they took the mailbox apart. On the street. With

126

a hand-grenade. While he stood there. He can meet nobody – because if he does, it puts them in danger and he knows that. That's the problem, darling.'

'His information – how crucial?'

'As I say. He's the one who knows everything.'

Therefore he'll know about Claire. Play this cool.

'Why don't they kill him?'

'He has told them that he has given sealed instructions to several anonymous people in case of his death. He did it when he first discovered what was going on. So they have to keep him alive. And he goes on tracking them. He monitors everything they do.'

We sat silently for a moment.

'Will he meet me? If I offer?'

Then Ruby said, 'Darling, you don't understand. He can't *make* an arrangement. But he may be able to fulfil one.'

'How?'

'Difficult. He can't risk contact. He can't be seen to speak to anyone. He can't write to anyone. He can't phone. There can be no contact. But he can tell us things that will keep people alive. He knows the claimants they've targeted, the ones they mean to –'

She stopped.

Ruby's room – I knew it so well, the swathes of cream lace and the blue flowers on the grey French wallpaper and the pinks and soft reds and the cream bed linen and the grey square pillows. In this room, with help from her, I saved my own life. I looked all around it.

When my ideas click into place I feel it in my hair. On the radio a soft clarinet crooned. In my mind the words followed the music. *Tea for two. And two for tea. And me for you. And you for me.* I looked at the blinds inside the curtains. Stiff canvas, cream, with faint grey flowers lit by soft lights under the pelmet. I looked back to the radio. Ruby followed my eyes as I listened to the song.

'Would you like some tea, darling? I may make a cup for myself.'

Her acuity never failed. I shook my head.

'Can anyone reach this "doctor"? I mean, with a message?'

'Maybe, darling.'

'Ruby. Listen carefully to what I have to say.'

Her eyes widened at my urgency and sudden energy.

All she replied was, 'This is Tuesday night, darling. Give yourself more time.'

'No, Ruby. Get the message sent. I'll fly tomorrow.'

'But flights – ?'

'Geneva's well served. Arrange it for Thursday. The afternoon. I'll assume it's fixed.'

Ruby looked away from me. 'Darling, please be certain you want to –'

'Ruby, I *don't* want to do it. But, well, you know.'

I kissed her cheeks and left. Mixed messages to myself.

If Claire finds out I'm helping Ruby's claim and not her own – ?

But this gives me a chance to know more.

But I'm going to Switzerland because Ruby's afraid.

But I'm not getting involved – just forearmed.

21

My pillow was drenched: I had been dreaming about motorbikes. Two hours of sleep and when I woke I missed Claire savagely. My hand reached to her pillow and I stroked it. How often have I placed my face between her sleeping shoulders.

Why did I agree to do this? Reasons and no reasons. This is all so unhealthy.

The travel arrangements took ten minutes: fly via Swissair, book in Geneva, they're an hour ahead (and they rise earlier). My taxi waited. Still no word from Claire, no message, no answer to my calls, no nothing. I telephoned one last time. No reply. I used to think I could tell when a phone rang in an empty house. Now I'm not so sure. For a moment I stood at the mirror, my face hurting at the loss of her. I had to breathe deeply, then concentrate. I closed my eyes . . .

Morning glowed along the streets. I turned and locked the door – and heard the motorbike. It roared in and its engine cut off. I dropped my keys. Shit! I've double-locked the door, I can't get back in.

Scrabble at my shoes for my keys. I can't see them. I can't run, there's nowhere to run. The cabbie's looking at me strangely. Is he in on this too?

I freeze. Slowly I bend and pick up the keys. Slowly I put the key in the lock again. It won't work, it sticks. I hear the boots hitting the pavement and then hitting the steps. I close my eyes and prepare to lash out. An arm wearing black leathers reaches past me and presses my doorbell. I spin.

The courier's a girl, she takes off her helmet and shakes out her hair. She has a tawny face.

I scream, 'What do you WANT?' *Dark they were and golden-eyed*.

She looks at me, thinking, Is he mad?

'Delivery,' she says.

'That's *my* doorbell,' I snap.

'Then you can sign, can't you?' She hands me a clipboard and a package.

I felt the package with tender hands. It seemed all right. Once a paranoid always a paranoid.

'Why so early in the morning?'

She shrugged. I signed and climbed into the cab, my hands shivering. Looked down at the label: 'Sender: Claire Newman.' Oh, Christ.

Nicholas

Why won't you help me? Will these files change your mind? This is what other families have gone through.

C.

No 'All my love', not even 'With love', no little joke or drawing, nothing. Just 'C.' Didn't even sign her full name. No 'Dear Nicholas', or 'Darling Nicholas', or even plain 'Darling'.

Again I think, Claire, the reason I won't help you is that I don't want you doing something that gets you all fired up and upset. Or that's my excuse. If I'm honest. Which I'm not. The people on the streets seemed to saunter. A flower seller set up her barrow and sprayed water on the blooms. I fought the shrivelling of my heart.

My life is choking me. Or will choke me if I lose my wife. I opened the package again and glanced at the documents – a dozen or more plastic folders, some with blue covers, some with grey. Each contained no more than two or three pages. All had been typewritten. They were claims, each carefully prepared. Claire knew how to put on pressure. I knew how to resist it. Or would know if my feelings let me.

Some said, 'Current name and address'. Some bore only initials. Some carried full flourishing signatures like old deeds and bonds. And some had been witnessed. What is this ache rising off them? The taxi swung out onto the M4. I put them away.

What am I doing? I know what I'm doing. Can I carry it off? I must. Not that I understand the core of all this – but do this thing and my life will ease. Silly notion. I sat back; coping with the airport will give me strength. Clarify this. Make Ruby safe. Get a fuller fix on Strafe. But above all take Claire out of the frame, make her give up this claim.

We decry the Swiss for their anality. Until we need planes to take off and land on time. Until we need privacy in our finances. Until we need to feel we are in the hands of people competent at what they intend. The Swissair flight took off precisely on time. It reached the gate at Geneva precisely on time. Do they make clocks and watches because they are so punctual? Or is it the other way round?

Children raced each other along the moving walkways in Terminal Two. Did I feel fear? Apprehension, certainly. What I felt most was pain over Claire. I think I dreamed of her but I can't be certain. Keep the fear coming, stay alert. I checked the other passengers.

Not many; a party of six jovial English, including the in-evitable 'Man Friendly to Everybody'; he insisted on joshing the ground staff. Two women bankers spoke to each other or their mobile phones. The married couple bickering easily in French had the casual air of young money. A rich woman with a receding hairline and a suede coat worth a few thou-sand pounds flicked through her half-dozen magazines. Four laddish businessmen travelling together talked loudly about websites. Japanese tourists with little floppy summer hats looked for – and got – attention. Four others chattered in to join them and became part of the process. An elderly couple walked slowly to the seats nearest the gate. Two American couples arrived, smiling and talking loudly. A tall flustered woman wrestled with too much hand luggage. I looked at her and remembered how endearing it used to feel when I met a woman who couldn't reach behind to fasten her bra and had to wrestle it round to the front, fasten it and then twist it round the back again. Like Mary Strait. Claire is more competent.

Why am I not at my drawing board? I stood from my seat and looked out the window. Or at home in Rye? Trying to sort out my problems with my wife? Because I'm in some sort of pain, that's why, and I think I can take care of it by doing something for someone who's not too intimately involved with me. Not any more, that is. By which I mean Ruby. Not Claire. I hope.

I think of a new word for myself – 'futile'.

22

How do we keep history away from us? Rediscovering it has become one of our industries. Look at Strafe's renovations – he wants them 'faithful'. Some day someone will found a movement countering 'Heritage' – a bureau that offers escapes from the past, a sort of personal Year Zero. I opened the first of Claire's folders.

This memory has beginnings with my celebrations of my ninth birthday which has begun happy and light-hearted. It is October 1942 and I was all night and all morning hoping for the afternoon. Papa said he will come home early from work and when he did, he had two gifts for me. He teased me which he liked to always do until Mama made him give the gifts to me and said stop teasing the child but she then advised me that I should wait carefully until all the family could enjoy watching the gifts being opened. Mama when she said this was wearing her big pink blouse, that blouse with such flowers on it I still remember them. Aunt Mayva came in her green dress and her stole draped over the shoulders of it. It was green silk, she said it was emerald but they talked about eau-de-nil and the stole was a blue which shouldn't look good with the dress but it did. Uncle Roder had his best grey hat and said the green was the colour of sour apples and they laughed and scolded him. Mama said we will invite Levi and Peter and Sala from the apartment next door. Sala is nearly my age and my closest friend but I was worried because they did not have as much money as us. After the Nuremberg Laws their father had no job and I was ashamed because Papa went out of our home every day to work.

A different hand (was it, I wondered, Clay Massey's?) had added freshly in the margin: *'The Nuremberg Laws of 1935 denied among other things the participation by Jews in any public office or employment.'*

Levi and Peter and Sala arrived soon. Peter had carved me a fish with a big tail. Sala baked me a cake, she put marzipan dots all over the top of it. Levi who was a surly boy had no gift for me and said it to me proudly. I told him never mind. Everybody was assembled and Papa called out cheers for me and I blushed and I had to make a little speech of thanks. I was allowed to open my gifts although I was a bit ashamed with Levi and Sala and Peter looking at me. Mama gave me a beautiful notebook she made and a pen. Papa bought me a small leather handbag down in the big stores near where he worked, burgundy was the bag's colour and in it I found a little round mirror. Papa said this was my first handbag and he said into it you will put half the world just like your Mama. Uncle Roder gave me some coconut chocolate sticks wrapped in silver and everyone said it was because he liked coconut as much as he liked chocolate. Aunt Mayva gave almost the best gift of all, she bought me a bottle of scent and showed me how to dab it behind my ears and at my wrists even though I already knew how to do this from watching Mama do it.

I flicked to the last page. The line for signature read, *'Dictated by H.G.'* No date, no address, no age. The stewardess who

134

served breakfast spoke her English with a strong German accent. I waited some minutes, looking out on the clouds. Pillows of softness. Distant, roseate battlements. Ways of escape. Down below us, to the left, an aircraft passed in the opposite direction, its speed the only way we see how fast we travel through the skies.

It was being a most exciting birthday. Mama's smile had no strictness in it because it is my day and we ate the cakes and the little bits of marzipan from Sala. Papa laughed at every joke and Uncle Roder and Aunt Mayva holding hands at the table and Sala asking again if she could smell my scent bottle. She took the glass stopper out of it and put her nose to the little curved neck of the bottle which was light green. I never knew whether the glass of the bottle was green or whether that was the colour of the scent and I was allowed to use so little of the scent I could not tell if it was a green liquid. Papa clapped his hands and told everybody I was playing something very special today. Aunt Mayva said she hoped I had been learning something new and would it be she prayed a Chopin *Valse*? Everybody laughed because they knew that Mamma had told Aunt Mayva I had been learning this *Valse* specially for her. I sat down on the stool and everybody was gathered round the living room. Sala sat on the floor beside me and Peter was also quite near her. Levi stood at the back of the room and he was not interested at all. His face was very spotty and he kept coughing while I was playing. Papa stood so much in the window that Mama had to tell him he blocked the light and I couldn't read the music and Papa moved to one side. I began to play and the music came out from my fingers just like I hoped it would. From the corner of my eyes I saw Mama begin to weep a little and pat her eyes with the handkerchief from the sleeve of her blouse. I finished and everybody clapped. Except Papa did not clap. I looked at him and he was staring out of the window down into the street. When he turned round to the room he said to Levi and Peter and Sala that they must go back to their own apartment, he said, 'Now.'

Long legs have not evolved towards passenger aircraft. I had a cramp in my knee. Easing it, I dropped the 'H.G.' folder. More irritation. I now had to move my tray to the next – empty – seat and scrabble on the floor. As I straightened I looked ahead and saw a man four rows in front look back, hard at me. Never saw him before. Christ, I'm jumpy.

Then Papa changed his mind and I thought this was strange and nobody moved and Papa gave no explanation. I know today that everybody there understood what was to happen although we did not know and we had no warning. The doorbell did not ring but we heard the steady thump-thump of two pairs of boots on the staircase and then we heard loud someone hard knocking on our apartment door. Mama looked at Papa with her eyes very full and sad and afraid. Uncle Roder and Papa moved towards each other in the middle of the room. They looked at each other's faces and each slowly shook his head. Uncle Roder put out a hand and steadied Papa and then they walked to the hall where the hammering on the door began again, it was noise which had not any rhythm in it as when Papa drums the table, he did so in a nice steady tempo. Papa opened the door and inside the room nobody said anything. I saw an awful look cross Mama's face as to Aunt Mayva she pointed out Levi,

136

Peter and Sala. Many times have I been afraid but it is not like that evening. Out at the door I could hear an argument and Papa's voice. Uncle Roder's voice was loud too and seemed to be trying to calm matters. Then I heard more hard bootsteps and a soldier stood in our living room. First he looked at me where I sat on the piano stool. Then he looked at everybody in the room and he smiled but it was not a smile of friendship. He carried a gun on his belt at his waist and as he stood with his hands on his hips he allowed his fingers to touch the gun. He said very clearly and not quickly, 'All of you must leave now. Please bring your coats. Do not ask me questions.' He was twenty-three about I think and his accent was thick, from the south and he would not look at us. I stood up and so did everybody. Mama said these children are from a different apartment and this lady does not live here either. The soldier walked to the table with his boots hitting the wooden floor very hard like iron. He took a piece of cake and ate it and gobbled some pieces of Sala's marzipan and said again everybody has to leave. He said to leave quickly, quickly. I thought it strange that he seemed so not concerned at what he was doing to us. I went to the table to fetch my new handbag which lay on its nest of opened wrapping-paper. I put my first scent into the handbag and the soldier said leave that. Go. *Raus, raus!* I became upset and Aunt Mayva grabbed me by the shoulders and said come with me we shall go together. But I sneaked the scent bottle into the bag. Mama stood outside the living-room door with my coat in her hand and her own coat over her arm and she was trying to take Papa's greatcoat from the hooks in the hallway. Levi, Peter and Sala came out with me and as they attempted to walk along the corridor to their own apartment the other soldier halted them and pointed that they must go down the staircase although they said they lived in the door that was behind him. We all walked down together and there was one soldier in front and the other behind. Out on the street they made us stand into two groups with Levi, Peter, Uncle Roder and Papa in one over there and I, Mama, Aunt Mayva and Sala in the other over here. We were told by the soldiers to walk in different directions and that was the last time I saw Papa or Uncle Roder or Levi or Peter, although I was looking back very much and the soldiers told me to look where I was going. Then I almost dropped my bag off my arm and it fell open and the bottle of my birthday scent fell out and it shattered on the stones of the street. I tried to stop but Aunt Mayva said you can't gather up scent and I never found out whether the bottle or the scent was green, maybe they both were green. We walked down our road and other people waited there. On the way we passed a man and a woman who stood there but when we passed by they looked away although I knew who they were. They were Herr and Frau Hiedler. My mother tried to say something to Frau Hiedler but the soldier said no talking please. Herr and Frau Hiedler had been told by the soldiers to stand there and see that we had gone because when we went they were told they will own our home. I found this when the war has ended, that these people were waiting for us to leave that afternoon of my birthday because they had been told they were to live in our apartment. They lived there together until Herr Hiedler died and Frau Hiedler is very old and lives there today.

I close the pages and put them on the seat beside me. I am unable to cope with 'H.G.' I don't want to cope with 'H.G.' Or any of this. Can't do it. An odd refraction gives me a hazy view of my face in the perspex window. I look failed and down. Ten minutes to landing. What the hell am I doing here?

23

No question. I should have turned back. Everywhere I looked I saw warnings. A bandaged man in a wheelchair. Two policemen in a corner of a corridor checking their guns. A woman, alone, weeping. I should have caught the next flight back but nerve failed me and cowardice cancelled cowardice. I feared being disliked, I feared disappointing, I feared breaking my word.

Go through with it. But keep control, keep giving myself options. For which reasons I went to the French side of Geneva airport. This gave me the choice of going to Montreux by the big *routes nationales* or by country roads.

Shall I call Claire? What shall I hear if I do? A sound of the phone being replaced? My own voice on the answering machine? Or, perhaps, Claire herself? Once before, after a coldness like this, our returning conversation began with her most fearsome question, 'Nicholas, do you love me?'

Why should that question so frighten a man? Of my age and experience? I can offer no reason. But it does scare me. When somebody whom I didn't love and whom I didn't even think I loved asked it some years ago, I got fazed. The self-inquiry lasted months.

Then one morning, in Rye, alone, I knew why it bothered me. My mother had asked it constantly – of my father, to whom she was serially unfaithful; of my brother Kim: 'Do you love Mummy?' But she never asked it of me: 'Nicholas, do you love me?'

I was there when she died. Didn't want to be, but there I was. What I most recall about it now is my abject terror

140

that her last words to me might be; 'Do you love me?' They weren't, as it happened. Her last words were, 'Darling, that light's too strong on my face.'

The relief when she died! I feel it still, the relief of not having to stand on that shifting ground or interpret those mixed messages.

I love the light in Switzerland. The sun shone hot as well as bright. How beautifully the Swiss drive, the best in Europe. Nobody followed me. As far as I could make out. At Ferney-Voltaire customs post the police said, Take the road to Lausanne. On the map it looks longer.

Small bonus: by not taking the autoroute I avoid tolls. Larger bonus – the road to Lausanne, via Versoix, Nyon, Rolle and Morges, runs by the lakeshore. Vineyards to my left, sparkling waters to my right and in the distance the haze of heat obscures the Alps. Who was the boxer my father liked – the 'Ambling Alp' they called him? Primo Carnera – yes! Glass jaw. Glassy stare eventually as he took it on the chin. My father said Primo hit the canvas harder than Primo ever hit an opponent. My mood eases. The sinister images fade. Except for the mountains on the far side of the lake: they look like teeth.

Lausanne came and went. In Montreux they boast of their micro-climate, claim they're warmer than Vevey, down the road.

I checked into the Eden Au Lac and got a room – 'Au bord du lac, m'sieu?' Now what? The pleasure cruisers criss-crossed the lake. Above them in the blue sky stretched the white laces of vapour trails. All I can do is wait. Lunch on the *terrasse* brought me *une grande salade* and a plate of grilled fish. All so precise: I doubt you will ever find 'wild' mushrooms in Swiss cuisine.

After lunch I strolled a little. Interesting bedfellows the statuary of Montreux – Freddie Mercury and Charlie Chaplin; plus innumerable grass sculptures of sheep, goats, cows, horses, all with horse-chestnuts for eyes. And a giant spider.

My mind raced. How shall I play this? Elizabeth's father was a spy and she told me his motto was, *Put yourself in the other fellow's shoes*. Will the 'doctor' have checked that I have arrived? He might need to. I will make myself visible.

A couple walked by, in their thirties. He had sideburns and a congenital limp. She clung to him, laughing and snogging. Her see-through blouse let her nipples take the air. Both wore brand-new matching trainers. Where have I seen these people before? Or have I? *Nicholas, stop.*

Lac Léman today is hazy. I should have brought binoculars. Claire enjoys her mild obsession with my telescope in Rye. Should I buy the house that has come up for sale in Church Square, opposite the old reservoir? Restore it, keep Claire occupied?

I set off, walking briskly. To make myself visible.

They were washing a train in the *gare* at Montreux. In a special booth, men with hoses and long brushes smoothed sprays of water down across the carriages – they might have been bathing a blue-and-cream elephant. The rack train to Caux waited on one side, with its little anodized steel buggy in front expecting to be pushed up the mountain. I looked hard to find the track – can that be it over there, almost vertical, up through the foliage of the hill?

Last time I came to Caux I was a student writing an acoustics essay. I cycled up, half-killed myself with the effort. Then almost killed myself again freewheeling back down.

The train set off to the minute. Mussolini was here. Old joke. Making the trains run on time. I once defended oily Hal Callaghan to Elizabeth Bentley who hates him.

'He makes the trains run on time.'

'Nicholas, dear, we are an architectural practice. Not a bloody railway.'

142

At Glion nobody came and nobody went on the bare plat-form. The rising track rose above the road. A car sat parked beneath a bridge with two people in it. Not going anywhere, just watching the train. Are they wearing trainers? And am I getting jumpy again? I looked behind me along the carriages: almost empty; some children; a grandmother with a Red Riding-Hood shopping basket; the nearest person to me is a middle-aged Japanese man, travelling alone and making notes.

Foliage brushes the windows. A funny black-and-white wooden cow laughs from the sill of a chalet.

Shall I get out at Caux? The building I chose for our 'meeting' looks like something from Disneyland. I know it from my past. But it's now a training school for hotel management who share it with Moral Re-Armament. I hope the acoustic is intact. No. Stay on the train to Rochers de Naye.

I can feel the teeth of the little train's central wheels. They rack themselves up the mountain. My spine melds with the ratchet of the rail.

Sparrows flourish in the gardens alongside. Far below I can see the white figures on the tennis courts and I can see the waters of the lake like grey shades of satin and off there in the haze I can see the urban necklace of Lausanne. Do the mountains contain powerful secrets? The Swiss hid their wartime gold deep within the Alps. Above Caux a huge, lone rock sits, its texture like an elephant's hide. We had an elephant's foot umbrella-stand when I was a child.

Soon we are too high for small birds to fly. These are snowy wastes in winter. I have been here then, watching the skeletons of the ski-chairs wobbling like commas up and down the empty skies and the stark, blinding-white snow ten feet deep mantling terrible crevasses.

The train slows but does not stop at the Buffet Col de Jaman. Oddly, the driver, before he takes this decision, turns round and looks at me. Don't be ridiculous. Nothing to do with me. How did they build these tunnels? What is it like when the snow falls and piles up against the tunnel walls? All along the trackside, like little sentries, stand the brushes for clearing the snow off the rails. The wooden chalets on the distant slopes have high legs like mannequins. I think of Claire whose thighs don't meet at the top. Signs keep telling me of a *Jardin Alpin* that has been established for *100 ans* but I can't see it yet.

At the terminus of Rochers de Naye I take decisions. I will have some chocolate. Then I will take the air. Next train's two hours hence. The restaurateur is a thin young man with good English. His drinking chocolate is excellent, if not as dense as Ruby's. And still I sense I'm being watched. Again I see my face reflected in a glass. Not a face I'd bet the farm on.

I wander outside and sit in the sun, gazing across the patchworked terraces of land where miracles of farming are performed every season of the year. A family walks by, hiking for their lives. Soon, a couple strolls down from the heights above. In the sunshine they sit at the next picnic table. He has a small moustache and she, complaining merrily of the sun's heat, takes off first her waistcoat and then her shirt. Sitting there in her white bra she is too sexy for my comfort. I walk away, thinking of Hitler and Eva Braun on their mountain. An hour to go before the train. On a rock I stretch and doze. My brain sees lizards. I know I am frightened – but of what?

The rock's too hard and the sun too hot. I go indoors for another cup of chocolate. They must think me mad: I should be drinking something cold. This time I am served by a red-faced, innocent girl. She *mercis* me mercilessly. Something's about to happen. I feel sure of it. But I'm wrong.

No, I'm right. She brings me a small packet of Swiss

wafer-chocolate. When I unwrap it I find a handwritten note, *'Go back to your hotel.'*

Christ!

You hear the rack train before you see it. Not for very long but very distinctively. I wondered about all the avalanche warnings up and down the mountain.

Same driver; no passengers this time; white-bra Fräulein and her Adolf remain on the mountainside and I am alone on the train. Down at the Buffet Col de Jaman the train stops and the driver gets out. For some reason I divine that he wants me to get out too.

'Go back to your hotel': I am still digesting the note. Soon I will react to this. The sinister images return. Broken branches end in spikes. I feel the rail in my spine. A trackside shed has a shattered windowpane.

Inside the buffet, the driver talks to a group of three men, all jovial and relaxed. Nobody greets me. I stand in the doorway looking out across these mountains of whose beauty I can never get enough. The men behind me debate the sandwiches in the buffet for weather like this. They speak of *jambon* and *tomates* and *concombre* and *salade*. Le Patron goes to his blackboard where he has scrawled the day's fare. I watch him – and I sense that I am expected to watch him. He begins to chalk words on the board. But that's all. Nothing else happens. I clamber back on the train. Soon I will need a lavatory.

The word 'track' hums in my head. The track is my spine. The track's a trainspotter's dream. Who is tracking me? And then, with the track dropping almost vertically down the mountain, I think again. This 'network' giving me these messages – is it on my side?

Or not?

24

Look, I say to myself (I am standing at the mirror). By any standards this is bizarre. You are in Switzerland. Involved in things outside your life's writ. You are now beginning to tremble a little. Your gut will be pumping torrents by tonight. Why are you doing it? Why are you putting yourself through this? And I answer slowly, I – don't – quite – know.

The lake changed from satin to glass. My room, on the fifth floor, had a corner window. I could see Caux up above. So near – a flight would take three minutes. Some time between now, it is the late afternoon of Wednesday, and tomorrow, Thursday night, I might even know what I am doing here.

Sitting in the room, with the curtains blowing in from the balcony's breeze, I weigh the stakes. I am doing this for – for what? 'For Ruby' came out too pat as an answer. And in the ethics of marriage that would be wrong anyway. For Claire? I could pretend.

I know it's not for Clay Massey. For Madeleine's memory? No. Okay – for history? Can I reach back into the past and feel the atrocities? I've just read 'H.G.' No – because I feel inclined, even obliged, to fence myself off from them.

Paralysis sloped across my mind. Everything in me baulked. Feeling like a spy prepared to eat his own notes I began listing the possible reasons I was here. Number them in order of importance.

I didn't do that. My telephone rang. Not a switchboard ring; to judge from the ringing sequence, the caller knew the direct number assigned to my room. And as I moved to answer it an envelope fell on the balcony. I picked up the envelope and answered the phone.

'Mr Newman?' A woman's voice.

'Yes.'

'Your table has been reserved for twelve thirty tomorrow in Caux. At the Buffet de la Gare. Please drive.' The telephone clicked off.

I opened the envelope – one ticket for an afternoon concert, at four o'clock in Mountain House. Ah, yes; that is what they call it now – 'Mountain House'. On the balcony the sun beat in. The circle is closing.

I rang Claire. She answered.

'Hallo?' Tentative, like a child.

I know what my problem is – I lack compassion. I was born without the compassion gene. What would happen, I wonder, if the human race was born without certain genes? Embarrassment? Compassion? Envy?

'Claire, it's me.'

Silence – and then, 'Nicholas, do you love me?'

'Claire, I love you.'

I picked the phone up like they used to do in American films before cordless and mobile phones were invented and I moved to the window.

'Where are you?' she asked.

'In Switzerland.'

'I promise not to ask what you're doing there.'

'I promise to tell you when I come home.'

'Nicholas, do you love me?'

'Claire, I love you.'

She put the phone down. I knew I would call her later and that it would be all right.

Time to recover. My neck dripped with sweat. Clothes off, into the shower, change, then a long walk.

25

To the east of Montreux stands Chillon, a castle built over several centuries. It's as dark and brooding as a graveyard poet. I walked there in three-quarters of an hour, paid my seven francs fifty and went in. The cool, huge rooms would buttress me, I hoped; the ancient stones and pillars support me.

Byron was here. He signed a pillar. Above the unremarkable first courtyard I looked out over the lake. How does one find a place in Europe Byron never visited?

Few things in life offer the pleasure of cut stone. I remember an old stonemason's tip: Once you pick up a stone you have to find a place to lay it. His other tip: To make something you have to break something.

In a long room with halberds and chain mail I crossed from the lake windows. Check the inland views. Watching for enemies – that was the brief here. Had the architect achieved it? He had. How did I know? I knew because parked on the forecourt below sat a yellow Porsche and standing beside it I saw Richard Strafe.

Snatch at calm. Distract myself to buy time. Look at the window – a mere slot, wide enough to fire an arrow. Strafe wore a black linen jacket and a shirt as white as fear.

A fibrillation kicked in. I took my pulse. Racing like a triphammer. And I have no pills. I put my back to the wall – as I am, so shall I be. Closed my eyes. Have to take a decision.

I decided to stay where I was. For twenty minutes I walked up and down that room. Tourists came and went; retired

148

couples, a small coach party, a pair of ageing women who might once have been whores, given the swing in their hips. A couple of pleasant-faced gay men spoke playfully to each other; a school group of twenty teenaged pupils heckled the teacher. From time to time I checked the window – there's Strafe's car but where's Strafe?

When there is nothing to do – do nothing. I inspected some halberds – again. Strolled to the far wall and gazed upon the waters of the lake – again. Then I decided to brave it. Followed the tour arrows to the next number, '10', a bedroom and dressing room, thirteenth-century *en suite*, so to speak. Behind me, footsteps on the hollow floors rang slow and deep. Two sets of footsteps. Mine – and someone else's.

I am a tourist here, therefore I will follow this tourist trail. And I saw the Bernese clock. And I recalled that in the Bernese Oberland my father once hit a man who called my mother a rude name. And this next room was a torture chamber, presumably torturers caused those marks on the base of the pillar. And what a sweet chapel, but they have denuded it of any sanctity.

Some skilled craftsman of the past made the marble pillars of the next chamber look like wood and the wooden pillars look like marble.

More latrines.

In the Hall of the Scribes I liked and disliked the medieval decor; 'European-Florid' – stylized and ornate and the leaves have long lost all connection with the natural world. Foot-steps still following me.

Let me try something new. As I leave each room I turn and look back. But nobody appears.

On and on I went, walking through the chateau and fondling its bastions and gripping its balustrades and patrolling its patrol galleries.

Now I shall try something else. In the Keep, hide round

149

the corner, make them think you've vanished, given them the slip, see if they'll rush forward. It works in the movies.

But in the movies there is drama. In life at that moment all I saw was an elderly man in an anorak and a boy in rubber-soled shoes. Grandfather and grandson. They strolled past me. My turn to follow them. Two more innocuous people I have never seen. After ten minutes or so they and I finished the tour.

When I got outside, Strafe's Porsche, Swiss number plates, still sat there, yellower than ever in the evening sunshine. I returned by the lakeshore, on the wide paved way beloved of the pedestrian citizenry of Montreux. Perhaps I will design a personal rear-view mirror. With a shoulder grip. To be worn by pedestrians – and paranoids. Bet the Californians already have one. Minutes later I saw, on the road above, Strafe's car drive by.

At the hotel I didn't take the glass lift, I climbed the stairs. Directly outside my door a burly, shaven man lolled like a rock in one of the two armchairs. He did not look at me.

I closed the door. Brine in my eyes from my own sweat. Ring someone. Don't. There's nobody to ring. Ring Ruby? And endanger her?

Sometimes (but not often) my own calm amazes me. It dropped on me now and brought presence of mind. I thought, If Strafe is here it means the stakes are high.

I telephoned his office in London and got through to his secretary. My plan is to tell her I heard he's in Switzerland and so am I.

'Oh, Mr Newman, hello. He's in a meeting next door – but he'll be out in twenty minutes.'

What-at?!! My brain begins to bulge. A glass of water. From the mini-bar. Do everything slowly.

I opened Claire's dossier. This will move my mind to a different problem. What is Strafe doing?! Is that a henchman outside the door? But I *saw* him, I saw Strafe himself! He's not in London, he's here. In Montreux. That can only mean Strafe wants to find out what I'm doing here. If he finds out I hope he'll tell me. Feeble joke, thin smile. But what's his connection to all this? Connection. Ruby's word. I'm baffled. And anxious. And angry. I'm going to ask him when I see him – if I see him – 'Look, Richard – what's going on, what's all this about?'

I didn't. The phone rang and Strafe asked, 'What you doing out there? Seeing your bankers?'

I think, Note the 'out there'.

'Where are you?' I asked foolishly.

'Where d'you think I am? I'm in my office. Returning your call.'

Do you recognize that moment when the left and right sides of your brain fail to meet in the middle? Strafe said to me, 'You ringing to confirm lunch?'

'Yes. Exactly.' Keep it flippant: I've done that all my life.

'Good. L'Arlésienne. Friday. My turn. Watch out for those gnomes. Tricky little fuckers.' And he laughed and went.

Call him back, Nicholas! NOW! Go ON!

The secretary put me through: it took no more than thirty seconds.

'You did say l'Arlésienne?'

'Yes.' Curt, this time. No joviality. 'Hey? Your money going to your head out there? No, I get it. You're on some fucking Alp and the air's thin?' He rang off.

I ran to the balcony. There's a man down there, a man in a black jacket and a shirt as white as – he's slipped round a corner. It's Strafe, I know it!

Sit down, Nicholas. This is awful. This is a kind of brain-washing. This is splitting my frontal lobes. Sit on the bed. Do something.

Open Claire's folder. Read another file.

My family home, in the ownership of us for four generations, possessed many and lovely heirlooms of an elaborate nature. We took a special pride in our drinking services from the city of Chemnitz where, as we were frequently informed when we were children, there had once been a famous glass-factory of the seventeenth century.

The signature on this one read, *'Ethel Saye'*.

The glass was shining a light pink colour and we knew that our family only brought it into service for very special occasions as the highest days and my father's birthday. In the service we owned glasses of the sherry kind and a fluted decanter of the sherry or the port or the sweet wine. This glass we used only for the adults and when it came to us the children we used for lemonade the fat pink tumblers and their large jug. All of us in our family knew the history of this glass from Chemnitz. It came from a house in France, in the south, and we knew it was of our family for many, many years.

On the 'last day', which is what I always call the day we were ordered to leave our home, it was sunny and I remember seeing the sunlight shining into the cabinet and on the glass where I often looked because I liked them so much. Everything was quiet and suddenly four soldiers were in our apartment and they looked around. One of them gave orders and we were allowed to put some clothes into a suitcase, we had to scramble and hurry and I had not a suitcase until my father emptied his valise for work. There were five of us, including my parents, and then the soldiers said we must leave. We halted then at his order when he asked my father where he kept his wines. My father said we only owned sweet wine and the soldier nodded his head like an officer although his uniform did not say so. My father handed him a sealed bottle of wine and the soldier asked him, 'Please open it.' While my father did so the soldier fetched our wonderful glasses from the cabinet and set them on the table. He ordered my father to pour some wine into each glass and the soldier called his colleagues. The four stood around the table and raised their glasses and one said, '*Sterben Juden,*' a toast I knew was drunk in Germany at the time, and the others laughed and drank from our Chemnitz glasses. Then they ordered us again and we left our home. When I returned in 1990 to our home, our Chemnitz glasses were still in their cabinet although I cannot say if they are all there. If I am to be given back my family home with such possessions as I can identify, I do not know whether I shall be able to drink from those glasses again.

A margin note: '"Sterben Juden" *means "Death to Jews"; it was a toast frequently proposed and drunk at family, official and ceremonial occasions throughout Hitler's Reich.*'

Wind feathered the lake. Someone knocked at the door. Jesus! What is it now? I walked silently forward and said, 'Yes?'

'Votre service, m'sieu,' said a girl's voice.

I opened the door and saw the pair of legs sitting outside – the shaven man. But brushing past me with a tray came the red-faced girl from the restaurant on top of Rochers de Naye.

She set the tray on the bed as I closed the door. Finger to her lips, she murmured in excellent English, 'Go out to your balcony and walk eight rooms along – the barriers between the rooms are quite low. I will wait for you there.'

She left the room, with her trademark volley of *mercis*.

My jaws hurt. I could feel the cold air of my flared nostrils.

Out on the lake a boat made a feathered 'V' wake. The balcony had become tiny and fraught. I looked along its length – no more than an unwide, flimsy shelf. Climbing over each little wrought-iron separator, I dared not look into each room I passed. Nor dare look down to my left, the sheer drop to the gardens. I heard myself make a small nasal 'cheep'. No one called out; nobody halted me. I lost count of the balconies until my red-faced friend waved to me. My neck was wet and I had a half-erection.

Inside the eighth room stood a large heap of bedding. She piled it high in my arms until it concealed my white face. Turning me so that I walked sideways she led me from the room. What could the shaven man see? Along the corridor from his chair a maid and a hotel porter piled high with sheets and pillows. Straight across the corridor she opened the emergency door. I went through it, dropped the linen on the stairs and waited.

Nobody followed.

'What do you wish to do?' she asked.

'I wish to –' I didn't know what I wished to do. Adrenalin helped. 'I wish them to know I can beat them.'

'Go out. Come back later. Walk in as normal.'

She smiled, finger-waved a small 'goodbye' to me. I walked casually down the emergency stairs to a corridor two floors down, took the lift and left the hotel.

At the corner of the *Grande Rue* I hailed a cab. The television executives who come to Montreux for the annual Comedy Awards spend most of everyone else's money in l'Ermitage. That night I spent a great deal of my own; superb food and a wine of the country. The rich surroundings settled me and I felt a stab of enjoyment. But there lies the danger. If I engage with this Zurück business Christ knows what can happen. Elation, that dangerous friend, surfaced.

I went with it, wrestled my mind away from the day's events. So there's a heavy thug outside my room – so what?

154

Think of Claire. Once again I shall try and compose my letter to her. But I can't. How can I write down the questions I need to ask? Claire, why do you shiver so? Claire, what is the name of your most frightening ghost? Claire, what's it like when you're up, not down? Nicholas, don't be so stupid! All you want to do is tell her you love her. Simply write that to her.

It didn't happen. The words didn't come. Slightly elated (for no good reason), I walked back through the empty streets of Montreux. Cartier's window showed a pair of diamond earrings. Seventeen thousand Swiss francs. Seven grand in sterling. Tomorrow I will buy them for Claire. Reflected in the window I saw the yellow car draw up behind me and I saw the driver look at me in his black jacket and I couldn't quite see him and if it were Richard Strafe he did not have time to get from London to Montreux in the few hours since I spoke to him, not even flying his own plane, so therefore I am now a dement.

Reception gave me a duplicate key. As I took the glass lift I thought, They can shoot me in this. I strolled along the corridor humming a song manically in my mind. The song was one I had been humming rather a lot, Donald Fagen's 'Ruby Baby'. Must remember not to hum it near Claire. *I got a gal and Ruby is her name.* No shaven man. Empty chair outside my room. *She's my gal and I love her just the same.* Or words to that effect. I smiled.

Inside the room I had this extraordinary, momentary sensation that I was dreaming all this. I opened the door again to check the corridor. Nobody there.

I rang Claire. Her sleepy voice welcomed me – and I fell asleep again. The night calmed me down; I slept better than I could have expected. But I did arrange furniture so that anyone trying to break in could not avoid sounding like war.

26

I am in the restaurant at the Buffet de la Gare in Caux. The little train passes by the window. I order *potage du printemps*. The muzak offers Poulenc. A Japanese waitress brings me a bottle of water, carrying it like a vintage wine.

Beneath my hand something flickers on the table-top, a dark shape. Odd. I look and can see nothing. When I look away it flickers again. This time I keep my gaze concentrated downwards. The flicker returns and I trace it: the hard shine of the knife has captured the reflection of a bird of prey. I look out of the window and there it is, circling above the *gare*. Sometimes in London I have seen bizarre reflections of aircraft in the sloped rear windows of cars. The bird of prey returns to the mirror of the knife-blade. And – I think I expected it – at that moment the door opens and in comes Richard Strafe.

I do nothing. I say nothing. Strafe sits at a table in the next room, on the other side of a wall. For a moment I wonder again whether my imagination is playing tricks. I look away, close my eyes, look back again and open them. Time to take my sanity from my surroundings – which is what an architect does: he takes stock of where he is.

This is what the restaurant looks like at the Buffet de la Gare in Caux, vertically above Montreux. The tables have undercloths of oak green. Triangulated across these lie smaller cloths of spotless white linen. M. le Patron evidently likes music; over the piano hangs a brown and cream coaching horn made of what seems like marquetry. Beside it hangs a percussion triangle, there's a guitar on a stand and on the wall to my left shines a little silver clock in the shape of the treble clef.

In the corner farthest from me sit a most elegant Indian couple, he a good deal older than her, each heavily involved with the other. They look like some Scott and Zelda Fitzgerald of the sub-continent and now I recall – Scott and Zelda whistled though here on one of their wild spinning tours and he remembered the 'fabled acoustic' of the Grand Palais ballroom.

Lunch proceeds. I gaze out of the window a great deal. Hang-gliders drift in and out of my view. The bird of prey has disappeared. Can it be true that Strafe sits in the next room? Can it be true that he pretended he was in London but was tracking me in Montreux? What is true any more? Discuss. At the end of the grilled lamb main course I go to the lavatory. I need to – and I can reach it without passing by Strafe's table.

The cutting edge of sanitary technology has reached Caux. When I press the flush button, the plastic seat revolves in a wonky circle, being force-cleaned through a sanitizing clamp.

On my way back I will find it difficult not to look at Strafe. I rehearse what I will say: 'Richard! So you've come to visit your bankers too!'

But he's not there and his table looks as if nobody ever sat at it. My bewildered cheese arrives, then the pudding, then the coffee. I have all the time in the world but my heart is beating so fast.

At three o'clock I pay my bill. When the credit-card chit returns, it is not in duplicate – it is in triplicate and on the third part is printed a small message: *'The Doctor will speak first. Do not attempt to meet him.'* Trying to look like someone without a care in the world, I saunter outside.

Nobody waits for the train. In the near distance I see a minibus drawing up at the main entrance to Mountain

House. From it climbs a small group of people, arriving for the recital. I am waiting to meet a man who may not exist. They are hoping to hear a pianist fill their souls. The world is a dangerous stage.

Time to make my move. I take the concert ticket from my pocket. At the door a girl of great natural charm whose name is Marianna ushers me into the Grand Hall and tells me that since I am the first to arrive I may sit anywhere I choose. I wander past the bust of *Frank N. D. Buckman 1878–1961* and look at the ceiling. Not changed much; the same Rameses red Egyptian terracotta with ochre lozenges and black friezes; the same outrageous plant-spears of foliage rising from the borders; the same sunburst whose plaster is now peeling.

Why is Strafe following me? I suddenly understand – or so I think. It has to do with Ruby. Jealousy? But how did he know I visited Ruby? And what nerve – jealous while he himself is making overtures to my wife. I sit in this huge room and I know with that familiar shudder that if life continues much longer in this bewildering splitting off of truth from illusion I am soon going to have difficulty in not breaking down.

The room rings to my step. Clasping my hands behind my back to look grave, I measure in paces the direction I need to hear what I have to hear. Now I choose my seat with infinite care. As I sit down I see a commotion at the door. Strafe has not done his homework. He possesses no tickets. The recital is sold out. He can't get in. I watch. He's trying a bribe. They rebuff him. I know what will happen – and it does. Minutes later he arrives in my peripheral vision, behind me, outside the building, on the horse-shoe terrace. From there, he will keep watch. But why? *Why?*

My mood swings between fear, self-recrimination and excitement. Act, I tell myself. Act like a spy. Or a hero.

This is your battle. You are a man whose wife is haunted by her past. Or the greater past. Act.

Silly man, Strafe. To find out what's happening he needed to be inside. Even then he would have had no guarantee, because this room has an extraordinary acoustic and I know how the acoustic works. It's a whispering gallery. I wrote a student essay about this room.

My instructions to Ruby were specific. When the 'Doctor' arrives he is to sit diagonally across from me. The acoustic is such that he can speak to me and I to him in tones pitched between low and conversational and we will hear each other perfectly but the people either side or in between will not hear a word we're saying. Nobody has ever explained it to me satisfactorily. Acoustics are a matter of luck and therefore an architect's nightmare.

In my hand I have a programme – Schubert. Schumann. Liszt. Debussy. In my mind I have a list of questions for the 'Doctor'. Soon the people drift in. It is twenty past three and, as I have arranged, I begin to fan my face with my programme. Nobody yet sits opposite – or at least nobody who looks likely. Yet a voice speaks to me.

'Yes I am here, what is it you wish to know?'

I look diagonally. No, nothing significant. All I see, forty feet away, is a man in his twenties. Not a doctor, surely; he's probably no more than twenty-two or -three; he wears a baseball cap turned backwards and still has acne. But he speaks again and this time I see his lips move.

'Yes, it is I.'

I murmur, 'We have limited time. Tell me about Zurück.'

'Yes. The word is as close to infinite meaning as a German word can get. I have lost count of its variations. In this case it means cynically "to retain". It was created to ensure that Germans "retain" the properties of Jews.' Monotonous voice.

'Why is it secret?'

'Yes. Because of the means it employs. And because it is now against the law in Germany to espouse any cause that echoes those old sympathies.' Almost a drone. And what is this with the word 'yes'?

'The means it employs?' I am speaking in a voice I might use to Claire in a restaurant if we didn't want the people at the next table to hear us.

'Yes. It kills people. It prides itself on its targets being unable to hide. And it kills them.'

'Did it kill Clay Massey?'

'Yes. Of course.'

'Why?'

'Yes, he was part of a committee helping with researches into the claims.'

Part of me felt cold. Part of me felt eerie. Part of me felt empowered. Next question.

'I am being followed by a man called Richard Strafe.'

'Yes, I can see him. He is outside the window.'

'Why is he following me?'

'He wishes to kill me. Not you.'

'Why?'

'Because he is Zurück.'

'What d'you mean?'

'He *is* the organization.'

'Why?'

'Two reasons. Strafe's father was a leading Nazi. He worked for Kaltenbrunner in the management of the camps. Secondly, Strafe himself has bought many of the properties from people who had been given them and who grew afraid they would lose them back to their original owners under the claims. The properties form the basis of all Strafe's wealth. And all his commercial interests.'

Concertgoers arrived in greater numbers. The 'Doctor' said, 'We may not have much time left.'

'How does Zurück operate, meaning – can I anticipate them?'

'Difficult, yes? They reward their operatives very richly. Drugs. Money. Freedom – whatever that is. That is why it is so difficult to hide from them. They can recruit anybody. Not one of their many murders has yet been prosecuted in any country.'

'How do I stop them?'

'Kill Strafe. That is the only way, yes? I must go.'

'Please! One last question.' I had to find out about Ruby. The 'Doctor' said, 'No.'

'Please.'

Again the ghost across the room said, 'No.'

I half-rose. He saw me and his lips moved. 'Ask. Quickly.' The words floated down that whispering tunnel of sound.

I said, 'Do you know any names on the Zurück target list?'

'Just one.'

This is it. How will I break it to her? Ruby, I'm sorry.

'What is that name?'

'Yes, the name of Claire Newman.'

Terror makes one unsure. My eyes went hazy. I asked, not trusting my voice, 'Claire Newman?'

'Her family once owned large property. She is known to be claiming.'

As desperate as a child I asked, 'Are you sure?'

'Yes.'

My mind is screaming as my voice is murmuring, 'But – do you know who Claire Newman is?'

Not another sound came along our channel of air.

27

For the next three-quarters of an hour I acted like a concertgoer. I gazed at the heraldic shields; I closed my eyes; I watched the recitalist's electric hair; I leaned back and studied the ceiling. Once I looked out of the window and saw Strafe sitting on the bench alone, staring in the direction of the huge circular windows. He looked cool. Inside, we sweltered.

Valentin Benois had a divine touch. His hands flashed and his head reared. But I quit after his Schumann and before the Liszt. Had anyone thought me rude I'd have told them, Liszt is too hot for me, too wild.

On my left stood tall doors with mysterious muslin curtains. If only they could give me some sort of tiptoed exit into a better world, some bright and ideal country, some land of eternal youth and sunshine. Ironic, isn't it? This is the building that houses Moral Re-Armament, an organization dedicated to a new Europe where Nazis could never rise again.

I looked to my right. All the chairs were full. No baseball cap. My ghostly, acoustic confidant had melted away.

Zurück. I reached my car. Zurück. 'To retain.' I flipped open the mobile. Eyes on the rear-view mirror. Pain in my chest. Gasp in my throat.

'Lemon?'

'Where are you?'

'On my way home. Everything all right?' My dull voice.

'More or less.'

'I'll be in the office tomorrow. Has my wife rung?'

'She's left a message on your mobile. She's gone to her friend, Lucinda's.'

'I don't think I have Lucinda's number.'

'She said she'll ring.'

'Anyone else?'

'Miss Hamer. She'll call too.'

Panic finally reached me. I couldn't start the car. Until I realized I had hired an automatic and that I had moved the shift out of 'P'. At last I rolled out from under the trees.

No Strafe. No yellow Porsche. At the end of the slip road I turned left: lots of cars parked for the recital but mine the only one in motion. A van, bearing the logo of the Swiss Hotel School of Management, came up the hill past Villa Maria. I waited until it passed me.

At the first downward hairpin I heard the roar and on the corner Strafe overtook me, almost forcing me off. He disappeared.

My mobile rang – it replayed Claire's message.

'Nicholas, it's me. Just to say I'm feeling much better and I'm off to Lucinda's. Lemon says you're not home until tonight and I think I shall see you in London tomorrow. I'll ring the flat tonight late. Travel safely. Much, much love.'

Under the railway bridge I turned the next hairpin. Is he here? I pulled in. But I can hardly see, because I am bewildered by fear and concern and my eyes are full of sweat again.

I'll wait a bit. My schedule gave me time to catch either the last Swissair or the last British Airways flight out of Geneva. Wait.

It worked. An hour later I drove on. No more Strafe. Then I recalled that a police car had passed me climbing the mountain. It must have passed Strafe too; perhaps he thought I had summoned it.

In Montreux I collected my bags from the hotel, laid them in the car, parked outside Cartier's – and then hit the road.

Strafe did not appear at Geneva airport. Nor on the flight. Nor at Heathrow.

Nor at Ruby's. She had two hours to go before she opened for the night. A barman or a waiter grunted and released the door on the buzzer. Down the hall I heard the snatches of music and the laughs of the musicians. All the lights were on, house, spots and effects. Ruby stood there, tights and leotard, talking to the band.

They started again and she came in on the refrain; *'Twas there that you whispered tenderly. That you loved me, I'd always be. Your Lilli of the lamplight.*

I watched until she saw me. Her face in the strong evening light, without make-up, still looked good. But when she stopped and ran over to me her eyes shone full of ruin.

I told her what I knew. Unedited – except for the part about Claire. Each word hit her like a blow. She fidgeted, unable to look at me, didn't want me to see her fear.

'Will you keep looking out for me, darling?'

Her words, her edgy look – I twisted away; I'm no good with direct appeal.

'Ruby, I sense you'll be safe.'

'I hope so, darling.'

Ten minutes later, when the cab dropped me at the flat, I walked around the block to check whether I was followed. No sign of anyone. Inside, I felt less safe than I had done heretofore. I rang Claire – no reply from Rye. As if by telepathy she called from Lucinda's almost the moment I replaced the phone.

I encouraged her to stay there. 'Come to town tomorrow.'

'Yes. I – I will.' Odd hesitancy. 'Yes, I was intending to.' Why the vagueness? 'So – we shall see each other? Nicholas, you sound funny.'

'Sore throat,' I said. 'Some Alpine bug. I might take the morning off.'

'Good idea. Don't you have a lunch?'

'Yes.'

How did she know? Perhaps I told her. Check the diary again in the vain hope I'd got it wrong. Tomorrow, Friday, said, *'Lunch: R. Strafe.'*

28

Who would sleep well in such times? Life's games were tearing me apart. If my reason, my sanity, is to survive, I have to fight back. And I don't have many weapons.

At midnight I telephoned the Clay Massey incident room. A bright-sounding man answered and I told him who I was. He said he had 'got me up now' on the screen: 'Ah, yes, sir.'

I said, 'I'm just checking to see whether there have been any developments. I've been abroad.'

'Nothing, sir. Several leads, but nothing.'

'No developments of any kind?'

'No.'

'Nothing at all?'

'No, sir.'

Do I tell him about Zurück? No. Not yet. Why not? Don't know. Maybe because on one level I'm a selfish, middle-class man who wants no trouble. Therefore the call did nothing for me.

After a long, hot bath I sat up, deciding to read and sleep, read and sleep. It sometimes works for me when I'm exhausted and that way I cheat insomnia. And comfort myself with the thought that in the morning I will draw.

It didn't work. Insomnia won. I had no place to put my thoughts. The fight began – between rationale and anxiety. For safety's sake, rationale must always win. But anxiety stops one from getting to the place of safety. Which, in all crucial moments, is the bottom line.

Eventually I reached it by means of rationale's great

helper, Time. I simply looked at my watch and thought, In seven hours and thirty-four minutes I will sit beside the man who means to kill my beloved young wife.

Unreal. This is not happening to me. I have died and am dreaming of life. A new thought. What are the stages of those who have terminal illness? Denial. Anger. I couldn't catalogue them – but I knew rage was in there somewhere. I raged. I will kill him. I will kill Strafe. Simple as that. Upon which thought I finally fell asleep.

And the depression of reality, isn't that another stage? When I woke, febrile and dozy, I knew what was real. The morning became one long shudder.

Hoping to upstage Strafe, I made sure, as I thought, to get to lunch early. He beat me to it. I watched him arrive just ahead of me, at a quarter to one. So I waited, used the time to seek calm and walked through the door at exactly one o'clock. He looked at his watch (as he always did), said nothing (as he always did when I was on time). Once I came late by five deliberate minutes and he pointed it out.

Table set for three. Three? And he had ordered a drink for me – the usual charade.

'No spirits at lunchtime, Richard.'

My voice sounded brittle. I looked at his neck. Take a fork in your hand, now, Nicholas, do it now, deep in the folds of his throat – do it! Take a knife from the table. No, not sharp enough. Use a fork.

'Don't be so poncy.' A favourite word.

'But *you* don't drink spirits at lunch.'

'That's different.'

'How is it different?'

'Because I'm not poncy. And by the way – I have nothing, zero, fuck-a-duck [another favourite term] in my diary for that French place, what'd you call it, for that Wednesday night. How were the Swiss bankers?'

Instead of saying, 'You tell me,' I replied, 'La Regalido.'

167

If he was going to dance this one slow, so would I. Then I added, 'I had a nice time talking to your wife a few nights ago.'

The blow landed. He winced in his eyes.

'How do you know Diana?'

'We have mutual friends.'

'Diana hasn't any friends. Who?'

'Ed Melchior.'

'You have some weird fucking friends.' He grunted, then added, '*Those* people.'

Claire once told me she could always tell when someone was being directly anti-Semitic by the way they said, '*You* people.'

Five minutes into meeting Strafe I was struggling worse than before, principally with the incomprehensible enormity, the unreality, of all this. I hadn't even begun to address how to protect Claire. And didn't rate my chances of success too highly. For a moment I turned away, closed my eyes tight and suspended all mental activity. Then I broke through.

Turning back, I grabbed his arm with a grip that surprised him. I said, 'Now. What was all that about?'

'All what?'

'Yesterday. The night before.'

He looked me in the face. 'What you talking about?'

'I'm talking about Montreux.'

'Montreux? What about it?'

'Why were you following me?'

He stared at me levelly. Am I dreaming? Is this a dream I'm having – maybe it's all a dream?

Strafe said, 'What the fuck you talking about? I haven't been to Montreux in years.'

I insisted, 'You followed me in Montreux. In a place called Chillon, there's an old castle. Then yesterday you followed me up the mountains to Caux and then afterwards you nearly ran me off the road in your yellow Porsche.'

Strafe sat back. 'Are you fucking joking?' The lizard eyelids fell and rose. 'Listen, you dick –' he was laughing – '*you* called *me* from Montreux. Are you on something?'

'Where did you lunch yesterday, Richard?'

He yanked out his mobile phone. 'Watch – my – lips. I spent all day yesterday and the day before with my personal financial adviser and my PA.' He hesitated. 'Want me to call 'em?' It was the only sign of doubt I saw in him and he dispelled it in seconds.

He rapped into the phone. 'Sheila. Me. Could you tell this dick where I was yesterday?'

He pressed the phone to my ear so hard it hurt.

A woman said in a whirring voice, 'Mr Strafe was here in his apartment at Butler's Wharf doing personal business.'

He snatched the phone back. 'Okay, Sheila.'

He dialled another number. 'Roger? Me. I've got a fuck-head with me doesn't believe me. Tell him where I was yesterday.'

Again his phone hit my hearing and a slow voice said, 'I'm Roger Palin and I'm Mr Strafe's investment adviser – we spent the past two days together in London strategizing.'

Strafe snatched the phone back, clicked it off. He looked around and saw the *maître*.

'Louis?' He waved. Louis came over.

'Louis, where'd I breakfast yesterday?'

'Here, Mr Strafe. Like you do every Thursday.'

'Thank you, Louis. Louis, how is your son?' Strafe waited.

'He is well, Mr Strafe. We are so grateful to you.'

He waved Louis away and looked at me again.

'Unless I have a fucking twin – whom I've never met – you're losing your grip.'

But he jumped from the table and walked out onto the street. I saw him look in all directions. His departure gave me time to think. I sank down in my chair, exhausted and dreadfully confused. Had I seen visions? Was I so obsessed with Strafe that I had imagined him? Imagined I'd seen him? The word 'dismay' is the colour of deathly grey.

Come on, rationale! Help me! I ran through a small range of possibilities. Is this The Big Lie? Or does he have a double? Or has he paid all these people to alibi him? Or am I losing it, as he suggested? Before I had time to choose one of those options he came back with no expression on his face. I looked at his barrel chest. Isn't there a karate chop to the heart that kills? There may be but I don't know how to do it.

Monster. And I have no control over him. I can but try. Jab at his throat? I'll do jail for Claire. I'll do twenty years.

No. I'm not able to. I'm not able to kill this man, I'm not able to kill anyone. Not even if I didn't know them and never saw them. I couldn't have bombed Dresden. Not even for my wife? Not even for such a vital and intimate cause as Claire's safety? No. And I knew it and I fought off the sadness that sailed in behind the realization. I have no guts. I have no idealism. I wouldn't even have been able to bomb the railway line into Auschwitz.

But, Jesus, I'm good at excuses and here comes my excuse (it's never far away). The excuse is – I may have to stay close to Strafe.

What in the name of Jesus Christ am I going to do now, this minute? The sweat is running down my stomach into my pubic hair. A man has some pride, some feeble courage, so – try a jab.

'I take it that by now the police have rung you?'

He treated it like a feather. 'For why?'

'Clay Massey, obviously.'

He said to me without looking, 'That's the third time you've asked me that question. Don't fucking ask it again. I said to you. I'm not interested in Massey. I'm glad he's dead.'

I suppose I had some vague, vain hope that had they

questioned him I might have been able to weigh in with Zurück. Shall I do it myself? Shall I come out in the open and hit him with it? No. I'll play some longer game even if I don't yet know what it is. Yes, I do. It's called cowardice and fleeing.

In any case, Strafe said nothing. I looked sidelong at him, at the pulse beating slow and strong in his neck. Part of me found his company exciting. I dislike that part of me. Then he turned and looked at me. With his face full on mine he searched my face with his eyes and he searched my eyes with his eyes and my eyes were the eyes unable to hold the gaze. I think I saw a flicker of disappointment in him. Like a man putting away a weapon, he folded his warlike hands.

'Now,' he said to me. 'Business.'

I tried again, my heart gasping for air. 'Hold on,' I said. 'Montreux.'

Strafe looked away from me, head to one side; I'd swear the lynx ears almost twitched.

'You didn't listen,' he said. 'I want to talk business.' Again he rose and went to the door and came back empty-handed; whoever he expected had some crucial importance to him.

I wanted to grab his arm again or let him see me clench my fist – or anything. No, couldn't do it. In the back of my throat I could feel the beginnings of a whinnying sound that I make when real fear hammers into me.

At which moment my mobile phone rang.

'Mr Newman, I *am* sorry, it's Mrs Lydiard here.'

I find the old-fashioned hotel manner so soothing. But the idea of the call felt not so good – probably because my awareness had so heightened.

'Not at all, Mrs Lydiard.' I rose from the table and stepped out onto Jermyn Street. 'What can I do for you?'

'I can't get into the house. Did you have the locks changed or anything like that?'

'Good God, no. If I'd been doing anything like that I'd

have asked you to get it done for me. When were you there last?'

'I went in on Wednesday. Everything was fine then.'

I thought, When did Claire leave? Is she still there?

'Are you sure my wife's not there?'

'No, sir. She rang me. She couldn't get in and she was going to London anyway, she was staying with a friend.'

Mrs Lydiard's details always tally, she's that kind of person.

'So you tried to put the key in?'

'Front and back.'

Some of those locks had a device on them preventing anyone with a wrong key from trying again. I told Mrs Lydiard this.

'No. I've got all your house keys on one ring.'

'How strange. Can you get a locksmith?'

'Is that what you'd like me to do?'

'Very much, yes. We're down on Friday evening. Any problems, call any time.'

'I hate to disturb you, sir, I know how busy you are.'

'No-no. Please!'

I finished my call and braced myself to return to the table. As I moved to the doorway a taxi drew up and out of it popped Claire.

'Hello! What a lovely surprise!' Then, as a reflex action I said, 'I didn't know you were lunching here.'

She said, 'But I knew you were.'

'Who told you?' and the maelstrom of fear whirled faster.

Before Claire could answer, Strafe bounded out of the restaurant.

'There you are, you peach!' He grabbed Claire and said to me, 'Now you know why the table's set for three.'

We went indoors, no choice really, and Strafe ordered champagne.

'Didn't you know?' Claire said to me.

'I knew nothing.'

Strafe said, 'Think of it as a surprise.'

'Think of what as a surprise?' I asked, coldly enough for Claire to know I wasn't best pleased and for Strafe to ignore my pique.

'The surprise that your wife is coming to work for me.'

Claire looked somewhere between pleased and non-plussed.

I said, with all the ice I could find, 'We haven't had a chance to think about this.'

'What's there to think about? She's not doing anything else exactly, is she? Are you?'

Claire said, 'I think what Nicholas is trying to say is that he and I haven't had a chance to talk about it.'

So that was what she meant when she said to me from the dark dawn sofa, 'Don't be angry with me.'

29

There comes a moment when the problems in life climb so high you can only stand back. You walk slowly all around them, you crane your neck to look up at them, even admire them perhaps in some perverse way. And then you turn away. You turn away because something in you says, Forget it, this is hopeless. Then you learn that you turned away in order to buy time.

Lunch with Strafe proceeded; nothing else for it to do. He sparkled – well, he would, wouldn't he? A story he told about taking the chairman of his Canadian company caribou hunting made us laugh until we wept. How can one hate someone who makes one laugh? How can one fear such a man? I looked at Strafe again and again and had this mad split – between wishing to hug him and wishing to cut his throat. Over and over I thought, Look at him! I can't believe what I know. Zurück? I know – I *know* – there is some mistake. Nothing else explains anything. This man does not intend –

Stop there, Nicholas. Maybe it comments adversely upon me but I liked this man, whatever his grossness, I liked his eagerness to be liked, I liked the warmth of his beam when it shone on me. But think – what happened to Clay Massey? A single shot to the forehead. The rosebud of blood. And the point about that board meeting must be the hatred in Strafe's eyes when he came back into the room after fleeing Clay's gibes.

So I sat there, looking at him, my mind unable to shape or believe the thought it can speak so easily now. Namely,

This man means to kill my wife – and perhaps kill another woman of whom I am unexpectedly fond – because he is descended from an old and savage evil which has never left the face of the earth. Old songs, sometimes I hate them, the way one hates a friend who's always right; *Who do you think you are kidding, Mr Hitler* . . .

I found I had returned to the theories I formed when Madeleine died. The evil was not snuffed out at source and therefore it got a purchase on Planet Earth. It still has that purchase. It will continue to. It is continuing. There is Claire breaking my heart with her sweetness and her innocent earrings like little gold manacles – and all she wants to do is pluck something back from the tide of history.

The worse thought returns, as worse thoughts always do. If this is not some mad mistake about Strafe, if this is not some mad mirage I'm living through in a deluded state of mind, I have very few options. In fact – I have only one. And, worst thought of all, I know myself well enough to be aware that I will never exercise that option. In other words (I say to myself mockingly), you see here before you, Nicholas, a man who doesn't have the guts to protect the only human he has ever deeply loved.

Somehow we got through the lunch. We laughed at Strafe's outrageousness. He gazed on me as though he loved me. Claire blushed at his compliments. I sat there – the lemon at the table. Why didn't I leave, taking Claire with me? Maybe I hoped that staying close would tell me the thing I most wanted to know – that I and the 'Doctor' were mistaken. But the lunch never told me that. Or anything like it.

I moved to the more immediate problem – how to handle Claire vis-à-vis Strafe. She received his charm with decorous hesitation. And, Jesus, he flattered her, he focused on her – an expert performance. He outlined for her, such shrewd psychology, the role he saw for her. How did he know of her low self-esteem? He carved out for her a job designed to boost her. She was to be his delegate to his clients, present and future, home and abroad; she was to be the face of company policy, 'An ambassador – to show what a class act looks like,' were his words.

'Let me give you an example, my dear' – emphasis, just slight, just enough, on the *my*. 'I've got a major international client who can't get his life under control. Brilliant business-man but every so often he goes off the rails. He suffers from a poor opinion of himself, says no one's got any faith in him. I want you to make him realize how brilliant he is.'

When we left Strafe she was walking on air, this child who, a year ago, was whimpering in pain, who can still be reduced to a frightened innocent by a misplaced inflection from me, who sometimes has to be helped out of the bath, who loses some garment or other every time she goes shopping. She looked radiant. And I felt completely caged.

What could I do? If I told her about Zurück and Strafe and the claims – and I knew how to make her believe me – it would shoot her off the rails. If I removed her, hid her away without telling her the reason, she would accuse me of jealousy, of trying to ruin her chances. If I let her stay close to Strafe – I would know not the day nor the hour. Clay Massey sat on Strafe's board. Clay Massey died.

The first dilemma struck immediately. On the street, in the sunshine, Claire said, 'Nicholas, I must go. You going back to the office?'

My brain shouted, No! I am never letting you out of my sight again and gasped the question, Will it be this afternoon? Will he kill her now, today, on the street? I kissed her forehead. Did my lips feel a rosebud bullet hole? Then for a flash – denial: I disbelieve it all; then that depression, that hopeless feeling like sludge.

She said, 'I need a touch of the old retail therapy – do you mind?'

We kissed again and, my mind filled with shrapnel, I watched her walk away, that lovely, long back. She deserves better than a man who can't protect her. I went to the office.

Where I found chaos to distract me. Bernard, the one who hums all the time, had resigned – as of there and then. He was at that moment, I was told, emptying his desk.

Hal had the wit to tell me.

'When did this happen?'

'Ten minutes ago. Tears 'n' fears, Chief.'

'Ten minutes ago?'

'If it was sooner, Chief, I'd have belled you. How were the gnomes?'

I looked at him. With an energy he recognizes and responds to I asked him, 'Hal, how did you know where I was?' Because I had told nobody.

Hal said, 'Your friend, Strafe. He was on the phone to the Straits of Dover. Very matey.'

My heart did that grim flip it was getting so good at.

'Is the Straits of Dover in today – why do you call her that, by the way?'

Hal grinned. 'Seen how wide she's getting?'

I almost laughed. 'Is she behind Bernard's fracas?'

'You're not wrong, Chief. She's been giving him grief. In lumps.'

'Where *is* Bernard?'

Hal displayed something unexpected – an intention to make me look good.

'Why don't you go and look for him, Chief? It'll send a message.'

I walked ostentatiously down the long drawing office. Bernard's a smoker, so he works near the door, ready to pop out for a quick fume. I like Bernard, even though he apes me; same spectacle frames as mine and now he dresses in black all the time. He had just about finished packing his satchel.

177

'Bernard, where are you going?' He looked at me and didn't answer. 'Hal tells me you've resigned.' No answer. 'Do you have a new job to go to?'

Bernard shook his head. Not humming today. He half-turned away from me. This man's in an extreme state.

'Bernard, put your bag down for a moment and listen to me. You have to turn round so that I can see you.'

In the distance Mary Strait watched, oozing belligerence and edge. I rested my hands on Bernard's drawing table.

'Bernard, can you list now, for me – or in your head – the jobs you've worked on in the last four years? No. I'll do it for you. You've worked on Whitechapel, you've worked on the Exchange Annexe, you've worked on the Killionaire's building; you did all the work on Emersons, you did Olivia Mossley's warehouse in Camden almost single-handed and she wanted to go to bed with you as a result, you did all the spec work on Johan Pearl's house. Those are the ones I can think of. What do they all have in common?'

He didn't answer.

I said, 'This is what they have in common. On all of them you worked close to me – the closest to me in the office. Now if you think I'm going to let you walk out – you can think again. Please unpack your bag and go back to work.'

He lifted his head. Tears in his eyes, Bernard who goes whitewater rafting.

I said, quite softly, 'Bernard, I'm not blind. I know what's going on. It'll get sorted. Come on.' In my mind's eye I saw myself with my arms around Claire. She made me capable of tenderness towards others.

Bernard couldn't cope. I looked at my watch.

'Quarter past three Friday. Okay. So you don't feel like unpacking your bag right now. Want to go?'

He nodded.

'On two conditions. One, that you call me over the

weekend; say, Sunday night? And two, that you tell me
– and only me – the full story.'

He blurted, 'Someone's feeding shit into my software.'

'What?' I looked up – and knew everything, as one does.
Mary Strait turned away. This means war. 'Are you the only
one affected?'

He said, 'Me and Henry' – Henry being the other draughts-
man/architect with whom I worked closest.

'Bernard, don't call me Sunday night. Let me work out
lunch next week, all three of us, you, Henry and me, and
we'll go through this. Now – enjoy your weekend. Think
up some nice revenge fantasies. And if you're going out to
lunch on Sunday, bring me the expenses chit.'

When I turned from Bernard, Mary Strait had vanished.

Lemon brought my messages and my mail. The French
paperwork had begun to surface – in reams; soon it would
be mountains. I couldn't face it. Message from Mrs Lydiard:
can't get a locksmith until tomorrow, Saturday. Fine; we'll
stay in London tonight.

Then Claire rings on the direct line.

'I got an appointment at the Sanctuary – but I'll be late.
Can you manage without me until ten?'

'Olive's for supper?'

I'm going to hold everything down to the norm as tight
as I possibly can. The Sanctuary's a good omen. She can get
cosseted.

When I put the phone down I asked Lemon for Dr
Hayward's number. My head had begun to spin. A sudden
fatigue kicked in.

'Lemon, tell nobody where I've gone. Back in an hour.'

I walked the bright street with the traffic hot and angry.

Hayward's a curious man, a mixture of cold and bawdy.
He squeezed the black rubber bladder and watched the blood
pressure meter. 'A hundred and fifty over a hundred. It's all
right but it's up a bit.'

179

If he's in a bad temper it shows. If he's in a good temper it doesn't. That afternoon he played it flat.

'I take it this is part of the Massey business? Saw your name in the papers, thought, "I know him." What exactly happened?'

I told him. Doctors who've been in the Royal Navy have the best attitude. Nothing shocks them.

Hayward reassures me. Sometimes he says little, speaks directly, wastes no time. Sometimes he talks non-stop and makes me laugh.

He asked, 'You just got married, didn't you?'

'A few months back.'

'Want me to have a look at it?'

I said, 'No, it's – I'm – fine. But thank you.'

'We'll check it when you come in for your annual.'

He did some more bits and pieces, eyes and ears and feet, asked me the usual bowel questions. Today was one of his days for talking.

'Had a man in here yesterday, his first wife just remarried, their divorce was World War III and he told me the day she remarried he had six major bowel movements. Six. Several kilos, he said. Kilos. First time I ever heard shit being calculated metrically. Told me it felt as if he got rid of everything.' He paused, then asked, 'I can't remember, were you married before?'

By now I was laughing. 'No.'

He took some blood, twisting the rubber tourniquet round my arm like a mechanic mending a tyre. 'You're basically okay. Ring me if you get any trembling fits you can't handle. Or headaches, sharp ones, with one locus.'

I asked, 'Why'd you say that?'

He asked, 'You're under pressure, aren't you?'

'My wife is a reformed addict.'

'Heroin?'

'She was into everything.'

'She's looking well on it,' he said. 'Saw her picture in something or other.'

'I'm always afraid she'll –'

'Stay close. Keep watching. How long's she off it?'

'Just under a year.'

'Yep. Don't take your eyes off her. And try not to let any pressure near her. Pressure's the danger, stress of any kind, an accident in the car, anything by way of shock, anything like that – just watch it.'

I stood. Taking my courage in my hands, I said, 'Can I ask you a really stupid question?'

'Usually, people who say that *don't* ask a stupid question.'

'No, this one's stupid.'

Hayward said, 'I'll be the judge of that.'

'What would you do if you knew someone meant to kill someone close to you?'

'Huh!' He turned away and thought, looked out of the window, tapped his pen rapidly on the other hand.

'I'm presuming that I wouldn't feel I could recruit allies.' He spoke like a man musing. 'I'm presuming I had no evidence and therefore no hope of help.' He stuck a finger in his mouth and chewed on it; he had a flake of skin on his bald patch. Then he turned and looked at me.

'I'd do one of two things. Or both, if possible. I'd become his shadow – I'd stalk him, I'd spy on him, learn everything I could about him, I'd know when his bowels move. And I'd either hide his target or stay by their side day and night.'

On the way out I rang Lemon from the mobile.

'Everything's fine,' she said. 'Most people have gone. I'll be here for an hour. Your wife rang just to say hello.'

'Where was she?'

'About to go into the sauna.'

'Lemon, my car's still in the garage, I'll go and bring it round. Then I'll sign the letters.'

The garage lies under the office building: room for one car only: part of the reason I took this lease. Steel door: locked at the bottom: I have a key, there's another in the office, in my desk. I open the door and haul the shutter right up – and I hear the rustling sound. Rats? No. Or – yes, in a way. The sudden breeze from the street blows some papers on the garage floor – papers that were strewn there when someone ransacked the Saab.

'Ransacked' is English understatement. In this case it means 'pulled apart horrendously'. All my papers scattered, most of them torn in half. The Artioli briefcase she gave me slashed to thin ribbons. My duplicate address book, all so carefully locked into the boot, systematically ripped apart page by page. My new organizer, into which I had programmed all kinds of measuring and calculating software, ground into the floor by the heel of a boot. My Barbour jacket trodden into the ground and defecated upon. They defecated on Claire's matching Barbour. And on everything else – I thought of Hayward's patient and his six kilos of shit.

No damage had been done to the car itself. The radio had not been ripped out. Seats had not been slashed. Nor had glass been broken. Every item attacked belonged to Claire or me.

30

I had the advantage of time. Back to the office. Say nothing. Return to the garage, clean up the mess. Say nothing. Especially say nothing to Claire.

I'm interested in our natural allies – such as sleep when exhausted, stillness when threatened, truth when accused, anger when attacked. Sometimes I think I prefer the hot variety – cold anger brings with it a kind of self-pity, a sort of 'And-no-one-to-help-me' whine beneath the ice.

As I raged on, scrubbing and hosing, it occurred to me that I had a fresh reason to go to the police. On wet seats, the car smelling of air freshener, I drove round there. Completely unsatisfactory. Fill in a form. They gave me 'So what' in trumps. Eleventh car 'incident' reported today. Since noon. Brilliant.

My mind wanted strategies. I said, 'Is this where the Massey Incident Room is?'

'The wha'?'

When I spelt it out they called someone – the woman detective who first took my statement. She found an empty office.

'Any European information?' I asked.

'Meaning what?'

I lied; invention is the response to necessity. 'I have a friend in the FBI. He's just been staying with me. Fascinating man. He tells me that every time there's an unusual killing in the United States they do something now they've never done before – they check with European police forces. You know, all these immigrants and that.'

183

'Oh, yeh.' She lit up and I drove on at her, looking for every button I could hope to press.

'Mr Massey being a Jew,' I said (I prefer to use 'Jewish' but here, in the very crucible of prejudice, might as well use their language), 'I would be checking the Germans to see if there's any pattern. You know, neo-Nazis and all that.'

'Oh, yeh,' she said again. Her eyes had the cunning of ambition and encouraged me to exert the first real pressure on Strafe.

'Mr Strafe must be upset,' I said.

'Mr Strafe?' she echoed. 'Who's Mr Strafe?'

'He's the bloke owns the company Mr Massey and I were directors of.' When I'm speaking to the police my grammar goes out the window.

She switched on the computer beside her.

'Hope I can get into our records from this.' She slammed the keyboard a little once or twice; we waited; the screen lit her face; she tapped.

'Naw, no Strafe here.'

'He must have given a statement,' I said. 'I mean he and I were the last two people to see Mr Massey alive.'

'What's his full name?'

Not only did I give her the name, I gave her the address and telephone number and mobile number.

As I left the police station I had one of those heart lurches. High risk – to put Strafe under pressure? Oh, shit. The depression of error hit me. I went into a shop and bought two bananas.

Eight o'clock. Now what? Claire not home for two hours. I thought about Hayward and his advice. Nothing to do at the moment. Then, not sure why – in the grip of some old memory perhaps? – I went to Ruby's and spoke to the voice at the buzzer.

'Is Ruby there?'

'Who's it wants her?'

'Nicholas.'

'She know you?'

'Yes.'

She was in a leotard again, and tights, grey and cosy.

'Hello, darling.'

'Hello, Ruby.'

'You look tired, darling. I'm just going to get myself ready for work. Got time to chat?'

'Sure.'

We went up in the lift.

'I'll just have a quick bath, darling, then I'll be with you.'

I sat in the hallway and we talked through the open door. Then she emerged in a robe and soon after called me into the bedroom.

'It's all right, darling.'

Call being stark naked 'all right'? Not really, not with my natural guilt. I decided to ignore it but I couldn't take my eyes off her flesh.

'Ruby, you're as lovely as ever.'

'Thank you, darling.' She looked at me. 'You're shattered, darling.'

'I am, Ruby.'

She walked over in her high-heeled pumps and nothing else and cradled my head. We stayed like that for maybe a minute and said nothing. I think I know why we need guilt: it produces adrenalin: I could become addicted. God, how those wide, stippled nipples babied me when my heart was dying. How could I ever explain that to Claire?

'Ruby?'

'Yes, darling.' Tiny ridged stretch marks where breast meets armpit.

'Strafe. And you. And your mother. In Berlin – Magda-what's-it-strasse – finish the story.'

'Not now, darling.' Brisk and final.

Weary, I gave in. 'Okay.'

She said, 'I was rehearsing "Lilli" today.'

'Again?'

'Always, darling.'

'I must come and hear it.'

She began to sing it for me, her voice as low as Dietrich only sweeter, her face in the sunlight of the evening, her eyes on mine, saying – saying what? I don't know.

I knew you were waiting in the street. I heard your feet. But could not meet. My Lilli of the lamplight. My own Lilli Marlene. And when she finished, through my own head in that cacophonous way things have about them ran Donald Fagen's line *Ruby, Ruby, when will you be mine?*

We kissed, very softly and briefly on the mouth, and then I said goodnight to Ruby Hamer with the brown eyes.

Nine o'clock. The flat, which I now entered with care, seemed fine. I checked the answering machine: Claire saying she'd be at Olive's about ten fifteen; Mrs Lydiard saying the locksmith will be in by noon. I called her and she sounded reassuring.

'We'll stay here till we hear from you, Mrs Lydiard – and then we'll go down.'

'No problems, as they say, and how's Mrs Newman?'

I knew she meant it – which is why Claire's belief that Mrs Lydiard hated her felt so troublesome.

'She's well, Mrs Lydiard, she's well, thank you.'

When it comes to Mrs L., Claire's crazy – but I mustn't use that word. I showered, flopped down and used my biceps to lift Auguste Mende's *Le Château Français*, all thousand pages.

Then, as sudden as flame, I changed my mind. Dr Hayward's talk made me do it. Scribbled a note to Claire in case she came by before going to Olive's.

dear one car broken into too boring for words gone to see
mister plod go to olive's and wait for me i'll be there by
eleven I like my body when it is with your body.

Several birds slain. Keeps Claire out of the house. Our
lower-case communication (because we read each other
e.e. cummings's love poems) tells Claire I love her. Eases my
slight guilt over kissing naked Ruby. And buys me time.

31

Next to the Design Museum I paid off the cab. It slipped away into the mesh of little streets. I stood, smelling the river. How good is my memory? And my nerve? Across the open space by the Thames ambled lovers and somebody's dog. Anyone following me? Smell of bleach from my hands after cleaning the car.

I found the address. We restored some of these blue girders and balconies, old warehouses – 'sexified', to use Elizabeth's word. I walked around the corner to the garage entry. The steel curtain was down and locked. I decided to hang around. Do humans have autopilot? Yes, they do.

Rosy evening; the late sun reaches odd fingers into corners down here, lanes and crannies that get sunlight at no other time of day. I studied the homecomers, the black suits, purple ties and chic of designer lives. I should jeer – I've made a name out of it.

A young woman in a flat opposite came to the window a second time to check me. She took a longer look this time and I moved. My mouth dried a little. What did I think I was doing?

Five minutes later a blue BMW Z3 came ripping in, slowing down. The change of gears cued me. I slipped along the shadow of the wall, half-ran across the street and followed the car into the underground car park before the steel curtain could descend again. The driver had no need to stop and I reckoned that the sharpness of the corners in the car park would keep his eyes from his rear-view mirror. Now all I had to do was wait until he left the area.

He walked past me, a few feet away, not seeing me. Too busy managing his keys and his mobile phone. Late twenties and doing well – wearing Paul Smith or Zegna or Ralph Lauren or all of them and steel jewellery to match. No hair, a tight, shaved head and a cocky, moneyed walk. I eyed him to the lift and did not move.

The planners had questioned the fire escape coming down to the car park. Building regulations originally forbade it. We got around them by saying the car park would never be locked, have no gate. The planners knew we were lying and we knew they knew – it happens on every job.

I needed the fifth floor – the penthouse. The staircase risers were higher than I remember. Now comes the test of memory – and – yes! Each floor has a tall gate leading to the fire escape, thief-proof in theory, but to those in the know, or who have locked themselves out, a tiny catch behind the hinge silently releases the hasp. All in place: well done, memory.

New problem: it's duskening and the penthouse lights blaze along the walkway. How can I see without being seen? I can stand at the pillar between two sets of windows or make myself as thin as possible.

I ducked under the first window and made it to the pillar. Stood there, well sheltered by shadow. I took stock. Can anybody see me? The shadows will hide me – unless somebody comes into the building opposite and switches on lights.

Relax. I took a chance and glanced quickly. According to memory it should be the kitchen. It was. Empty now, but still alive. A coffee mill sat on the island; a coffee packet yawned open; food bags from Harvey Nichols patrolled the counter.

I turned to my right. This room had been the central selling point, the vast 'lounge' as we were asked to call it. It runs the length of the entire building. My mind grinned at the surge of voyeur's adrenalin. A song floated into my mind from somewhere: *Some folks say some farm boy. Up from Tennessee.*

There he is! Head bent over the long table. I once cursed that table: made of Italian oak, that's the third version. Some flaw in the wood caused the first two to clot the seasoning oil into blobs.

He wasn't alone. With him sat a secretary I had never seen at his offices. She handed him documents to scrutinize. I couldn't see what they were. *Taught it all to Ruby.* I twitched back to the wide window to look at him again. The secretary walked behind him along the long room. *Then just let her be.* Then, in comes the shaven man from my bedroom door in Montreux. The Big Lie! The Big Liar!

Strafe's phone rang. I watched him answer it. He stared in my direction. I doubted he could see me – but I moved to the fire escape.

By now the car park lay in thick darkness. I remembered – no exit! For security reasons we never included pedestrian access from the street to the garage. Could I risk going up to an entry floor and waiting until somebody left? What if Strafe came down in the lift?

Not a good idea. I would have to wait until a car arrived. *If* a car arrived.

Think again, visualize the specifications, see the drawings. Isn't there a small service room, a sort of short, blind corridor – unlocked and unlit? My key ring has a tiny torch. Yes, that's where we housed the electrics. Now – there's an emergency button somewhere, it raises the metal curtain. I found the utility room and directed the little torch's coin of light. On the floor near me was an old paint tin into which I nearly stepped. Directly above my head jutted the metal box with the fuses. I pressed the button for the door: nothing. Try the lights – risky, but try it. Nothing. The fusebox had suffered a short or something.

Ten minutes passed. My mobile had no signal. Twenty minutes. I'm getting cold. And worried. The walls were moist with condensation.

Then I heard the lift and somehow knew it would carry Strafe. It did. He flipped on the low-level light at the switch beside the lift door and looked all around. I could see the yellow Porsche – but he didn't walk towards it. He walked towards me. I ducked behind the cars. Crazy. This is crazy.

Four feet from where I ducked Strafe stopped. I saw his legs but not his head. What is he doing? My bladder's leaking. Strafe leaned against the car that hid me. Leaned casually, like a man about to chat. I could see the shiny shoes and the clean floor beside him. Next I saw his hands. He began to do them again – those he-man press-ups. I saw his face in profile – down, then up; down, then up. Had he glanced sideways he'd have seen me. He didn't. But I believe to this day that he saw me, that he was taunting me. Slowly I moved my hands to my crotch. I did it as a small boy when I thought I would wet myself.

I heard the lift machinery. Strafe straightened, grunted and walked away. He greeted someone and continued to his car. The other person went to their car and they left the car park in convoy.

Before the steel curtain sank again I slipped out of the car park behind them. I was back once more in the little streets where, as Oliver Twist knew, there are a thousand hiding places.

32

In the cab I calmed myself down with a promise. I promised myself, Soon I'm going to survey all that's happening to me. See whether I can make sense of it. From Claire's relationship with my old, dead friend Antony Safft to Ruby's recent kiss. From the past in which I found Claire to the history that killed Clay Massey. From the might of Nazi power to the might-be of Richard Strafe. I must apply some thought; I can't fly on autopilot for ever. And then I must plan my strategy for keeping Claire safe. If I can.

I called the flat, got the answering machine, left a message.

'Hi, it's me. I'm on my way – are you there? You're not. See you in twenty minutes.'

When I walked into Olive's – no trace of Claire. Looked at my watch – ten to eleven – where is she?! Jesus!

Then – the relief! – I saw her, not at our usual table. I waved and walked forward and Olive intercepted me.

'Isn't your missus looking lovely?'

'Isn't she?' I enthused, my mind racing with thoughts of, But what am I to do? Keep her by my side day and night? No, kill Strafe, kill him! Work out a secret means of doing it. Plan the perfect murder. Don't be daft, Nicholas, you know you haven't got the balls to do that. In cold blood? No, nor in hot blood. Maybe I should hire someone? No way, you'd never cope with that.

I kissed Claire and I kissed her again. She looked wonderful. Seemed calm and stable, too, and I can't have looked too flustered after my 'adventure', or she might have commented. What was I thinking of, playing prowler like that? Claire said she had ordered the minestrone risotto; I ordered cod and chips and we had a light Veneto red.

'What a day!' I said. 'I'm sorry I'm late.' No matter what her problems, every time I see her my heart turns a little in excitement.

'How's the car?'

'Boring. Don't ask. Your Barbour's gone, I'm afraid.' It had. I dumped it. She made a mouth.

I said, 'But I've got something for you,' and slid across the table the Cartier box from Montreux in its little black envelope.

'What is it?'

Gift-giving had become one of my means of measuring her mental health. When well, Claire revelled in the smallest token; when down, she shrank; she possessed no register in between. Tonight she revelled.

'Oh, Nicholas! Oh, no!'

'Diamonds dearly bought for ladies.'

She laughed, as happy as I had ever seen her. 'I know that, my father says it. It's from card-playing, isn't it?'

The diamonds shone. Claire shone. Love has become a drug which we take for one simple reason: when present in its full abundance, we don't need anything else. She and I held hands across the table and just smiled at each other.

'You look so lovely.'

'Diamonds on the soles of her shoes.' She bopped a little. 'Thank you, thank you – thank you.'

One of Claire's eyes goes a millimetre out of true when she's emotional.

We began to talk.

'Wasn't that some lunch?' I said, deciding to lead.

'Amazing. What do you think?'

'About the job?' This has to be played like a cello.

'Yes. But I also mean – Strafe and everything that comes with him.' She blinked.

I said, bravely, 'I think you can handle him. He's besotted with you.'

Claire said, 'I don't want to do anything that'd upset you.'

I demurred. 'No-no-no. Look – I have so much to tell you. Oh, by the way, Rye. No locksmith yet.'

'Surprise-surprise.'

'And you'll love this. Mary Strait.' I told her about Bernard.

'But you like him?'

'More to the point – he's bloody reliable.'

'So what's happening?' She fingered the diamonds. Ice, the gangsters call them, rocks.

I said, 'Someone in the office is fouling up the software he has adapted for his own use. So that when he prints out – I presume – or when he opens his screen in the morning, things fall off. In other words, someone's trying to make him look an idiot.'

Claire leaned forward, her eyes gleaming. 'Listen.' She looked around, mock-furtively. 'I have a cunning plan.'

I laughed, but I listened and she brisked up.

'Why don't you take on Lucinda as a temp secretary? Trust me.' She tapped her nose.

'Lucinda with the golden eyes and the nice line in oral sex?'

She laughed. 'She is completely – but completely – amoral and I think we need a bit of that.'

I thought, Oh, sweet Claire! If you but knew . . .

'What's the state of play on your "paperwork"?' I asked, trying not to sound too careful.

Swift change from light to shade. 'Can we postpone it?'

Her anxiety flattens me.

'Of course. How was the Sanctuary?'

'Wonderful. I wish they had a Sanctuary for boys.'

I laughed. 'Naw. Girls' stuff.'

So there we sat, late on Friday night in London, a husband and a wife ordinarily unwinding for each other the details of their week and looking easily into each other's eyes. A normal and likeable picture – except for one tiny detail: the husband knows a man who wants to kill the wife. Possibly means to do it quite soon. The husband hasn't done a thing about it. In any case he hasn't a clue what to do. Or if he does know, hasn't the nerve to do it.

Sometimes I think I will forever regard that evening, that dinner, as the most perfect a couple can have. By which I mean, of course, a couple consisting of Claire and me. I relished it like a Death Row dinner because I knew that from the moment we left the table all the rules had changed. A vile possibility had come among us like a spook and it needed dreadful vigilance.

On the street I looked fore and aft, like some sort of scared, hamfisted bodyguard. Is this cabbie okay? Or am I to infer menace from his moustache? This could get comical. Or lethal. Surreptitiously I double-checked every door and window in the flat and saw Claire safely into bed before me. During a night of the lightest dozing, I rose several times. Claire had long gone to sleep.

Eventually I also drifted into some kind of strange coma. At ten o'clock in the morning I woke, surprised to find I'd been sleeping. Immediately I checked. She stretched beside me, drowsing awake also. We lay there, warm and tangled, grunting a little, not saying anything. Time to make tea.

When I came back into the room she looked like the smallest of small children, sleepy-eyed and disarranged. I have a friend who believes the benchmark of all women is how they look when they wake. He'd give Claire eleven out of ten. Like Sammy Davis Jr gave Elvis.

We sat and talked idly about nothing much. We yawned

and drank our tea. We held hands. Then she slid down again and fell asleep. I climbed into bed beside her, got my arms around her and sat upright, dozing. Some time later I woke and realized I had been in a deep sleep and I also comprehended two things: that so far we had not been attacked and that we can't go on for long like this.

But what am I to do? Hide her away? Send her away? Keep her by my side day and night? Quit work and stay at home? The killer question (forgive the pun) wailed, Yes, but how long, O Lord, how long? Today I cannot grasp what I went through. When I think of it, of that casual terror, I find myself unable to define the word 'unreal'.

Claire woke.

'I am declaring hunger,' she chirped. 'This is national hunger day.'

I called the options – scrambled eggs, boiled eggs, poached eggs, fried eggs, an omelette?

'I gather you're offering eggs, M'sieu.'

'Shrewd woman.'

'Omelette please, M'sieu.'

'Then it's the Molière?'

'The what?'

'D'you know about Elizabeth David's omelette? A restaurant in Avignon?'

She began to 'la-la-la' the Marseillaise and marched out of the room. Back she came in one of my tee-shirts and stood beside me in the kitchen. Impossible to dice cubes of Gruyère with that kind of distraction – and I almost forgot the spoon of cream.

Thoughts and feelings raced. This must be what it's like for a man who's about to be charged with some grievous crime but doesn't want his wife to know. Or who has lost his job but still goes out to work every morning because he can't bear to tell his family he's been sacked.

While other soundtracks attended to the cooking, or

admired Claire, or registered hunger, that same frantic track rushed to take in every eventuality. Being watched. Followed. Poisoned. Mown down in traffic, shot, pushed, being firebombed. I could be killed with her. Better in a way. But that's selfish. And when? When will this happen? When will 'The Attempt' be made? Today? Tomorrow, Sunday? Next, say, Thursday? At, say, twenty past eleven in the morning? Or six in the evening?

I now know one of the attractions of murder. The murderer does something we can't ordinarily do – he gets a crucial grip on time. Somebody else's time. Soon it will be Claire's time he grips. My time. Which means that, from now, this moment, day after day stretches ahead with unrelenting dread.

Yet, in and out of the picture faded the notion that a dream had been born, inside which I was walking around, that it was not real and would soon end. I assume now that such dream notions are the mind's relief. For such long moments I rested, comforted by denial and disbelief.

Another rescue device began in me, too, something out of character. I began to settle for the immediate, the short term. I, who planned everything in my life so far ahead, found myself looking forward no more than an hour or two. And, chillingly, being grateful for each hour.

That eased the pressure. A little, not a lot. But you can always tell a true crisis, because when you iron out one facet, the ghastly others stand revealed. My next problem now magnified itself. If Claire cottoned on to an inkling of what I was doing – watching her every step, checking her every move, being with her every moment – her own implosion might damage her as easily as Strafe's madness.

I caught my thoughts in mid-air when I heard the word 'madness' in my head. This might be a way to address this crisis. Were I to see Strafe as sane – not a chance. But were I to assume him mad – I might change the odds in my favour. Enable myself to plan more clearly. Give myself the confidence to out-think him.

This thought-experiment brought an immediate result. I began thinking up moves to keep Claire in my constant sight.

'Put your knickers on,' I said. 'I'm taking you to the Tate. Before they move half of it.'

'I'll go without knickers,' she pouted.

Out in the street, I looked all around me, checked the cabbie's face. But I somehow breathed easier. I also found inside myself an underlying stratum of cold objectivity like a foundation plate of thick, blue steel and it hardened me.

Perhaps I *might* find the courage to kill Strafe. By all the laws of Nature I should – especially if, as I suspected, he reckoned I never would. We reached the Tate and I put the worst of such thoughts on hold. Safe for a time; the Tate checks all bags.

We stood and looked at Rodin's *Kiss*.

Claire whispered, 'We can do better than that.'

We went to the Rothkos.

'He makes me weep,' I said.

'Weep?' She was puzzled.

'The simple expression of complex thought.'

'Let's go see lovely Modigliani,' she said.

I said, 'You only like him because you look like a Modigliani,' and that pleased her.

I knew why I had chosen the Tate: apart from the searching of the bags and the safety in numbers, it stimulated the part of my intelligence I most enjoy.

Claire asked, 'What's your favourite piece here?'

She had tied her hair in a high, short ponytail. Wave after wave of affection rolled over me. And rolled me over, because on each wave rode a white horse of terror.

'Come and I'll show you.'

We walked to the Matisse *Snail*.

'This?' She looked surprised.

I said, 'On balance.'

'Why?'

'I don't know. No, yes, I do know. Let me think.'

We stood for a moment. The rough rectangles of colour seemed, as I stared, to whirl ever so gently and in a moment I fancied that the entire painting began to spin slowly within itself. But unlike the spinning motion inside my spirit with which I am so familiar (and which now had taken on the pace of dervishes), Matisse's effect promoted tranquillity rather than the opposite.

I said, 'Several reasons. Because I love Matisse. Do you have any idea what he went through? And that remarkable wife he married. Because he took chances. Reticent. Awkward. Driven. And difficult. But he had the heart and soul of an adventurer and I love him for that. Because the snail carries its house on its back and I love it when I'm asked to design somebody's house.'

Then I paused as a new thought struck me and with it came a new view of myself.

'But perhaps most of all because of something I haven't thought of before. If you look at it – it reminds me of something I learned at school. When the Roman legions came under attack they covered themselves top and sides with their shields.'

'The *testudo*,' Claire murmured.

'You know about it?'

'Girls did Latin too.' She grinned.

'This reminds me of that shape,' I said, 'and it must appeal to me in some way.'

'I like your shell,' she said, taking my arm. 'It's the first thing I saw about you.'

We lingered another minute or two. Nobody disturbed us. We soaked up those wonderful colours. How to put the entire light of the Mediterranean on the back of a snail.

Only when the gallery announced the end of the day did we leave. Outside, people milled, couples looking for cabs, students hoping to grab dates, school parties waiting for their coaches, pensioners sinking slowly down the steps. We crossed the road to look at the river.

Flow gently brown Thames. I had fallen in love with Claire all over again. A tide splashed the walls not far beneath us and along the wall a pipe hung out a silver tongue of water. I've heard it said you truly know how much you love someone when you know you're about to lose them.

33

Unless we get lucky we usually have few possibilities. And never when we most need them. In the taxi, with sweat running down into my coccyx, I counted my options. They amounted to the sum total of almost nothing.

Option One: stay in the flat or at Rye. To what end, and for how long and with what explanation? And with what amount of safety?

Option Two: talk to the police. Oh, yes, I can see it now: Excuse me, Superintendent, a man I met in Switzerland told me that the distinguished chairman of one of our country's largest property companies is about to kill my wife because his father was a Nazi, my wife's a Jew and she wants to get her hands on property he owns because it belonged to her family before the war. I see, sir – so what's this man in Switzerland look like, and where and when can we talk to him? I can't tell you what he looks like, Inspector, I never met him and you can't talk to him. Never met him? So can we phone him? No, Sergeant. I did meet him but I don't know what he looks like, I mean I spoke to him across a ballroom during a concert, I mean there's this peculiar acoustic in this former hotel –

Do you know the 'Methought' moment in *A Midsummer Night's Dream* when Nick Bottom, having awakened from his spell, thinks about trying to tell everyone that he was made love to by Titania, Queen of the Fairies? And he perceives the impossible incredulity of it all? Precisely.

I sit in the cab, holding Claire's hand and chatting idly. You can tell a woman's quality by her profile.

On to Option Three: disappear. I could say to Claire, Fancy a round-the-world trip? And she'll say, Great, starting when? And I'll say, Starting now. But what do we do when we come back?

Option Four: face Strafe, look him in the eye and say, Zurück. I know everything. Forget it. He'll do one of two things – deny it outright or, worse, say to me, Yeah, so what you gonna do about it? I'll say, I'm going to check all your property purchases, everywhere, and he'll leer and say, Don't be so ludicrous.

Option Five: persuade Claire to give up her claims. Then tell Strafe she's done it, say to him, Forget it, she's abandoned all that. No, I know she won't do it. No result likely there.

Which leads me to Option Six, the crunch option. Kill him. It really should be Option One, shouldn't it?

Cowardice and nerves aside – if I did possess the guts how would I go about it? When I supervised the Opera House reconstruction in Belfast the builders told me of the 'accident' rate. Especially in the shipyards. If a hammer drops from high enough, no hard hat in the world will save the skull it falls on.

But I don't have an ocean liner being built. In fact all I have for Strafe by way of accident potential at the moment is a chateau in France.

At which thought I shouted, 'Yes!'

She looked at me.

I said, 'Where's your passport?'

'In the flat.'

'So's mine,' and I began to laugh in a way I knew she would find infectious. I'm about to buy a little time.

We raced into the flat, asking the cabbie to wait.

'I'm not telling you,' I cried. 'It's a surprise. You're always saying I'm not spontaneous.'

She laughed and laughed.

Heathrow's Terminal Two serves more airlines – more ways of escape. Watching my back all the time, I stood behind Claire as she looked at the flight screens.

'Choose!'

'Oh, Nicholas, I can't!' She sounded intoxicated and so did I because my bones felt we had given somebody somewhere the slip. Running from shadows. Strange feeling.

Pretending spontaneity, I chose Lyons.

'Nicholas, why Lyons of all places?'

'Why not?'

We raided the duty-free shops. Claire bought four pairs of knickers, some toiletries, a light dress and a holdall. I echoed her purchases and also bought a new charger for my mobile phone. We stood at the departure gate looking out at the late heat of the day.

Claire said, 'This is deliberate, isn't it?'

Her question almost caught me off guard. I was still checking every passenger and every possibility.

I said, 'I just want to show you something.'

She grinned and said, 'Not here, too many people.'

'Don't be lewd.'

'But you like it when I'm lewd.'

I said, 'Lavatories before the flight?'

'Yes, Daddy,' and we entered adjoining doors. I wanted to call Ruby and for the moment I felt safe about Claire. Just for the moment.

'It's me.' To Ruby's answering machine. 'In case you're worried. Remember where I was the day before Berlin? I'm spending the weekend there. Call you later, just to check.'

But I knew Ruby would be all right. She had the survivor's mark on her.

Think, think. It'll be ten o'clock tonight before we get into the centre of Lyons. But you can tell a great hotel by the way it copes with the unexpected. Two hungry Brits won't cause much of a problem. From Heathrow I booked Villa Florentine.

My brain had begun to work at its best. From now on every move I make must work on more than one level. The Florentine, small and grand in the old city, offers superb privacy. Claire's good spirits are thus maintained. I buy the time distance gives. And if I guess right I might get a chance to drop a hammer on somebody's head.

On the flight Claire said, 'Oh! The locksmith!'

I said, 'I didn't check the messages. Never mind, I'll page them from France.'

The reception manager remembered me. He bought our giggling impression and saw before him either an illicit weekend or a bashful honeymoon.

They gave us, in our room, the most stunning dinner. *Avocat Fauré*, grilled pigeon, dry, woody *chèvre* from Grenoble and bowls of the Midi's cherries. We rolled into bed and each other.

In the morning the hired car came and we left. I love the hinterland of Mont Ventoux. We lunched under the trees in a big old house near Mondragon, watching the silent cars on the distant, shimmering autoroute.

Claire said to me, 'Have you thought any more about Strafe's offer?'

I batted it. 'Have you?'

'You have to admit – he's made it very attractive.'

'Yes,' I said, wondering when to sow doubt.

'How is he to work with?'

I answered (nothing else I could do), 'He's an operator. I've never seen such force.'

'Do people make money with him?'

'If they agree to be driven as hard as that. So far I've agreed.'

The wife of the anxious chef brought us salads, with their child studying us nearby.

'He hasn't quite said what he wants me to do.'

I said, 'He wants you to be decorative, he's not a fool.'

'Very sexist of you.'

'No. Very sexist of Strafe. Very appreciative of me.'

She sat back and stretched. 'Isn't this wonderful?' she said. 'Where's this something you wanted to show me?'

'Tomorrow. And wonderful is the right word.'

'Oh, you sweetheart!' Claire sang, and my heart seized with pain as if someone had stomped on it.

34

I had begun to assume – probably since Montreux – that we were followed. Or else, in protection mode, I had automatically factored in such a possibility. All my decisions now took account of Strafe. He knew I had stayed at the Regalido. Therefore we couldn't go there. I knew his familiarity with Arles. No dice either.

I chose Mas de la Brune. Got a room overlooking the approaches. I think I also chose it for a strange, not entirely mad notion. In those outcropped hills of limestone and thorny *maquis* around Eygalières, stretching up to St-Rémy and Les Baux, the Resistance harried Strafe's crowd. I think of it as the only romantic part of me, that family memory. My father fought all the war with partisans.

'Tonight,' I said, 'we will have an omelette Molière at the Café Molière.'

We didn't. Much though we traipsed Avignon we never found the Café Molière. We ate at Christian-Etienne and walked in the moonlight by the ramparts of the Popes.

Something peculiar happened next morning at Mas de la Brune. I went down to swim. Claire was asleep. After thirty sybaritic lengths I went back to the room.

Empty.

I tried not to panic; it would prove impossible to explain. Instead, still dripping, I went looking for her. She came swinging along the corridor.

'Oh, I went looking for *you*,' she said, 'and then I followed your wet footprints and realized you'd come back,' and she giggled and put a 'shhh' finger to her lips. We had reached the door of our room. Inside Claire stopped me.

'Guess who's having breakfast on the *terrasse*?'

She looked at me in a peculiar way; Claire has many offbeat expressions, most of them to do with psychological debris inside her. This look I had not seen before.

'Who?'

She struck a dramatic drum-roll of a gesture and announced in an American accent, 'Your friend and mine. The one. The only. I give you. Mister. Richard. Strafe!'

What is it called, that condition in which you see words as colours? 'Synaesthesia', isn't it? I see, not words in colour, but emotions. This feeling I call 'white' – as in heat, terror, seeing a ghost.

I lied; 'Let's not say hello to him just yet. I've ordered breakfast here, I thought we'd sit on the balcony.' Then I fudged. 'But there's some problem with the phones, I think I'll gee them up in a moment.'

I showered and dressed, easy, unhurried. But Claire said to me, 'For goodness' sake! A man your age ought to have learned how to do up his shirt buttons –'

'What's Strafe wearing?' I asked casually.

'An enviable lime-green jacket,' she said.

'You should have been a fashion journalist.'

'Was he serious when he offered me that job?'

'Did you say "Good morning"?' I dodged.

'No, he's engrossed – and I know enough about men not to disturb them when they're reading their newspaper.'

'I've got no evidence for that,' I said and left the room.

The terrace looks out on the gardens. There's one angle where you can see the terrace without being seen. I took the long way round, across the car park.

No good; a tree hid the crucial table; I could see an arm in a lime-green jacket but nothing else. Closer approaches brought me along the same trajectory. I had no option left but to enter the hotel and go to the terrace.

Perhaps if I did so very quietly Strafe wouldn't hear me. No, a vain hope. On his form so far, he had probably seen Claire, may even have planted himself so that she could see him. Since Saturday night, therefore, he had followed or traced us in some way. Which meant he was ahead of us at every turn. Comes a time when paranoia seems an ally.

I found a promising corridor. I could see where it opened out on the terrace. I softened my tread. But just as I rounded the corner, a cheery boy said, 'Bonjour m'sieu, voulez-vous un petit déjeuner?' and everybody looked up.

Including Strafe. Except that it wasn't Strafe – nor anything like him. This man, in a lime-green jacket, had a thin head and a long, lean frame. He had the same hairstyle as Strafe and perhaps that same air of contempt. But no, not Strafe.

Back in our room, breakfast arrived and Claire lauded my – mythical – effectiveness. I had a brief hour of near-release. A simple meal with glistening conserve and golden breads, and the brightness of a clear Provençal morning – timeless and enriching. But no matter how I relished it I could not escape the overhanging shadows. This running from doom can't last.

'Will we say hello to him?' she asked.

'You sure it was Strafe?'

'But . . .' She thought for a moment. 'He might want to tag along.'

'Good decision.'

In the car I kept puzzling the 'Strafe' sighting. Claire sounded so certain. Whatever her difficulties, she makes few errors. Maybe some of the pressure on me was getting to her. Or – should I open up the whole subject: the claims, my visit to Berlin, Ruby, Zurück?

The thought blanched my mind, yet it fought to be heard. It argued that Claire had been through several mills, some of them all at once. Might she not be tough enough in adversity to fight this one? Indeed, mightn't the bigger danger put her other problems in perspective? The blow that nearly breaks us makes us.

Then a voice inside me blared – Oh, come off it! We're talking here about someone who wants to kill her. Who has offered her a job so that he can get close enough to kill her. Because she's trying to take from him the basis of his fortune.

I heard again Hayward's warning: *no pressure*.

'Claire, I'm going to stop and ring the office.' I needed displacement.

'And Rye,' she reminded.

'Jesus, yes!'

Instant problems. Instant feeling of disturbance. I paged the answering machine at the flat and found several messages from Mrs Lydiard: *'Mr Newman, it is most important that you get in touch.'*

Which I did immediately, or tried to. Line busy. I waited and finally got through.

'We're in France, Mrs Lydiard. What's the matter?'

'Oh, sir, I hope I haven't done the wrong thing.'

'I'm sure you haven't, Mrs Lydiard.'

'Only, the locksmith wasn't able to make any headway and he gave as his opinion that the locks had been tampered with and because I couldn't get hold of you –'

I interrupted, 'Yes, I'm sorry –'

'So I rang the police and they've told me – and they want to talk to you, sir, as soon as possible – they think there's someone in the house.'

'*In* the house?'

'In the house. Were you expecting anyone?'

'There can't be! You mean inside?'

'That's what I said, sir, I mean I wasn't sure if Mrs Newman had somebody coming to stay and had forgotten to say or anything like that –'

'No, Mrs Lydiard, not at all. Are you absolutely sure?'

'Oh, yes, sir, I mean nobody down here would make up a story like that, I mean –'

'No, of course not, what I'm asking I suppose is whether anyone's seen anyone.'

'The police say they saw an upstairs curtain twitch and I know for a fact that some furniture has been moved because the small back dressing room, you know the one with the fleur-de-lis wallpaper that I'm so fond of, the room where Mrs Newman keeps her coats? Some furniture in that room has been moved across the window.'

Mrs Lydiard's adenoids had never annoyed me until that conversation.

'Mrs Lydiard, we have a flight back tonight from Lyons and I think I shall come straight down to Rye. Can you book me a room somewhere locally? In case I can't get into the house?'

'Sir, the police advise coming here by daylight, they say they're so short-staffed by night that there'll be nothing they can do even if you file a breaking-and-entering complaint. And if the house isn't in any danger.that we can see. I'll keep dropping by to look at it – then tomorrow should be fine, don't you think?'

How shall I keep Claire from knowing? *No pressure.*

I climbed in the car and said brightly, 'How much do you know about seventeenth-century French chateau architecture? Because you're about to get a crash course.'

Whereupon I launched into every barred spur, donjon and *dans-oeuvre* I ever saw, every architect whose name I ever traced on an old drawing, Jean Lejuge, Clement and Louis Parent, Rodier, Mansard, Leonardo da Vinci's plans for Chambord and Leonardo's death (according to legend) on the very day the builders started work . . .

When that line of manic chat dried up I showed her the bull statue at Tarascon and recalled every corrida I'd come down here to see. She had fallen silent and I did register the fact – but although I didn't dismiss her silence I never probed it. And then I drove into the chateau's avenue.

There's a gleam in the trees on the left, a yellow gleam. He'd parked the Porsche at an angle. Beside it he stood looking at us like a basilisk. He wore a lime-green jacket. Claire never saw him.

35

What synaesthetic colour is desperation? People talk of 'black despair'. Desperation is white, acid like foul sour milk. Sometimes I wonder whether desperation isn't the feeling I know best. It seems to have been part of my being since I can remember. Desperation at the mood in the house as my father asked desperate questions about who had called during the day; desperation as my mother gave us all desperate glances trying to quell us into silence. Desperation on the day they heard the news about my brother Kim hanging himself from the rafters of the school bookroom. The quiet, chrome desperation of the icy days and nights that followed his funeral, when I lay in bed and heard each parent sob in separate rooms. Desperation at Cambridge where I was never good enough socially to join anything successfully, always the hanger-on. Desperation in the early days as an architect with Elizabeth Bentley, and she so cool and smooth and capable and connected. Desperation as I first made the acquaintance of women. Will I get it up? Can I keep it up? And then the long, shivering desperation when I began to discover that I was unable to sustain affection for any woman for longer than the first few jousts in bed. Except Madeleine. And Ruby. And, above all, Claire. Even to them I came across as an iceberg, and they damaged their hearts on my icy reefs.

Desperation after desperation after desperation – but nothing like the desperation now facing me under the blue skies of Provence. Richard Strafe is here, out in the country in this isolated site, and so is his target, my wife.

I thought I was here in secret. Instead I have delivered her to him. And here he is, waiting for us, like a butcher with a steel and a knife.

Am I so transparent? Or is he so skilled? In which case we might as well lie down now and die. I drove down the avenue to the chateau trying to make my tongue and my palate and my breath work so that I could say to Claire in words that didn't come out of my mouth as a hoarse groan, What do you think of that, then? Is not that the most beautiful building you have ever seen in your whole pretty life?

I know what I expected. I expected her tomboy whistle. I also expected her to say what she always says when she sees something wonderful, like the full moon or the setting sun: 'I want it, I want it, I want it!'

That is not what she said and I – foolish, unseeing me – had no expectation whatever of what she eventually did say. Nor did I pick up that her silence beside me, and her slightly lifted face, defined her sense of desperation. She knew where she was – and I didn't know that she knew.

To begin with she didn't speak. Fine. I was busy checking the rear-view mirror. No yellow Porsche, no Strafe, only the sunshine and the trees and the oxbow of the river.

'The river Gard,' I pointed, still waiting for her over-whelmed cries of delight.

'As in Pont du Gard?' Strangled voice.

'Yes.'

Now, of course, I assumed she said little because the chateau stunned her – as, again, it did me, or would have done had I not been shaking like a leaf. How Claire didn't notice my trembling amazed me. Maybe the shaking didn't show on the outside.

Suddenly – if at last – it struck me that something was wrong, something serious, something different. Has she seen Strafe? Is she having one of her flashbacks? She grabbed my arm (it hurt) and gasped, 'Stop the car. Now, Nicholas, please.'

Half-irritably I said, 'I was about to stop anyway.'

I parked a few yards from the grass knoll. She almost threw herself out and walked forward, arms raised to the skies as if making an offering. I heard her say, 'God! God! God! God! God!' What is this? An excess of emotion at the sight of such beauty – but I knew it cut deeper than that.

I followed her, my eyes again bathed with the beauty of everything. But on alert this time, thinking, I must keep my mind working.

Claire put her hands to her face and shook her head. The familiar current ran through me, the panicky urge to ask, Are you all right?

'Nicholas, d'you know what this is, ohh-Jesus-ohh?' More a moan than a question.

'Yes. It's the chateau I'm restoring –'

She grabbed me, her eyes beseeching. 'NO! Nicholas – Jesus – NO!! Don't you know what it is?'

'Yes. I said, I mean, it's the –'

How feeble I sounded.

'Oh, shit, you don't know, do you?'

'Claire? What is it? This is the chateau I'm restoring for Stra—'

'Nicho-LAS! No! No! No! This is one of the properties on my claim form. This is mine!'

214

36

People who have difficulty loving can't deal with the un-expected. I had everything planned and ready; show her where the deer came out that first day; explain the structure to her, the pavilions, the lack of a barbican or any surround-ing wall, meaning this was either a peacetime building or the owner had an army; point out the escutcheons, the rustication, the underfloor drainage from the house to the Gard, the lead and brick linings they used to keep the cellar temperatures constant. She loves those details – but how can she appreciate them here?

Reactions spun through me. I didn't know. Why didn't I know? But Strafe told me he bought it from an entailed French family. What do I do now? She was so happy in the car. Look at her now, trying to cope. Where in the name of Christ-as-a-child do we go from here?

Another shock – gunfire, two shots close by. Behind us, direction of the avenue.

'The bloody French,' I said, trying not to run. 'Every bloody Sunday.' But this was Monday afternoon. No prizes for guessing the gunman.

Claire stared at the chateau, winding her hands like grief, murmuring something over and over. I walked closer to listen: she was saying, 'So this is what it looks like. So this is what it looks like.'

She once told me, 'When you don't know what else to do with me put your arms around me.' I did that now and to my surprise she sank into me.

'Let's go inside,' I said and she raced across the open ground towards the parterre.

The young deer came out!

'Aaaah!' We both shrieked and stood back as it bounded away.

The red, leggy, innocent body wheeled and hurtled towards the trees, with its little white scut. I knew what would happen next. And it did, and it shocked us. Two more shots rang out. The fawn fell, kicking one leg haphazardly in the air, twitching for a moment. Then it died.

'Oh, Jesus!' and Claire ran in the direction of the fallen animal.

I grabbed her.

'No – there may be more shots.' She saw the sense of that. 'Leave it,' I urged. 'C'mon, let's go inside.' She flailed her arms, as if trying to keep her balance, she didn't know what to do.

Tears hadn't fallen – just as well: from the moment she begins to weep, no matter where we are, no matter when, disintegration follows.

No doors had been locked. That would change, I reflected, once work began.

'This is *my* house. This is *my* house. This is *my* house. I know more about this house than you do,' she cried to me and sounded almost hostile. 'I know more about this house than anyone in the world. My great-great-great-grandfather owned this house, his name was Lucius!' She shouted his name. I followed her; the unravelling of all this could wait.

The ballroom seemed to soothe her a little. She touched everything, making sure it was real; the painted swags, the delicate panelling. 'Four hundred rooms. Including a special room to soothe babies. Did you know that?' Yes, she did know it and yes, she was hostile.

We climbed the stairs. She ran along the gallery like a

child, stopping from time to time to check the silvering on the great mirrors. 'This is mine. This is my house, this is my property. Mine.'

I watched her, the long legs, the swinging mane of thick hair, the rangy, vulnerable back. Keep her out of his sight, I urged myself, out of his sight. Strafe killed the fawn, I knew it; he did it to show me. I listened – no car engine; where is he?

'Claire – Strafe told me he bought this from a raft of French families.'

'This is *my* house.' Quieter – and more determined.

She found a long wooden bench with flaking gold paint and sat. I looked down at her but she didn't look back up at me. She wasn't wild or anything; she was fixed, vigilant. As she stretched out I moved away and leaned against a windowsill, out of vision from anyone below but able to watch the parterre from an angle.

Strafe appeared, hands in pockets; he's hidden the gun in the trees. He looked up, scanned the range of windows – he knew exactly where we were. I watched him cross the parterre to the walk beneath me. When his head quit my view I turned, hoping the window would open easily and some loose masonry might make itself available.

Both worked. I opened the casement and shoved down a huge clod of ancient plaster and slate. It hit the ground and I heard the quick shuffle of someone below.

Claire jumped. 'What was that?'

Had it hit him? I thought not. At least it sent a message. But, thoughtlessly in my desperation, had I made our situation worse?

'Falling plaster, I'm afraid. Bit of a problem along here.'

Her great strength – and she doesn't necessarily know this – has been her instinct; she always knows what to do. She climbed from the bench.

'I want to go now.'

The remark was an iceberg: eight-ninths of its meaning lay beneath the surface.

She meant, But I will be back.

She meant, Richard Strafe will never get his hands on this.

She meant, This is worth any fight I have to put up.

She meant (I feared), And I will come and live here with or without my husband, whatever the conditions.

For a moment she stood in front of me. She put her arms around my neck and pulled my face to her cheek. We stood as if glued together. I could feel her cheekbones against me, pressing so hard I can't recall if I felt her body – yet her body was the Claire I knew best.

We stepped apart. The game had truly begun. I knew it for sure that afternoon. And it had changed in the first move. There was a minute-to-minute coldness in the air. I hadn't expected that – but I hadn't defined any expectation. How could I? I had only just learned the stakes.

It seems incredible to me now. How can I think so calmly of that situation? The sunshine was black with gold in that early summer weather. I went through each hour of each day not knowing which moment would bring catastrophe. Soldiers who have checked minefields say that it's extra-ordinary how ordinary mortal danger becomes. But I'm not a soldier and I don't need minefields. At one level of my life I'm simply a man who likes to do the crossword at breakfast.

We walked the sward towards the car. Strafe did not appear. If Claire had successfully hidden so much from me so far, she might also be hiding from me how much she knew about Strafe. Such as, he's in there, somewhere in the building and he may choose to attack at any moment.

And yet we walked almost casually to the car.

Claire said, 'I want one last look.'

Her attitude seemed distant but stable – and determined. She turned. I decided to protect her by driving the car around in front of her. She could lean against it and survey the chateau safely. I sprinted to the driver's door and then jumped back. On the passenger seat spread a mess of blood, flesh and feathers.

Better tell her. 'Claire.' She turned. 'Something awful's happened. A bird crashed into the car window.' I began to haul the mess away. 'No, don't come near, I'll do it,' and I scrabbled up handfuls of guts and stickiness. Last night's underwear and handfuls of grass wiped everything else.

She accepted the facts of the car calmly enough and lay on the grass, her face towards the sun. I thought, Good, impossible target lying down. How quickly one learns to think like a killer. A moment later she called out to me.

'Nicholas, if someone wanted to kill me, what would you do?'

37

Flight: uneventful. Mood: unsteady. Claire: quiet. London: welcoming. Chelsea: still safe. But I knew – and Claire knew – that I never answered her question, 'If someone wanted to kill me . . .'

I knew why I didn't answer – because I couldn't give what she wanted. The shame felt as chilling as the desperation. In the flat we moved around each other like a pair of animals who had just met. We had no capacity to talk to each other at that moment. I decided to break the news to her about Mrs Lydiard's message. If we went down to Rye it would take her out of London and keep her by my side.

Again she surprised me.

'Ye-es. I was afraid of something like this.'

I stared at her over our sandwiches.

'You were *what*?'

'If you think hard,' she said, 'you'll probably know what I mean.'

'If I think hard?' I stared at her. No. Nothing came. Brain not functioning. I had put myself on hold when we came home, when I double-locked the door of the flat behind us.

'Claire, they think there may be somebody in the house. *Inside.*'

She nodded. 'I know. I heard you.'

'But – but?'

'Captain's Wife?' she interrogated.

'What about it?'

'Think.'

The young man in the rollneck sweater. The Peeping Tom.

'You mean, him?' I kept down my annoyance. 'That *would* be a bit extreme. And if you recall – we never talked about him.'

'I know and I'm sorry. But I did tell you his name.'

'You didn't.'

'Mason Quinn. "Mace" for short.'

No matter how much I love her, Claire makes me feel more isolated than when I lived alone with no relationship. Perhaps I always avoided love because of the loneliness it generates.

'Why d'you think it might be him?'

How much more can I take? Not much.

She dusted the crumbs from her fingertips, wiped her face with paper from the kitchen roll.

'It's a long story.'

'Is it serious – if it is him in the house?'

'He's a bit tricky. But I can deal with him.'

'Tell me the long story.'

She began in halting reluctance, but not (I observed thankfully) distressed, nor even under pressure.

'I met Mace when I first did drugs. He had been living in a squat, somewhere out there, Enfield or Hackney, some place, you know what I mean. Terribly well-connected family and all that. I was, well, as you know, I had met Philippe and was working for the company. Philippe and I hadn't got together at that stage, it was when he was working in London, but he and I had – we had "observed" – each other. He told me afterwards he was biding his time.'

We had scarcely spoken of Philippe since his death, apart from one dangerously painful visit to the house by the Seine to fetch Claire's possessions. I feared mentioning his name. Now I saw that she seemed to have risen above that trauma, too.

221

'Mace got emotionally fixated on me because I didn't dis-approve of him. Not that I was in any position to disapprove of anyone. And then he got, well – he got physically fixated. Is all this going to bother you?' she asked me anxiously.

Claire thinks I'm the one who's jealous of the past. I shook my head.

'But you don't still fancy him?' I asked rhetorically.

She sighed and continued. 'I mean – really fixated. We went away for a weekend together and it became a week, then a week and a half and I kept calling in to the office, saying I wasn't feeling well, you know the usual excuses, food poisoning, flu, all of that. The truth was, Mace and I were doing this daisy chain of expensive hotels in a ring around London. We'd ring up and book a suite and pay with credit cards and arrive and get stoned out of our heads, because thanks to my connections I had unlimited supplies. And naturally enough the inhibitions fell away and naturally enough we got more and more used to each other and naturally enough we got – he got – more and more involved.'

She had begun to sing-song a little but out of embarrass-ment rather than distress. I watched her like a hawk.

'He wanted to marry me and give up all the stuff and settle himself down and go back to Oxford and finish his degree, all of that, and he said I was his ticket to his future and would I do it? Trouble was – I couldn't. I was too fucked up. And then with Antony's blessing – indeed urging – Philippe, at just the right moment for him, wrong moment for Mace, put on the pressure and I fled with Philippe to France. Where you, eventually, found me.'

Claire stopped, took a knife, cut into an apple.

'Mace went ape. A.P.E. Lost it. Totally and completely and comprehensively. That's how I know Lucinda.'

She looked uneasy.

I said, 'D'you want coffee or tea or nothing?'

'Don't. I need to finish saying this.'

I sat there, watching her.

'Lucinda knew where to find me and she rang to say Mace had come around. He talked and talked, about me, about him and me, about our future. Lucinda listened and I gather they both did some stuff and then she went to bed with him, which, when she told me, not only didn't bother me at all – it took the pressure off. Until.'

She stopped, her apple as yet uneaten. When I met Claire, with Philippe Safft on the streets of Oradour, I tried to pin down her voice. Best I could do was a young Judi Dench, not quite as cut-glass as a Royal, but undoubtedly crystal. The voice proved a problem when helping her recovery: I could not believe those horrors being told in such elegance. Again I waited; it's something I have learned to do.

'Lucinda got up at some stage during the night to go to the lavatory. When she came back Mace was awake and standing in the middle of the floor. He reached for her and she said she was exhausted or something like that and he strolled away. And that's how she put it – I remember her words, "he strolled away". He came back a moment later and said to her, as if he'd never seen her before, "Where's my Claire?" Lucinda, on instructions from me, said she hadn't a clue. And Mace, who had been hiding a pair of scissors behind his back, took them out and stuck them in his own throat.'

I closed my eyes, then opened them to see how she coped: so far, so so-so.

'Miracles happened that night. An Asian surgeon in Hackney General. Nobody knows how he did it. But he sutured the jugular – or something like that, I've never quite enquired.'

I said, 'The poor boy' – and didn't mean a word of it.

'He was eighteen and now he always wears a rollneck sweater. As you saw.'

I asked, 'Is he still doing – ?'

Claire shook her head. 'I don't know. Haven't seen him. That night at the Captain's Wife was the first time for, I don't know how long.'

'Did you ever see him again – I mean at any length?'

She nodded. 'Twice. I went to see him in hospital. Had to. Or felt I had to. But – bad idea. He got all upset, nurses had to be called. And then –' She grimaced. 'I met him again. On the street. In Paris, would you believe, of all the bloody luck.'

'What happened?'

'He must have heard I'd gone to live in France. Obviously he came to look for me. He saw us on one of the little streets coming up to the Place St-Sulpice. I saw him coming and next thing I knew – bang.'

She fingered her nose. So that was the cause of the broken nose!

'Oh, my God.'

She said, 'I forced Philippe to let him go.'

Silence, broken by me biting the bullet and saying, 'Therefore we have a problem.'

Claire said, 'I don't know. He looked quite sane that night. I know his outburst sounded mad, but – I don't know.'

What she didn't know was that he had stalked us down Lovers' Lane. Yep, we had a problem.

'We'd better start working out how to deal with it,' I suggested.

'I think I know how.'

'Oh?'

'In fact I think I know why he's there. Something I said to him during our rampages. And foolishly I repeated it when I went to see him in hospital.'

'What was that?'

'I said that I'd always give him a roof over his head and a bed for the night and a coffee in the morning to get him started again. You know the kind of mantra kids get into. And he's obviously remembered it.'

'Which means,' I said, figuring it out slowly, 'he's clinging to it. Which means his mind's not been in a good state. Which means he's still –'

Claire interrupted, 'Still on the old routine.'

She went to bed and I, exhausted, stayed up for an hour, trying to work out whether tomorrow I should take us both back to Heathrow and leave the country, make a clean breast of it, tell Claire everything at the airport, get her to drop her claim and begin a new life with her on the west coast. Or Australia. Or anywhere. Ordinarily not difficult to do once you set your mind to it. I wish she hadn't seen the chateau.

38

Instead, we drove to Rye, mostly in silence – a silence born in me of weariness; a silence born in Claire of, I think, apprehension and self-blame.

My new 'instant' system of making no plans helped again. I decided: think of nothing: make no provisions: prepare contingencies. First, get there and sort it. But I saw that each of us packed a heavy suitcase. I don't quite know why I did. And, as I was discovering almost by the minute, I couldn't speak for Claire.

Somewhere en route I handed her the phone.

'Want to kill two birds with one stone?' She questioned me with a look. 'Talk to Lucinda. Ask her when she last saw your mutual friend. Ask what she knows about his current state. And tell her to call Hal, we need a temp, say I said so.'

Claire grinned. I felt better too – some normalcy restored.

Lucinda knew nothing fresh of Mason Quinn. Vaguely heard he had a job with someone, some kind of minor executive job, like a runner with a film production company, something like that. When Claire suggested Lucinda take the job with Bentley Newman I heard shrieks of laughter. She closed the phone.

'If you knew what we gals have got hidden up our flowing sleeves.'

We rolled into Rye at noon. Thunder clogged the air. Out over the Channel the heat haze looked red. By arrangement we met Mrs Lydiard near the house but out of sight. She stood by her car, talking to a policeman. When we arrived he spoke into his little squawker.

They had some facts. The mystery occupant was male; he had shouted what Mrs Lydiard called 'offence' when she halloo-ed through the letterbox. No answer from the phone; the police had left some messages. He got in across the roof, prised up a slightly ajar skylight.

No damage done, so far as they could establish. The 'occupant' had remained concealed all day. That information inflamed me. Dangerous – not a time to lose control.

A more uncomfortable thought surfaced. This 'occupant' has his uses. He'll keep Claire and me close to the police. And keep Claire by my side day and night. We'll be out of the vulnerable mainstream of our lives. This is a situation in which we can hide. Let's not rush things. More than anything, whatever its pressures or implications, this was a new crisis. Many an old problem is solved by a new one. I made a mental note: Don't seem too unconcerned. But lead it, lead this situation hard; milk it.

A new policeman arrived, plain-clothes, the rank of Inspector. I broke the news to him, said we thought we knew the 'occupant', that there had been a family history with him, an unstable young man. In some misguided way he might be confusing our house with his home. I thought we should let him know we had arrived in the area. Within reason we would wait upon his wishes; he would probably open the door to us.

Inspector Sinker ('Not a very promising name,' Claire said later) responded carefully. He defined the extent of his powers. If we had acquaintance of the occupant this made it 'domestic'. He could only order what he called an 'action' if we requested it. But we could be overruled if, in his judgement, life or other property seemed endangered. By, for example, fire.

'We should, of course, advise you before taking an action and we would take such an action as guaranteed us positive but safe entry.'

'Like what?' I asked.

Cautiously he said, 'It is not unusual to recommend armed presence at such moments.'

To which I replied, as I watched his sandy eyebrows, 'But there is no need for that yet?'

'No,' Inspector Sinker agreed.

(Claire observed later, 'By "domestic" he also means they'd do nothing if you and I were hammering each other's brains out.')

That was how we reached our first decision. Which was: do nothing. We now had to decide which of us should let Mason Quinn know we had returned. Neither of us doubted the 'occupant's' identity; the ring of truth is a liberty bell. We deferred our next move and went to Colson's Inn with Mrs Lydiard. She had reserved their only – and warm-hearted – suite.

Where, from the window, I could see part of my house's gable. It twanged at me but I felt eased. Unthinkable that Strafe could follow us to this Merrie England coaching inn. If the French had failed to obliterate it in the fourteenth century, I felt sure it would look after us two frails. I now know that like the bereft or the terminally ill, we protect ourselves in great danger by using denial, or a sense of the unreal.

The inn proprietors sensed novelty afoot; Rye is a small town. With the menu came a complimentary drink; Mrs Lydiard's nous had clinched discreet care. Over lunch Claire and I debated how to approach the house. Claire said that a police approach might unsettle 'Mace': 'He's terribly sensitive, like all druggies.' At which I felt but did not voice, Sod that! This little shit's in my house.

We checked options: leave a message – he most likely had the volume turned up on the answering machine. Possibly. Shout through the letterbox? A bit threatening. A note – but would he read it?

Claire believed we should wait, sleep on it. But I sensed she had taken a decision. We finished lunch silently. I set about the business of running the office by phone, while not telling them where I was. To Hal I said we needed a new temp. He told me Lucinda had already called.

'Interesting girl,' he murmured; Lucinda's gifts travel fast.

For the rest of that day I went into limbo. I was exhausted by the whole appalling Strafe business. Not to mention the chateau – which we didn't. I lazed, watched television, declined food, dozed.

At half past ten, with darkness full, I thought of taking a walk – but Claire might want to come too. Difficult. Or she might not. Also difficult. Suddenly a foul humour swept through me like a plague and my spirit felt infested and in ruins.

39

A desert followed next – that is to say, long expanses of dull, treacherous time. We had nothing to do and limited power. Of this extraordinary limbo, only I knew the whole story. To cope I summarized endlessly to myself. It kept me from speaking, therefore from saying too much.

Around the corner stood our home with all our possessions. Yet we had no access to it. That aspect I could at least share with Claire. I could not mention the moment-to-moment recurring visions that had been haunting me – of a man, a woman, a figure of some kind or other appearing, a biker, a waiter, a waitress, a pedestrian – and suddenly every dream I was bringing to maturity would be shattered, every tender investment snuffed out and a lovely creature extinguished. How would they do it? A knife, a traffic accident, poison, a car-bomb, two barrels of a shotgun like the deer? No, this is getting out of hand, this is my Claire. I will protect her. That is why I have not made immediate and violent moves to get this little shit, her former lover, out of my house. The maddest things are often the sanest.

My festering gave way to sentimentality. Behind which arrives unreasonable rage. But, said the loudest soundtrack, Perhaps unreasonable rage might prove beneficial? No. Not to me.

Mid-morning – this was the second day, Wednesday – Claire said to me, 'How about this? How about me leaving a message on the machine?'

'Saying what?'

'Saying something like, "Hello, Mace, this is Claire and

230

I know what you're doing. All I ask is that you take good care of the house for me. And when you want to leave – close the door. Nobody'll harm you, the police aren't even on the case, they can only do that if I make a complaint and I'm not going to do that." Or words to that effect?'

'Worth trying. But – if it doesn't work?'

Claire splayed herself down in front of me totally naked. I couldn't work out why a body that so distracts me also helped me to concentrate. Her flesh-planes shifted as she emphasized.

'Point is – if it doesn't work, at least he's already under pressure. Because he will have received and rebuffed an approach. Therefore each approach, if we escalate it just a little, is going to put him under further pressure. And under pressure people do things that let other people make their moves. Meaning us.'

No breakfast yet; I had to avoid food, given my stomach's gripe.

'And then?'

'Then we see, Nicholas. We could make our next move a response to his.'

'Example?'

'Example – if he says or does nothing – by which I mean if he doesn't pick up the phone when next I ring – I leave a message saying we're close by.'

'How much time between the messages?'

'Don't know. Don't know yet.'

I groaned.

Claire rang the house at half past four in the afternoon.

'Why now?' I asked.

'Sugar dip,' she said. 'With Mace's history – bad, bad sugar dip. I know about sugar dips. His resistance'll be low.'

I listened; she spoke carefully, pitching between warmth and authority.

'Mace, hello. It's me, Claire. You there?' Pause. 'Mace, if

231

you're listening can you pick up? No? Okay, I'll just leave you a message. We know it's you and that's fine, you're welcome to stay as long as you like and I think the freezer is pretty well stocked. If you want to quit, just leave, close the door, nobody'll come near you. There are no police, no nothing, they'll only come if we make a complaint and I'm certainly not making a complaint against you. I'll call again just to see if you're all right. If you want to speak to me, fine, if you don't, that's fine too. I haven't forgotten what I said – "bed for the night, roof over your head, coffee to get you started in the morning" – take care and I send you my love.'

I felt my jaw clench. She finished and said, 'Come on, let's lie down.' And the hours simply stretched and stretched and stretched, in a slow, baffling welter of haze and inaction and confusion and fear and anger and futility and inertia . . .

We put Wednesday and Thursday behind us. On Friday afternoon, slightly later, Claire called the house again. I, meanwhile, had been jotting down all kinds of options. Was he receiving phone calls, was he making phone calls? If so could we ask the police to monitor them and if so who would we discover to be his contacts? Could it even be that his strings are being pulled by Strafe? Boy, did I rip into myself for that little bit of self-indulgent paranoia . . .

I watched as she made the call. She stiffened and said, 'Mace, is that you? Hallo?' Then she waved the receiver at me, 'Picked up, said nothing, put it down, cut me off.'

'Now what?'

I let Claire lead. She knew him and it seemed to be energizing her. Against the odds she remained stable.

'We wait,' she said.

Confinement caused our principal suffering. I had argued that we stay in the room as long as possible, to remain available. Now I offered a drive into the country, a walk on the marshes. (My private thought – on the flat open ground

232

around Rye I'll be able to see people coming. I had also made up my mind to end this nonsense – I would call on my old contacts in the police, men who knew and trusted me.)

An hour later she called him again.

'Mace, it's me. Just saying hello, I'm around and when you're ready to talk that'll be fine.'

My head fumed. Why is she being so nice to him? I knew she was right – keep it calm. But I hated it.

She turned from the telephone and said thoughtfully, 'I think I'm going to leave it at that for a day or two. If I don't try again he won't know what to make of it.'

'Fancy a drive on the marshes?'

'Won't they need to find us?'

'I'll call from the car.'

In fact I didn't; we went to the Snave Dower. Claire ate like a trencherman. I ate lightly and carefully – my stomach still buzzed – and we laughed over the appalling dinner we had with Elizabeth.

This time Claire said in the car on the way home, 'Ahem – don't we have unfinished business?'

I laughed, but winced at the memory of our coitus interruptus. Then she staggered me by saying, 'At least if we get interrupted this time we'll know who it's *not*.'

'What-tt?!'

She said, 'Nicholas, I saw him, but I thought you hadn't and I was too embarrassed to say anything. I knew it was Mace.'

Same lane, same gateway, same soft night weather – but alas! For once, my dependable body let me down, even with Claire's incentives. She took my inert state as a personal slight. Always the same. I am not permitted variation. When we got back to Colson's she began a withdrawal. I never would have anticipated the consequences – nobody could.

40

In the next hour my feelings shifted. My discipline lapsed. I began to hate Mason Quinn. Needed to hate someone. Unsafe to hate Strafe: hatred would destroy my objectivity. The bizarreness got to me. Here I was in this cosy inn – but I was here for a vile and invasive reason. Which was also protecting Claire. Define the word 'paradox'. I can define it. Uncertainty leading to bolshy anger. To rage. And yet I somehow got back some eerie sense of safety, which I thought I had lost for ever in the ghostly acoustic of Caux.

Claire took a long bath. With the bathroom door locked. That's one of the familiar barometers. She's endearingly fastidious in her bathroom habits but typically she'll open the bathroom door as she's climbing into the bath in case I wish to come and chat to her – as I usually do. So I sat there and watched some late-night film about a failed businessman turned spy, whose wife, long thought dead, returned to accuse him of murder. The usual lousy fodder.

My mind drifted to my house. I mused on the things I love. *He* walks among them now. Touching my telescope. Fingering my clothes. Reading my books and probably not putting them back on the shelves, probably losing the bookmarks from their pages. Will he have tried my Doge's Palace jigsaw? And will he jam the pieces together as the three-dimensionals frustrate him?

On the sofa table in the Square Drawing Room I keep my collection of antique slide-rules. They enchant Claire. I have a Marquess and a Berkhold and a Hoffmann and a Jury – all fragile, all valuable, all absorbing, delicate instruments that have measured glorious plans. What will happen to them?

He's squatting. In my house. Every break-in or squat tells lurid tales. Pictures slashed. Glassware broken. Defecation. Thuggery. This is a mad ex-druggie, obsessed with my wife, he's a former suicide effort, for God's sake. I didn't know it's possible to suture the jugular: what a shame.

And anyway, what was that rampage of theirs like – him and Claire? I know the good hotels of the Home Counties, have stayed in several of them. Four-posters. Balconies. Vast Victorian baths. Can't bear that thought. Keep my thoughts on my house. That little shit. With no sense of responsibility. A drop-out, a no-good sponger who thinks it's all right to indulge any fantasy he can think of, who sees nothing wrong in moving into somebody else's house and taking it over, as much as saying, 'This is my house now.'

I began to pace – and that's one of *my* familiar barometers. Time, perhaps, to speak my mind a little. I mean, hang on here, I give Claire the best of my attention. Completely sensitive to her every need. Look after her to the very best of my ability. I don't see why I shouldn't attempt to recover my property from someone who has no right whatsoever to it or its contents.

Then – Jesus-and-gin, the insurance claim! Imagine how the underwriters will twist and cheat on this one. Friend of the family – blah. Not strictly a break-in – blah. Damage caused by, so to speak, a family member – blah-blah. Too late to say otherwise, we've already told the police.

I got so carried away I almost rapped on the bathroom door to call, 'Claire, I need to speak to you!' I forbore.

When she came out her mood had deepened as though she had tracked my change of temperature. She swept past me in a towelling robe, climbed into bed and switched out her light. Not a word – and the air above her head seemed grey and empty; the power of her moods never ceased to astonish me.

Now I decided to bathe. As I undressed my mood snapped.

'Claire, I think I want to take some action tomorrow. Something more direct than leaving messages on the answering machine.'

Muffled, she replied, 'Mace is very frail, he might snap.'

'Very frail?! He's in my house, for Christ's sake, that's how frail he is, climbed on the roof, yanked himself down through a skylight. And look how he's imprisoned us, he's got us holed up here in a hotel fifty yards from our own front door! No! Not bloody good enough.'

Silence.

'Claire? Do you take my point?'

Not a word, not a gesture, not a move.

'Claire?!'

'I don't want to discuss it.'

'Oh, fuck this!' I yelled and slammed the bathroom door.

41

Surprisingly, given the anger coating my skin, I slept. To be awakened by the telephone. Time? Watch says a quarter to eight, grope for the phone, aware of something odd.

'Hello?'

'Nicholas, it's Claire.' Formal, distant.

I checked the bed beside me. Gone, long gone.

'Where are you?'

'I'm here, at home, in the house.'

'You're what?' Fuzzy brain, fuzzy voice – but not fuzzy much longer.

'Mason let me in. It's okay.'

I jumped up. 'It's not okay. What did you do?'

'I knocked on the door and said it was me. It's okay.'

'Claire, it's not okay, I'm coming straight round there now.'

'No, don't do that, Nicholas. Listen.'

I listened, forced myself.

'Mason's quite upset.'

'Claire, for Christ's sake –'

'No, *listen*. This is delicate, it needs attention, he'll heed me.'

'When's that little shit leaving?'

'Nicholas, one thing at a time. I've persuaded him to have a shower. That's how I'm able to talk to you.'

My shower, the best Aqualisa can supply. With the thirty-centimetre antique brass rose I bought in Tours and had the piping adjusted to – *my* shower. And *my* everything else,

237

soaps, Floris, everything. I don't think I can control my rage
– but I must.

'Claire, you're not listening to me. When is he leaving?'

'I have to talk him down a bit first. He has this notion
he's going to live here with me, just the two of us.'

'Claire, this is mad!'

'You know I don't like that word. Anyway – I have to go
along with it for the moment.'

'How's the house? Has he done much damage?'

She held back a little. 'Untidy, that's the best word.' I
knew she meant chaos.

'Claire! Darling! Please! Let me in.'

'No, I can't. Uh, he's coming' – and she put the phone
down. Cut me off.

There's a scene in *GoodFellas* when Robert De Niro hears
they've killed his friend. He kicks the telephone kiosk, he
kicks it and kicks it. I've spent my life using such scenes
from films. They help me when I want to avoid expressing
strong feeling. Now De Niro stood in the room with me and
he kicked for me like a wild horse.

When the kicking ended and I came back from the cin-
ema, so to speak, I stood in the middle of the room. Try to
think. I sat on the bed. Press each of my toes to the floor.
Nobody to talk to, to ask. No advice I can take – this has
an emotional dimension. And no police because this has a
'domestic' dimension. I looked down at my toes. Counted
them as I pressed.

Next the images began to flow. He has come out of the
shower. Probably wearing my robe. His neck scar. Claire's
sympathetic to physical blemish. I'm not. It helps her, I
presume, to cope with her own inner scars.

Will he say to her, 'I need you'?

Will she say, 'I know'?

Will she let him hold her?

My eyes are hazing. She might try and explain it to

238

me later. As pity. Sympathy. Management of the passing moment. A spasm of violence seizes me. Sometimes I understand killers.

Where are they standing right now? In our room? In the kitchen beside Mrs Lydiard's full fridge – if 'Mace' hasn't demolished it and its contents? Will they lie down on the couch where we have lain so often?

Of all my physique, my eyes concern me most. I blinked and blinked, as though full of dust motes. And visualized tearing Mason Quinn's eyes out. One after the other. Plucking them out as they do in that unwatchable scene of *King Lear*. Only more savagely. I grabbed my spectacles, tore on some clothes and ran.

In Church Square I slowed down. Not a person in sight. No cars parked anywhere, nothing unusual in that. I look at the house. Can just about bring myself to. All curtains tightly drawn. All blinds down. All grilles closed, Fort Knox. That was how I planned it. My wish for Claire's security has shut me out of my own life.

Claire sometimes disturbs me when we meet men socially. She's too relaxed with them. Especially if they flatter her. And they usually do; they're round the honeypot, aren't they? Strafe's a case in point. She could have kept a better distance from him. She doesn't mark out her boundaries.

Now she's in the 'safety' of her own house with a former lover. But I thought she feared him. How she hid her face from him that night at the Captain's Wife. I must have been wrong. If she's gone in there now she can't have feared him. And if, when we go out socially, she has boundary difficulties, oh Christ, what will she be like in there now?

What was their relationship? How many times was he inside her? How many? Fifty? A hundred. I know I'm not a jealous man – but how many times? His hands on her face, between her thighs, his fingers, his mouth. It doesn't matter that it was in the past. It happened. I don't want it to have

239

happened. And if she finds that letting him near her again is the only way to resolve this crux – will she do it? I used my right hand to grip the left. Each finger felt like a stick of gelignite.

I'm on the pavement, I take a step forward. Now I can see the house. I stand and watch it for a moment, surprisingly nervous. Then I call up my reserves of strength, walk firmly to the door and ring the bell.

No reply.

I ring again. No reply. I ring a third time. No reply. Nor any sound from inside. No shuffle or rustle. Not a whisper. No sense of anyone even bothering to try and divine who might be at the door. I bang the lion's head knocker. Hard as hammers I bang it. Not a sound. It echoes down the hall and through the house, an echo with which I am very familiar and which I love. No response of any kind.

My letterbox came from a brass founder in Dagenham. I specified it wide and deep to take blueprint tubes. Down on my hunkers, I pressed the flap open. I should have been able to look down the hallway but something hung over the box. A cloth? A carton? I couldn't quite make out. When I squeezed my fingers in I couldn't tug it away.

'Hello!' I called. 'Hell-ooo?!'

No answer.

Now what? I didn't want to call out the word 'Claire' – too intimate. And I certainly didn't want to call out, 'Mason, oh Mason, it's me, Mace! Coo-eee!' I really wanted to shout, 'Open this fucking door!'

Defeated. I stood upright. And then stood back. Play them at their own game? Yes. I'll buy a camp bed. Arrange for Mrs Lydiard to supply me. Camp on the doorstep.

Heartened by this positive thought I stepped away. Then I understood the pressure it would put on Claire. And a new soundtrack murmured this to me: You said, Play *them* at *their* own game. You're already thinking of them as an alliance. You don't trust her to handle this, do you?

Defend myself against this inner whisperer. She isn't stable yet. Her mood swings cause problems. The guy may be dangerous. The guy *is* dangerous. But a more aggressive voice inside me said, Listen. She's out of the way of Strafe. As long as she's in there Strafe can't get at her. This is the gods, old son, coming in on your side. Don't look a gift horse in the mouth. And she can probably handle this nutter, she knows him from way back . . .

Food cures confusion. I left my own doorstep, returned to Colson's and ordered breakfast – for two people; perhaps I wanted Claire in the room with me; perhaps I didn't want the inn to know she'd gone.

Think, Nicholas. Bacon and egg helps me think. What is the thing most bothering you? Hold on, go through it again. Claire's actually safe at the moment. If you call that 'safety'. She's out of circulation. And she's actually competent and has come through savage fire to marry me and attempt a life together. I have these plus factors rooting for me. Repeat the question: What's the thing most bothering you, Nicholas?

Answer: *I don't know what's going on in there*. It's that I don't know what he has done to my house. To my possessions. I don't know when it's going to end. It's that, essentially, I am powerless. Trapped by my wife's frailty. And her former lover. But above all I don't know what's happening in there and I know myself well enough to know that within twenty-four or forty-eight hours that will be driving me crazy . . . Anyway, I haven't been able to think straight since Caux.

But at the same time – I want no fuss. I just want him out of there. Fast. And I want to be in control of that happening. I want it to happen without calamity or bother, with nobody knowing anything. I want to be there when it happens. Jesus Christ, I could have done without this.

I love that house. Ruined when I bought it, a total ruin. I had to bring in every service afresh, drains, wiring, the lot. It had lovely basic features, though, and details which only another architect would appreciate.

My builder called out to me one day, 'Look, China [which he called everyone]. You haven't clocked this.'

I remember the weather: also summer, roasting hot. We climbed over piles of materials on broken floors to the southern wall (the house faces west). One of his men had stripped away some facings.

Derek, the builder, tapped the wall. 'Those Jacobethans, they knew things, see?'

'What is it?'

'A duct. I'm sure they didn't call it that, but I'd call it a duct.'

'Water?'

He grinned. 'Knew you'd like it, China. Seen one before. The heritage chap said it was a kind of air conditioning.'

We then walked out to the exterior. Derek showed me rows of small bricks with angled perforations.

'Prevailing wind,' he said. 'Little of it gets in and mostly blows this angle in summer.'

At the time I felt faintly uncomfortable lest the rooms feel draughty. I trusted Derek. He said we could always cover the perforations should we need. No draughts, nothing but a coolness in summertime that I now attribute to what Derek called, 'Me little perforations' – from a commercial for tea-bags.

I finished my own breakfast. Claire's bacon and egg – I ate that too. God, I hope she's all right. As if she read my mind, the phone rang.

'It's me. I'm okay.'

'Good.' But I said no more because she clicked off.

So the game will be – stay here to take her calls. Fine. Same question though – for how long?

Caux, Zurück and the dreadful fear for Claire and of Strafe – and now this. The walls are moving towards me.

No. I must do something. Why am I thinking about walls?

42

Senior policemen speak opaquely. Inspector Sinker looked around my suite.

'They do this sort of thing well, sir.'

Did he mean the owners of the inn? Or the architects, or the decorators? Or the suppliers of the furnishings?

'Yes,' I agreed.

He accepted tea and waited; I had, after all, asked to see him.

'There's been a development, Inspector.' He looked interested. 'My wife's gone into the house.'

'Ah, yes.' I couldn't tell whether he knew.

'She went in this morning. She's phoned me twice. Everything's okay, she says.'

Inspector Sinker never struck me as a fool, just, well, opaque. His nose bends slightly; he looks as though he has to sniff sideways

'She also says, Inspector, that she'll keep in touch with me. By phone. Here.' I pointed to the telephone by the bed. He looked at the phone.

'The occupant – acquaintance is a strange business, sir.'

'Yes, that's true.'

What did we feel like, sitting there on armchairs facing each other? A pair of negotiators, I suppose. I wanted something from him. He sensed he might not want to give it. I waited, as one does in a negotiation. He buckled first.

'So – that's all right then, is it, sir?'

I waggled my hand in an iffy sort of way.

'Theoretically, Inspector.'

I took off my spectacles to wipe them. He watched everything I did. And made the next move.

'Well, as I pointed out to you and the young lady – it's your home, sir.'

'Young lady' – not, I noted, 'wife' or 'your wife'.

'Yes. I was grateful for that, Inspector.'

He checked to see whether I was winding him up, then relaxed. We paused again, like members of a gentlemen's club.

'Inspector, were I to ask for assistance, say?'

An experienced negotiator knows when the moment has arrived. A skilled negotiator knows how to counter that moment.

'Well, as I believe I explained to you, sir –'

'Perhaps I mean advice more than assistance.'

'Always happy to *advise*. But, as I say, sir, it's your home and as it seems, it's currently occupied by the young lady's acquaintance and now by the young lady herself.'

Sharp eyes; in fact, he's very sharp; he gives the impression of being lazy but he's not.

'There's a difficulty here, Inspector. I'll be completely open with you. I need to know what's going on. Inside the house.'

'Won't the young lady convey that to you, sir?'

My brain had daubed my crux in words a foot high. If I tell the police Mason Quinn's history (not to mention Claire's), they'll raid the house for drugs.

'She might be overheard while she's on the phone, Inspector, she's being cautious. But let me put something to you.'

I told him about the ancient ducts. He smiled.

'Yes, I remember that, sir, the tea-bags. Everybody said it at the time. "Little perforations."'

'Inspector, tell me about listening devices?'

He got my drift. 'We rarely have occasion to use them

down here. But I have seen them in use, I was a young officer at the Balcombe Street siege. They're quite effective, I gather, sir.'

'And the police who use them, Inspector. Are they very skilled?'

'Oh, it's not the police, sir. I mean, yes it is, but it isn't any more. It's all privatized now, sir.'

'You mean you can hire them?'

'I believe so, sir. But if it's a matter of safety – I mean.'

Waving my hand in a gesture that I hoped spelt dismissiveness and understanding all in one, I said, 'So presumably I could hire them.'

'As I say, it's your house, sir.'

'That's what I thought, Inspector. Do you have a company that does this sort of thing?'

'I'd need to think about that, sir.'

He called me an hour later as I sat in the room doing nothing; not even a pack of cards to play patience. The company whose name he gave me had 'wide experience'. Then he added something that hadn't crossed my mind: 'They're also very discreet, sir. It's how they make their money. They don't talk to newspapers or anything.'

'Any advice on how to handle these experts, Inspector?'

'If you'd like, sir, I'll drop by unofficially when they're in place. That is, if you select that option, sir.'

To help me decide I rang the house. Claire didn't answer – and a dilemma slammed me head-on. I didn't know whether to leave a message. Would it provoke 'Mace'? And if so, provoke him into what? He must know that I know about him and Claire. What is the mentality of an obsessed, druggie former lover? How in Christ's eyes should I know? I called the number Inspector Sinker gave me and spoke to 'Dennis'. With, as he advised, 'two "n"s'.

246

43

Dennis with the two 'n's' arrived at nightfall. As arranged. After a long preliminary conversation he and I walked to the corner. I showed him the house. He strolled past while I waited. I heard a clock chime ten.

Dennis came back.

'Who owns that bare patch of ground?'

'I do.'

'That's the blind side of the house.'

'Yes.'

Two hours later the big van came in on the lower level. I walked down the steps from the Gun Garden. Not a light showed in the house, front or back. And Claire hadn't called all day. My mood swung. I was firm. I was distressed. Soon I was more distressed than firm.

Dennis's team – his 'operatives' – didn't allow me to see what they did. They asked me to show them the 'little perforations' and seemed pleased.

'Makes our job easier,' Dennis said; the others never spoke. He asked me to return to my room at Colson's. When they had set up he would call me.

The call came through at half past one. In the silent night I walked down to the van, which had a furniture removals logo on the side. Impossible to see the van from inside the house. Therefore it could stay there as long as it liked. If needed.

Again the eerie reality of it all tried to kick in. I was about to eavesdrop on my own wife. And her former lover. In my own house. That I had owned for years. This surveillance seemed no more than a step I felt I had to take. The utter bizarreness of it did not reach me.

Dim lights inside the van. They waited for me. The range of equipment looked like a television rig. Big sound desk, several monitors with grey images. Not only had they planted tiny listening devices inside probes through the perforated walls, they had also inserted some sort of micro-cameras. One screen showed the Long Drawing Room and the second showed what we called Nelson's Room, because from the exterior you could see where one window had been bricked up and we said the room had only one eye.

'Any – results?' I asked, not knowing quite how to put it.

Dennis said, 'Some. Where do you watch television?'

I said, 'Damn! It's in the only room surrounded by other rooms. It doesn't have an exterior wall.'

Dennis nodded. 'Explains it. We can hear it. And we've had one sighting. The lady came into this room and sat over there for a few minutes, then went out again.'

On the fish-eye monitor he pointed to the sofa in the window space of the Long Drawing Room.

'How was she?' I asked.

''Course we can't see her face. The definition doesn't give us that. But she seemed all right.'

'Anything else about her?'

'No. Normal, I'd say. She did one slightly unusual thing. She left the door open and then came back and closed it very deliberately.'

I said, 'I wonder why.'

'Dunno.'

'Where are they now?'

'The television's still on. Wanna listen?'

One of the 'operatives' handed me a pair of large padded earphones. Dennis watched me, his moustache shiny. I sat there eavesdropping on my own wife watching television in my own home. Too much. Not able to take it. I rose quickly, handed back the earphones.

Dennis asked, 'D'you wanna stay, d'you wanna go?'

'Any developments – call me.'

I went back to Colson's in a frightful state – edgy and tearful and rather broken. I thought, If you don't get hold of yourself –

So what can you do to pull yourself together? You can't speak to Claire. But why don't you communicate with her another way? How? Write to her. You've always said you would.

Yes! I'll write her that letter. The one I tried to write and couldn't. I'll tell her all about me. I'll say how I love her. How I mean to go on loving her. My letter will have in it all the force of my dear father and all those people of his breed. Silent heroes at war. Decent men at home. I want to be like them. In the writing of the letter I'll see if I measure up. Acute shock brings me back to adolescence.

My dear, darling Claire

I'm writing this letter in our suite at Colson's late at night. You've now been in the house – our house – with your friend almost twenty-four hours and I have been steeling myself to cope with it. I miss you terribly and I thought I would try and tell you what it's been like having you in my life.

You know I'm not good at communicating emotion. If this 'crisis' makes me face that fact about myself, then it will be for the best. Also, I have decided to let you handle this. I will stand back and keep a loving eye on you in so far as I can. In this, too, I have to train myself, because I have never been good at trusting others and the fact of trusting you now to get us all safely out of this, to get us our house back, to see to it that you and your friend will be all right, has led me to think a great deal about myself and how I've gone wrong and how, therefore, I can take steps to make sure I don't go wrong with you.

In the past I haven't divulged what I feel about anything – I mean, about anything crucial. Until you came along. I know you're probably saying to yourself, 'Well, he would say that, wouldn't he?' but it's true and there it is. I suppose I should qualify it by saying I have made the greatest effort of my entire life where you are concerned. That, I expect, is partly why you're on the receiving end of such bitchery from Elizabeth and Mary Strait and on those other occasions when we've met people from my past. They once wanted from me the emotional effort I'm clearly putting into you and they know I never gave it to them.

I don't want to provoke in you the reaction that says, 'Ooh, hark! I am the lucky one!' What I'm trying to say here in my cackhanded way is that since I met you and fell in love with you I seem to have taken a decision (if one can take decisions in such subjective areas) to try with all my energy to overcome my shortcomings and emotional backwardness.

For instance, I've been trying to keep embarrassment at bay. I simply don't know what to say to you after we've made love. Or before, or during, either. And when you say to me as you so often and generously do, 'I love you' – I don't know how to respond. And the embarrassment piles on more embarrassment, because I am embarrassed at not being able to respond, as well as embarrassed at not having responded.

For instance, time after time I want to look across at you and say, 'I love you, I think you're wonderful' – but I can't do it. My mouth won't form the words.

For instance, I want to tell people how I love you, what

I think of you. Instead, I don't mention your name unless I have to.

For instance, if we part on the street after lunch or when you come to the office with me, I stand and admire you as you walk away. But I'm unable to tell you that.

Perhaps you can now understand why I like buildings so much, why I become joyful when I am in somewhere like the Miracoli in Venice, or Hagia Sophia in Istanbul, or the Arènes at Arles, or Paestum? They're 'safe' houses for me, in the way a spy is repatriated by being brought to a 'safe house'.

Until I met you those of my feelings that could be called delight or wonder or beauty were safely met by buildings. Buildings don't ask questions or need responses.

Does this all sound frightfully bleak? If so, I'm truly sorry. I regard this as a love letter – but I know that I am not getting anywhere near what I set out to do, namely, explain to you why I love you, and how it has come to pass that I love you so desperately and excitedly. At the same time I want to try and persuade you that what I sometimes seem, i.e., distant and unresponsive, is about as far from what I may be feeling about you at that time as it could possibly be.

I think about you all the time. I worry about the age difference between us. I feel that younger men can bring a smile to your face the way I can't, even though I know the age difference isn't too vast. And I worry about your family's past. How can I know – even though you've tried to tell me – what it is like to have all one's geniture wiped out by the Nazis? Like millions of others, I remember – and always will – the moment on television when Dr Bronowski bent down and scooped up a handful of earth at Auschwitz and said something like, 'These are the remains of my people.' But that merely enabled me to give a response that made me feel better about myself,

*that enabled me to say, 'See! What a right-thinking chap
I am – I think the Holocaust was dreadful. Hitler was a
scoundrel.'*

*The reality, as I'm discovering through you, is very
different. Sometimes I see that gap, that vacuum in you,
and I try and push it up along the scale until it reaches six
million dead. And then the whole thing becomes as infinite
as space, and I realize that what I have always thought is
true – that we can never know enough about it. Because
we can never truly know about anything unless our own
blood was involved. And then I have to try and stop a
self-defeating vicious circle from forming.*

*My dear, darling, Claire – here you are. A long
rambling letter from your emotional cripple of a husband
who, in terms of loving his wife the way she needs to be
loved, is still afraid of falling over. So all you're left with
is a man who loves you and who hopes that you will
continue to say to him 'I love you' – even if it doesn't
always get you the response you might dream of.*

*But even though I find it difficult to say it with my
mouth, I find I can say it in writing – I love you. I love
you as much as any building I have ever loved and that is
the closest I can come – or ever will come – to what I feel is
the truth.*

Your devoted – Nicholas

When I finished I thought I would feel enervated, in need
of a drink. Five o'clock in the morning. No – I felt airy and
alert. Nevertheless I knew I had better get some sleep so
I bathed and slept like a child. Evidently I had resolved
something within myself. My last thought was, There's so
much she won't discuss – the chateau, Clay Massey, the bits
and the pieces. But I had a picture of the loving smile on
Claire's face as she read the letter and I wondered when I
should push it through the letterbox.

44

The next two days twisted like hot metal. Every dice felt loaded. To the office I pleaded illness. Told Hal to put Mary Strait in charge of Strafe's chateau. Suggested she bring Elizabeth in on it. I quite like the dynamics of that. And I can always take the job back from them when all this ends. If there's still a job in it. They said Strafe hadn't called. Aha! He's tapped the telephone in Rye. Paranoia is the fastest-growing plant on earth.

Nevertheless – he hadn't called. Therefore he was nowhere near us. Relief from that pressure swept through me like a breeze from the Channel on these stifling, humid days.

Inspector Sinker contacted me to say he'd been down to the van – 'Not officially, you understand, sir' – and considered everything well in hand. He seemed keen to tell me he had checked the legalities and that he found nothing wrong; the van 'wasn't causing an obstruction'; the observation was 'a private matter'.

Dennis called me every four hours by arrangement. Nothing happening, he said; no sound inside the house; distant conversation only, or television. It occurred to me to suggest in my letter that Claire move the centre of the house's activity to the Long Drawing Room. But I couldn't come up with a good subterfuge in which to frame the suggestion.

She didn't call. Not once. Nor could it have been possible that I missed the call – the team had monitored the telephone. Therefore I had no idea of events inside the house. Neither Claire nor Mason Quinn had come close enough to any of the listening devices to give us a sense of the state of play. Nothing in my life ever felt so eerie.

Paradoxically I felt freer to move. I bought a pack of cards, had lunch, even got my hair cut. All the time, unknown to the world at large, my house stood there like a pocket of the universe or a separate little planet with my wife isolated inside it. In the hands of – or, I hoped, in charge of – a strange young man who wanted to live there with her for ever. To cope with that set of thoughts I had to jump firmly on myself.

At midnight on the third night I went down to the van. We reviewed progress. One of the listening devices had packed in. Another kept picking up some loud intermittent sound. The team felt frustrated. It kept happening in a room where they half-heard the most promising talk. Just as a pattern became established, this noise cut in and almost ruptured the microphone. I solved the puzzle: one device had lodged on the grille at the back of the fridge.

That, almost more than any detail so far, wounded me. It gave a picture of a 'normal' life. Who's cooking for whom?

I said to Dennis, 'What do you think?'

'Someone's trying to keep it all normal.'

But was he trying to humour me? Anyway, that meant what? A long game? Therefore I must merely endure. 'Endure'? 'Merely'? There were moments when I thought the sun was travelling backwards in the sky.

We reviewed the positioning of the devices and decided – expensive – to escalate the coverage: more devices in other walls. Pain loomed; one of the locations would probably tap into our bedroom – or a bedroom likely to be in use. I feel ashamed that I experienced a near-pornographic quickening.

Dennis counselled his team, 'Quiet with the ladders.' They fed more micro-listeners into the perforations. I split inside me. Between, Is Claire safe? and, again, Mason Quinn's been inside her in their vivid past, probably more often than me.

What if she thrilled more to him than me? He's younger. He knows her. What if, since those rampaging days they spent together, he had some hook in her, the hook of sex? And back again swung the thought, She's in danger inside the very house I brought her to as my wife.

Calm down, Nicholas.

I didn't suspect her of wanting sex with Mason Quinn. But she may feel she has to cut a deal with him. In order, say, to keep him calm. My head in a red spin, I left the van and walked slowly back to Colson's.

In half an hour the telephone rang.

Dennis said, 'Ah'm, got something to report. Definite movement, not in any way worrying. But worth a look, I think.'

They'd added extra cameras; five screens altogether. There's Claire! Where's that? That's the upstairs corridor. I'm looking at her. She's wearing jeans and a sweater. Her hair is swinging loose. I love her.

Voyeurism is compelling. Whatever the pain, I could not stop looking at her. She seemed to be listening. Why there? I figured it – because that's the most private telephone point in the house, the one outside our bathroom. She's hovering, she's waiting for something. On another screen I could see Mason Quinn. He's in the Square Drawing Room and he's working on my jigsaw.

Such a flash of rage – on the palm of my hand I found gouges afterwards from my fingernails.

'What do you think is going on?'

Dennis pointed out the fish-eye details. 'The lady keeps picking up the phone. It's like she wants to make a call. Only she feels the gentleman will hear her. And, look, he keeps coming to the door and listening.'

As I watched, those two scenes kept being played. Then I knew Claire must be trying to call me.

'I'd better get back in case she gets to make a call.'

'D'you want me to record across the phone intercept?' Dennis asked.

I nodded and he began, 'It'll be extra –' and I snapped, 'Put it on the bill.'

'It'll be ready tomorrow.'

Racing back to the inn, I thought about how Claire looked. She seemed all right; no trace of that stiff movement she has when under real pressure. I felt so tender towards her. Then I thought, If she doesn't feel pressure she must be feeling relaxed. But if she's feeling relaxed that means she doesn't hate being there. Every avenue of thought became a cul-de-sac.

No call came. Obviously she hadn't given him the slip. I lay awake, in limbo. My Hell, when I die, will be a passive place where I can do nothing.

Next morning I took my letter to Claire but went first to the van. Dennis's face told me he had results.

'Struck gold, really,' and hastened to say, 'in our terms, that is.'

All the screens showed empty; I was looking at the different rooms and the closed doors of the upstairs corridor. He snapped a video into a machine.

'We're now across all output. This is timed – you'll see.' The time-code said, '07:51.'

On the screen nothing appeared and then I heard a voice – Mason Quinn in astonishingly clear sound.

'Claire, where are you?'

Claire's muffled voice answered, too distant and too brief to discern what she said. Mason Quinn appeared in the corridor, half-staggering along.

'Been at the sauce, I reckon,' Dennis opined.

'Claire, I want to see you.' He knocked at our bedroom door.

Such incongruity between the clarity of the sound and

the fuzziness of the visuals. I could tell Mason Quinn was wearing a tee-shirt and probably nothing else – Jesus!

Now he banged on the door. She opened it but stayed inside the room.

'C'mon, Claire, you promised –'

And now Claire came into the corridor, pulling the door behind her. Fully dressed, same jeans and top – which angered him.

'Hey, you're still in your clothes, c'mon give us a hug.'

Claire leaned across and hugged him, keeping the lower half of her body away from him the way women do when they embrace other women.

'Lemme into bed.'

'No, Mace, I'm not feeling well.'

'Claire, I'm desperate.' He grabbed her as she began to ease away.

'Mace, tomorrow. I promise.'

'No, Claire, now. I want you, Jesus, I want you.'

I could feel the eyes of the van watching me.

On the grey fuzzy screen these figures swayed back and forth, grabbing and evading, grabbing and evading. His voice cut in again.

'You promised me, Claire. You promised me you'd let me fuck you whenever I needed you.'

There's that filthy porn strobe across my mind again. What causes such thoughts?

'Mace, but that was then.'

'No, Claire. "For the rest of our lives," you said.'

'Mace, tomorrow, I promise. Tomorrow, Mace. You know how fastidious I am.'

He seemed to accept her not untypical excuse. (I thought, I know she's lying.) She began to steer him along the corridor. They vacated the lens. The tape went on recording the empty space. Five minutes passed. Claire came back, went into the room and closed the door. In my mind, I could feel my arms encircling her. I patted the letter in my pocket.

'Best result we've had,' Dennis said, 'court-of-law stuff, that.'

'Is that it?' I asked, hoping it might be.

'No. One more thing.' He spooled the tape forward. 'Nearly missed this.'

The time-code said, '08.43' and Mason Quinn walked along the corridor. He hammered the door and called in a wretched voice, 'Claire-Claire-Claire-Claire-Claire-Claire-Claire-CLAIRE!' Just when I thought he might break the door down, he subsided. He sank to the floor, screwed himself up against the opposite wall, hugged himself, weeping like a child.

Claire appeared, still fully dressed. I thought, She's sleeping in her clothes. She knelt to him, took his head, cradled it and began to coo soothing sounds. I couldn't look but I had to. My brain felt as if someone was pelting it with stones. She's never done that for me. I'll kill this fucker. Claire, this isn't the way to keep a distance! Then, more rationally, I thought, What's going on here? But I said it aloud, not knowing I had voiced the question scorching my brain.

'He's gotta be on something,' Dennis said. 'That's what we think.'

It made sense. Mason had a supply. Claire hadn't joined in. When he couldn't have her, he had a hit instead. Then, stoned, he went after her again – a vicious circle.

'Anything else?' I asked.

'No. Odds and ends. But that's the best so far. We keep going?' Dennis enquired.

I agreed. On the way back to Colson's I changed my route. Climbed the steps, cut through the Gun Garden, into the square. Life seemed so normal. The sun shone. Cars gleamed. Curtains billowed through open windows – except at my house. *My* house.

Feeling like a thief – and then angry at that feeling – I shoved my letter through the door. If I had reckoned right, Claire would call me while he slept off his fix. I could tell her I had written her a love letter. Back in the room I sat as still as a graven image.

She called in twenty minutes, whispering.

'He's asleep.'

I almost betrayed everything by saying, Yes, I know. Luckily I caught myself. Not time yet to tell her we're listening in.

'Are you all right?' I whispered.

'I'm fine, really I am.'

'What's happening?' The base creature inside me, the part of me I most revile, wanted to check up on her, see whether she lies to me. Plus, she hadn't answered my rhetorical question as to whether she still fancied 'Mace'.

Claire whispered, 'I'm still in my clothes. He keeps wanting to sleep with me. I'm trying to persuade him I have a period and then I'm going to try and persuade him that it's safe to slip out for a walk.'

'How is he?'

'He's being persistent at the moment. The first two days he sat watching television. The hardest thing is – he has a supply here.'

'What about food?'

'We've just started into the freezer. There's enough for a month. That's part of the problem – we don't have to shop.'

'How are you feeling?'

'Oh – I don't know, I don't seem able to listen to myself. It's all so unreal. Nicholas, I'm so sorry about all this. I'll apologize fully when I see you.'

'Look,' I said. 'You seem to be doing fine. I'm trusting you to handle him. You'll know what to do. I've written you a letter. It's in the hall.'

She almost squealed. 'Oh! I'll sneak down and get it now. He's chosen to sleep in the television room.'

'Are you warm enough? Is there anything you want me to do?' I was whispering too.

'Stay near, go on loving me, that's enough. I love you, Nicholas.'

'I love you.' And I tried a stratagem. 'I'll think of you lying on the sofa in the Long Drawing Room. Where we lie.'

'Oh,' she said. 'What a lovely idea. Think of me tonight at eight o'clock. I'll go there at that time and lie down on the sofa so that you can look at your watch and think of me. I love you.'

'Claire, I love you,' I said.

At a quarter to eight I sat in the van like a man on a high wire. Dennis said they had nothing to report; some movement along the corridors, the television again, the lavatory flushing, but the mood seemed peaceful. They heard distant conversation and what they thought was something falling, but it seemed like something dropped accidentally, a pan perhaps, and directly afterwards they had seen 'both parties' behaving normally.

I never knew I owned so many clocks. The mantel clock in the Long Drawing Room always reminds me of Claire. Its peaceful chime set the tone the first night we ever sat across from that fireplace and looked at each other.

Now it chimed eight o'clock. The door opened and in walked Claire. She went to the sofa and lay down. A moment later, like a tame animal, Mason Quinn came in. He stood over her where she lay.

I heard her say, 'Mace, could I have a few minutes to myself?'

'Sure, Claire, sure.'

He left the room. If only she knew I could see and hear her. In the fish-eye I saw her stretch. She rose, went to the window and looked out. I could have sworn she blew a kiss to the world but perhaps that is what I wanted the gesture to be. She came back and lay down.

Then I heard a wild shriek. Mason Quinn came running in like a Berserk, shouting, kicking furniture, screaming, flinging himself around. All of us in the van jumped to our feet. The technicians had to grab the incoming sound levels. Claire jumped up from the sofa.

I heard her say, 'Mace, what is it, what's the matter?'

Shouting, 'You fucking bitch, you lying, fucking bitch!' He waved something in the air.

Dennis said, 'What's that?'

I said in the dull tone for which I am justly famous, 'It looks like a letter.'

Even to someone so subjective as I was it became riveting. Mason Quinn danced in rage – literally danced up and down, like a man in a western when the bandits are firing six-guns at his boots. He screamed, he punched the sofa, he shredded my letter, shouting incomprehensibly.

Claire kept saying, 'Mace, Mace, it's all right, it's all right. Really it is, it's all right.'

'You promised! You fucking promised!'

As we watched she got hold of his arm and then his other arm and slowly she began to talk him down. He seemed as unstable as wet dynamite. I couldn't bear to watch but I had to. Dennis and his men were glued to the screen but I saw that Dennis cast eyes at me.

'What do you think?' I finally asked Dennis.

'I'm glad he's where we can see him,' he answered carefully.

'Should I give Inspector Sinker a call?'

Dennis nodded. 'Not a bad idea.'

They patched me through to the Inspector's mobile. He told me he was 'just finishing a Neighbourhood Watch meeting out Playden way' and that he'd 'drop straight in'.

He did. The scene in the Long Drawing Room had calmed.

261

I heard Claire tell Mason Quinn to sit there and she'd make him a sandwich. Lucky bastard, I thought, to get that offer from 'the best sandwich-maker in captivity', as she used to call herself. We ate a lot of sandwiches. They were the sort of food she could guarantee preparing; her cooking too often collapsed in tears.

I began to shiver again and felt a diarrhoea attack starting. When I was eight years old, one of the horses got flu and died. My father had to peel me off the great bulging chestnut body lying cold in the stable. The consternation unhinged me. I felt like that now. At which moment Inspector Sinker arrived.

Dennis played him the shrieking video. I explained that I had written a letter to my wife and dropped it in. She had telephoned me and seemed calm. This had been the first difficulty. Sinker looked at the footage.

'Run it again,' he said.

He watched, wearing headphones, while I kept an eye on the other screens.

I heard Claire announce, as she always did to me, 'A star-spangled sandwich, the last of its kind, in a never-to-be-repeated offer. To you, sir, at the knockdown price' – and she corrected herself, because at that moment she always said to me, 'at the knockdown price of one kiss' – but to Mason Quinn she said, 'at the knockdown price of – nothing.'

Bless you, I thought. Jesus!

The Inspector stood listening. What I now began to appreciate was that for much of the time Mason Quinn and Claire said nothing to each other. He ate his sandwich like a pig.

I said to Inspector Sinker, 'What did you make of his violence?'

'It's instability, really. I don't expect he's dangerous.' He added, 'He doesn't have much by way of previous form.'

My head rang like the bells of madness. 'You know about him?'

He nodded, 'We found his motorbike, he had been observed for days here, he was riding around. Bike with big lightning flashes on it. We've got his bank accounts and we've even tried to get hold of his employers.'

The air turned chalk-white.

'Who are they?' I asked, doom-ridden.

'He's paid by a man called Roy Jewell. Can't get hold of him, we're waiting for the bank to get back to us.'

45

Lightning flashes. Clammy Roy Jewell, Strafe's nasal finance man. The sound of circles clicking shut. Deep in the night they brought in the vans. A team of three advisers came from the Metropolitan Police, plus a psychologist (female), a rapid-response force of snipers and a caterer. It might as well be Hollywood – high drama, big back-up.

I froze. My mind refused to function; my eyes began to hurt; my hands and feet felt unexpectedly cold; a cold sore had already burst my lip.

Dennis and his team, retained now by the police, moved up a gear. In fact, Dennis's pragmatism jolted me out of my frozen state. He approached me, consulting his watch.

'Just to confirm, Mr Newman, that as and from twenty-two thirty-eight you ceased to be our client in this matter. I've confirmed it verbally with the Inspector and you'll be billed only to twenty-two thirty-seven.'

I nodded and said mechanically, 'Thank you for all you've done.'

'No, sir, thank you.' He then did something that warmed me – he patted me on the elbow and said, 'We'll do our best to get you a good outcome, sir,' and he nodded at me.

The Inspector asked me to stand by. When two other officers joined him the place began to hum. Sinker assumed responsibility for the entire operation. He delegated in slow, precise phrases, and said everything twice. The others wrote it down. I, who love detail, lost interest. Only the news blackout caught my attention and I was too fazed to comment.

Misery remains my principal memory, plus appalling stomach pain. Dully I answered the questions relating to the house's layout. The operation was under way – huge, stealthy and distant. Although I remained in the van, I had become a spectator in my own life.

Odd to be commended for intimate knowledge of one's own home. Odder still to be praised for describing one's wife. The psychologist entered everything I said about Claire in a laptop computer and began to sort the data into headings which she would not let me see. I said nothing about a history of drugs.

She and I watched the video of Mason Quinn's outburst.

'What d'you think?' I asked.

'He's very unstable. She's very capable,' she replied – perhaps too freely. She distanced herself thereafter.

Activity rasped throughout the night. A town official got called from his bed; they threw cordons around the entire area; Church Square closed off, the Gun Garden sealed.

I said to Sinker, 'But if he looks out of the window – I mean, he'll see everything, the cars, the cordons, won't he?'

Sinker nodded in agreement. 'I hope so. He's meant to. But people in that situation often don't look at the outside world.'

He asked me to stay in the van. But I sensed that he had removed himself from me. This felt devastating. I had become dependent on him, had almost begun to elevate him above the ordinary police powers his training had given him. After I had told him about the bike with the lightning flashes, about the killing of Clay Massey and about Claire and me being stalked by Mason Quinn, he changed. No longer a policeman advising a member of the public, now he was an officer forging links in the chains of command.

Details chilled me. I overheard Sinker speaking to the snipers. They verified calibre of ammunition, style of weapon.

Tear-gas and other possibilities came up, as did pressure points if the building had to be stormed. Most chilling of all, they asked me about sightlines in the event – they spoke candidly – of 'armed response'.

At nine o'clock in the morning, with Rye now awake and people learning that some 'incident' had begun in Church Square, Inspector Sinker ran his first ploy. I thought his tactic wrong.

He phoned the house. The answering machine kicked in.

'This is the police,' he said. 'It is exactly nine o'clock. We would like you to open the door now, please, so that the owner may return to his home.'

I winced. Not how I would have done it. Not at all. It created risk. Mason Quinn could blow. Sinker saw my recoil and ignored it.

Nobody in the house responded. During the night Dennis's team had added extra listening devices. They intended to wire the entire building. They had also lowered a probe with another camera down one chimney. It produced poor results – plus it ran the risk of being seen.

Sinker waited five minutes, then left another message.

'This is the police again. It is exactly five minutes past nine. We would like you to open the door now, please, so that the owner may return to his home.'

Once more he waited five minutes. Then he left the next – identical – message. He wanted the repeated ringing (our machine was set to pick up after four rings) to wake up Claire or Mason Quinn.

On about the eleventh message I called, 'Look. Top right.'

Everybody stared. That monitor showed the corridor nearest to Claire's room. She emerged, still fully clothed, picked up the telephone, listened, replaced it immediately, then walked along the corridor and out of that camera's view. Her much-loved lope in the fuzzy grey monitor: I closed my eyes.

266

'Where's the answering machine?' Sinker barked.

I answered. 'Downstairs lobby. Not covered by a camera.'

'Can we hear it – if she plays it back?'

I winced at Claire being called 'she'.

Dennis answered. 'We'll hear enough to know if she's playing back.'

In a flash of idiocy I wished to shout at him, 'Don't call her "she". She's "Claire" for Christ's sake!'

In a moment we heard the answering machine. Claire cut the output volume, afraid to wake Mason Quinn. What will she do now? I guessed she would spool forward. Spot-check at low volume. Then erase. In seconds we heard the tape whirr forward, then the last message: *'This is the police calling you, it is exactly nine fifty-five.'* Followed by the goose-gabble of the tape being erased as it rewound.

'Smart girl,' Sinker said. 'What'll she do now?'

I guessed Claire would drift softly back upstairs and call me. That's what I hoped she would do. In a moment we saw her back in the corridor walking on tiptoe. She picked up the telephone outside the bathroom door and – superb intelligence if personally disappointing – did not call me.

Dennis checked fast. Someone called, 'She's dialling one four seven one.'

Claire had pressed the service identifying who last called. And if you press 'three' it dials the last caller. She pressed. The phone rang on the van's bank of equipment. Sinker picked it up. Dennis, bless him, handed me earphones.

'This is Inspector Sinker. Are you uninjured?'

Claire whispered, 'Yes.'

'Is the other occupant uninjured?'

'Yes. Asleep.' I closed my eyes at the sound of her whisper. 'But I'm afraid I'll wake him up. What do you want me to do?'

'Can you persuade him to leave? Calmly?'

'I don't think so.' Then Claire asked, 'Is my husband with you?'

Everybody reacted. I could feel their emotion reaching me. Sinker handed me the phone.

'Claire, it's me. Are you all right?'

'Thank you for your lovely letter.' All this was heard in the van.

'Not at all. How are you bearing up?'

'Nicholas, what's happening?'

'The police are here. For your safety.'

'I can't say much.'

'How is he?' I asked, afraid to hear the answer.

'It's – tricky.'

A technician waved, pointing to his headphones. I knew he meant they had picked up waking sounds from elsewhere in the house.

'Claire, don't stay too long on the phone.'

On one of the screens, the door of the Long Drawing Room opened. Mason Quinn looked in. Then he walked away. We saw his legs climbing the stairs. On her screen, as I watched, Claire whispered into the phone.

'I love you,' she said and hung up.

Mason Quinn ambled along the corridor. He tried Claire's door.

'Claire? Claire?'

Sinker moved. I knew I wanted to stop him – because I knew what he was doing. He rang. Mason Quinn picked up the phone on impulse.

'This is the police. It is ten o'clock exactly.'

I watched, shaking like a leaf. Dennis punched up the sound on the speakers. Mason Quinn ripped the telephone from the wall. He went crazy. Screaming, whirling, kicking. Kicked the walls. Picked up the telephone again. Smashed it against the wall. Took a large Middle Eastern dish (given me by a Lebanese client), hurled it along the corridor. We heard the smash as it hit the wall somewhere.

Claire emerged. He screamed at her. 'Did *you* call them? Did you?'

He tore at her hair. She grabbed his arms. He threw her to the floor.

And I launched myself at Inspector Sinker, kicking and punching and shouting, 'You – fucking – IDIOT!!!'

46

The officers who forced me outside calmed me down.

'Why did he do it? Why in the name of Christ did he – I mean –'

'Sir, this is a police investigation.'

'You must not interfere, sir.'

I said, 'A blind deaf mute could see that was the wrong thing to do. The whole point is to avoid provoking the guy. Why did he do it, for Christ's sake? Why not adopt a softer approach?'

The psychologist came and stood beside me. She said nothing. I knew from her demeanour that she agreed with me. Or, at least, didn't disagree. I raged up and down. She talked to me all the time.

'Inspector Sinker – very experienced officer – there are measures laid down – recognized procedures – they've been effective before –' and so on.

'But he's made it worse,' I said. 'We might have got Claire to get them out shopping or something.'

'Inspector Sinker – knows what he's doing – extensive training for this sort of thing – psychological methods – to get the best result – minimize danger –'

'But he's maximized the possibility of danger,' I said. 'I mean – oh, JESUS!!!'

She took me by the arm and walked me away towards the Ypres Castle pub. The morning sun shone on the fat winding snake of the water below us, on the oily, rust-coloured iron of the industrial sites, on the scrublands and on me.

I said, 'What happened – after that?'

'She calmed him.'

'Where are they?'

'They're in the downstairs room – they're on the sofa – she's talking to him – we can hear it all – she's doing the right thing.'

'I want to go back in.'

'Let's walk for a bit,' she said, her way of saying I wasn't going to be allowed back in the van.

We walked. Back and forth. No farther, no more.

'Go back to your hotel,' she said.

'I must see what's happening.'

She said again, 'Go back to your hotel. I will talk to Inspector Sinker' – on whom I think I landed a punch. I certainly caused havoc for a moment or two. Heard Dennis shouting, 'Mind the desk!' They overpowered me.

This is awful. Any moment now the feelings will converge. Guilt and embarrassment and shame and anxiety and dread and worry and paralysis. But why did Sinker take no thought? Sure, I saw what he wished to achieve. Open a dialogue with Mason Quinn. But he didn't take into account the wild instability.

The psychologist, whose name was Rosie, looked at me carefully.

'Perhaps a little routine back in your life – some food – this is a good moment to do it.'

'I have to see what's happening to my wife.'

'Leave it for a bit. You'll view it differently.'

She judged well the distance between warm and cold.

'Are you trying to tell me he won't let me back in?'

Rosie said, 'I should have a bath. Get something to eat. Shall I get someone to go with you?'

I gave up. 'No. It's okay.'

As I walked back I saw the size of the police operation. All streets leading up the hill closed. Police cars across each entrance to Church Square. Uniformed officers everywhere. Knots of people at barricades, rubbernecking.

How are they going to keep a news blackout on something as big as this? How am I going to keep sane with no one to talk to? No means of knowing what's happening? Worst of all, no trust in the police to handle it?

At Colson's they typically asked no questions. They knew something. The police told them the square had to be closed off. I hit the suite like a tornado and began to pace up and down, unable to get control.

Food helped. As did a bath. But I had no idea what to do. I searched and searched for any advantage in the situation. None – other than the news blackout. The event had imprisoned me totally. It took away my ordinary powers of managing my life.

Nothing had so disabled me since Madeleine's killing. Then, I felt besieged by my own guilt. I am now besieged again. My house is besieged. And my wife is the hostage in that siege.

Try the other extreme. Try saying, She's not a hostage, she's a willing participant. She's there in an effort to break an impasse. No, the fact is, no matter how we dress it up, she's being held hostage inside her own home. And if she tries to leave she will endanger herself.

Use the logic of drawing. Join the lines until the pattern becomes evident – what's it like to be under siege? It doesn't take a genius to grasp it. The powerlessness is what offends.

There's another factor. The Stockholm Syndrome. Where a hostage fell in love with her captor. She's going to sleep with him! I know it! She has to! How else can she survive? In that oak-beamed inn room, wearing a white towelling bathrobe and draining the last of my coffee, I knew only a dread – that dread mixed with the numbing pain of grief when everything inside turns the colour of pewter and every human voice sounds drab.

Will it help, I thought, to hear the words of the situation in my own ears? Speak them anyway and see what happens. This is what I said out loud: Strafe had, after all, got to my wife, whom I was supposed to protect. She hadn't yet been killed because Strafe's young hitman had once been her co-junkie and lover.

End of story. Full point. Anything else is a lie. I am the one under siege. Again. It keeps happening. What have I done in a past life?

Next thought process: how did I lift that inner siege of myself all those years ago?

Ruby. Where is she? Might as well. I called the club.

She answered. 'Darling, where are you?'

'Ruby, a dreadful thing has happened.'

47

Some time in the afternoon Ruby phoned from the London road. I gave her directions to the edge of the cordon. And I stowed all traces of Claire in the wardrobe.

To get Ruby in as far as Colson's I had to ask the police. Nobody halted me and I reached the door of the van. Sinker had gone. Another, older man had taken over. Team of two, I guessed, twelve hours on, twelve hours off. The psychologist had also gone. So had Dennis.

Sinker's replacement shook hands. He said dryly, 'I hope you're not going to take a smack at me.'

I said, 'I'm sorry about that.'

'Earby' he said he was called. He replied, 'I don't think there's hard feelings.'

When a vital event affecting you is taken over by the police it feels as if you don't exist. Your emotions are homeless. You feel, I'm a bystander in my own life. You ask, How do I re-insert myself into my own story?

I took advantage of the fact that I faced a new team. Best to keep quiet. Establish myself with them. Do nothing. And say less. Just watch. Ask intelligent questions. Make helpful observations.

The screens seemed the same. Fighting a rising nausea I asked, 'What's happening?'

Somebody pointed to the sofa. 'That's him.'

I could see a shape. The definition lacked sharpness. 'Been there for several hours.'

'Asleep?' I asked.

'If you'd call it that,' someone said.

274

Earby remarked, 'He's had some sedatives.'

I picked up the irony.

'Oh?'

'Never thought I'd be glad to see somebody using them.'

'What happened?' Sometimes my mouth feels full of cricket ball.

'He lost it. At one stage he began –' and Earby stopped.

I said, 'You have to tell me everything. It's worse if you don't.'

He took a decision without looking at me – and he continued: 'Blokey began to hit her. We thought of going to megaphone status but that would reveal we were looking at them. Then we formed an opinion that she might get control of it. And she did.' He looked sidelong at me. 'Cool lady, your wife.' That released me. He acknowledged my status vis-à-vis Claire, the first to do so.

'Then what?'

'She stood over there.' He pointed to the fish-eye dimensions on the screen. 'Right beside the microphone, you'd swear she knew it was there.'

I said, 'She knows about the perforations in the bricks. I've shown them to her.'

He smiled with satisfaction. 'That explains it. It's almost as if she's giving us instructions. She's speaking very slowly. As if she wants to make sure somebody else is picking up what she's saying.'

I said, 'She's very bright. She'd guess we had listening devices.'

Like one of those toy dogs on the back shelf of a car he nodded his head repeatedly.

'Where is she now?'

'Upstairs.'

'But how did she get away from him?'

Earby said, 'He's using. Heavily. She helped. Bit of an expert – she a nurse?'

275

I said, 'No' – thinking how Claire and I would laugh at this. Thinking, *If* Claire and I get the opportunity to laugh again.

'They both asleep?'

'Not only that. She came down to check him, then spoke slowly. It was definitely for us to hear. She wished him pleasant dreams, she said she was now going to sleep for several hours because she was very tired and could he please not wake her up.'

I almost exploded. 'But why doesn't she come out while he's drugged? Why don't you go in?'

The inspector said, 'I get the impression she's locked in. Or barricaded. Where are the keys for the window grilles kept?'

'Just inside each window. But out of arm's reach from outside.'

'So he's found them all. That's what we thought. She did go looking for something near the windows.'

'So she's a prisoner?'

'That's right.'

'Have you phoned again?'

'We have no phone contact. He's ripped it out. Or done something.'

'Why not go in now?'

The inspector said, 'Because we're not too sure of the state he's in. A loud noise might make him worse. Besides, there's –' and he hesitated.

I waited.

'D'you keep guns, sir?'

'No.'

'A replica?'

'I loathe guns.'

'Then I'm afraid he's got a firearm in there, sir.'

'Have you seen it?'

'That's what it looked like.'

Oh, please Jesus, no! Now it became plain. They have had to put on kid gloves in case he kills Claire. And, given his state, in case he kills himself. Thanks, Strafe.

Everyone picked up my realization. I felt their sympathy. That explains the wait-and-see tactic.

'You know about food and things?' I asked. 'Plenty of it in there.'

'That's part of our difficulty. In a siege situation providing food is part of building a relationship.'

'Is there nothing we can offer them?'

Everybody in the van had been listening to my questions. Everyone laughed. The inspector explained, not without humour.

'There's one thing he needs – or soon will. His supply's running low. If we were prepared to send him in some raw heroin – he'd join the police the moment he came out.'

I thought of joking, 'Well, I'm sure you've got plenty of it.' I didn't, but I was recovering some strength. And I laughed more than Earby's wit warranted. It's a thing I do when I'm under pressure. They laughed with me. What they didn't know was my desperation. Raw heroin going into that house? The number of times Claire said to me she'd rather die than go back . . .

But, Jesus, maybe she has already? Ask bluntly.

'Has he insisted she join in?'

'The drugs?' What else did he think I meant? 'Yeah, good question. We'd kind of expect him to. The only reason he hasn't offered or insisted is – like I said – he's running low.'

We talked some more. About patterns being established. What they expected next. The timescale things were happening on. When the next development might come. What it might be.

'Your wife's keen to give him food,' Earby said. 'Very sharp, that. Counteracts the worst of the drugs. How does she know to do that?'

I lied, 'She used to be a social worker. Sort of posh volunteer, you've seen them.'

Futile of me. He had made up his mind by now. But I think I may have been storing up things to make Claire laugh when she came out.

I added, 'I need your permission, by the way – I've got some moral support arriving. Want to get them though the barriers.'

'Yeah, no problem.'

Nothing else happened on the screens or on the microphones. When the call from the cordon came, I walked away from the van, my head full of snakes.

Ruby stood at the tapes. Again she dressed to her sense of occasion, a summer dress. You'll always pick out Ruby in a crowd.

People are strange. Some waited all day at the police lines. Everybody asked what was happening. I led Ruby through once the constable had radioed the van. Her company soothed me immediately and the snakes slid from my brain. I registered surprise that I felt such little guilt about Claire. Who would hit the roof if she knew.

We had tea in the suite. Having offered no more than broad brush strokes on the phone, I now told her every detail. Mason Quinn meeting us. Following us. His motorbike in Clay Massey's death. He was the courier. The payments from Strafe's finance director.

Ruby's face took on the look of somebody watching a gripping film. The brown eyes widened. She sat back.

'But what about you, darling? Who's looking after you? How must you be feeling? Your poor lip – cold sores are caused by stress.'

'Ruby, my whole body feels as though it will burst. I don't know what to do.'

'This is all my fault.'

'Don't be silly.'

'They photographed you outside Zurück, I bet that's what happened.'

'Nonsense, Ruby.'

'And they followed you, darling. Strafe's doing all this – how awful!'

'One day, when it's all over, will you answer any question I ask?'

'I will, darling. I promise.' She took my hand. 'I know what to do now, darling.' I looked at her. 'We lie down, darling.'

'Ruby, no. I can't. I mustn't.'

'Easy, darling.' She became slightly brisk. 'I mean only loving and care. It will be good for you, it was before. Look, we just lie down here, in our clothes. I will hold your dear head.'

Just like Claire cradled Mason Quinn. Why am I doing this? Pre-emptive strike? Is it because Claire's about to do the same? She may already have done. How do I know? Revenge, too; why has Claire done this to me? Pre-emption and revenge – how a man excuses adultery.

Anyway, I need it.

Ruby knew I liked her body. I knew what she was doing. And I didn't stop her. She then lay on top of me as I lay in my clothes and my hands roamed her naked back. In time we lay in each other's naked arms.

Ruby kept saying, 'This is right. This was always right, yes, this is right. There's a belonging between us, darling. That's why I've trusted you so much, darling. That's why I came to comfort you when you called.'

I think I screamed. She bit my shoulder.

We lay in the dusk and talked. I asked her to tell me the rest of the story. Might as well possess all the details. I no longer knew what lay ahead. She told me, more succinctly than I expected.

'Liese was my mother, remember? Alexander and Hana, yes?'

The family who were given Alexander's and Hana's apartment raised the three-month-old baby Liese. Who grew up with them, not quite a secret but not exactly an open family member. At age fourteen – and before – she was their housemaid, a Jewish girl among defeated Germans. When she was sixteen the father of the house made her pregnant – with Ruby. Whom they then raised, because soon after the birth Liese died. Ruby choked on the words.

'Died?'

'Yes, darling.'

'Do we know how?'

'Too painful. Let me move on, darling. I grew up there. There was a boy, of the natural family. That is Richard Strafe, the man you know. He was my playmate and then my tormentor.'

'Ruby, don't say it. Don't tell me.'

'You've guessed, darling. But at least I didn't get pregnant. And I got away. All he took from me was my opinion of myself.'

I took her in my arms again. And thereby defined my ambivalence. My body, of which I am so proud, reached to Ruby. Claire, who needs its solace, had now been betrayed twice in an hour by that gift of solace. In my own defence I can say one paltry thing. I wept afterwards. Ruby said I needed to. Said she didn't and said that anyway she had so few tears left.

48

I vowed not to tell Claire. Deep cringing shame. And yet –
and this is not a justification – I can understand why I did it.
It also freed me to say, If Claire in her circumstances now has
to do the same thing, succumb to the pressures in the same
way, I will understand. That's what I solemnly told myself.

Ruby left, soft as thistledown. I lay in the dusk, guilt
stinging me like prickly heat. I hated Strafe. Desperately
I wanted to see Claire, in a way I had never felt before. I
wanted to hold her, be with her, listen to her, talk to her,
remember her.

A memory coursed through my head: Claire's description
to me of what heroin did for her.

'There is a cloud I sit on. Where everybody loves me. And
where my family does not mourn this frightful history. The
shame of being persecuted. The humiliation of the camps
they took my grandparents to. The way they died there.
Or the worse humiliation of the world's undecided pity,
the world's ambivalence. And there's a worse shame than
that, the shame of having survived. Which is ridiculous
given that I wasn't even born then. My mother suffers that
shame. Sometimes she doesn't speak to anyone for weeks.
No resentment or acrimony, just silence. And then there's
perhaps the very worst shame of all – the shame of trying
for some kind of feeble redress so long after the event. Some
apology, some retribution. That's why I do what we call my
"paperwork" – which also has a trap in it. I know that when
I hear I may get my claim granted – I will feel ashamed that
I asked for it.'

The eyes prancing, the voice sing-songing.

'You can't know what it's like, Nicholas, to be in "the descendant", you who have always been in "the ascendant". It feels unbearable. And therefore you have to do something. In my case, I had to *take* something, some chemical. To effect a change. It's like cookery. That's why every meal I attempt collapses. I used to be a brilliant cook. Cooking is all about chemical change. Those were the words I said to myself, I used to say, "I need a chemical change." See how hard it is to live without the stuff? Imagine how hard it is not to go back to it. Look – we've met people, you and I, who don't advertise that they are Jews. They don't deny it – possibly. But they don't proclaim it. Which they should do. Think, Nicholas – what would it be like if you felt shame at the very memory of your family and your ancestry? That's why I look for this cloud I can sit on – so safe and so far away from everything. Life was soft and funny and I loved everybody and they loved me. I'd have been sweet to Hitler. He'd have cuddled me on that cloud. Cloud "H" I used to call it. Until it became my own personal mushroom cloud.'

I shan't forget where Claire made that speech – sitting on one of the high stools at the breakfast bar. We were having breakfast on a Saturday morning before setting out for Rye. She had bathed and dressed. The sun shone in her hair. Her words flowed as though rehearsed, but with a passion no actress could convey.

She spoke as though she had one statement to make. And expected me to know when she had begun that statement, when she had reached the middle of it and when she had said it all. I said nothing. Not just because I had nothing to say, but because what on earth could sound valid or important after that? And from my own wife?

I don't know whether she intended an effect. But her words, and perhaps even more powerfully, her whole demeanour, the kind of huge, sad, wavy flame as she

282

spoke, determined me never to pass judgement on her again. For anything.

That, at least, became my sincere response. And my committed intention. I also swore inside me that I would never be unfaithful to her. Lying on the bed in Colson's 'Ancient Coaching Inn of Rye', I felt my face harden with shame as though caked with drying slime.

Ruby was gone. The night approached. I had a shower. It produced in me one of those ancient 'wash-everything-away' feelings. I stood beneath the streams and sprays and regretted that I possess no religious faith. It could wash my guilt away biblically. Or so my fancies suggested. Wash, wash, wash. *Forget it, Macbeth or Pontius Pilate or whoever you think you are, you lousy, cheating heel.* Groucho Marx had a saying: 'Time wounds all heels.' Perhaps it will wound me, too. It was wounding me then.

A practical mind has its uses. The only good thing about a feeling as vile as guilt is that it soon turns into a determination to improve. To improve I always try and do something. In that practical side of me dwells my guardian angel. Or my benevolent daemon. Or my fairy godfather. Practical aspects to a problem – and therefore practical solutions – salvage me so often. I've given it much thought and I think it simply comes down to the fact that it's good to have something to do. The thing I wanted to do now was to cause the end of that siege.

I ticked off possibilities. Do it myself. Use the 'cherry-picker' the police had brought to the rear of the house. Force open the skylight. The chimney's wide enough for Father Christmas – what about that as a possibility? No. I had it 'sealed' with a wire grid to keep out squirrels. Too noisy.

No secret passages, the police had asked me that. No connection to other houses – I bought the house for its utter detachment. No stealthy access through the garden, no silent entry through the windows with their steel, sliding grilles. Nothing would get me in easily, swiftly or silently.

What about a psychological solution? No communication with Mason Quinn: stalemate. Building a relationship between besieger and besieged is crucial. No chance so far. He had killed the phones. Face it – this could continue indefinitely. Mason Quinn was pursuing a 'husband-and-wife-at-home' fantasy with Claire.

I carry several permanent images in my mind. Some are geometric, such as the classical assembly of sphere, cone, cube. To which I became so subject that I eventually had to design a building around it.

Some of my images come from childhood – the farm courtyard in Herefordshire with the clock and the dovecote. Or my mother standing on the steps leading down to the lawn, the skirt of her summer dress blowing – I see it in monochrome.

There's a helpful image that comes from the school science lab. Spill a blob of mercury – the teacher called it 'quicksilver'. The blob forms a perfect sphere. Press down on it. It immediately escapes and regroups – into several other little perfect spheres.

The same teacher showed us how to make primitive telephones: two lids from shoe-polish tins and a length of string; every schoolboy knows it.

He said, 'But all communication doesn't have to be two-way. Sometimes it's enough to say something and the way it is said makes it a fact. That is what teaching is.'

It probably went over our heads. But I came to know what he meant. Think something. Think it hard. Send out that thought like a beam. It works, I've known it to work.

I returned to the van, arriving at handover time – Sinker from Earby (I bet his juniors called him 'Earwig'). For a moment the officer at the door halted me; then Sinker intervened and beckoned. I hadn't seen him since I'd thumped him. He and Earby stood side by side, each wearing head-phones. Both watched the screens intently. Rosie, the psychologist, slipped to my side.

'There's been a development,' she murmured. She watched my face closely. Did she think me unstable?

Sinker beckoned that I should be given headphones. He made way for me to stand between him and Earby. I scanned the monitors and quickly found the active room as my ears adjusted to the sound. In the fuzzy grey screen, Mason Quinn and Claire moved around the Long Drawing Room. They were like animals in a dance.

Claire was saying, 'But if it's to be long-term, Mace, then you have to give me time to refocus on you. Give me time to concentrate on you again. You understand that, don't you? You were always good at understanding things I could never say to anyone else. I mean, I can't have a situation – or, rather, *you* can't have a situation – where you think I'm thinking of somebody else.'

Her voice still had that same calming note – not pleading, not cajoling. She aimed to sustain a level of intelligent consideration. She evidently believed she could keep him under control.

As I focused, Claire came closer to the camera. Now I knew the reason for the changed mood in the van – she had taken off her clothes. So had Mason Quinn.

49

Nobody looked at me – at least not in a way I could see. I was inches taller than both officers. My height is important to me – it has always been. At that moment it had no use. Some situations in life can never be catered for, not by instruction leaflet, briefing or advice.

But I believe that in such blasting moments we discover what we most believe. At that moment I learned that I believe in retribution. Not in the predictable way, meaning the retribution I wanted to bring down on the head of Mason Quinn. Too simplistic, that response. I meant something else; I meant that I had been dealt retribution for my infidelity to Claire.

That thought gave me surprising relief – not immediately. Immediately all I felt was an animal's pain, brute and mute and dreadful. My beloved child, as I often thought of her . . . Her naked body gave us an innocence we relished. I know I idealized her – but I was glad to idealize her, given all the women I had trashed one way and another. Now I was being paid back for trashing her.

A further pain hit me – that my behaviour had brought this new development down upon Claire. But that thought became too much and I had to abandon it or scream my head off. Nor could I acknowledge my groin's filthy response to seeing my wife naked with a naked man. And neither of them knew I was watching. How many murders have sex in them? I bet more people are killed for sex than for money. Unless you count war.

Someone broke the silence in the van. I thought, I know

that voice – then found it was mine, asking, 'When did this happen?'

Earby said, 'About forty minutes ago.'

About the time I was in the shower, trying to wash Ruby away.

'Did you see it happening?'

'Yes. Happened in that room.'

Will they tell me – or must I ask? Earby told me; he had kinder instincts and, I think, felt uncomfortable at what might have been Sinker's revenge – or natural sadism.

'Blokey insisted. Not violently. But he made it clear.'

'Was there further violence?'

How is my tongue, my breath functioning? How can I be so calm?

'Some. She stopped it.'

'How?'

Earby smiled; he spoke in a tone only I could hear.

'She told him that she could never marry a man who hit her.'

'But how did he get her – ?'

'She may be making a concession.'

'Why do you say that?'

He hesitated. 'He was very insistent – on admiring her.'

I looked once more. She stood, back to camera, that long, incomparable back, the thighs that don't meet at the top. Such unease in me, such unforgivable excitement.

The open air made me stagger. My brain was scattered to the winds that now blew in from the marsh. Lights winked at the Ministry of Defence danger zone. Beyond them blinked Lydd airport. We never did pursue that fantasy of going to Heathrow and just catching a plane to anywhere. I know Claire at first thought we were doing just that when we flew to Lyons – was it only last weekend? But I knew we were merely escaping, keeping her safe from a deeper, viler past. Now look at me – I can't save her from the past or the present.

Earby came out. He stood for a moment, then walked over to me.

'Your wife's remarkable, sir. That's what we all think.'

Steeling myself, I went back in the van. All had resumed their seats. I divined that nothing much had happened. Sinker pointed to the screen of the upstairs corridor.

'They're in there,' he said, meaning our bedroom.

'Inside?'

'Yes. Listen.'

I could hear sounds, but not sounds that disturbed me – sounds of doors or drawers opening.

Then I heard Claire's voice asking, 'This?' The transmission came across less distinctly than the one downstairs.

Rosie said, just behind me, 'I think she's trying on clothes.'

I said, 'That explains the muffled quality. They're in the inner room, the dressing room. How did that happen?'

'Persuasion,' Sinker said. 'She persuaded him that she owns lovely clothes. That a wife likes to dress for dinner to please her husband. He bought it.'

'What now?' I asked.

Sinker looked at Rosie who gave nothing away.

I pressed. 'D'you expect developments?'

Something had been planned; the mood had changed. Earby had been evasive and uncomfortable. Rosie fiddled with her clipboard. Another man, whom I had not seen before, sat at the back of the van. Dennis seemed embarrassed.

'Have you decided on a way forward?' I asked.

Sinker said, 'Police operations come under the Official Secrets Act.'

Hold it, Nicholas. This is not a time to blow it, hold your fire.

'Inspector, that suggests you're planning an operation.'

My practical mind came back to me; my brain hit a power surge. Of course! With a news blackout they could do what they liked. They're going to send in a team. What's the awful phrase they use, 'extreme prejudice' – meaning they don't care whom they kill. When will they do it? Four o'clock in the morning usually, the weakest, lowest moment of the day.

I decided to gamble.

'Inspector – the media have been on to me.'

I had him down for an ambitious man – and I got it right. His eyes narrowed. I listened hard to the output from the microphones. At that moment Claire and Mason Quinn appeared in the corridor, she walking briskly ahead of him. Both wore clothes, she fully dressed, he in what looked like one of my bathrobes.

'I have a very good recipe for steak,' she was saying, 'and we'll have that red Sancerre you liked at lunch.'

Such clear microphones; I could hear every nuance of that crystal voice. The tactic played on – Mr and Mrs Normal; her voice, though, had a brittle edge. I saw why.

'What's that at his waist?' I asked – but I knew because they had already told me; it was just the shock of seeing it that called for verification.

The newcomer at the back said, 'It's a common-or-garden Fabrique Nationale machine pistol, heavy calibre, which means it can take your face off.'

The police meant to go in during the night. Mason Quinn's gun justified their decision.

'Do you know whether he has ammunition?'

Sinker answered, 'We have to assume so. Mr Newman, I believe we now must ask you to leave –'

Desperate measures: 'May I make a telephone call?'

Sinker hesitated, then said, 'They've disconnected the telephone.'

'I'm not calling my house.'

289

Dennis pushed one of the many phones in my direction. I spoke so that everyone could hear.

'Bernard? How are you?' I listened.

Few people could have been more surprised to hear from me at that hour of the night than my draughtsman who hums all the time. His well-meaningness towards me felt like warm milk.

'Bernard – that message you gave me last week?' By now everyone looked puzzled. 'From the Home Secretary. Could you repeat what he said?' Bernard wittered on, repeated everything he had already told me and I said, 'Thank you. I'll explain later.'

I then turned to Sinker and said, 'Inspector, I'm alerting you to the fact that my wife has a serious medical condition. I will go as high as I can and as far as I can to protect her.'

Sinker swatted me aside. 'I must ask you, sir, formally to leave – this is a police operation.'

He didn't believe my threat. Therefore, said my stark mind, Mason Quinn will kill Claire.

Sinker continued, 'If you don't leave, sir, I shall be forced to have you removed.'

I said, 'If I have to leave here now, I'll spend the rest of the night bringing a kind of pressure to bear that you never dreamed of.'

My father told me that the *Prominenten* of the Third Reich all agreed privately on one thing: the closer you got to Hitler the more you needed to fear him. The point being: abusive authority only fears a greater and more abusive authority. Sinker hesitated. I turned on my energy. And a formal form of words.

'If you don't believe me, Inspector, I will within the hour have taken some kind of *ferocious* step to have you removed from this operation. On the grounds that you mean needlessly to endanger life. And I will also personally

290

break the news embargo. You can begin to imagine what I will say in public.'

I kept my eyes on his. Got him! He flickered – and looked over my shoulder to where Rosie sat. Something in her face halted him. He rose and beckoned to the newcomer. They went outside.

I said to Rosie, 'I hope he's not going to make the mistake of misjudging me.'

She said nothing and left the van. I knew I had won. Sinker did not reappear for fifteen, twenty minutes. The two watching officers logged everything they saw or heard. But not, I think, my words. When Sinker came back he sat down without a word and put on his headphones, picked up his clipboard.

Claire and Mason Quinn didn't reappear that night. The kitchen microphone proved ineffectual. We could hear sounds of cooking and loud conversation, mostly from him. The distortion obliterated the words. From the timbre of Claire's tone she kept listening, soothing, reassuring. This, I thought, is going to shatter her.

After dinner they went to the television room. He appeared briefly in the Long Drawing Room, the gun no longer at his waist; Claire must have persuaded him to put it aside. For the rest of the night and on until the morning we heard only the distant television sound.

50

Cock-up has far more power than conspiracy. If Cock-up wanted a fruitful opportunity it had only to come here, now, to Rye. Everything waited for it – frail woman held by unstable armed man, trigger-happy cop in charge. Greetings, Cock-up!

By now I felt like an amoeba, no form, no shape.

Earby came back on duty. He and Sinker went outside. I saw them, once, when somebody entering the van held the door open. They stood in deep conversation. Earby held a piece of paper.

Sinker's mood had changed – deflated but wouldn't wish to show it. My mind played tricks, because my eyes were so tired. Sinker's profile reminded me of Hitler's *Gruppenführer*, the awful Heydrich. Sinker had the same unusual physical characteristic, the almost womanly broad hips on a tall slim figure. Reinhard Tristan Heydrich. But perhaps I only imagined he looked like Heydrich; perhaps *in extremis*, to cope with my enemies, I have to demonize them.

Earby came in and sat.

'Quiet night, I gather,' he said.

I nodded. My eyes felt infected, my ears sore. I went out for a look at the day. Things had returned to 'normal' – but I mightn't be able to hold them that way.

Tea and bacon rolls came; everything tasted like glue. As I munched I let my eyes wander over each screen. This house was to have been mine for the rest of my life. How defiled shall it feel? My possessions, my space – all depredated.

Earby said to me, almost nonchalantly, 'We think it's possible to create a way of speaking to them inside the house.'

'I thought it must be.'

'The chimney –' he indicated the Long Drawing Room monitor. 'The wire grid has got apertures wider than the "little perforations" and we can get something down. Mind you, it'll sound strange to them.'

'When will it happen?'

'It has happened.'

'When?'

He looked uncomfortable. 'During the night.'

Which meant that my hunch had not only been right but close-run; men had gone onto the roof.

'Did they put anything else down there?'

Earby didn't answer.

'The airflow inside that house, the general ventilation – anyone would smell a gas of any kind before it affected them.'

He said, 'No gas. There will be none.'

So what had they intended? A drop of some kind of gas to stupefy or render unconscious? And then break in with the armed-response team?

Earby looked along the control panels where Dennis was signalling: the house was waking up.

Waking up too hard and suddenly – the Long Drawing Room door burst open and Claire marched in, still fully clothed as she had been last night in a long dress and simple top.

'No, Mason, no,' she called and he erupted into the room behind her, naked. She stood in the window and said in a schoolmarmish way, 'I'm not having this conversation with you until you put some clothes on.'

This might have been farce – but things had changed. Claire seemed less sure.

'Fuck you,' he screamed, 'I'll put something on, you fucking tease!'

He ran. I felt myself urging – Barricade the door! Push the sofa across! Instead her hands were fiddling with her hair and she jerked her arms – bad, bad signs.

He came racing back, still naked, and now he waved the gun like some cowboy.

'This is what I'll wear, Claire, you promised, you promised. You've been dragging me on! You're nothing but a cock-teaser!'

He might have been a child – and he acted like a child. Jumped on the back of the sofa, down into its well. Ran to the curtained window. Grabbed Claire. Forced her down on the sofa. I couldn't now see her – but could see him above her shouting, 'Look at it, look, see Claire, I have two pricks. See!'

'Mace, this isn't a good idea.'

Her voice had cracked. 'Mace, please put it down – please.'

Earby said softly, 'We have to take some decisions.'

I said, 'Isn't this a room where they can hear us?'

He looked at Dennis who checked and nodded.

Earby picked up the phone with the military attachments, pressed a button on it and said, 'This is Inspector Mike Earby. Hello, Mason, and hello, Claire, I'm just getting in contact to see if there's anything you need, to see if you're all right.'

He spoke softly but firmly and I thought, If I were in there I'd want to come out and meet him.

I watched Mason Quinn. He spun around as if God had spoken to him. What would he do now? He stopped, not sure what he'd heard, tried to locate the sound; he looked at the curtained windows, he looked around the room – a cross between a jungle man and some kind of frightened animal.

Earby spoke again. 'Hello, this is Inspector Mike Earby. Mason and Claire, we're just trying to make contact, to see if there's anything you need.'

Mason identified the source of the sound, the chimney. He raced across the room to the fireplace, couldn't see anything and he began to scream, 'Where is he? Where is he?'

Claire rose from the couch, trying to put herself together. She had deteriorated in the last twenty-four hours.

'Mace, it's a speaker, a sort of radio arrangement, sort of loudspeaker, it's probably outside the building.'

'No. It's here.'

He cocked the gun, struggled with it and aimed it. Earby sat still, waiting. I guessed his thoughts. If he spoke now we might lose the speaker and the microphone and the camera in that room. I urged silently, Claire, come over, calm him, say something.

She stood beside him and began to stroke his hair.

'If we tell them we're all right – they'll leave us alone,' she said.

'Don't be stupid, Claire, don't be so fucking stupid. How can we tell them?'

'Fix the phone,' she said easily.

He spun and shoved the gun into her face, screaming, 'You just want them in here. That's what you want.'

'No, Mace. Let's just speak to them. Look, I'll go and speak to them. You can come and listen to me.'

She eased back. He took the gun down. She stroked his hair – and split my feelings. I knew she did it to keep things even, yet I resented it with blind rage. She had never done it to me.

Mason Quinn stood and listened.

'Are they going to speak to us again?'

Earby reached for the button. I put out a hand and stopped him. He glanced at me with irritation.

I said, 'Do you want him to know you've got microphones in there?'

Earby paused. He rethought, then spoke.

'Mason and Claire, this is Inspector Mike Earby again, I

hope you can hear me. If there's anything you need give me a ring.' He read out a telephone number. 'I'll give you that again at the end of this message. But give me a ring.'

Very calm.

'We can't get through to you so perhaps you've left the phone off the hook so as not to be disturbed. Or if you like, we can rig up a means of you talking to us.'

Very clear.

'So ring me – and if you don't ring me I'll assume the phone's out of order. And we'll rig up something comfortable.'

Very slow.

'Do you need food? Some cold drinks in this hot weather? Anything else? I'm here if there's anything you need.'

He repeated the telephone number.

I watched Claire. She spread her hands out.

'See, Mason. We're all right. Really we are. Why don't you ring him. Or would you like me to?'

He waved the gun again, pointed it at the ceiling and I thought he might fire. I knew that if he fired I had a problem. That would give the police the excuse they needed to go in mob-heavy.

Claire said, 'There's a cordless phone in the hall. Why don't we see if it's working?'

She edged back a little, then reached out and took his hand as though he were a little brother.

'C'mon, Mace, you're good at this.'

We could see them in the hall; she left the door of the room ajar. Their words had grown indistinct – they had drifted between microphones. He gestured, she made calm movements – then picked up the telephone and handed it to him. He refused it. She walked back into the Long Drawing Room holding the phone. Perched on the arm of the sofa, she spoke, projecting her words.

'Mace, shall I ring them? Some orange juice for you. I'd

like some cranberry juice. Wouldn't you like a fresh steak? I'd love some salmon.'

My heart lifted to her.

'Shall I ring them?' she asked again.

'No,' he screamed. 'No-no-no-no-NO!' He held his head as if in pain and bent over a little, the gun still dangerous in his hand; the barrel hit her slightly on the shoulder.

'Look, Mace. I'd rather we had spoken to them on the telephone than have them think the phone's out of order and then they'll drop a microphone in or something.'

I winced – had she taken a risk? He straightened up, looking at her.

'You mean they could eavesdrop on us?'

'Yes,' she said carefully.

He laughed. 'We could put on a show for them. They could hear us making love, you groaning, Claire, d'you remember how you used to groan and the people in the next room would knock on the walls 'cause you were making so much noise when you were coming?'

My heart sank and jumped in one movement. His remark disclosed an intimate past I found scarcely bearable. And yet it spoke of the immediate past, meaning he had not – they had not . . .

Earby murmured to Rosie, 'He's quite far gone, isn't he?'

Rosie said, 'Yes. Very.'

'Any pattern?'

'He's in a kind of stop-go pattern. He'll go dull for a moment, then activate again.'

As if on cue Mason Quinn threw himself on the sofa and left the gun on the floor. Would Claire pick it up? Would she use it? She looked at it, then edged around in that direction. He may have suspected her because he reached down and took the gun from the floor, pressed it in behind his body. Claire knelt beside him, I could see her head.

'Mace, I'd love some cold drinks.'

'We emptied all those hotel minibars, do you remember, Claire?'

'I remember, Mace.'

'The times we had, Claire.'

'The times we had, Mace.'

'You used to blow me, Claire.'

'The times we had, Mace. Mace, can we have some cold drinks? Please?'

He twisted himself off the sofa violently and ran down the room.

'Stop putting pressure on me, Claire,' and he began to yell meaninglessly; his decibels hammered the microphones.

'Mace, I'm going to the bathroom,' Claire said.

She went out and up the stairs; in a moment the corridor camera picked her up. He screamed on, then realized she'd gone and raced after her, hammered on the door.

We only heard muffled words from Claire but they made him stop and he collapsed in a pose we had seen before – crumpled against the wall, his eyes on the door from which Claire would emerge. He aimed the gun at the door.

Tension rose in the van. I had thought it couldn't climb higher. Before speaking to them again Earby had to wait until they came back down to the Long Drawing Room. I depended upon Claire to get them there. She waited – and waited. Mason Quinn dropped the gun and sat on the floor. Claire didn't emerge from the bathroom for nearly an hour.

Earby scribbled out what he intended to say. He checked it with Rosie. Claire and Mason Quinn came slowly downstairs and into the Long Drawing Room. He sat on the armchair – my chair – and she faced him from the sofa.

'Mace, you're all right, you are,' she said gently.

'Claire, nobody was ever like you. Nobody was ever like you were to me.'

'Mace, we had wonderful times.'

298

He reached down, took the gun from his belt and pointed it at her.

'Claire, I've got the shakes, bad. I need you. You have to come over here. On your knees. Like you used to.'

'Mace, I've got a bad tummy upset. That's why I was so long in the bathroom.'

'But Claire,' he said mock-pleasantly, 'I have the cure here.'

'Mace, later. Please?'

'Claire – on your knees. Now,' – and he made some gesture with the gun that I didn't see.

It scared Claire. She slipped off the sofa very reluctantly. On her knees she began to cross the few feet of carpet to where he sat.

'That's it, Claire.'

Earby has the habits of a fastidious man; I had watched him arrange his food, his cups of tea. Now he spoke.

'Hello, Mason, how are you? Hello, Claire. This is Mike Earby here again. Hoping you're both all right. Haven't heard from you. I assume the phone isn't working. I'm just about to rig up a microphone. So's you can ask me for anything you need. There are shops nearby.'

The heat outside made the van an oven. I thought of the huge back-up services; police at cordons; traffic rerouting; armed-response units waiting; the tentacles of the operation I couldn't see and would never know about. My gut said, This is the point of no return.

In the room Mason Quinn jumped to his feet and fired two shots at the fireplace. The noise cost us one leg of sound.

Claire jumped up and grabbed his arm. 'No, Mace! Didn't you hear?' She forced his arm down. 'Didn't you hear?'

He screamed, 'I heard! I fucking heard!'

And held the gun to the bridge of her nose.

51

The police say they want all sieges to end in anticlimax. They claim that's the way they like it. But they don't always get what they like – because they also enjoy their guns.

No guns this time. Claire came out at nine that night, stumbling and unsteady. They switched on a floodlight. To give the marksmen a clear shot. She turned her head away. I knew she was alone and I beat them to it. Claire saw me on the pavement running forward from the police. She tried to run towards me but her motor function had gone. She wobbled like a child. I held my arms out for her, pulled her into me.

'Nicholas, I'm sorry, I'm so sorry, I've let you down again, I'm so sorry, I keep letting you down.'

Someone brought a blanket. Four big policemen formed a wedge around us. No attacker could have touched us. One or two of them patted her shoulders.

An hour earlier I had seen the beginning of the end. Earby didn't believe me when I said it was ending. This is what happened.

Claire looked at Mason Quinn down the barrel of his gun. The wrong way down the barrel. She then gambled – she lost her temper. Or pretended to. She began to call him every name under the sun.

He couldn't handle it. First he bridled. Then he wilted. She accused him of not allowing her to have a cold drink. And she told him if he had ambitions to live with her he'd better sort himself. He jumped from the sofa and ran to the kitchen, came back with a six-pack of Pepsi.

Claire made him break two open. She drank from hers and instructed him to drink. Clutching her can, Claire went to the bathroom upstairs. By now he'd have granted her anything. She told him to sit until she came back. He sat, docile and frayed.

I knew. Upstairs she doped his drink with her sleeping pills – the pills I counted every day. She swapped cans when she came back. I saw her do it. In time, when he fell asleep, she murmured to the microphone in the fireplace, 'I know where the door key is. I'm coming out now.'

On the pavement, in our huddle, Earby said to her, 'Is he asleep?'

She nodded.

Earby asked, 'Is he alive?'

She nodded again. Then she said, 'I want to wait until you fetch him.' She didn't want them to damage him. Arms tight around each other, she and I stood there. Men with guns escorted men with a stretcher. Minutes later they took him out. We walked forward. He was strapped down, handcuffed, ankles manacled.

Claire stepped over to him, as did I. He had begun to wake up. She clasped his hand.

'Mace, I'm sorry.'

His bleary eyes didn't focus. I looked down and couldn't hate him. His gaze found me.

He mumbled, 'Sorry, mate.'

I suppose I should have made some gesture – touched his shoulder perhaps. I didn't.

The police wanted Claire at the station. I objected. And objected again. That battle lasted almost an hour. Claire, wrapped in anoraks and blankets on one of the hottest nights of the summer, sat shivering and weeping in the van like a destroyed creature. Someone had screwed up – no ambulance arrived.

Strange people appeared. The police deferred to one man. Younger than me, bland and quick of speech, he carried some huge clout. Home Office civil servant, I reckoned; he never spoke to me.

I bargained with him through Earby. My wife's astuteness, I said loudly, saved lives. They demanded undertakings from me. When he overheard me asking Directory Enquiries for Raymond Colville's number the bland man gave in. Colville had been MI5's house doctor. I had known him since he rebuilt his house. His past services to me saved lives. I took Claire to him last year when we got her back from the Berlin gang.

We put her to bed in the London Clinic at three o'clock in the morning. Colville met me there. The clinic fixed me a bed in Claire's room. Colville, after close examination, gave her a gentle but heavy sedative – and found a large drink for me. Within minutes of his departure I swarmed into Claire's bed. I held her as though I might never see her again.

She said, 'That was a lovely letter.' She kissed me. 'Nicholas, I'm sorry.'

I put a finger to her lips. And dared sleep only when she did. I told the night nurse to call me at seven – not enough sleep but I wanted to be awake before Claire.

The police had asked to talk to her as soon as possible; I had said, 'When she's ready.'

So much to do, so much to work through. Would we go back to Rye – could she bear to? Would we live there again, unhaunted? Earby had sealed the house. This, the aftermath, ran the greatest risk of media force. I wished to avoid that.

And the court hearings to face – all of that, with Claire the leading witness. It won't happen for many months but what effect will it have on her? Will Mason Quinn's lawyers trawl Claire's past? How far back into hell had she already gone? In the ambulance she tried to call her-self 'calm'.

Something else she said shrank me: 'I kept on hoping you'd come crashing through the window to rescue me.'

52

Cowardice kept me awake. I hadn't done a thing. Which didn't surprise me. But look at what my cowardice had caused. Had I confronted Strafe headlong and behaved with some balls – none of this might have happened.

And cowardice carried me up to the next level. I no longer have to feel a failure. It's over. The Mason Quinn connection will sink Richard Strafe. That's him cancelled. The relief! When will they arrest clammy Roy Jewell? Now we'll know whether he's smiling or sneering. And when, after that, will they arrest Strafe? I can testify in Mason Quinn's trial, that's what I can do – but how will that affect my business, my reputation?

Claire woke at ten. By then I'd fielded two calls from Earby's team. First they wanted to see Claire. I told them to call Colville. Their second call apologized for the first. Colville had clouted them with his MI5 friends.

I told her this as she sat up. She got astride everything straight away.

'Thank God that's over.' She yawned.

'How did you know it was?'

'I woke during the night and saw you asleep.'

'Why didn't you wake me?'

She smiled. 'It was enough to see you. I went back to sleep.'

'How are you feeling?'

She grinned. 'Better than I thought I should.'

'Isn't it all so weird?'

'Weird,' she agreed.

'How do you think he'll feel?' Couldn't put Mason Quinn's name in my mouth.

'That, Nicholas, is something we'll have to face. He'll forever be obsessed with me, I fear.'

'So if you needed him to testify to anything –'

But a nurse interrupted and fetched me to the telephone and Earby greeted me and enquired as to Claire's health and mine and we murmured one or two words about the extraordinariness of it all and we agreed to meet as soon as possible – and then he stunned me.

'The young man.'

'Yes?'

'He died during the night.'

I don't believe this.

'Convulsions and a heart attack. That's the first report. Post-mortem this afternoon.'

'What happened?' This is dreadful.

'Nothing much. His lawyer came and went. Perfectly civil, the whole thing. Then this morning – found dead.'

'Did he say anything?'

This is devastating.

'No. We hadn't taken a statement. Hadn't even charged him. We were going to start in on him this morning. So there we are. Nice neat end in a way. Don't wish to be callous, sir, but your wife won't have the ordeal of court.'

'Yes, of course.'

Jesus! Our lifeline gone! Our shield against Strafe! Hammered by the gods. Plus I had to field Claire's reaction.

'Trouble?' she asked.

'Yes.' Play it straight with her, every doctor and psychologist had told me.

'What's up?' – her oblique voice.

'Mason Quinn.'

'Don't tell me, let me guess. He's dead.'

'How did you know?'

305

'I knew when you went to the telephone, I thought, "Mason's dead."'

'My God.' I had nothing else to say.

She sighed. 'It could have been me. Or I might have killed him.'

'You okay?'

Claire said, 'Relieved. Ten years in jail, he'd still have been after me.'

I decided to postpone telling her about the bike and Clay Massey's death.

Thereafter the day passed in a half-blur – of Colville, flowers from the police at Rye (for Claire, not me), a call to Colson's to tell them I still needed the suite (they said a newspaper had been sniffing for me) and some dozing by both of us.

Claire looked amazing – fresh and sharp and together. For long stretches of time I sat near her, taking us down from all that happened. We held hands tight.

I kept saying, 'Extraordinary business!' My vocabulary seemed stuck on that phrase: my delaying brain had put Strafe on hold. 'Extraordinary business.'

'D'you think we might live abroad?' she asked.

'Are you worrying?'

'We do seem to attract problems.'

I said, 'Maybe we should stay and change that.'

'Abroad is different,' she said. 'It breaks connections.'

'The outer life mirrors what's going on inside us. I'm certain it does.'

'What does that tell us?' She stroked my hand.

'In my case it tells me I haven't faced up squarely enough.'

'To what?'

'To what's wrong with me.'

She asked softly, as though afraid of intruding, 'And what do you think is wrong with you?'

'I don't know. And that's the core of the problem. It's

probably why I fell in love with you. Somehow I must have believed that through you I'd find out what was wrong with me.'

She didn't say to me, 'There's nothing wrong with you.'

She didn't say, 'You're too hard on yourself.'

She didn't say, 'I don't find you too wrong.'

Claire, many things, some difficult, was never fatuous.

We decided on three more days in the clinic. If, after that, she needed more care – fine. The nurses organized a hairdresser, a beautician, a masseuse. We went out for lunch once; en route she bought a blue linen dress in Marylebone High Street.

That afternoon a massive thunderstorm broke over London. The lightning danced like a savage along the sky. When the rain hit the windows Claire said, 'That's it, that's the end of it,' and fell asleep as suddenly and finally as a full stop.

I stood at the window, liking the force of the weather. To the west, sulphur-yellow clouds boiled in the sky. Overhead, the black canopy passed on its way out to the North Sea. Using the Thames as a guide I followed it in my mind – Westminster, Tower Bridge, Greenwich, the Thames Barrier, the estuary, Chatham and Gillingham, the Isle of Sheppey.

I thought, Perhaps it won't die over the sea as storms do. Perhaps it will go on – across Holland, across Germany, into Poland. Out there it will pound its thick rain into the earth. Earth that holds the remains in bone and ash of the ancestors of my wife – whose shame at their fate still cripples her.

By the time the storm finished I knew what I meant to do. What I had to do. What I should have done before.

53

The media never got the story. They tried – and tried hard. Whatever they ran lacked detail. Nobody leaked – and the bystanders they questioned in Rye had no details. I returned no calls. Journalists rang the office. All callers were referred to the police in Rye. I told Lemon to close down all questions. From inside as well as out. It died before it was born.

We called Claire's parents from the flat. Fran, no fool, said she'd been worried. Massive deception needed – we had 'been to France and Claire caught a bug'.

My mind scarcely encompassed it – had we been through all of that and nobody knew? One day we might tell them. Or might not.

Practical problems. The car's in Rye. We both need clothes. When will the police have done with the house? Colson's must be paid. Our suitcases remain there.

I wanted not to go to Rye; I wanted – I *needed* – not to let Claire from my sight.

Mrs Lydiard took over. Her son drove my car with our suitcases to London. I met them at the flat, began to regroup our lives. Then, Mrs Lydiard staying with Claire until Lucinda arrived, I reached for Ruby.

We met in a pub on Peter Street. She looked frail and closed. I thanked her for coming to see me, told her the outcome. She said nothing, smoked five cigarettes in half an hour, lighting one off the other.

It seemed she didn't want to speak to me. After a while she asked, 'The young man. How do you feel?'

'I'm glad. Dreadful, I know.'

She dragged on her cigarette. 'You mustn't say things like that, darling' – and turned her face away from me.

We sat there for several minutes. I tried to break through her barrier.

'Ruby, I still have – there still is – there remains – the matter –' I kept hesitating but my determination to say it drove me on. 'Strafe. I have to address it.'

'Please, darling. Please don't say anything.'

'I must tell the police.'

She shuddered. 'That will involve me, darling.'

'But Ruby –'

She rose in mid-cigarette. We walked out into the street. I took her arm but I felt it tighten in refusal.

'Ruby, would you like to come back with me? Meet Claire. We'll all have dinner.'

'I need a cab, darling. May I call you?'

'If you need anything, Ruby.'

She climbed into the cab and neither waved nor looked back at me. My heart hurt. But I felt some relief, too. What if she'd rhapsodized? What if she'd said she wanted to carry on where we'd left off in Rye?

The evening lightened when I fetched Claire from the clinic. She had invited Lucinda for supper. My intuition, a scalpel since Rye, said, Safe for the moment. Tonight we go to Aylesbury and hide there. By the time we resumed normal life I believed everything would be settled, with Strafe neutered, or afraid to move or, with luck, under charges.

I said, 'Lucinda, you do indeed have golden eyes.'

'And that's all you're allowed to confirm,' Claire hissed with a grin. She brought Lucinda into the joke. Who then reported on Bentley Newman.

Hal had fallen for Lucinda, to Ms Strait's disgust. The air hung with Hal's 'innocent' questions – boyfriends, tastes, ambitions. Lucinda played the role of ingénue, 'desperately interested' in architecture, 'hoping' to become a draughtsman, in time 'rise to' the rest of the qualifications. Hal couldn't believe his luck.

She was timing it, she said. At the moment (she told Hal) she'd stay on the south coast. But 'a friend had asked her to house-sit' in London. Hal's beady eyes, she said, 'glinted like bottle-tops'. Lucinda also had a nice line in phrase-making.

I asked openly about Strafe. His office had been evasive. While I was 'ill', Lucinda said, he had called once, then not at all.

Claire fidgeted. I dropped the subject.

Lucinda caught a train home. Claire and I drove to Aylesbury. We seemed cheerful and thoughtful. I checked the street outside, the car's underside, my mirrors. Nobody followed us. The night streets lay quiet in the heat of the summer.

Claire said, 'May I ask a favour?'

'Anything. Turkish delight. The perfumes of Arabia. Diamonds –'

She interrupted, 'Dearly bought for ladies, I've got those.' I waited. She said, 'Could you take the motorway?'

I looked at her. Claire's the eternal passenger, never shows the slightest interest how we go.

'Sure. Any particular reason?'

'In case you need to drive very fast.'

'Claire?'

'You mean – explain.'

'Well – yes.'

She said, 'Mason told me.'

'Told you what?'

'Everything. While we were watching television. He reckoned the house might get bugged. That's why he went wild about the telephone, so he told me with the television sound turned up.'

310

'What did he tell you?'

'He told me Strafe had sent him to kill me. Completely bluntly. Told him I had stolen from Strafe. Seduced him and cheated him.'

'I feel I should stop the car.'

'He knew you knew.'

'Were you terrified?'

'No, Nicholas. I knew Mason wouldn't kill me.'

'Are you terrified now?'

'No, Nicholas.'

'But –'

'You're going to say we have no witness, no evidence. Leaving Strafe free to do as he wishes. But no, I'm not terrified. I'm alert, but that's different.'

'Why aren't you terrified?'

'Because, Nicholas, I know you'll kill anyone who wants to harm me.'

54

We grow, if we're lucky, in front of our own eyes. For many years I doodled question marks. This led to a long phase of boxes. Then geometrics, then pine-cones, then animals. The change was visible. Ditto the great inner questions. We all have, I expect, one recurrent question we ask ourselves. It changes as we mature, as we have breakthroughs – or breakdowns. My earliest recurring question (and it stayed with me for years) ran something like, 'Will this ever get better?'

I grew a little when I found the question had become, 'How can I make this better?' The breakthrough didn't feel immediate. But something profound altered in me – and it lasted.

Since marrying Claire the question had settled down to, 'Where do we go from here?' This was its best form so far. Practical. Accommodating. Useful. Encouraging. It brought me onto the best plateau I have patrolled – the plateau of 'Do the next thing'.

The 'next thing' now came easily to me. With Claire safe among her parents, on the following morning I drove from Aylesbury to Butler's Wharf and rang the bell of Richard Strafe's apartment.

A man's voice called through the intercom, 'Who is it?'

'Nicholas Newman to see Richard Strafe.'

The words sounded as if they strolled from my lips. But I should say that in the car my face had been a sheet of water. I needed long minutes of composing myself when I parked.

'He's not here.'

'Where is he, please?'

'I don't know.' The intercom clicked off.

Press it again. Hard and long. 'Yes?'

'I want to see Richard Strafe, please.'

'He's not here.' Then a woman's voice cut in. 'Who is this?'

'Nicholas Newman to see Richard Strafe.' This felt mildly farcical.

The buzzer opened the outer door and they opened the inner. I recognized the man (as I expected to) from Montreux. The woman was the PA whom I had seen the night I spied here.

Tightening the muscles of my jaw (and of my sphincter), I strode at them: 'Where is he?'

Neither knew what to do.

'He's not here,' she said, an attractive, jittery woman with pearl-drop earrings.

'He won't be,' the man said in an accent so thick it delayed the meaning of his words.

Behind them the room looked like a packing operation. My hopes soared a little – not a lot, this needs caution.

'I need to see him.'

'We don't know where he is,' she said.

In truth I hadn't expected to find Strafe there. But I wanted him to know I was looking for him.

Next stop his office. The receptionist knew me. No, Strafe had not yet arrived.

'Is he expected?'

She called through and relayed to me, 'No. Not today.'

'I need him urgently.'

But nobody could find him. In the car I puzzled, then rang Ed Melchior, who proved perfectly happy to give me Diana Strafe's number and address.

'Oh!' she said, when I rang the doorbell. 'Come in!'

Competent woman; integrated and organized. She looked me up and down.

'I wondered whether I might see you again.'

She didn't waste time enquiring where I found her address; simply poured coffee and sat down.

'You want either Richard or me – and I know which I'd prefer it to be. Not that you should take that as flattery.'

Dry, hard humour. I bet she was too much for Strafe.

'Richard, I fear,' I said, trying to keep it as light as possible.

'You've seen the papers?'

'No-o?'

What bombshell now?

'He's been answering questions. But being Richard nothing will stick. Shareholders won't like it, though.' Then she said impatiently, 'What's he doing hiring young tearaways with drug problems?'

'Eh?'

'Gossip. His finance director has admitted to some dirty work. Some young thug they hired has just died of an overdose.'

The spin materialized: Roy Jewell, the company secretary, will take the fall.

I said, 'How much do you know about Richard's wider world?'

Diana Strafe said, 'Nothing.'

'I need to see him.'

She shifted.

'I need to see him urgently.'

Another shift. 'I don't know where he is.'

'If I don't see him this will get worse. I've been to Berlin recently. And Switzerland.'

Strong conduct: she did not look afraid and she did not come on to me.

'He's in the Ritz,' she said. 'In the Pelican Suite. I don't care if you tell him I told you. But I prefer not to have him contact me.'

'Point taken.'

She wanted to say something else. I sat silent. She looked at me.

'What's Richard's great gift?' she asked.

I had some wry thoughts I could have offered her.

'Business?' I suggested. 'Genius for property.'

'But what's the gift behind the gift? Everyone has one.'

I said, 'That's several hours of conversation.'

'Richard's true gift is for capitalizing on disaffection. All bullies have it.' Diana Strafe dismissed me. 'I think I've told you enough.'

More than enough. At the Ritz, Strafe himself opened the door because he had been expecting me and said so.

'Putting yourself about today, Nicholas?'

Odd: he seemed quieter, almost a touch mellow.

'Looking for you.'

'And you found me. How are you, Nicholas?'

He beamed at me – in another mode, at another time, I'd have done anything for this man. The day he invited me to sit on his board I left his office floating a little, thrilled at his wanting me.

I looked at him across the ormolu desk. The suite doubled as a posh office.

'It's over,' I said. 'I've come to end it.'

He beamed, like a delighted child. 'I haven't the faintest idea what you're talking about.'

I know those shirts – that tiny herringbone white-on-white from Camiceria SanMarco in Venice. One cufflink said 'O' and the other 'K'. Time for a wry joke.

'O.K., Strafe – stop.'

His eyes never narrowed. Nor did he flinch in any way. He laid his hands like a priest on his desk. And simply smiled.

'Stop what, Nicholas?'

'The police have been questioning you. I've been to Berlin. I know about Zurück. And, as you know, I've been to Switzerland.'

'So you have!'

'So you admit it.'

'So you told me!' He beamed again, like someone enjoying my company. 'I'm glad you called, Nicholas. I was going to write to you. But I can tell you now. I'm moving some of my operation to Spain. Oh, not for ever. And Spain's not so far away, is it?'

Strafe didn't swear that morning, didn't show his bully-bluster side. He remained elegant, poised and powerful – considerate, with just the right level of regret.

'Listen to me, Nicholas,' he said and he walked around the desk to sit in the armchair next to mine. 'I owe you an apology.'

A chink? A crack with light coming through?

Strafe said, allowing himself to show some fake discomfort, 'I can be unparliamentary in my speech. I've been too overt about your wife. Meant as a compliment, you understand.'

Those eyelids – the way they drooped. He's a crocodile.

I rasped, 'Tell me about Magda Zemendstrasse.'

'That's why you're such a good architect! You do your research. I was born there. Number one hundred and eighty-three.'

'And Ruby Hamer?'

'Dear Ruby. I'm like all men – I like women. Sometimes I can only deal with them impersonally. Isn't that why clubs like Ruby's – and indeed women like Ruby – exist?'

He sat back, relaxed and expansive. Not that I'm any judge but I believe no psychologist in the world could have faulted his body language. I never took my eyes off him – but as I'm no mongoose, not for a second did he look uncomfortable.

'Why did you want to kill Claire?'

316

Not a flicker. 'Do you know who your wife reminds me of? What's that actress, the very beautiful one. I can't remember her name –'

'When are you leaving?' I cut in.

'Ohhh – I don't know. Perhaps at the weekend. I've got some property down there ready for me. A friend of mine is driving down from Arles to see to it.' He looked at his watch. 'In fact, she should be at the Spanish border by now. Wonderful thing about driving in Europe, when you come across a road border between two great nations. So exciting.'

I asked, 'Are you relinquishing your interests here?'

'Good God, no! Now, Nicholas, why would I do a thing like that?'

'Strafe – you must NOT come back. And the chateau is ours. And my wife – is mine.'

I tried to say it levelly and I tried to say it with force and I tried to say it like a man who would kill for the thing he loved. But Strafe laughed, in that pleasing, inspiring way of his.

'My dear Nicholas, I do like you.' He reached out and touched my arm.

On his desk lay a stiletto paper knife. I can move very fast when I want.

I didn't. Instead I said, 'I know what you've done. You've understood that many people won't want the Jews to reclaim the confiscated properties and therefore the existing "owners" would rather sell at a loss than surrender their anti-Semitism.'

He leaned forward to interrupt. I said, 'Shut up!'

Strafe looked at me, a hooded and different look.

I hammered on. 'This was not so much Kaltenbrunner as commerce. You've been buying up these "bargains" knowing you'll have to be compensated. Knowing you have enough money to mount legal challenges. You might even be successful. But you'll certainly sap the energy of the claimants. And you'll get something out of it. In other words, Richard, you've found yourself a scam. And Clay Massey knew it. He knew it was going on – he may even have joined your board of directors to track how you did it.'

Strafe sat back; I had said my say; all the truth had come tumbling out. Although I had been guided to the rudiments of his operation down that whispering tunnel in Caux, I didn't quite know that I knew so much. Diana Strafe had finally unlocked it. As her husband might have said, Wives can be lethal.

I looked across at him. He was gazing straight ahead, into the glowing room.

'Come on, Richard. It's over.' I put all my urgency into the words.

'Oh, Nicholas, you are so lurid.'

55

I said to Claire that night, 'Strafe's gone. Or going.'

She looked sceptical and afraid.

I said, 'It's true. Shareholders have more force than police, it seems.'

Claire said, 'But he's still alive.'

At dinner she sparkled – but I reckoned it a show put on for her parents. In bed she turned to me, buried her face in my chest and said not a word. We had not made love since the events of Rye. Nor did we make love that night, nor any of the next ten nights we stayed in Aylesbury. In fact we had little exchange that meant anything. She slept a lot and we spent the evenings with her parents.

We all went out to dinner once, to lunch once and then Claire and I went out to dinner together. Always, she controlled the conversation, kept it to light matters.

I went to Rye the second weekend. Claire needed clothes and I needed to see the house, to see Mrs Lydiard, to gauge how far we remained from restarting our life. The police wanted some details – exact dates and times, damage done in case of a claim, general background. Dennis had called a number of times; 'Little invoice here, Mr Newman, be most grateful, eck cetera.'

I hate it when people say *eck* instead of *et* cetera; I hate it when people say 'pacific' instead of 'specific'.

When I met Earby again, I marvelled that I had ever felt so dependent on such an awkward man. And when I saw the house again I marvelled at Mrs Lydiard. She had removed not just the physical traces but the very *feeling* that anyone had intruded.

New spectacles she had, red frames. She said to me, 'I heard wonderful things. About you.'

'Oh?'

She smiled, 'Oh, yes.' Then she whispered, 'The police are dreadful gossips, you know. Worse than hoteliers. And they said you were so good about it all.'

'Mrs Lydiard, I sometimes think it never happened. That I dreamed it.'

'Why don't you take a little break?'

'Where would you go, Mrs Lydiard?'

'Well, my old boss, Mr Hilton – he said that there was only one place a hotelier could have a holiday and that was San Tropp, he used to call it.'

'Mrs Lydiard – what a good idea.'

I rang Claire, who said, 'Lovely, but I'd like to spend a night or two at home first.' She confused me for a moment – and just as I was about to remind her she was at home, she said, 'I mean our home.'

Her use of the word 'home' thrilled me and I burbled, 'You can't believe how well Mrs Lydiard's done things.'

But Claire, I felt, would see ghosts here. As would I. I already knew what my ghosts looked like – those wretched screens, that wretched van, the grey naked shapes of Claire and Mason Quinn and, in the guilty darkness, Ruby.

Whom I now rang; she's always at the club on Saturday afternoons. A man answered and Ruby took the phone.

'Hello, darling.'

'Ruby – are you all right?'

'Yes, darling,' but she sounded terribly flat.

'I'd love to give you a holiday, Ruby.'

'Thank you, darling, but – you know, the club.'

'Strafe's pulling out – has probably left by now.'

'That's good, darling.'

'Wouldn't you like a break, Ruby?'

'Are you taking one, darling?'

320

'Thinking of St-Tropez. Next week, probably. Look, Ruby – I really would love to give you a treat. Why not take a break?'

'I can't, darling.'

'Lunch, then?'

'Leave it a bit, darling.'

'Your lease? What's happening?'

'Darling, I'm sorry, I have to go, I'm auditioning pianists – all right?'

56

Delayed reactions protect us. They allow us to retain objectivity just as the pressure comes on. Give us time to regroup. To prepare our response. To cope. If I could, I would urge all the people I value to develop delayed reactions. I would also warn them. When the time comes for the deferral to end – expect to be hit with force.

Mrs Lydiard left the house. I was standing in the window of the Long Drawing Room. Maybe that's why I reacted so heavily. It seems fair to suspect myself of timing these things, the ultimate control freak. Certainly it frees me to have any reaction I want when nobody's looking – tears, sweats, confusions. I sat down and let it roll over me. Including – again – the remorse of having slept with Ruby.

It took an hour or so. I felt some relief. Except from the guilt. I said to myself, You've smeared things. You must do something to repent, to atone. I couldn't clinch the thought – because another feeling, larger and more menacing, lurked somewhere. I identified it as rage and I gave it full rein to see where it was taking me – I saw myself from overhead, filmed myself like a camera. The guilt and the rage had some connection to each other and to my cowardice.

I phoned Claire.

'How would you feel if I stayed in Rye tonight?'

'I'll be fine.'

'Would you mind?'

Dine at Colson's. Thank them as fully as I needed. Unwind. Restore my possessions to myself. Restore myself. Then take action. Somehow I knew everything that would now happen.

For a time I wandered around the house. The damaged telephone socket had been replaced. No trace of any other damage. I checked the chimney-breast, which had taken two rounds of ammunition. It seemed black and content, usual quota of soot. I didn't look too closely. Illusions also help.

Was there a smell in the air? Fear's odour? I unlocked and peeled back all the grilles. Opened every window. The curtains billowed in like a bride.

At eight I went to Colson's. Outside Henry James's house a party of Japanese listened to a guide. I wondered what they made of the orotund Mr James and tried to remember my tutor's rhyme.

'Claire?' Good signal on the mobile.

'Hello.'

'What was that rhyme – d'you remember? "In Heaven there'll be no algebra" – we talked about it once.'

She continued it. '"No learning dates or names. But only playing golden harps –"'

I chimed in: '". . . And reading Henry James."'

We laughed.

'Claire, I love you.'

'Nicholas, I love you.'

Twelve Whitstable oysters and thick brown bread. Mason Quinn saw Claire naked and held a gun to her face. Did he also fu— *No, kill that thought*. Loin of lamb with mint leaves and a redcurrant jelly that was more tart than I expected. I slept with Ruby, broke my solemnest vow to myself – of fidelity. Then a deep Stilton with digestive biscuits. And a syllabub as big as my head. Who caused all this to happen?

The inn was quiet. I drank no wine. A sober couple, staying for the weekend, sat at the next table and talked about her mother. Among the darkening tables and the deep panelling a zing began. I knew that sound – the zing of my antennae. Yes, this is over, or is about to be. I looked through the window and saw them as I had seen them before – in their jeans and identical trainers.

Rage scratched at me. I wanted to go out and kick them. Tell them that should they wish to go about their vile pathfinding, she shouldn't wear blouses that draw attention to her and he shouldn't limp. Also, please wear old trainers. And now that you've tracked me again as you did in Switzerland, go and tell Strafe I'm ready for him.

Instead, I paid my bill, and again thanked the Colson family on my behalf and on Claire's. As calmly as a hangman I went back to my house to sit and wait.

57

In the silence and the dusk, I read it all. Strafe could no more let me go than he could change his own blood. This had gone beyond Claire and the properties. He'd bound himself to me. In some bizarre way. Clients can be peculiar. It feels as if they resent the creativity. They may be buying it but they know they'll never own it – only the proceeds of it, but that's not the thing itself.

Strafe's advance upon Claire had more tangible reasons. Property. Money. Sex. The usual reasons people kill people. In his case his great scam also sprang from a birthright of political evil, evil not yet described fully enough, not yet explained deeply enough.

Those motives, though, had a disposability; he could give them up. As the Mafia say, 'It's only business.' He couldn't give up the reasons he wanted me – he didn't even know what they were. I'm not sure he'd have understood them.

I can stab at it; I can say that Strafe locked on to what he couldn't have. A psychopath, certainly, but was he any more psychopathic than many a captain of industry? Check out one characteristic of success – 'charm'.

Strafe's murderousness was different. That roared into action when someone threatened his wealth-base – hence Zurück. But with me he had nothing tangible. He didn't want me for what I am, Nicholas, the man, Newman, the human being. At some level Strafe wanted my taste, my aesthetic sense, my creativity. I doubt he'd have put it like that. He could see that I owned some kind of force and he could hire it, pay for it. But he couldn't reach out and grasp it and take it into himself, to have and to hold. And therefore if he couldn't have it, nobody could. That's crude – but it's what I know.

He bound it up – never consciously – with all kinds of other things. Such as Claire. Such as the beauty of the chateau in Uzès. Look at his desire to have dinner with me and then the failure to turn up. Now I understood the puzzling moment at the board meeting when he asked me to defend his choice of tie.

I often thought about that. And I often thought about his impeccable appearance, the dandy, the beau in him. It represented, I think, an almost suicide-making need to control appearances. Since I make my living creating appearances, I triggered something in him. Perhaps I reflected him back to himself.

Unfortunately, psychopaths interest me compellingly. Therefore, perhaps I attract them. At the Ritz, Strafe did his best to tell me he had called a halt. I suppose I believe he meant it. What I hadn't allowed for was whether he could deliver it. To himself. I suspected he couldn't – that's why I wanted to stay in Rye for the night.

Strafe's invitation to join his board always puzzled me. I had no value to him as a director. He was already paying for what he bought from me, design, property and planning advice, surveying. Clay Massey queried it too, in his oblique way, referring to my silence that afternoon and my inexperience as a director at that level.

Our relationship always lacked boundaries. Strafe, not I, tore them down – he was always too familiar, too personal. Just like his father's dreadful friends tearing at the fabric of Jewish society, Strafe could not bear any place to which he was not admitted. That included my reserve. I must have seemed to possess much that he desired and envied.

If he only knew – but no point in telling him. Strafe concluded from our meeting at the Ritz he could not now, ever, deal with me again. Therefore, I guessed (and rightly), that his rage would turn first inwards and then towards me. I prepared for him. And if all his strange, psychotic reasons for liking me were not enough to produce hatred, he now had the practical, concrete fear that I could ruin his game.

My dream-house will always have its workshop. In Rye it's down beside the cellar. I had it so heavily padlocked that Mason Quinn failed to get in there. With the night still balmy and the curtains still blowing, I went down to the workshop.

I corked the neck of an empty wine bottle. Using a vice and a hammer, I broke the bottle in half, so that it had jagged edges. Turning the corked half upside down, I poured in half a cup of acid I'd once bought to experiment with copper etching.

Strafe's a vain man. Attack his face. That'll give me the swiftest victory. I thought all these thoughts and did all these things with complete serenity. No doubt, either, why I was doing it: he made me unfaithful, he made me break my promise – to myself – that I'd never betray Claire. I had done and now he'll pay. Someone has to.

When I had finished I strolled upstairs and with my free hand rang Claire goodnight. I began to switch off the lights. My last act took me to the Square Drawing Room, where I sat in the dark, the jagged, upturned half-bottle of acid in my hand, waiting rubber-gloved by the open window.

Strafe came when the church chimed two, when the owls had taken a break, when not a sound nor a puff of wind roughed the night. I heard the growl of the Porsche. He cut the engine and coasted in. He cut the lights too; he must be some driver – that corner of the square's very dark. Or else he knows the square.

I had no fear – none at all. Just a kind of deadly cold. Perhaps there's a psychopath in me too. 'Sociopath' the Americans call it. I watched him through the window, knowing he couldn't see me. He looked at the parked Saab, then the house; he leaned on the corner like Harry Lime but he didn't strike a match. Instead, he found the time-switch on the street lamp. I tried to remember. Sometimes those timers control just one lamp standard, sometimes six. This one controlled six and Strafe caused darkness.

Who's the advantaged one? My eyes focused quickly, therefore I've got the edge – from sitting, waiting, in the dark. Strafe moved and I saw him. I had him completely tracked.

My problem lay in how he'd approach. That depended on how much he felt in control. I guessed he'd want this to be quick; anonymous, therefore surgical. What weapon? He carried nothing. Didn't need to – his hands once throttled an Alsatian dog on a beach.

And what point of entry? I meant to entice him; doors double-locked but two windows and their grilles open. That seemed psychologically predictable of me. He would think I meant to air the house. And he would believe I had thought him gone to Spain. I enticed him to one of two entries: the upstairs bay, easily reachable from the flat roof. Or, better, the ground-floor front window four feet from where I sat.

A breeze blew the curtain and Strafe stopped to check. He reached the Saab, on which he laid a hand. Perhaps he's not coming, perhaps he's going to nobble my car. No, he's coming; I know the shape of his confidence. He stepped onto the grass – sensible; I'd have done the same.

Sound of breathing – but it's my breathing. I cool it and breathe through my nose. In. Take a count of seven to do it. Draw the cold air up through my nostrils. Hold it in for seven. Exhale – through my nose – for a count of seven. Keep doing it. Inside my mouth I count my top teeth with my tongue. I am so cool. No brine in my eyes now, although my hair's a swamp.

Strafe stops on the lawn. He's two yards from my window.

I know what he considered – he considered it almost too inviting. His next move will reveal his true opinion of me.

Not a very high opinion, evidently. He came willingly to the open window. This is telling me he doesn't believe I could play such chess. He turned his back and looked all around him. I could have told him – no worries, chum, nobody'll see you. He looked to the house again, then looked down. In my mind I'm saying to him, Come on, Strafe, there's a little coping down there, see it, there's a border, you can lever yourself up via that, the sill's not very high and anyway you do all those heroic press-ups, you'll be well capable.

As though he heard me he looked down at the coping. Then he looked up again and tried to peer into the room. I couldn't be seen; I had made certain of that; I was standing now, to one side, in the lee of the room behind the bay window's groyne. He will climb in now, then he'll take a moment to get his bearings. A sudden flash: irrelevant detail from one of the claim forms in Claire's folder: Nazis got compensated for any repairs they did to the properties they confiscated. Jesus – what a nerve.

There's a light somewhere. It's the porch light two doors away. In its glow I can see Strafe's nose, the shadows of his eyes. He's about to clamber. Has he worked out where I'm 'asleep'? Mason Quinn will have telephoned him in the days before the siege with all the details of the house.

I know when to move. I'll move when he's halfway into the room, at that heaving, fulcrum moment when he's across the sill, neither in nor out. He takes one last look around; come on, Strafe, you don't need to look around, there was a siege here last month and they still don't know about it, these people keep themselves to themselves.

He decided – and hauled himself up. The curtains swished a little about his huge head and he parted them while checking his balance and the depth of drop into the room inside. I struck. Bottle and acid. The attack had to include both – in his face and neck, acid followed by bottle. Blind him and sever the jugular all at once. I missed. Caught his shoulder – but the acid splashed up into his face. I was pleased that he screamed.

58

I've been told that psychopaths flee the danger they create.
Strafe ran. He ran diagonally; he's heading for his car. NO!
he's not getting away, I want him, I want him DEAD!
I want him stone, fucking dead! This bastard made me
betray Claire!

The acid burned the curtains. I could smell it.

Strafe's a fit man. My car's nearer. His car's faster. He's
roaring away, lights full on – and now I'm in the Saab and I
know Rye better than him. Okay, Strafe. He's down the hill
at the train station and he veers right, fuck, why's he done
that and not the London road? Because he doesn't know
the way and he's confused, that's why.

For half a mile now he's going to be under the town lights.
But, by the same token, so am I. What's the rule the Free
French told my father – Wherever you are, whatever you're
doing, keep the enemy in your sights.

I know where he's going, he's heading for the A259
which means he's heading for the A2070 which means
he's heading for the M20 which means he's heading for
London or the Channel Tunnel.

He's turned off. To the right. But that's Camber – and
Camber's nowhere. And that's Lydd and there's nothing in
Lydd except the little airport and that's closed at this hour.
He's driving like the hammers of Hell. Good driver. But he's
taken the wrong road because I can see him all the way.

Hell! Strafe flies aircraft. Boy's comics and boats for the
coast of France and small planes waiting in the dark. Strafe's
got one waiting. I see him. He's half a mile ahead and racing,

racing. A Porsche keeps the driver close to the road: the tarmac enters your coccyx. A Saab keeps you higher, you can see farther. Strafe uses all the road and he can afford to because tonight not so much as a candle lights the sky.

On this road every Sunday and now almost every day you can see the little covens of birdwatchers with their innocent binoculars twitching the sky for new hope, or the coming of the Messiah. Meaning the lesser bustards and crested larks that are now breeding in the north of France (if the French haven't shot them all on Sunday mornings). I sometimes stop and watch, too; down here we get the lovely mathematics of starlings and gulls.

It *is* Lydd! My schoolboy comics were right – he's going to Lydd airport! He swings right like a jackknife and he's roaring up the little scrub road – he's doing well over a hundred. I could have waited and watched. By now I don't think I want him. By now he's gone for ever. He will leave us alone, I've defiled him, broken his mirror. But the fancy of a small aircraft hooked me and I followed at a distance.

If there is a small plane – I can't stop him. Makes sense too, fly to France, then down to Spain. Follow, watch and wait.

Strafe's lights lit the forecourt. In the little terminal building there's a dim security bulb. The Porsche's beams now light the restaurant: *Biggles*: *Family Lunch on Sundays*. Strafe races off the forecourt apron down the rough ground by the fence. He's looking for an opening. I know he won't find one and he knows I know, because he sees that I've stopped beside Biggles.

He stops too, he gets out of the Porsche. I watch him. He looks through the fence, he looks back at me. If he's thinking of getting through there I'll nail him – I'll nail him with the car, or by kicking him into submission. Aha! So I do want him! He comes back from the fence. This is one agitated man. I feel a flash of disappointment; I wanted him tougher than this. He wheels the car round and the rough ground does its axles no favours.

Slower than he went down by the fence, Strafe comes back. What's this? He's driving towards me. I'm parked head-on to him so that I can keep my beams on him and he comes at me. He swerves in front of me, accelerates past the nose of the Saab and I'm too late – he throws something and shatters my windscreen. Shittttt! A wrench from a toolkit. Nicholas, you stupid, stupid man! I've got shards of safety glass all over me. Quit this. Go home.

Strafe's gone. I see his tail-lights turn right at the bottom of the road. The wrench landed through the passenger side. Did he hope Claire might be with me? That refuelled me. I hauled and punched at the sagging, shivered screen in front of me, hammered a socket in it with my clothed forearm and, frozen by a blast of the summer wind, revved the Saab and took off.

No sign. He's gone to Romney. And then he's heading up to the M20.

You fool, Strafe! Never try to lose a man who knows his way around a blueprint, because there's a good chance he'll know his way around a map and I know this flat hinterland like I know my own drawing board.

Like parts of my life falling away the glass keeps shivering and breaking. I cut back towards Lydd and if he sees my lights in the night sky he'll think I've given up. Then I kill my beams and cut across the marshes.

Sometimes there's a gas that comes up here at night and gives a glim. Not universal, but if it's there it haunts. If it's not, the marshes are as dark as plague. That night the glim came and went but it helped me, moonless and dimmed, halfway to Brenzett.

And I saw him again. He had slowed down. Somewhere beyond Old Romney he began to figure I had given up and he relaxed. If I turn right I can cut straight across him. I did

– but by the time I got to the larger road he had vanished. Straight over I went, looking left and right – no sign.

Down here, the tiny, flat roads bisect each other, little more than lanes, and sometimes they become farm tracks, or sometimes they open out into better roads. I know them all and I know how to get back onto the road and pace Strafe, harry him. Put the boot down like a trucker; the Saab handles well, though I loathe the car. She throws around corners, good centre of gravity, otherwise I couldn't keep her at eighty on the marsh avenues. The glim comes up again and I am travelling so fast I feel I'm in a hovercraft, skimming the ground.

I know what he's done. He glimpsed my half-lights in the fields and knew from my speed who it was. I'm freezing now. My lips are hanging numb from my face. And still the windscreen keeps dropping into my lap. Plus – I have wet myself and that's all turning cold in my crotch.

But then – the skin on the back of my neck crawls. Jesus-Jesus! Strafe's behind me. Right behind me. He's driving without lights. Using my lights to follow me. The old Mafia trick. I mean – right behind me. I mean – five feet, I mean three feet. Jesus!

I can brake. That could kill us both. I can accelerate. He's a liar, so he'll just accept the challenge. I can't get away from him, he's got a hundred and fifty in that engine, a hundred and sixty, I've got a hundred and thirty before the wheels splay.

Look down, Nicholas, do your cameraman's trick of seeing yourself from above, it always helps you. It'll help you now.

Okay, I'll look down.

I'm speeding through the countryside at night and in my slipstream there's a long, low unlit object like the fastest slug on earth keeping pace with me and matching every gear change. That's what I see – death a yard behind me.

The view from on high helps. My cameraman tells me

what to do. Drive, keep driving, stay on these roads, confuse him, he's going to miss a bend soon. Go, go for it, accelerate. Yes, he'll keep up, yes, he'll be right behind you, but the first moment he loses five yards you've dented his confidence. And you can put on your beams and enjoy this because you know he's not armed, otherwise he'd be shooting at you. I did two things at once – I switched on the beams and hit the accelerator.

He slipped, I saw him slip. Sure, he came roaring in again and now of course I could hear the Porsche through the hole in my windscreen. Christ, my face is freezing. The *Sunday Express* when I was a child had a huge story they ran for weeks about Christ's face appearing in the snows of Austria. That's what my face feels like – and that's what my windscreen looks like.

That's the gateway where Claire and I stopped – Strafe, you bastard! Twice Claire and I stopped there to make love. The first time your young thug stalked us and the second time my fear of you made me impotent. I swung the car and roared ahead.

He's there still. Every twist and turn. He's hoping to make me crash. I switched off my own lights. Don't know why I did it – but I did. Didn't know where I was going, depended on the glim and not having a windscreen to look through – and then I heard the screech of metal and the clang! and the awful, awful scraping sound.

It wasn't me. He wasn't behind me any more. I switched on my headlights again. Then I slowed down and no, he's not behind me. I stopped.

Stop, look and listen. Old highway code. On a marsh path. The night is so still I can hear the darkness.

I reversed the car into a gateway and drove slowly back. The yellow Porsche was on its roof, the wheels spinning. I stopped and kept my headlights shining. Getting out carefully. Looking all around me. Dropping to my knees to one side of the beams. Inside the Porsche I saw Strafe's head. His hand moved. This car will go up in flames any moment. I ran forward.

A smell of petrol made me cough. I got down on my knees and grabbed Strafe's collar. He knew what I was doing and he assisted by pushing upward. No seatbelt, story of his life, I guess. Haul. Haul. You can get through any space as long as your head fits through: every architectural student, police cadet and trainee housebreaker knows that. I got Strafe's head and then his shoulders out of the car window and he pushed the rest of the way.

He couldn't walk. His legs had broken. I dragged him and dragged him – to the wide grass margin, a safe distance from the Porsche. Will the tank blow? It didn't. The summer night air was warm on my iced face.

Strafe tried to get up on one elbow. Huge cut on his forehead. His shirt had ripped away and his skin underneath had savage blisters. But not the car, I realized – my acid.

He failed to lift himself. We said nothing. He tried again, failed, tried to lift his shoulders. I grasped his problem – he needed to breathe. I squatted, one knee kneeling, and held him up. He leaned back against me, gasping for air.

'Where are you injured?' I said.

'Nicholas. Trust you,' he said and wheezed a laugh.

'Save your breath.' I meant it.

He misread me. 'Don't be dramatic. That's your problem, you know.'

He heaved and wheezed.

'I told you it was over,' I said. 'Why didn't you stop?'

'Don't leave me here.'

I continued to squat. He put his head against my shoulder. Tried to ease his limbs. I have a thousand questions to ask him. Minutes passed. He pressed heavier against me, his entire posture asking for comfort.

'Take it easy, Richard. I'll call an ambulance.'

'Don't go.'

He caught my hand and put it to his cheek. I kept it there.

'Nicholas. It wasn't all – I wasn't all – I –'

He didn't finish it. I didn't know what he meant.

His left hand came round, clawing for me. The cufflink on the torn, flapping sleeve said 'No'. The other one probably said 'Yes'. I let him grip my arm and then he clawed again and I took his hand.

'Nicholas. Whose voice do you – ?'

His mind had begun to wander. No grip. No grip in the hand that half an hour earlier intended to crush my throat. He held my hand like a girl. Or a child.

'This was so wrong,' I said. 'All so wrong.'

'Some of us –' he tried to say something. 'Some of us – My father –'

'Easy, Richard.' Be kind to him. Can always be harsh to him later. If there is a later. 'Take it easy. Rest a little.'

'My head's sore.'

'I'll get some help sorted. Rest first.' I pushed open his neckband a little, made his head more comfortable. His mouth opened again, like a goldfish. He was desperate to speak. I stroked his hair.

'Nicholas, stay with me –'

I thought, Nothing changes.

His fingers with their square fingertips tightened on my hand. But then he began to shake and rasp. The skin tones changed. He heaved the barrel of his torso. Heart attack!

I lowered his head to the grass, spread him, ripped open his shirt, began to press but he tried to scream – the pressure I was exerting to save his heart burst the blisters inflicted by the acid. He clutched again.

'Don't.' He clawed for my hand.

He said, 'Nicholas.' Then, with perfect lucidity, 'It's beautifully quiet out here, isn't it?' Then he asked, 'Isn't it quiet here, Nicholas?'

And then he died. No movement, just a tiny loll of the head. Somewhere a bird cries a faint 'awk' and I know it's also the sound of Richard Strafe's soul leaving his body.

I went on holding his hand for about – how long? – five minutes. Didn't know what else to do. His jaw was falling slack. Blood on his forehead. In a bed somewhere, warm and, I hope, calm, Claire lies safe. My eyes filled with tears. If these tears fall they'll be for all of us . . .

Somewhere a light climbed the sky and behind me a car drove across the marshes. It saw my headlights and the upturned Porsche. A young couple got out, homecoming from somewhere more convivial than this great, grey graveyard.

The young man said, 'Oh-ah!' and called to his girlfriend, 'Stay where you are.' He said to me, 'Sir?' – and nothing else. I was still kneeling cradling Strafe's head.

An hour later I walked through my own front door. The phone rang.

Claire said, 'I couldn't sleep. I was worried about you. I rang and rang. I hope you're all right.'

For a bitter moment I found myself counting and saying to myself but not to her – Darling Claire, you've spoken four consecutive sentences beginning with the letter *I*.

But I didn't say it.

Instead I said, 'I was restless so I went out for a drive on the marshes.' Then I said, my voice cracking open, 'Claire, Jesus-God, he's dead, he's just died.'

59

Claire is pulling on stockings. She draws them slowly up each leg. I can't bear it and she knows it and she grins.

'And to cheer you up even more,' she says. 'Guess what's happening this afternoon?'

'Tell me.'

She blew a trumpet sound and said, 'Lucinda – with the golden eyes – and the nice line in oral sex – is taking Hal – to her bed. Da-rah!'

'No?!'

'Yesss!'

'How come?'

'He goes to football on Saturdays. But as he put it to my friend Lucinda – today Hal is playing the *indoor* game. An away fixture.'

'I don't believe it!'

'You can believe it. And don't you feel better already?'

'Infinitely.'

We were in Aylesbury. Claire had had a wonderful afternoon: she baked Elizabeth David's chocolate cake: total, moist success. Earlier, Fran and she had made a hat for a neighbours' daughter's wedding. I watched them as they did it, sitting together on a rattan sofa in the conservatory; they looked more like sisters than mother and daughter.

I said, 'You should wear the hat while you're putting on the stockings.'

'I think you're a pervert, Mr Newman.'

'Does Hal have any inkling?' Claire laughed and shook her head, her tongue stuck out as she smoothed the stockings upwards. 'This is all carefully planned,' I said. 'I can tell.'

'Of course it is,' Claire said. 'You're the one who postponed St-Tropez so you could have your office meeting.'

'When will we know – and what's going to happen next?'

Every week I promise Claire that I will win the pen prize for the Saturday crossword and every week she interrupts me while I'm doing it.

'Nicholas, you will know nothing. You will simply do as you are instructed on Monday. Nothing more, nothing less.'

Four across. Grandeur of Sally in spring. Easy-peasy-japanesy, 'majesty'. A jest is a sally. 'Jest' inside 'May'.

Inspector Sinker dealt with Strafe's crash and I dealt with Inspector Sinker. I find one thing unusually helpful in controlling clients – pile them high with information. Like Mrs Lydiard does. Tell them things they don't need to know, shower them with statistics, pour facts at them. It controls them because they can never say they didn't know. Few people relish this tactic less than an ambitious policeman who does not wish to have swum out of his depth.

Thus, Sinker and I agreed to close down everything. Richard Strafe's death and all associated with it became a road accident. End of story. And Clay Massey's death was down to Mason Quinn – same gun. And the lawyer who visited Mason Quinn gave him a suicide pill. Very Nazi. Who was the lawyer? Nobody knows. From the – inadequate – description it was Strafe.

On Monday, I telephoned Ruby. She should be allowed to breathe free. A man answered.

'No, she's not here. No, the club is closed. No, she didn't say. No, there's a problem with the lease, I'm just waiting for the storage people.'

I put the phone down and for the first time since early

May began to think about serious enjoyment. Whatever happened at the office meeting, I couldn't lose.

They all poured into the boardroom, Elizabeth in her richest black and white, Mary Strait gleaming like a Ruritanian soldier in some sort of tunic, Hal Callaghan looking – well, creamy. And oily. I could see them all through my open door.

And then I saw Claire. Stunning. In black and yellow she sashayed through the drawing office, walked through my door and gave me a smackeroo of a kiss. I had last seen her in Aylesbury, in the bath.

'What are you doing here?'

She laughed, she couldn't stop laughing, then reached into her handbag and handed me a small tape recorder.

'Nicholas, I'm about to give you your instructions. Do you agree to carry them out to the letter?'

I looked at her. 'I suppose I must.'

'Indeed, you must.' She laughed again. 'This is primed,' she said, 'ready to roll. When I go, as I am about to, you're to call Hal in here. You're to close the door and you're to ask him to swing his vote behind you at this meeting. Am I right in thinking his vote will give you back your controlling interest?'

'Hal won't vote for me. He's discovered the power of the balance of power.'

'He'll vote for you,' Claire said and laughed again. 'Just press the playback button.'

'The playback?' I reached for the tape recorder and pressed it but she snapped it out of my hand.

'Certainly not! Do what you're told. You will only play this when he refuses to vote for you.'

'Claire, I've got to hear it first.'

'Nicholas – you agreed, "to the letter". Right?' She went, waving a cheery goodbye.

Oily Hal ambled in, looking ever so pleased with himself.

'San Trop, eh, Chief? Going topless, then?'

'Hal, close the door.'

He closed it.

'Hal, I want you to vote for me this afternoon.'

He sucked his teeth with more regret than a banker. This tosser. I had built him. From primary school, from being a messenger at Bentley Newman into practice manager and a bloody good architect in his own right. Hal was sacked three times by Elizabeth. And reinstated each time by me.

'Oh, Gawd, Chief, I mean – lookit.'

'I'm serious, Hal, I want to get back control.'

He sat down, oozing, oiling and greasing – and enjoying every iota of refusing me.

'Well, point is, Chief – you know what I was thinking, I mean apart from the fact that the ladies would have my balls on a trowel, I mean, the democracy you always wanted – it's really beginning to work – I mean, really, really – I'm getting very proud of it –'

'Hal, I surrendered my shares temporarily and out of goodwill. I need your vote –'

'Listen, Chief, let me give you another way of looking at it. I mean – fact is –'

'Fact is, Hal, are you going to vote for me or not?'

'Chief, I'd love to, but you know how it is –'

'Hal, I require your vote.'

He grew quasi-dignified, power touching him. 'Look, Chief, I think it's no bad thing that we now have such equality.'

'Hal, are you going to vote for me, yes or no?'

'Chief, look. I can't. My conscience wouldn't let me. There is a kind of morality involved and you know I'm serious about that sort of thing.'

Looking at him and smiling and saying, 'Yes, Hal, I understand,' I placed the tape recorder between us on the desk and pressed the 'Play' button and I heard Lucinda say, *'Ooh, Hal, that is – seriously – delicious – just . . . oooh, pwooh!'*

342

I smiled and asked, 'How's Pam keeping? And the boys?'
Quick study, I am.

We had a wonderful meeting. The voting came. Mary Strait looked puzzled that I seemed so light and clear.

'Who'll count the votes?' I asked. 'Mary, perhaps you should.'

She still didn't get it. Knew there was something – but didn't know what.

I voted for me. Bernard voted for me. Henry voted for me. As did all the men in the drawing office. Elizabeth voted against me. Mary Strait voted against me. Lemon voted against me but embarrassedly; they'd have made her life hell and I didn't mind, I had done my counting. The rest of the women from the drawing office then voted against me, one by one, with grave faces suggesting responsibility when in reality they were shafting me. The vote tied.

Mary Strait smiled, 'Down to you, Hal. Again.'

Hal picked his teeth with his triangle of cardboard. Elizabeth beamed at him.

'Yeah, well, I'm with the Chief,' Hal said sulkily. 'Continuity and all that, he's the one brings in the bacon.'

I looked at Mary Strait the way chess players are supposed to look at someone they've just slaughtered. She didn't look at me, just blushed very red and turned to Elizabeth.

Who said, loud and petulant, 'Why do we have to have this *flavoured* bottled water? I don't like it.'

By the time we finished the meeting, with Lemon smiling at me under her eyelashes and Bernard and Henry unable to stop laughing and Hal as brooding as Hamlet, I was back in the saddle and deciding things, such as a new voting system in the future, one that took account of the senior partner, and new rules about smoking inside the building instead of people having to dash out into the street – and a new telephone system with a full-time receptionist, and I said,

343

beaming to Hal, 'That new girl, Lucinda, she might be good at that, she's very welcoming . . .'

A sting in the tail – isn't there always?

Elizabeth came up to me afterwards.

'Give my love to San Trop, dear. I remember it so well. Might even drive down and see you. But I don't think so. You look tired, dear, everything all right?'

'*Drive* down, Elizabeth?' I know her so well. 'From where?'

'Oh, I wouldn't be doing the driving, dear. Mary would, you see we're going to Uzès.'

Oh, no. And she knew that I knew.

'You're right about that chateau, dear, I read your report, it's the *most* wonderful house, I think Mary will make such a lovely job of it and besides, she doesn't *need* to be an architect all her life. Interesting price, too. And yes, I think it must have been Bougier. Or Leonardo.'

60

I am gazing at the high white parenthesis of a seabird and enjoying that the word 'azure' comes from the 'azu' in lapis lazuli. We're sitting in La Pinède on the balcony of room eleven looking out at the yachts in the port. Claire asks me to spell it out.

'They were going to move the whole practice to Uzès. If it hadn't been for Lucinda I'd not have been able to stop it.'

'But how did Elizabeth get her hands on the chateau?'

'Amazing contacts.'

'You mean – she was able to move fast enough after Strafe's death?'

'Something like that. Or he began to sell it when he knew things were unravelling – and he'd have approached Elizabeth, that's just the kind of mischief he relished.'

'As, Nicholas, would Elizabeth.'

I love the way Claire uses my name all the time.

'She would certainly have known how to do it. No complications. Got a bid in fast and got it accepted.'

Claire leaned back. 'Did you see, by the way, his death is being called suicide?'

'He was driving suicidally.'

'Bloody hell,' Claire said. 'This is going to go on for years.'

'I know.' Aunt and niece in full flow – I can almost hear them.

'Can we stop her?'

I said, 'You can. I can't. Does your claim have legal status?'

'Not yet.'

Wish this hadn't happened; I want Elizabeth in my life; relationships that go wrong always damage other connections.

'We must get you a career,' I said, as though thinking aloud.

'Yes.'

'Any thoughts?'

'Don't know. That chateau – something historical. Art. The history of painted furniture. Something like that.'

After a silence, she rose and stood at the balcony rail. It became a long silence. Then, adjusting her towel, she turned round and smiled at me.

'I want to say something.'

Her face was in shadow.

'Yes, Claire.'

'You think, Nicholas, that you're the lover in this relationship and that I'm the loved. But you're wrong.'

Then we had a very long silence.

In La Pinède you forget that St-Tropez in August has more tourists than the rest of the world. Blue, blue water and high, golden sun and for lunch a *brochette* of the lightest fish and a musty Chablis and a *gaufre* whose honeycomb they lined with crushed cherries and cream. It took away some of the pain.

'I love you, Claire.'

'I love you, Nicholas.'

We clung to La Pinède for three days. That first afternoon we went to bed after lunch, with all the windows open. Distant mopeds buzzed, angry they could not be with us; a dog or two barked; some woman nearby laughed – the sleepy, sexy sounds of love in the afternoon. Everything we enjoyed about each other returned, the smells, the small local sounds, the tickles of hair. I licked Claire's sweat. If a shadow fell across our bodies, the shadow of Ruby, I turned it away.

346

Before dinner we sat on the balcony once more, had a drink, talked about Lucinda, laughed about Hal and dreamed of coming down here, maybe buying a house up in the pine-covered hills.

'Brigitte Bardot lives here,' Claire said.

'Not now. She moved to the Alpilles. But Colette's summer house is here; I'll show you tomorrow.'

'Tomorrow,' Claire said, 'I'd really like to go to the Beaux-Arts museum.'

'We might just saunter and look at the yachts.'

She sipped her drink. 'Nicholas, I must ask something.'

'Yes, Claire.'

'You won't like it.'

'Try me.'

'Your friend, Ruby.' Claire looked out at the harbour. 'I was afraid you went to bed with her. I mean, during the – Mason and that. You know – the tension.'

I said, 'I never left Rye.'

We were golden with each other that evening, we laughed so much that other diners smiled. I can see Claire's face and the slight miscuing in one of her eyes. We fell asleep so entwined I can't work out how we disentangled.

Claire has a huge capacity to be made happy, even after horrors. I knew the depths of her lows and perhaps dwelt too much on them and thought not enough about her high moments – when she sings and smiles and makes stimulating, intelligent enquiries about life in general. Interesting how the women in the office – at least those who didn't have some agenda or other – all liked her. And the men. I often knew when she had arrived to see me because I heard sudden bursts of laughter from Lemon or someone. So different from prosaic, dull-voiced me.

And now she lies asleep, snuffling a little, in my arms. I thought as I too fell asleep, That's it. Whatever lay within me and within her, drawing down such forces upon us, will

347

be expunged by the sun and sky and the loving . . . And in the morning we will play at being tourists . . . and we will go into St-Tropez and walk the curved port . . . and gape at the yachts with their little folded helicopters aboard . . . and lunch in some place with checked tablecoths and I shall eat an impossibly huge feast of *crustacés* . . . and we shall wander into the sweet Beaux-Arts, past the sour-faced man at the door and gaze at Matisse and Corot and Dufy and Seurat . . .

Which is exactly what we did.

'Don't you want to go shopping?' I asked at lunch, winkling out a winkle.

'Nope.'

God, I love this woman. Look at her – have you ever seen anything so pretty?

As we finished she said, 'Second thoughts. I want to buy some sandals. You stay and relax, I'm boring when I'm buying shoes, meet you in the Beaux-Arts.'

'Where's the sandals shop?'

'To the left, you know –'

'Yes, I think I will dawdle.'

Kiss.

I finish. I leave the restaurant. I know what I'm going to do. I'm going to sit on a quayside bollard and watch for Claire. Have the pleasure of seeing her from a distance without her knowing I'm looking at her. Then I'm going to follow her to the museum, some yards behind, loving this view of her, enjoy watching her. Inside I'm going to show her one of my favourite Matisses, the one of his daughter with her young friend.

But something's bothering me. No, a whole heap of things is bothering me. I hate loose ends and I have suddenly become anxious and nervy. Am I so insecure that the moment Claire leaves my sight I get the vapours? I can't believe that I'm actually starting to look for a couple wearing brand-new trainers and the man is limping.

Curiously, I miss Strafe, his vitality. Now *there's* a tangle, a whole bloody Medusa of loose ends. Strafe being Ruby's half-brother. I never got to the bottom of that. Was I pleasant enough to Ruby in bed in Rye? Why has she gone off me? Not that I want her – but I don't like that she doesn't seem to like me.

I suppose Strafe hired the skateboarder. And the Clay Massey gibe about his tie was the last straw – given that Clay was also threatening Strafe's wealth. Call me a fool but I don't believe Strafe would have killed Claire. Strafe liked beauty, he loved it, even if he was as crass as creosote. That's why I never panicked. There has to be a reason – because I'm quite a good panicker when the occasion demands it. Who rubbished my car? Need I ask? Wonder if Claire knows about that too? Wonder how much Claire knows that she's not saying? Zurück. Is it closed down? Oh, fuck, who cares. Enjoy the sun.

I look up. There's Claire. She'll not see me because she won't expect to see me and she won't be looking for me. She's walking with that sexy lope down the street, and now she stops to look in a window, walks on and looks in the next window, I shall tease her about this later. Quaint architecture, St-Tropez, the little streets that radiate up from the port still echo the original fisherman's village. Wonder where Matisse and his family stayed – could be there, that little row of houses across from Claire and behind her. Christ, my stomach's acting up. Last time I felt this type of pain was the night they told me about Mason Quinn's motorbike. I shift on the bollard. Beside me on the quay there's a satellite dish from one of the yachts. Funny, isn't it, how the pedestrians on one side of the street mirror the actions of the pedestrians on the other. I've been thinking about mirrors. My life must have improved. I've got back control of the practice – which suggests I've got back control of myself. Yes, that woman over there is a mirror of Claire's actions. The outer life being the mirror of our inner. Peaceful people are peaceful people. Turbulent lives have turbulent inner lives. You can't be peaceful on the outside and chaotic on the inside, at least I don't think so. Nor the other way round. Look at a blueprint. The calmer the drawing, the calmer the building. Calm. Calm my stomach, please, someone. Calm. How is it that great sportsmen seem to have all the time in the world? I'm always banging on about it. Joe DiMaggio had a lazy swing, look at McEnroe's economy of movement, Viv Richards or David Gower at the wicket. Calm. No. I have no calm. Because Claire moves on and the mirror movement moves on. It's not an abstract movement, it's that other pedestrian and every time Claire stops, this woman, several yards behind her and on the far pavement, she stops too. No, it's an illusion. I'm wrong.

Calm down, Nicholas.

No, there is no calm! NONE! It *isn't* an illusion – because as Claire comes out of the little street and crosses the broad swathe in front of the port and moves towards the gateway of the museum, the woman follows her and stops at the corner to see where Claire's going. No, I'm getting paranoid, this is just a tourist like the rest of us. She's wearing white capri pants, a striped top and shades, she's following Claire, I swear she is, no, I'm not getting paranoid, she *is* following Claire, it's a woman with a mane of hair tied back, it's a woman whose springy walk I know, it's Ruby and she's following Claire!

Now I know everything.

Ruby knows we're here. Only Ruby knew I was in Montreux. Ruby never congratulated me on my marriage. And skirted all my mentions of Claire. And when I called she had closed the club . . .

I watch. Claire swings across to the gate of the Musée de l'Annonciade and Ruby – yes, it is Ruby – follows her at a distance. And I follow Ruby. Claire buys a ticket, so do two, three other people directly behind her and so does Ruby and five, six people later, so do I.

But then I start to move faster because Ruby's carrying a bag, the small, square leopardskin handbag she had in Berlin, only now it's bulging.

Claire's on the stairs. Ruby's after her, hanging back a little, waiting for some people to come down. I move in behind Ruby, two steps down, and she never sees me. At the top of the stairs I see Claire ahead, she's gone deep into the gallery and Ruby's hanging back eyeing her. I sprint around two people and turn back to meet Ruby face to face. For a second she doesn't know it's me. I grab her forearm.

'What have you got in the bag, Ruby?'

Ruby jumps back. She looks up at me – we used to joke about how I towered above her. She struggles but her heart isn't in it and she looks away and she says, 'Sorry, darling.'

We stand aside, I force her to take my arm like a wife, we move downstairs to the lower gallery where the light of the Midi never reaches and there's a dark and exquisite Braque on the far wall.

'You're shaking, darling.' As casually as she might mention the weather, as cool as a – what?, as a killer.

'Ruby, you must tell me. If you don't, I will kill you. I mean it. I will kill you now. Here. In this gallery. Tell me. It was you, it was always you?'

'Sounds like a song, darling.'

She looked away, brittle and distant, then sought one of the two chairs. I sat in the other.

'Give it to me.'

She handed over her bag. I took it.

'Don't open it, darling.'

Therefore I opened it – just a little. I could see the glass tube of a syringe. Ruby prattled at me, seeing my dismay.

'I know you'd kill me, darling. I've always known you could kill a woman. But not a man.'

351

'What in the name of Christ did you think you were going to do, Ruby?'

'It's been done in the past, darling. Quick jab. From behind. It's been done by others. To others.'

I looked away in despair. A schoolgirl drifted past with a notebook. The attendant looked at us churlishly. I closed the bag.

'Ruby – I think I know everything. But I need to hear it from you.'

Her brown eyes. Her forearms. That lovely, jiggling bosom.

She looked at me. 'If I go away, darling? If I promise?'

'Come with me.'

She took my arm again and we walked into the sunshine, past the instant portrait painter and the woman selling boat trips and the man with the pottery and the garish pictures of St-Tropez on a dozen easels. I held the bag a little away from me.

'I promise, darling. I mean it. I will go away. For ever.'

Her voice had fallen.

'Tell me it all,' I said. 'Now and finally.'

'I lied, darling.'

Almost made me laugh. 'About what?'

'The Liese story, darling. Clay Massey. Being afraid of Richard. All of that.'

'So what's the truth?'

'Did you believe the Liese story, darling?'

'I found it hard to imagine that a young couple would leave their baby –'

'I told Richard you wouldn't believe that, he said you would, that you had no feelings –'

'But, Ruby, I know about people and their houses. You did live in that property. Magda Whatsit-strasse. It shone out of your eyes.'

'I did, darling.'

'And did Strafe?'

'Yes, darling, I told you he did.' As if I must know when she was telling the truth.

'Were you brother and sister?' I asked.

'Yes. Devotedly. And, darling, he knew I loved you. He was jealous. But he also wanted me to have you. And so did I.'

'Ruby, I need this, I need to know everything. Caux, Zurück, every bloody thing.' I said it so intensely that passers-by noticed.

'Not here, darling.' She was afraid of me now.

Beyond and behind the public telephones a small café keeps its tables out of doors all year. We walked down the quay and took a table, ordered coffee.

'Ruby, begin.'

'Darling, why didn't you marry me?'

I said, 'Is that what all this is about?' She looked away. 'Ruby!' I grabbed her wrist. 'Look at me.' She turned to face me – and waited. For a second I thought she had begun to milk the pause as she did with her songs.

'Darling, I wanted you to marry me. If she died, you'd turn to me again.'

'Ruby, forget that. Zurück, first.'

She sighed. 'Zurück was only an investment company. For Richard's holdings in Germany and Austria.'

'But the "Doctor"? In Caux? All of that? I kept getting messages in Montreux.'

'My idea. The Doctor's my nephew. I wanted to try and tip you off about Richard. That's all I was trying to do. In case things went wrong –'

'But he meant to kill my wife –'

'It's you I was worried about, darling. If something went wrong and you were hit by mistake –'

'I don't believe you, Ruby.'

'No, darling. I'm lying again.'

Ironic? Perhaps. I could feel my exasperation boiling.

353

'Ruby – how much of what happened in Switzerland was genuine?'

'I thought you knew more than –'

'More than what?'

'More than you knew, darling.'

'Are you Jewish?'

She gave me a look like glass. 'No, darling. Not at all.'

'Did Richard follow me to Switzerland?'

'Darling, we laughed about that. We couldn't believe you didn't guess about satellite phones.'

'And all that stuff with the waitress – and the climbing along the balcony?'

'Stage-managed, darling.'

'The skateboarder. The trashing of my car. The break-in at Rye.'

'Like I said. Stage-management, darling. It's how I make my living.'

I felt my pride stung hard. 'So you helped to kill Clay Massey?'

'It was that young man.'

'But you were in on it.'

She bit her lip. 'Well, I didn't do it, darling. I didn't even know Clay Massey.'

'But you said he was your dear friend – oh, Jesus, Ruby, how am I ever to know what was true and what wasn't?'

'I'll tell you what was true, darling. It was true that I loved you. And still do. And always will.' *Underneath the lantern by the barrack gate.*

'Ruby, I need to know one piece of truth from you.'

'That's a piece of truth, darling. That's a huge piece of truth.'

Her eyes filled with tears. I thought, People will think we're lovers quarrelling. *Darling I remember the way you used to wait.* These bloody songs.

'No, Ruby. This is the piece of truth I want to know. Is it

354

over? Is it finally and completely over? Is Claire – my wife whom I love and cherish – is she safe?'

'Did you love me, darling?'

The tears at last began to roll. *'Twas there that you whispered tenderly.*

'Ruby, I won't let you go unless you tell me – and unless you tell me in a way that I can know it's true.'

She placed the back of her hand to one wet cheek, then the other cheek. In a moment she stood from the table. *That you loved me, you'd always be.* She looked at me sideways, the sort of look people give when they think you're not watching them, a look full of fright and reproach and loss and love. Ruby standing in the spotlight, doing a Dietrich. *There were in real life two girls, one was a grocer's girl called Lilli and one a doctor's daughter called Marlene.*

She looked at my mouth now and my hand where it still caught her wrist and she disengaged. Then she hoisted her shoulders a little and, never glancing back at me again, she began to walk and then, in a little while, broke into a kind of half-run, so purposeful, so urgent that men looked at her curiously in her striped top and white capri pants. I watched her all along the curved front of the port. And then Ruby disappeared, somewhere under the citadel, by the old *marché*, in among all the jewellery shops and estate agents and bijou restaurants. My hands, resting on the table, had bruised each other. I reached down, took three hefty little stones from the ground and dropped them into Ruby's bag, then walked to the quay and dropped the handbag in the water.

Inside the gallery I found Claire sitting upstairs. My relief felt uncontrollable – with the added bonus that she doesn't need to know any of what's just happened. I moved so that I could feel her forearm touching mine.

'Is that the Matisse you mean?' she asked.

I looked. 'Yes.' Two young girls, one visiting the other,

355

captured in an afternoon's moment of russet and a touch of foliage green. One's wearing a hat.

'Look,' Claire said. She pointed.

A window opens in the wall on that side of the gallery. It looks out on the port. Through it we could see all the terracotta and blue and white of St-Tropez and the sea and the sky and the boats.

Claire said, 'I didn't know it was a window at first. I thought it was a painting.'

I said, 'Real life as still life.'

Claire mused. 'I've never liked the French term for still life. *Nature morte*. Too macabre.'

'I don't like it either.'

We walked downstairs; she tucked her arm into mine.

Outside, we stood for a moment, in the Musée forecourt. Claire put up her hand and stroked my hair. Somewhere, far away, there's a red deer running across green, open ground . . .

She said, 'I'd like an ice-cream.'

Across the street the sun caught the colours in the freezer cabinets, more pastel, more fleeting than the oils of Matisse and Seurat. We surveyed, trying to choose from the plastic rainbow of strawberry and banana and chocolate and lemon.

'Did you know,' I asked her, 'that pistachio ice-cream is one of my great passions?'

She chose a coconut sorbet and we moved away to find an open space. I was unable not to touch her – her arm, her hand, her shoulder, anything so long as it was her skin.

Claire licked in silence while I concentrated hard on the flavour of the pistachio, feeling the full pricklings of tears in my eyes. I wear light-sensitive spectacles; they go dark in sunlight. The traffic policeman flapped his brilliant white gloves at a confused car. An elderly man passing by, in his cream linen jacket, looked at Claire and enjoyed what he saw. She nuzzled her head into my shoulder.

'Nicholas?'

'Yes?' I rested my hand on her bare nape beneath her hair.

'Has Ruby gone now? For ever, I mean?'

Utterly thrown I muttered, 'I think so.'

We stood there and looked out at the blue of the world. Claire rested her cool forehead at my neck.

The Amethysts

Frank Delaney

An astonishing psychological thriller of great force and pace

The Amethysts is a novel of intense power. Frank Delaney uncovers the roots of a great twentieth-century evil through the fractured vision of Nicholas Newman, successful architect and Modern Man. The brutal murder of his lover proves to have a meaning so profound that it dramatically alters Newman's whole life. New values forced upon his consciousness become the central issues in a riveting novel which draws the reader to the disturbing conclusion, 'Sometimes only the unspeakable teaches us how to love.'

'The fusillade of shocks, and the crescendo of menace and confusion are contrived brilliantly. Frank Delaney's new novel cannot fail . . . inescapably gripping and sinisterly erotic . . . the pace rarely flags. *The Amethysts* is taut, tense and full of threatening emotional power.'

Daily Telegraph

'Delaney effortlessly hooks the reader . . . This mix of John Fowles-cum-Ian McEwan turns flammable.' *Guardian*

'A compelling novel, written with pace, verve and imagination.'

Mail on Sunday

'A psychological thriller as harrowing as it is absorbing . . . powerful, almost poetic prose style . . . always intense, emotional and uninhibited. This novel may prove unforgettable.' *Sunday Telegraph*

'An unusually sophisticated thriller . . . elegantly written and compellingly plotted.' *Sunday Times*

'The action pans across Europe with pace and verve, but all the time resonant with dark undertones . . . gripping.' *The Times*

ISBN 0 00 649952 X

Pearl

Frank Delaney

It is lunchtime for the powerful. Successful architect Nicholas Newman waits for his friend Antony – who never arrives. Instead a courier brings a package containing a knife. An hour later Newman meets his new client, the brilliant Black Pearl, Dutch international footballer and Premiership star. In the interlacing connections that emerge and mystify, nothing will ever again be as it seems.

Soon the past rises to dictate the present and control the future as the horrors of a violent death drag Newman back to a Nazi atrocity in France, and the links into modern football hooliganism and neo-Nazi thuggery rip his life open.

'The build-up of menace is deft and convincing . . . Delaney's fusillade of shocks, eroticism and sustained terror assails the reader from every direction. The elements of his novel are straightforward enough, but lifted by emotional power into something exceptional and utterly gripping.'   *Daily Telegraph*

'A taut, fast-moving thriller with a neatly wrought ending as architect and soccer superstar find their fates interlinked in a mad dash across Europe.'   *Irish Independent*

'Delaney has skilfully concocted a blend of adventure thriller and psychological mystery.'   *The Times*

ISBN 0 00 651324 7